SENS

Ronal

What do you see . . . ?

When the mutilated body of a young
the outskirts of Los Angeles, the detec ..... ~~deny the~~
similarities between this murder and one that occurred a year prior. Media
outlets are quick to surmise this is the work of a budding serial killer, but
Detective Bill Renney is struggling with an altogether different scenario: a
secret that keeps him tethered to the husband of the first victim.

What do you hear . . . ?

Maureen Park, newly engaged to Hollywood producer Greg Dawson, finds
her engagement party crashed by the arrival of Landon, Greg's son. A darkly
unsettling young man, Landon invades Maureen's new existence, and the
longer he stays, the more convinced she becomes that he may have something
to do with the recent murder in the high desert.

What do you feel . . . ?

Toby Kampen, the self-proclaimed Human Fly, begins an obsession over
a woman who is unlike anyone he has ever met. A woman with rattlesnake
teeth and a penchant for biting. A woman who has trapped him in her spell. A
woman who may or may not be completely human.

In Ronald Malfi's brand-new thriller, these three storylines converge to create
a tapestry of deceit, distrust, and unapologetic horror. A brand-new novel of
dark suspense set in the City of Angels, as only "horror's Faulkner" can tell it.

9781803365664 | 15 April 2025 | Hardback and E-book
$29.99 | £19.99 | CA$39.99 | 432pp

PRESS & PUBLICITY

UK PUBLICIST:
Bahar Kutluk
bahar.kutluk@titanemail.com

US PUBLICIST:
Katharine Carroll
katharine.carroll@titanemail.com

RONALD MALFI

SENSELESS

TITAN BOOKS

Senseless
Hardback edition ISBN: 9781803365664
E-book edition ISBN: 9781803367606

Published by Titan Books
A division of Titan Publishing Group Ltd
144 Southwark Street, London SE1 0UP
www.titanbooks.com

First edition: April 2025
10 9 8 7 6 5 4 3 2 1

A CIP catalogue record for this title is available
from the British Library.

Printed and bound in the United States.

This one's for me.

what do you have?

"Abandon all hope ye who enter here . . . "

—BRET EASTON ELLIS, *AMERICAN PSYCHO*

PART ONE

HIGH DESERT

ONE

Once, when Bill Renney was a teenager, he had been bitten by a Southern Pacific rattler while partying with some friends in Antelope Valley. He hadn't seen the thing at first, merely heard the ominous, inexplicable maraca of its tail, then felt the hammer-strike against the bulge of his left calf muscle. He had just set down an Igloo cooler full of beer and ice beside an outcropping of bone-colored stone when he felt the bite, and for a moment, in his confusion, he thought he had snapped a tendon in his leg. But then he saw the beast—four feet of sleek brown musculature retreating in a series of s-shaped undulations across the sand—and he knew he was in trouble.

His friends had loaded him into the back of a Jeep where someone tied a tourniquet fashioned from a torn shirtsleeve above the wound to slow both the bleeding as well as the progression of venom through his bloodstream. Renney pivoted his leg and could see blood spurting from twin punctures in the otherwise pale, mostly hairless swell of muscle, in tandem with his heartbeat, and the sight of it made him woozy. As the Jeep sped across the desert toward civilization, Renney could feel a burning sensation traveling from the puncture marks up his leg, combined with a moist, roiling nausea in his gut. By the time the Jeep pulled up outside the nearest medical facility, Renney was vomiting over the side.

The experience—now over three decades in the past—had left behind a pair of faint white indentions in the tender meat of Bill Renney's left calf. It had also left him with a healthy respect for the desert, and for all manner of creatures that resided there.

On this morning, the desert was alive. As he drove, large black flies swarmed in the air, and he periodically turned the windshield wipers on to swipe their smudgy, bristling carcasses from the glass. Beyond the shoulder of the road, the occasional coyote would raise its head and scrutinize the passage of Renney's puke-green, four-door sedan as it rumbled along the cracked, sun-bleached pavement. When he finally eased the sedan to a stop, he could see the boomerang silhouettes of carrion birds wheeling across the bright blue tapestry of the sky.

Two L.A. County Sheriff's Department SUVs and a few Lancaster cruisers were parked on the shoulder of the desert highway, their rack lights on. An ambulance sat at a tilt off the blacktop, next to a solitary green road sign that read, simply, LOS ANGELES COUNTY LINE. Two paramedics and a uniformed officer stood before the open rear doors of the ambulance, their faces red and glistening from the heat of the early morning, the chrome plating on the ambulance reflecting the sun in a spangle of blinding light. Farther up the road was an old Volkswagen bus, sea-foam green except for where the scabrous patches of rust had taken over. One more officer stood there, talking to a young couple who looked like Woodstock refugees. Beside the bus, bright pink road flares sizzled in the center of the roadway, but they were nothing compared to the sun that blazed directly above the desert.

Bill Renney popped open the driver's door of his unmarked sedan and swung his feet out onto the blacktop. With a grunt—he really needed to get back to the gym and lose the burgeoning spare tire that had been expanding around his waistline this past year, ever since Linda had passed—he bent forward and tucked the cuffs of his pants into his socks. Much like everything else out here in this desolate wasteland, the ants could be merciless.

He got out of the car, swung the door closed, then casually swept aside his sports coat so the officer and the two medics standing by the ambulance could glimpse the gold shield clipped to his belt, right beside the nine-millimeter Smith & Wesson M&P. The officer nodded at Renney then went back to talking to the paramedics. *Flirting*, Renney thought.

He nodded, too, at the uniformed officer standing with the couple beside the VW bus. The couple was young, the guy maybe in his early twenties, sporting ratty Converse sneakers and a tank top with marijuana leaves embroidered across the front. He had what looked like tribal tattoos on his biceps and the feathered blonde hair of a surfer. The woman standing beside him looked even younger— nineteen at best, if Renney had to guess—and she was wearing a loose, cable-knit shawl over a neon-green bikini top, and, despite the rising heat of that early morning, appeared to be shivering. They were both in handcuffs.

Renney stepped between the two SUVs and out onto the valley floor, where the blacktop gave way to hard-packed sand, spiky tufts of sagebrush, sprigs of desert parsley, and the prickly pompoms of scorpionweed. The sun was high and bright and directly at his back, stretching his shadow out ahead of him along the rippling contours of the earth, and making it appear as though he were traversing some alien landscape. He could feel the intensity of the morning sun as it bore a hole in the center of his back.

He was suddenly craving a cigarette.

A group of uniformed officers stood beyond a scrim of sagebrush. They were maybe thirty, forty yards from the road, but their collective stare as Renney approached was undeniable, even from such a distance. Renney could see that they were all wearing paper masks over the lower half of their face, just like people did back when that whole COVID shit started.

"Detective Renney," one of the officers called to him, the man's voice slightly muffled behind the paper mask.

Renney checked his watch as he advanced toward the officers and noted that it was just barely after seven in the morning. He took another step, and a horde of blowflies was abruptly congregating around his head; he absently swatted at the air in an attempt to disperse them, bobbing and weaving his head like a prizefighter. Another step, and a prong of sagebrush grazed his thigh, *thwick*, causing him to jump and take a quick step to the side. He searched the ground at his feet for any signs of snakes.

"Watch out for the anthills, too," one of the other officers called to him, pointing toward Renney's shoes.

Renney froze in midstride. He glanced down again and saw crumbly mounds rising up from the desert floor like booby traps. Beyond the anthills, a set of tire tracks wove a clumsy arc across the floor of the valley. He made a mental note of the tracks as he stepped over them, careful not to disturb any potential evidence.

"We called dispatch first, but Politano here suggested we ask for you by name," said the muffle-voiced officer who had warned him about the anthills.

"Which one's Politano?" Renney asked.

A young-looking male officer with short, raven-black hair raised his hand. "That'd be me, sir. I remembered you from last year. Your name, I mean. We met briefly at a press conference." His voice was also muffled behind the paper mask; Renney realized now that they were wearing them to keep the blowflies out of their mouths.

"Right," Renney muttered, although he did not recognize the young officer with the mask on. "So, what've we got?"

"She's maybe in her early to mid-twenties, if I had to guess," said Officer Politano. "We didn't check for any ID or anything. Frankly, sir, we didn't want to do anything until you got here."

Officer Politano nodded down at the reason Bill Renney had been summoned all the way out here so early this morning.

There was a body on the ground. Adult female. Caucasian. Beneath the unforgiving glare of the sun and through a cloud of frenzied flies, Bill Renney could make out a turquoise halter top, and a pair of faded denim shorts that were frayed to tassels at the hems. What at first looked like a bruise on the left thigh was actually a tattoo of a rose, with a tendril of thorns running down the length of that pale, fly-bitten leg. The feet were bare, but a bit of gold jewelry caught a sunbeam and sparkled along one slender ankle. The woman's head was turned at an angle away from Renney, so that he only saw the nest of dusty, knotted blonde hair at the back of her head. The one arm that he could see from his vantage was crooked in a position that propped the left hand into the air. All five fingers from that hand were missing, the wrist and forearm stained in striations of dark blood.

A sinking sensation overcame Bill Renney. It felt like he was suddenly plummeting down an elevator shaft.

Jesus Christ, he thought. *What the actual fuck?*

"Those two up by the road spotted the body about an hour ago," said Officer Politano, who nodded in the direction of the VW bus and the young couple in handcuffs being questioned by the police officer at the shoulder of the highway. Politano lowered his mask and Renney saw that he was indeed young and fresh-faced, and he thought maybe he did recognize him after all. Maybe from Palmdale, although he couldn't be sure. "They were driving by, doing a little day-tripping, when they saw vultures circling something on the ground," Politano went on. "Guy said he could tell it looked like a person out there, and his girl agreed. He got out and had a look. Then the girl, she called it in on her phone. We asked them to wait for us to arrive, and they did. The girl said they kept honking the horn to keep the vultures away, which mostly worked."

"Why are they in bracelets?" Renney asked.

"Well, they gave us permission to search the van. We found some coke."

Renney stepped around to the other side of the body.

He wanted to see the face.

"The body probably hasn't been out here for very long," Officer Politano continued. "A few hours, tops. The vultures haven't done a job on it yet."

No, the vultures hadn't, but this close to the body, Renney could see large red ants coursing up and down the corpse's pale thighs, flossing between the exposed toes with their dark blue nail polish, and creeping in a conga line across the bloodstained front of the turquoise halter top. The blowflies, too, had collected in the corpse's hair, so plentiful that Renney could hear their orchestral hum.

He knelt beside the dead woman's head.

Jesus Christ.

A second officer cleared her throat and said, "We thought maybe coyotes could've—"

Renney shook his head. Said, "No." Said, "Coyotes didn't do this." Then he turned his head and spat tiny flies from his mouth.

"I didn't think so, either," said Politano. Something clicked in the back of the young officer's throat as he said this. He'd kept his mask down around his neck, as if in solidarity with Renney.

The dead woman's nose and eyes had been removed, leaving behind a trio of empty, bloodied sockets. This gave the corpse's face a disconcerting jack-o'-lantern appearance, albeit one smeared in a crimson sheen of dried blood. Ants swarmed all over while some large beetle with an iridescent carapace lumbered along the rise of a stone-white cheekbone—the only part of the corpse's face that was not covered in blood. Renney was cautious not to touch the ants as he reached down and brushed aside a tuft of tangled blonde hair. Blowflies exploded in a smoggy cloud and disseminated into the air.

Son of a bitch, Renney thought, just as a nasty muscle tightened in the center of his chest.

The woman's left ear had been removed, as well. Both ears, Renney assumed, although he could only see the one side of her head at the moment. There was dried blood along the neck, too, and the skin there had purpled, but the flies were not making the area easy to study.

"I saw this and I thought of that other one," said Officer Politano. "That woman from last year, I mean."

Last year, Renney thought, and he could feel a cool sweat dampen his brow. *Son of a bitch.*

"The fingers look like they were sliced off with a knife or a razor or something, maybe bolt cutters," Officer Politano continued, then he glanced at the other officer, and added, "Not coyotes."

Renney said nothing, but Officer Politano was correct. Same with the nose—it had been removed, along with all the cartilage, from around the nasal and vomer bones. The eyes had been gouged out of their sockets, while the one missing ear that Renney could see had been sliced away like someone sliding a sharp, hot blade across a brick of butter.

"You were the lead on that case?" the female officer asked him.

"I was," Renney said, thinking now, *I am.* "Is that a helicopter?"

"What, sir?"

Renney raised an index finger above his head, in the approximate direction of the sound of incoming rotors. He did not take his eyes off the body.

"Oh," said the officer. "Yes, sir. They're searching the area."

"Radio in and tell them to keep away. I don't want them blowing sand all over the place."

"Yes, sir," said the officer, and then she was jogging back to one of the SUVs.

"Any footprints in the vicinity?" Renney asked the remaining officers.

"Only the guy's footprints from when he came out here to have a look at the body," said Officer Politano, once more nodding in the direction of the Volkswagen bus and at the young couple in handcuffs. "Prints matched the treads on his sneakers. We took photos. No one else's that we could see."

"Night winds blow the sand around, cover things up. How far out did you check?"

"I personally canvassed about a hundred square feet around the victim before you got here."

"They see anyone else out here while on their drive?"

"The couple in the van? No. Not a soul, sir."

"What about any vehicle tracks in the sand? You guys find any?"

"No, sir."

"I noticed some tire tracks over by those anthills."

A beat of silence simmered in the air between the officers.

Renney looked up at their dark silhouettes plastered against the inferno of a blazing desert sun. He lifted an arm to shield his eyes from the glare. Sweat rolled down his face.

"That was me," confessed one of the other officers, who had also removed his paper mask now—another guy Renney thought he recognized from Palmdale. Or maybe Lancaster. These young guys all looked the same. "I drove out here when we first arrived on scene, sir, but then thought, well . . . I mean, I went back up to the road . . . I realized I'd compromised the scene, sir, I just . . . I wasn't thinking . . ."

"Someone go unhook those two," Renney said, jerking his head in the direction of the Volkswagen and the two hippies.

"Uh, sir," stammered one of the officers. "They had about two grams of cocaine in their—"

"I don't give a shit about the coke. Unhook them and ask them to come down to the station to give a proper statement. Do it before they manage to rub together whatever brain cells they still have between them and ask for a lawyer."

"Understood," said the officer, already moving back toward the road.

Renney looked back down at the corpse's mutilated face. From the inside pocket of his sports coat, he pulled out a pair of latex gloves and tugged one on. He brushed away the swarm of ants along the lower half of the corpse's face, then pressed his thumb to the chin. He gently lowered the jaw until the mouth hung open, then peered into the cavity.

"Tongue's gone, too, isn't it?" asked Politano.

"It is," Renney confirmed. Indeed, it had been severed, leaving behind a pulpy, bloodied stump. Not as neat and clean as the removal of the nose, ears, and eyes. Harder to get at, he supposed. As he stared at what remained of the tongue, a rivulet of ants spilled out from one corner of the corpse's mouth, and Bill Renney yanked his hand away, the thumb of his latex glove sticking briefly to the dried blood on the chin before releasing with an audible snap.

"She's cut up the same way as that other woman from last year," said Officer Politano, and it was not phrased as a question. Something clicked once more in the young man's throat. "Isn't that right, detective?"

Renney exhaled audibly as he rose to his feet. His armpits felt swampy, his throat dry. He still craved that cigarette. As he dusted the sand from his knees, Officer Politano's handcuff chain rattled, and the hairs on the back of Renney's neck stood at attention. He glanced around for any evidence of approaching rattlesnakes.

"Detective Renney?" Politano said, perceptibly clearing his throat. "She's in the same condition as that other woman we found out here a year ago. Isn't that right, sir?"

"It would seem that way," Bill Renney admitted, and to his own ears, it sounded like a confession.

The chief M.E. with the County of Los Angeles Department of Medical Examiner was a tall, sterling-haired man in his late fifties, named Falmouth. He reminded Renney a little bit of Pierce Brosnan without the accent. According to Falmouth, the parts of the victim that had been removed—her nose, eyes, ears, tongue, and the fingers and thumbs of both hands—had been done so postmortem. There had been two implements used to remove these bits: a crude blade, like some dulled hunting knife or razorblade, had been employed to dig out the eyes, and carve away the nose and ears. Possibly the tongue, too, Falmouth concluded. The fingers and thumbs, on the other hand ("No pun intended," Falmouth muttered stoically), appeared to have been removed with an altogether different implement—something, according to the medical examiner, like a set of bolt cutters. Just as Officer Politano had surmised, Renney noted.

"Tell me," Renney said. "Tell me—what are the differences between this body and the one from last year."

"Quite a few, actually," said Falmouth, "from a forensic standpoint, at least. For one thing, the cause of death is different. The woman from last year died from exsanguination—blood loss from her wounds. This victim, however," he said, and he peeled back a layer of white sheet to expose the corpse's face, now mostly swabbed clean of the dried blood by rubbing alcohol, yet still looking skeletal with its missing pieces, "died of asphyxiation. Look—see here?"

With one latex-gloved finger, Falmouth addressed a vague gray outline around the corpse's nasal cavity and mouth. To Renney, it looked like dirt or some other debris.

"What is that?" he asked.

"Remnants of some adhesive," said Falmouth. "Something sticky had been placed over her mouth and nose, causing her to suffocate. After she was dead, her killer went to work on her."

Renney leaned closer and examined the gray flecks of adhesive around the corpse's mouth and nasal cavity. He hadn't noticed them back in the desert when he'd first studied the body, given all the dried blood and blowflies swarming around the corpse's face, but he could see it clearly now.

"All adhesives contain long chains of protein molecules that bond with the surface of whatever they're sticking to," Falmouth explained. "I've already scraped some off, sent them to the lab."

Renney nodded.

"There are ligature marks around the wrists and ankles, too," Falmouth went on. "This woman was bound at some point. That differs greatly from the body we examined last year, as well, which showed no signs of that victim being bound or even held against her will."

"Can you tell what was used to bind her?"

"I'll have the lab confirm that, as well, but I'm guessing some sort of rope, based on the fibers I extracted from the abraded flesh. At least on the wrists, anyway."

"Her feet were bare when we found her. Maybe you can check the soles of her feet to see if you can determine what sort of location she might have been kept in?"

"Already have. Just your basic dirt and grit, I'm afraid."

"Right," Renney said.

Falmouth reached over the body splayed out on the stainless-steel table and gently turned the corpse's head on its neck. Renney imagined he could hear the tendons creak. The blonde hair had been shorn away close to the scalp, and despite the Braille-like topography of the skin due to countless insect bites and exposure to the cruel elements of the desert, Bill Renney could clearly make out the ragged cut around the ear canal.

"All these amputations are a little hastier than the ones on the previous victim," Falmouth explained. "See how the flesh pulls away, as if the ear was only partially severed but then torn the rest of the way, maybe by someone pulling at it? Do you see how it was ripped here? The way the flesh pulls down toward the jaw line, like a hasty rip. These little loose strands of jagged flesh?"

"Yeah, I see," Renney said, following Falmouth's latex-gloved finger as it traced the wound.

Falmouth lifted one of the corpse's arms by the wrist. "Same with the fingers. The cuts from last year were made precisely at the junction of the middle and proximal phalanx. These amputations are hastier; the implement used cut straight through the bone and not at the joint."

Renney stared at the irregular shards of bone poking up from what remained of the fingers.

"The woman that was found last year had all these elements removed from her in an almost surgical fashion. The person who had done that had been careful. Precise. Artful, almost. A scalpel was used, was my conclusion, except for the fingers, where I believe the assailant had utilized something more proficient to break through the carpometacarpal joints—something like a sturdy hunting knife or something of that ilk. The amputations on this victim are much cruder, which I find interesting, since they were removed postmortem where her assailant could have taken his time." Falmouth shrugged, placing the wrist back on the table, then added, "But those differentiations could just be circumstantial."

"Meaning what?" Renney asked.

Falmouth arched his slender, steel-colored eyebrows. "Meaning the killer could have been in a hurry this time, for whatever reason."

"What about any fingerprints or DNA left behind?"

"No fingerprints from the assailant that I've been able to find, which just means he could've been wearing gloves. I've swabbed the body for trace DNA, found some hair folicles and evidence of desquamation—the shedding of dead skin cells—but so far there haven't been any hits. It's possible the assailant isn't in the system."

"That's a big difference from last year, too," Renney said, although more to himself than to Falmouth. The crime scene last year had been impossibly clean, with no trace DNA left behind. "So, do you think this is the same guy who killed that woman last year?"

"Anything's possible," said Falmouth, spreading his arms. "The details of how the first victim was found were—"

"Those details never made it to the press," Renney finished. "Right."

"Exactly. So, in my estimation, to have all these same ... elements ... removed in such a similar and specific fashion, not to mention the location where the body was found—"

"Yes," Renney said, cutting him off. "I understand what you're saying. A copycat killer wouldn't know those details because they were never public."

"It's just that even with the discrepancies, Bill, the similarities are all there. I wouldn't bet on a coincidence, is what I'm saying. But you're the detective."

Renney pointed to a darkened, mottled tract of flesh along the victim's thigh—something that hadn't been there when he had first come upon the body in the desert, because now the rose tattoo was incorporated into that bruising, which hadn't previously been the case. He would have noticed. "What's all that?" he asked. "Are they bruises?"

"This?" Falmouth said, tracing the pattern of darkened flesh along the victim's thigh. "We call this discoloration a 'postmortem suntan.' Dead skin cells react differently to the sun's UV light."

"I once dated a girl like that," Renney said. The comment made Falmouth chuckle, but Renney could still feel some expanding discomfort uncoiling in the center of his chest. He kept hearing Falmouth's words echoing in his head: *It's just that even with the discrepancies, the similarities are all there . . .*

"I would conclude that this body was left in the desert sometime just before dawn," Falmouth said. "The coyotes and vultures hadn't gotten to it yet. Bugs will do damage at any hour, but birds and mammals tend to wait a while to make sure what they're going after is actually dead. Still, you're looking at maybe a three- to five-hour window, at best. Probably less." Falmouth cleared his throat then added, "The desert is unforgiving to a body."

Renney thought of the countless bovine skeletons that littered the desert floor, straight out to the Mojave, all the way out to Las Vegas. Thought of the pinwheels of vultures that were always visible somewhere on the horizon, waiting patiently for some poor thing to expire.

That terrible muscle in the center of his chest constricted again.

Fifteen minutes later, as Renney walked slowly down the long, tiled, echo-chamber corridor of the DMEC, he happened to glance up at a television mounted on brackets to the wall. On the screen was a newscaster standing before the solitary green road sign that read LOS ANGELES COUNTY LINE, an expanse of high desert in the background. The chyron at the bottom of the screen said: BODY OF FEMALE VICTIM FOUND MUTILATED IN ANTELOP VALLEY.

" . . . where, less than a week ago, the body of an unidentifed young woman was found mutilated in the spot you see right over my shoulder," said the reporter. "For the people who live out here, they are reminded of an eerily similar murder from the year before— that of thirty-two-year-old Melissa Jean Andressen, whose body was discovered in this very stretch of desert."

A still image of Melissa Jean Andressen appeared on the screen, and Renney recognized the photo as the same one the department had circulated to the media in the days after her body had been discovered last year—an attractive woman in tennis whites, dark hair as full as a lion's mane around her head, smiling beatifically. Her eyes were green and radiant and heavily lashed. *She had been very pretty*, Renney thought.

"Andressen's killer was never brought to justice, despite the efforts of the L.A. County Sheriff's Department and the hefty reward posted by Andressen's husband, prominent Hollywood psychiatrist Dr. Alan Andressen."

Melissa Jean Andressen's photo was replaced by one of her husband. Alan Andressen was smiling, too, only there was something reserved about it—as if smiling did not come naturally to the man. Renney supposed that was true, although he knew it was unfair to pass such judgment, since he'd only known Alan after the murder of his wife, when the man was at his worst.

"For a while," the reporter continued, "Dr. Andressen was the only suspect in the murder of his wife, but he was ultimately cleared by police early in the investigation. Now, with the discovery of this new victim, locals and police alike are starting to wonder if the two murders may not be connected. As for any specific similarities that might connect these two murders, the Los Angeles County Sheriff's

Department has not released any details to the media. Sarah Sullivan, Channel Eleven News."

The broadcast switched to sports, but Renney hardly noticed. There was a tunneling in his vision now, coupled with an eerie auditory exclusion. He'd been in two shootouts during his tenure on the force, and the way time seemed to slow down and stretch, providing only a pinpoint of light at the end of his narrowing vision, like staring down a long tunnel, was very similar to how he now felt.

He stood there, sweating.

Her name was Gina Fortunado, twenty-six years old, originally of San Bernardino, California, but recently having resided in a one-bedroom apartment in downtown Los Angeles. A schoolteacher, single, and a graduate of UCLA, she was last seen by some girlfriends the day before her body was discovered, while they all had lunch at some vegan joint on Alameda Street. No one that Bill Renney could readily identify—including the girl's parents, who still lived in San Bernardino—had seen her since.

He visited her parents at their modest, single-family home on Magnolia Avenue—a cheery stamp of property bracketed by towering palm trees and with a cluster of vehicles in the driveway. The house was hot, the windows stood open, and electric fans turned their heads in nearly every room. Gina's parents had filed a missing persons report after several days went by with no contact from her, and her father—a tall, quiet man with a deeply seamed face and gray, pensive eyes—positively identified his daughter by the photograph of a rose tattoo on her thigh. During Renney's visit, Gina's mother sat in the living room surrounded by daughters and nieces, her eyes foggy and distant, her movements like those of an animatronic slowly losing power. There was a grandmother there, too—a wizened apparition who rocked ceaselessly in a chair by the window, a string of rosary beads in her gnarled white hands. When the father meandered into the living room to sit beside his wife, Renney wandered around the house, gazing at photographs of Gina and her sisters, Gina and her cousins, Gina in a high school cheerleading outfit, Gina at the beach, Gina leaning against the hood of someone's Camaro. She had been pretty and bright-eyed.

"She wanted to be an artist."

Renney turned around, startled by the voice. It was one of Gina's sisters, looking at a particular image hanging on the wall from over his shoulder. He followed her stare to a framed watercolor painting of a blossoming red rose.

"She painted that?" Renney asked.

"When she was only seven. Isn't it spectacular?"

"Very impressive."

"She couldn't make a living as an artist. That's why she went into teaching." Her gaze left the painting and settled on Renney. He could feel the weight of her stare pressing against him like something tangible. "Who would do such a terrible thing to my sister?"

"I'm going to find out," Renney said, and then he left that place.

Several nights later, Bill Renney arrived home to find a man standing on his porch. He called out to the man as he slowed his gait moving up the walkway toward the front of the house: "Hello? Can I help you? This is a private residence."

No response.

Renney was cradling a soggy paper bag of fast food against his chest, but managed to slide a hand toward his hip, where his service weapon remained concealed beneath his sports coat. There had been a string of burglaries in the neighborhood lately, and Renney supposed it was only a matter of time before his number was called.

The man said nothing—and it was certainly a man; Renney could tell by the cut of the figure's silhouette—but instead this person drifted along the length of the porch, momentarily vanishing among the shadows collected at the corner of the house, where the light of the lamppost on Canyon Road was unable to reach. But then the man reappeared, and proceeded to descend the porch steps, stopping halfway down when he spied Renney staring back at him.

Renney paused in midstride.

About a year had passed since he had last laid eyes on Dr. Alan Andressen. Yet it wasn't the passage of time that prevented him from immediately recognizing the man, but rather Alan Andressen's overall appearance. As Alan stepped nearer to the light of the streetlamp, Renney could see that the man had lost too much weight, and that his clothes—Lakers sweatshirt and wrinkled chinos—hung from his frame as if from a clothesline. A few more paces, closing the distance, and Renney could make out patchy, unshaven jowls, and dark crescents beneath the man's sleep-deprived eyes. Alan's mouth was a firm slash, and something in those weary eyes glittered wetly.

"Doc," Renney heard himself say. "What are you—"

"I saw the news," Alan said. "Is it true?"

With the exception of a dog barking its head off somewhere in the distance, the street was otherwise quiet at this hour. Still, Renney did not want to be standing here in the open having this conversation.

"Listen, Alan—"

"You should have called me."

"For what reason? To upset you?"

"Christ, Bill. Is it true? What they're saying on the news about that girl?"

Renney fished his house keys from his pocket. "Come inside and we'll talk," he said, moving around Alan on his way to the porch.

It was a two-bedroom bungalow in Van Nuys, bookended by used car dealerships and pawn shops, and within spitting distance of both the 405 and the 101. The house had seemed perfectly adequate before Linda had died, but it now felt too hollow and empty to Renney, particularly in the evenings. After Linda's death, he had considered getting a dog to help fill the void, but he concluded it wouldn't be fair to keep some poor animal locked up in a house all day (and sometimes all night, too, given Renney's chaotic work schedule). In the end, he had settled on a fish tank, one of those fifty-gallon jobs, and he had sprung for the saltwater tropical fish because they had struck him as more festive than the typical freshwater ones.

He dumped the greasy pouch of fast food on the half wall that separated the living room from the kitchen, then went directly to the tank, lifted the lid, and sprinkled some fish food onto the surface of the water. A school of striped cardinalfish recalibrated their position in the tank and made a beeline in the direction of the food. The soft burble of the filter brought Renney a modicum of peace, if for only a moment.

His and Linda's wedding photo hung on the wall beside the fish tank, a glossy eight-by-ten in a cheap frame. In the photo, Linda looked young and resplendent in her white gown, the shape of her collarbones like the carved slats on a cello, no evidence of the cancer that would ultimately claim her looming in her future. He didn't look so bad himself in his rented tux—about twenty pounds leaner and missing the silver streaks that now grew like kudzu at his temples. *Kissing your white spots*, Linda used to say when they'd first started sprouting, and she would kiss him there.

When he turned around, he found Alan standing in the open doorway. In the stark light of the foyer, Alan looked nearly skeletal, and not just because of the amount of weight he'd lost since Renney had last seen him. The man's skin was the pallor of bread dough and his hair had receded quite a bit, expanding the real estate of his pale, sweat-dappled forehead. His mouth looked too wide for his narrow face, as if his teeth had grown, somehow.

"Shut the door," Renney told him. He set the container of fish food down and went into the small kitchen, where he opened the fridge and took out two bottles of Coors Light.

The front door squealed shut, but when Alan didn't appear in the kitchen doorway or over the half wall, Renney ambled back out with both beers to find him still standing in the foyer, staring at him. The man's eyes looked like burnt flashbulbs. He had his hands on his hips, and his shoulders came to abrupt points beneath the fabric of that oversized Lakers sweatshirt. He looked like a haunted house.

"I couldn't find any specific details online," Alan said. "Only whatever cursory bullshit they've been saying on the news."

"We're keeping the details pretty quiet for the time being."

Alan rubbed the heel of one hand across his forehead. "Was she cut up the same way? Was it the same?"

"You don't look well," Renney said, by way of deflecting the question.

"Don't give me that shit. What the fuck's going on, Bill? Was her face all cut up? Her fucking fingers removed? Tell me."

"There are . . . some similarities, yeah," Renney admitted. The words felt hot, like they came out of his throat on a gust of steam. "The body parts, the way she was cut up, yeah. Pretty much the same."

"Goddamn. Then you know what that means," Alan said, his voice shaking. Renney could see the anguish on his face, a year's worth of unmitigated grief compounded with the burden of this new information, each emotion stacked precariously atop the next, like some terrible Jenga tower. "It can't be a coincidence. No details were ever released to the public . . . "

"That's right," Renney said, though his tone was tempered. "We never released the details of your wife's murder to the press, Alan—the way she'd been . . . the, uh, specific details, is what I'm saying. No one outside the police department, the medical examiner's office, or the district attorney knew what condition your wife was in when we found her."

"So it's the same fucking guy."

"Alan, let's not jump to con—"

"To have this girl show up in the same way, all cut up like that, in what's pretty goddamn close to the same location . . . " Alan went on, ignoring him, and then his voice cracked and he could not complete the sentiment.

"It's unusual, sure, but I guess anything's possible," Renney said, realizing they were Falmouth's words coming out of his mouth. He wasn't so sure he could believe them, however. Not now. Not about this.

A humorless laugh trembled out of Alan Andressen's throat. "Fuck's sake, Bill. After everything that's happened, you can't just be straight with me?"

Renney sighed. There was a bead of sweat tracing down the center of his back, right between his shoulder blades. He was still clutching a beer bottle in each hand, but he suddenly had no taste for it. He extended one to Alan, but Alan just shook his head then glanced away from him.

"Listen to me, Alan. The man who murdered your wife is *dead*. This is entirely something else." Renney himself didn't believe this—he wasn't sure *what* he believed at the moment—but he didn't want Alan spiraling deeper into a hole. He didn't trust where that might lead. "I spoke at length with the coroner. There are more discrepancies than similarities. Whoever killed this woman, it was a hasty job, nothing like what happened with your wife."

"Yeah? So, what? This is all just some big coincidence?"

"It could be," said Renney.

"Well, I don't believe in coincidences. Not like this. It's too similar. It's too close. Which means my wife's killer is still out there." Alan's voice had gone reed-thin and slightly hoarse. "That the son of a bitch has been out there all this time. And if *that's* true, then what you and I did last year—"

"Stop," Renney said. "Just stop it."

Alan turned and stared at him again. The flesh beneath his eyes looked nearly black, like someone had slapped him around a day or two ago. "Look at me, Bill. Look me straight in the eyes and tell me this isn't the same guy who killed my wife."

"Like I said, I spoke to the coroner—"

"Ah, fuck it. And fuck you, too. I know you don't believe that bullshit. You're just fucking patronizing me, like I'm some goddamn child you can manipulate. I know what this means, and I don't have to spell it out for you, either."

"Get what happened last year out of your head. This girl's death has nothing to do with your wife's murder. That guy is *gone*. Move on."

Alan's face tightened. His mouth became a lipless slash. "Yeah, right," he said, his voice low and breathy. "Real easy for you to say."

"It's been a year, Alan. You don't look any better."

"You should have fucking called me," Alan said.

A moment later, Bill Renney was standing alone in his house, feeling the emptiness of the place pressing down on him like a physical thing.

TWO

E than Hawke was standing by the buffet table holding a bottle of soda water and talking to a young actress whose name Maureen could not immediately recall. There was music on the stereo—Loverboy, "Working for the Weekend"—and the chatter of guests' conversations created a lively hum in the air. Maureen herself was drinking a vodka tonic with extra lemon—her third of the evening, just to take the edge off—and she was planted in one corner of the living room that mostly kept her out of everyone else's way.

She'd spent that morning instructing the caterers where to set everything up, clearing out extra space in the fridge, and fretting over the placement of the glassware on the wet bar and the linen napkins and silverware on the buffet table. By the time Greg had come in from the golf course, tanned and cheery, she had already rearranged the silverware about a dozen times—so compulsively, in fact, that the caterers had relocated themselves to the far side of the room where they had watched her with a collective expression that suggested she might be a little unhinged.

She just wanted everything to be perfect.

On the surface, it was a party to celebrate Maureen and Greg's engagement. But Greg Dawson was a man of many layers, and one look at the guest list informed Maureen that this party was, at its core, much more strategic than it might appear at first glance. That was Greg Dawson's style: allowing for things to appear capricious and indulgent and lacking in discretion on the surface, when in reality there was an elaborate and disciplined choreography at work behind the scenes. Structures, delicate as strands of DNA, laid one atop the next, an entire procession of calculations, of chiming silverware and glugging pours of booze, of mouths breathing in synchronicity, each mouth a train tunnel bored into the side of a mountain, languages traversing invisible, breathy tracks, a distance to these people that signified a closeness, a *party*, a sense of—

Her mind was whirling again. She forced herself to take a deep breath and calm down.

The party was free-flowing now, with upwards of eighty guests, each one strategically curated from Greg's Hollywood rolodex. He had split from Miramax the previous year, before he and Maureen had met, to form Canyon Films with two old law school friends; at the moment, he and these two partners were in the homestretch to get Canyon Films' latest feature, *Hatchet Job*, financed. A screenplay was in the bag, an established director had thrown his hat into the ring, and Greg Dawson was owed enough favors from a few well-known actors all over town to feel confident that he could get some above-the-line talent onboard, too. He just needed the last few straggling investors to commit . . . and he had determined, in that inimitable Greg Dawson way, that his and Maureen's engagement party might just prove the perfect tool to get the job done.

She watched him throughout the night, from what felt like a safe distance: a man well past middle age, confident, a thing that could be shiny and appealing when necessary, staunch and direct a moment later. She admired his grace—was that even a male trait, something to be admired?—and registered his progression throughout the party with the same steadfast dedication and scrutiny as a Navy admiral tracking an enemy sub. *Greg Dawson lives here. Greg Dawson goes here. Greg Dawson exists here.* Stranger, still: *I live here. I go here. I exist here.*

Vodka tonic number four.

It was a gorgeous night, cool for so late in the summer, so most of the guests had migrated out onto the back patio and were having drinks by the pool underneath the stars. From where Maureen stood, still taciturn in her corner of the living room, she could see through the open sliders David Duchovny charming one of the young female caterers beside the manicured hedgerow that overlooked the lights of Los Angeles. A few feet away from Duchovny, someone popped the cork on a bottle of champagne, and Maureen watched the champagne geyser and gush in a milky spume down the length of the bottle. A man in a silk jacket leaned toward another and whispered something into this man's ear, some passable secret shared, handed off, conspiratorially, beneath a dangling, luminous network of Chinese lanterns.

Greg was across the room now, talking with a handsome couple by the stationary wet bar. As with most of the guests that evening, Maureen thought she recognized the couple, but she couldn't put names to their faces. (She was not "Hollywood," which, Greg had said on more than one occasion, was what he found fascinating about her—"Well, that and your lovely caboose," he'd add, and then he'd laugh.) As she stared at them, Greg turned and caught her eye, gave her a sly wink. Energy crackled in the air, bridging some invisible gap between them. She liked looking at him from a distance, knowing she was the one going to bed with him at the end of the day. She liked thinking that such a well-respected, talented, energetic man found something equally as appealing in her.

Greg collected his drink from the bartender—a lowball glass of bronze liquid swaddled in a damp cocktail napkin—and pointed in her direction, just as casually as you'd please. The handsome couple looked over at her, their faces bright. The man eyed her head to toe while the woman smiled vacuously at her. Greg said something to them from the corner of his mouth, his eyes on her, too.

Maureen smiled back, then instantly felt unsettled and on dangerous display, like something targeted in the crosshairs of a hunting rifle. She took a swallow of her drink and made a beeline for the kitchen.

Two young women in starched whites were placing smoked trout croquettes onto a silver tray, while a third woman was arranging crystal stemware on the countertop beside a case of Dom Pérignon. There were two rows of Sterno cans on the counter, as well, slightly misaligned; Maureen set her vodka tonic on the kitchen table, then drifted over to the Sterno cans and proceeded to tidy up the rows. There was an odd number of cans, and that realization caused her back teeth to tighten. Agitation funneled through her like a sickness. She quickly began to rearrange them, making three perfectly even rows, five cans in each, *one two three four five*, then found herself navigating toward the crystal stemware, so many glittery flutes, and not even an attempt to set them in clean, precise rows, just discarded haphazardly on the countertop, their randomness an affront to Maureen's senses. She could almost *hear* their discordance, like a sour note being played repeatedly on a piano.

She began to line the champagne flutes into perfect rows—so precise that their circular bases touched, creating a diamond shape at their center, and that the tops of the flutes were all equidistant from one another. Yet there was a design in the crystal, a pattern that rolled like an ocean wave, multiple prisms refracting the lights of the kitchen, and Maureen suddenly needed those ocean waves to align, to roll into one another, peaceably, so that to look upon the entire collection of champagne glasses was to look upon a consistent and satisfying rolling ocean wave that—

The women from the catering company were staring at her as if she'd lost her mind.

"I'm sorry," she said, taking a step back from the rows of champagne flutes. She realized she'd left fingerprints on some of the glasses. "You're all doing a wonderful job. I'm sorry. I'm sorry. Thank you. Thank you all."

She grabbed her drink off the kitchen table then retreated back out into the living room.

Pat Benatar was on the sound system now, and Ethan Hawke had meandered over to the wall of Greg's vinyl record albums. A woman in a tiara and sandals was gesticulating wildly before a group of swarthy men, her false eyelashes as lavish as palm fronds. She had a conspicuous mole in the center of her chest, right between her breasts, which looked almost strategically placed to draw attention to that particular section of her body.

Maureen looked toward the other side of the room and spotted a slender, attractive woman in a tapered black suit, with short, dark hair sculpted to her head, standing by herself in one corner. She wasn't drinking or eating anything, and in fact, was simply staring at Maureen through the crowd. Maureen nodded and smiled at her, which was when the woman began drifting through the throng in her direction. The men at either side of her appeared to part without noticing, as though some mental telepathy had just taken place. As she approached, the woman narrowed her dark eyes and leveled a finger at Maureen, a gesture that was simultaneously intimate yet indulgent.

"I know you," said the woman.

Maureen blinked, and said, "Oh? Yes, you do look familiar. Have we met before?"

"No, we haven't met," said the woman. "But you're Maureen Park."

"That's right."

"I've read your book."

It was almost as if she'd misheard the woman.

"My book? Really?"

"Yes. It was angry and visceral and daring and wholly feminist. You made me cry at the end, too, by the way, but I also shouted and laughed out loud. Just when I thought you were going for the throat, you went for the heart. But then, to my surprise and delight, at the very end, you circled back around and went for the throat again. It was very well done."

"Really? Wow, thank you. That's very kind of you to say."

"A shame you haven't written more." The woman smiled. She wore a gold cross on a slender chain around her neck which, Maureen noted with some intrigue, hung upside down.

"I could swear we've met each other be—"

"Looks like you're about to be swept away," the woman said, cutting her off. She was staring over Maureen's shoulder. "We'll talk again. Congratulations on the engagement."

Maureen thanked the woman, then watched her float back through the crowd until she lost sight of her.

"Hey."

Maureen spun around, startled, and nearly spilled her drink on Greg.

"What's with the jitters? You doing okay?"

"Peachy," she said, and took a drink. "I just met a fan."

"I'm your biggest fan, you know," he said, slipping an arm around her and giving her a squeeze.

His tan looked good on him, healthy, and made him appear younger than his fifty-eight years. He wore a rose-pink linen shirt and casual slacks, thatched loafers with no socks, and a gold Chopard wristwatch that cost more than Maureen's first car. He was in good shape, which was the first thing Maureen had noticed about him when they'd first met, only a handful of months ago, he on one side of a bar, she on the other.

He administered a swift kiss to the top of her head, a gesture that somehow made her feel both cherished and insignificant at the same time. That was Greg Dawson's specialty: the subtle insinuation of juxtaposition into everyday life. She supposed it was something she might grow weary of in time, but that realization didn't bother her now. "You've been standing in this corner all night, babe. You look like you're in the penalty box."

"That's not true. I was just in the kitchen, checking on the food."

"That's the caterers' job. People are going to think you're the help."

"I don't know what to say to half of these people," she confided.

"Oh, Maur," he said. "Half of them are dull, and the other half only talk nonstop about themselves, which makes them dull *and* lacking in self-awareness."

"I just want to make a good impression."

"You're the classiest woman here, Maureen."

She nodded in the direction of the young, handsome couple Greg had been talking to moments before, still standing by the bar. They looked like cake toppers. "Who're they?"

"David and Sophia Gilchrist. He's a nobody. She's the money. Her old man was some hedge fund guru."

"I'm starting to think maybe you need some actual friends in your life."

"Hey. These *are* my friends."

She frowned at him. "They're acquaintances with deep pockets."

"Maybe you're right. But listen, this is an important night, all right? It means a lot."

"Don't stress out about the finances, I'm sure you'll get everything you need. These people adore you. You've got them practically digging in their wallets right now."

"No, Maur, I mean it's an important night for *us*. You've been hiding from everyone all evening, me included, when all I want to do is show you off. Let everyone meet my beautiful bride-to-be. You look lovely tonight, by the way."

Earlier that day, she had gone upstairs and crawled into a battery of dresses, each one more unflattering (and expensive) than the previous one. In the end, she had settled for a pair of black Tuleh slacks, a sleeveless taupe blouse, and a pair of open-toed slingback shoes. Glancing down at herself now, she noticed that the polish on her toenails could have used a touch-up, and there was an unsightly crease in her left pant leg.

"These people just make me uncomfortable," she said.

"I told you to invite some of your friends, too."

Maureen's friends—her *real* friends, the ones she grew up with—were all back in Wyoming, and anyway, she'd stopped being close with them long ago. But she did feel bad for Greg, who was very sweet and handsome and who was trying very hard, and she wanted to make him look good in front of these people. She could have tried harder, she supposed; could've invited the girl from the yogurt place or maybe some women from her Pilates class, not that she knew any of them well at all.

"You're right," she said. "I've been a wallflower. Introduce me to some of these deep pockets, yeah?"

He laughed, and she could smell cigarettes on his breath, a habit he'd told her he'd quit. "Shhh, don't call them that. It's our secret."

"Mum's the word, baby love," she said, and pantomimed zipping her lip.

They went out through the open sliders and into the night. The air smelled of chlorine from the pool, and the music was louder out here on the wireless speakers hidden from sight within the hedgerow. Greg led her over to a group of men and women standing beside the outdoor bar. The men were dressed as if they were at a luau while the women looked a bit classier—all sharp edges, designer apparel, and sidelong glances.

Introductions were made in a frenzy, and with the exception of Barry Whitlock, the screenwriter who'd penned the *Hatchet Job* screenplay, Maureen could keep very few of the names straight. The men shook her hand and congratulated her on the engagement while the women demanded to see Maureen's engagement ring. More than just a little self-consciously, Maureen held up her hand and allowed the gaggle of women to flock around her to inspect the engagement ring that Greg had purchased for her just a few weeks earlier.

"Christ, Greg, it's the size of a walnut," said one of the men as he peered over at the ring while one of the women gripped the tips of Maureen's fingers as if in a trap.

"It almost didn't come in on time," Greg said, and to Maureen, he suddenly looked like a child confessing to some shameful inadequacy. "I wanted to give it to her in Bali, and the timing wasn't lining up. I had to call a guy I know in New York who called a guy *he* knows in South Africa. Can you imagine the rigmarole? I was sweating like a hostage hoping the damn thing would show up in time for the trip."

"Bali was wonderful," Maureen said, pulling her hand away from the woman's viselike grip. "Greg and I had such a nice time. It was all so wonderful."

"How did you two meet, anyway?" asked one of the men.

Greg snaked an arm around Maureen's waist, tugging her close to him, and said, "At a nightclub. I saw her and my heart just stopped, Roger. She swept me off my feet in an instant, and without effort, and I just knew right then and there I was going to ask her to marry me. I'm saying, in my mind, that very night—it was a done deal. Game over."

"Game's just begun," said Maureen.

The man who'd asked the question broke out in a shark's toothy grin. He turned his attention to Maureen, and said, "I bet you felt the same way about our Greg here, am I right? Love at first sight? Just like in the movies?"

Greg liked to dress up the story about how they met. In actuality, they had come across each other at a restaurant in the valley, where Maureen had been bartending. Greg had been waiting for someone who had never shown up—a flaky investor, it turned out. At the time, Maureen thought he had been waiting on a blind date or something, and when she thought he'd been stood up, she had felt sorry for him. She gave him a martini on the house and they chatted for a little while. Then he had paid the bill—leaving an embarrassingly large tip—and left, only to come back twenty minutes later to ask for her phone number.

"Oh, absolutely," she told the man. "It's been a whirlwind romance, Hollywood-style. What else could it possibly be?"

One of the women smiled at her and grazed Maureen's forearm with a set of acrylic nails in some strange signal of approval. It caused a shiver to race up Maureen's back, but she did her best to hide that fact. Her drink was getting dangerously low. Which one was this, anyway? Number four? She was losing count.

"But *you're* not Hollywood, are you, dear?" said the woman.

Maureen felt a nerve jump in her lower eyelid. "No," she said. "I'm not."

"Maureen's a novelist," Greg said, while rolling around the ice cubes in his glass.

"Well, just one novel," said Maureen. "It was a long time ago."

Greg said, "She's working on something now, you know." He glanced at her. "Aren't you, Maur? A new novel?"

"I don't know what it is," Maureen confessed. "It's just an idea, really. I'm seeing it through."

"Tell us what it's about," said Barry Whitlock, the *Hatchet Job* screenwriter.

"Oh," Maureen said, "I wouldn't want to bore you all."

"Nonsense," said one of the women. She spoke the word in a way a snake might: *Nonsssenssse...*

"Maureen, dear," said Whitlock. "I've spent the sobrietal bulk of the evening excreting small talk with investment brokers and entertainment lawyers, not to mention the better part of a year penning a paint-by-numbers screenplay about a masked serial killer who's got a hatchet for a hand, all for your beau here, which, I'll confess, while occasionally entertaining, could often prove an exercise in artistic prostitution—"

"Christ, Barry," Greg said, laughing a bit. "You ungrateful bastard."

"So, please, dear," Whitlock continued, unfettered. "Do me the courtesy—nay, the *necessity*—of rescuing me from the doldrums of my own personal hell and please, dear, regale me with your tale."

Maureen gave them all a timorous smile. She noticed the woman wearing the inverted cross standing just beyond their circle, partially obscured in shadow, watching her attentively.

"Go on," Greg told her, also smiling.

Maureen took another sip of her drink, then said:

It's about these two people having an affair. They check into a motel room one afternoon and find a religious altar against the wall, opposite the bed. It looks like a big, mirrored vanity but it's got a hassock for kneeling, and it's lined with votive candles and little plaster statues of the Virgin Mary, and there's a large crucifix hanging from the top. The candles are already lit, as if in preparation for their arrival, like someone knew they were coming. It makes them uncomfortable, of course, so they call down to the front desk and ask if they can get another room, but the motel is fully booked. No more rooms available. And they don't have a lot of time, they're both on a lunch break, you know? So, without another option, they decide to just stick it out. But the mirrored wall of the vanity is directly opposite the bed, and each time they happen to look up and glance at it, they're reminded of the thing being there. And they see themselves, of course. At one point, the woman gets up and blows out the candles. The man gets up and moves the plaster statues of the Virgin Mary off the thing, puts them in the nightstand drawer, next to the Bible, which makes him even more uncomfortable, even though a Bible in the nightstand of a motel is nothing unusual. But here they go, each one stowed away like a dirty secret. They pry the cross off the top of the thing, too, and bury it in another drawer. Or maybe in the closet; I don't really remember. But, you see, they've just been . . . heightened . . . to feel uncomfortable because that altar is right there in the room with them, reflecting what they're doing back on them, and it's just so goddamn strange. And the act of moving those items has only made the whole thing resonate more with them. It's like they've created their own discomfort at this point, you know? And then at one point, the woman, she happens to glance up again at the mirror, only this time she notices that the mirror has begun to—

She stopped immediately when she saw what appeared to be a look of consternation on Greg's face.

"Well?" urged Barry Whitlock. "What happens next?"

"Yes," said the woman, who had previously been squeezing Maureen's fingers while scrutinizing her engagement ring. "What has the mirror begun to do?"

"Babe," Greg interjected, clearing his throat, and squeezing her once more about the waist.

Maureen shook her head, confused.

"The first thing you need to learn about gatherings like this," Greg explained, "is that you never tell any of these soulless thieves all the details of your work-in-progress."

The guests laughed. Over their shoulders, Maureen could still see the woman with the dark, sculpted hair whom she'd spoken with in the house standing just beyond them. She just kept her eyes on Maureen, as if she possessed x-ray vision, and was bent on studying the structure of her skeletal system.

How do I know her? she wondered.

"Greg's right, you know," said one of the men, a fellow in a garish Hawaiian shirt with initials monogrammed over the breast pocket. "We're all soul-suckers here. We're all vampires. Hollywood is filled with us, my dear, and we won't think twice about sucking your creativity dry. We're like a contagion."

"A disease," said the woman who had been studying Maureen's ring.

"And you should exercise extreme caution," finished a grinning Barry Whitlock, desperate to add his own two cents.

"Son of a bitch." It was Greg, and the tenor of his voice felt off— it had gone deep, bassoon-deep, and somehow distant. Maureen looked at him just as his hand dropped away from her waist. He was staring at something beyond her, across the patio, and his face had gone pale despite his tan.

"Greg, what—"

"Son of a *bitch*," he said again, and then he was stalking away from their little circle.

Maureen turned to see what Greg had been looking at: two young men stood at the edge of the pool, one in front of the other, as if there was some rank in their numbers. The one in front was tall and lean and athletic looking, dressed in a navy-blue blazer and a partially unbuttoned Tommy Bahama shirt, loose-fitting linen pants, and with a nest of dark, explosive curls atop his head. He had the strap of an athletic duffel bag casually slung over one shoulder, and a glacial, dissociative expression on his sharp-featured face. The young man standing behind him looked less severe—he wore baggy Levi's and a concert tee, a wedge of sandy hair knotted along the left side of his cranium.

Maureen watched Greg approach the young man with the duffel bag. Greg was heated, his face red, and he leaned very close to the young man's face as he spoke, his voice too low for Maureen or anyone else to hear. Greg's words seemed to pass through the young man unimpeded, and the young man's expression never faltered. Greg took the young man by the shoulder, but then dropped his hand when that yielded no reaction. Then he poked the young man in the chest as his spoke with a duo of fingers—*thump thump thump.* The kid getting thumped hardly registered this interaction; he was, Maureen realized, staring directly at *her.* Behind him, his friend's eyes were as large and wide as billiard balls.

"Excuse me," Maureen said to the guests, and then she detached herself and floated over to where Greg was still thumping the young man in his solar plexus with two stiff fingers. "Greg, what's this all ab—"

The young man getting finger-jabbed by Greg took a step back. Greg's arm hovered in midair, desperate for something else to poke, a vein throbbing at his right temple. His face was crimson.

"You blew through twenty thousand dollars this summer," Greg was saying to the kid. He kept his voice low, but there was no mistaking the anger in it. Those poking fingers still stuttered, unanchored, in the air. Eager to resume contact.

The young man turned away from Greg and looked sedately at Maureen . . . though, in a way, he had been looking at Maureen the whole time. Unlike his friend, who cowered behind him with his billiard-ball gaze, this young man's eyes were red-rimmed and sleepy-lidded, bored almost, and as she stared at his knifelike, angular features, a calculating little smile insinuated itself across the lower portion of his face. She saw teeth arranged in perfect symmetry beneath the hawkish blade of his nose.

Without uttering a word, the young man leaned toward her and wrapped his long, sinewy arms around her body, pulling her close. He reeked of marijuana and overly strong aftershave lotion, and his slender, too-tall frame against hers felt geometrically uncomfortable and misaligned, like a wooden puppet dressed up in people clothes.

Too shocked to say or do anything, Maureen just stood there and allowed this kid's overlong arms and long, blunt fingers to infiltrate the places and spaces and creases along the back of her blouse. And when he finally disengaged from her—because that was what it was, a *disengagement*, like something mechanical and lacking in human emotion undocking—Maureen took a step back from him, creating further distance.

"Maureen," Greg said, running a hand through his hair, his face still on fire, "this is my son, Landon."

She elicited a barely audible sound that could have been misconstrued as approval, and then she Bataan-marched the simulacrum of a smile onto her face. Forced it to remain there. Said, "Landon." Said, "Hello." Said, "I've heard so much about you."

Landon's lazy smile stretched even wider. He jerked a thumb at Greg, and said, "I've told this old cocksucker to stop talking about me to people."

"You're supposed to be in Europe for another three months," Greg interjected, his gaze locked on his son.

Landon shrugged. "We ran out of money."

"What'd you spend it on? Drugs?"

"Good to see you, too, Pop."

"You could've called."

Landon looked around the patio, seemed to spot Duchovny by the bar. "Is this a homecoming party? You didn't have to do all this . . ."

Greg reached out and snared Landon by the lapel of his blazer. He peered into the boy's red, bleary eyes. "You're stoned right now."

"You're astute."

Landon's wide-eyed friend took a sensible step back, as if anticipating some physical altercation on the horizon.

"Don't fuck this up for us tonight," Greg said, dropping his hand from his grown son's chin. "Take your bag and your friend and go to your room."

"Me and Uptown are hungry," Landon said. He was still glancing around the patio, taking in all the sights now, as if just noticing them. On the hidden speakers, Billy Squier was singing "Emotions in Motion," and a girl in a pressed white uniform nearly approached them with a tray of drinks, but then sensed blood in the water, and wisely pivoted to a group of other guests. "I think maybe we'll sit down and have something to eat."

The kid behind Landon—Uptown—raised a hand and, bashfully, said, "Hey, all."

"Just get the fuck to your room," Greg demanded.

"You know what," Maureen said. She reached out and placed a hand on Greg's shoulder. It felt like touching a steel bolt beneath the fabric of his shirt. "Why don't I fix you boys a couple of plates and then you can go upstairs?"

Landon's bleary eyes settled back on her. He looked nothing at all like Greg, she realized—he was too rangy, too ungainly, and lacked the confidence and self-possession of his father—and there was a glimmer of arrogance deep in his muddled stare that made Maureen want to cross her arms over her chest. In fact, she did so.

"That sounds good to me," Landon said. Then added, "Mom."

"Oh, for fuck's sake," Greg said, turning away from his son. He still had his hand in his hair.

"I've got this, honey," Maureen assured him.

"No one's got this," Greg said, and then he negotiated away from them, halfway down the patio to where another bar was set up. He quickly ordered a drink.

"Come on," Maureen said, and she led both young men back into the house, and over to the buffet table. They said nothing as she stacked food onto two good china plates—croquettes, fried asparagus, sheaves of smoked salmon, caviar, dates stuffed with goat cheese, a dollop of chaat masala, pickled shrimp, cucumber salad, a few fingers of prosciutto shortbread, phyllo-wrapped brie with anchovies. When she looked up, she saw Landon extracting a full bottle of Dom from a silver ice bucket, dripping water along the carpet, a damp handprint on his Tommy Bahama shirt. His friend was standing nervously beside him, alternating from one foot to the other, those glassy, billiard-ball eyes roving anxiously around the room. Whatever chemicals they'd pumped into their bodies, they were getting worked over pretty good at the moment, she could tell.

She extended the plates out to the two of them. Said, "Landon, honey, it's so good to finally meet you. If only we knew you were coming home tonight, we would have—"

"Hey," he said, cutting her off. "Wanna hear a joke?"

The plates still in both her hands, hovering there in the space between them, Maureen blinked, then said, "Sure. Okay. A joke. Go for it."

That too-wide smile reappeared along Landon's face. Staring at her with his red-rimmed, messy eyes, he said, "A priest, a rabbi, and a dyslexic guy walk into a rab."

She said, "A what?"

"That's it. That's the joke. You don't get it?"

"She don't get it," said Landon's buddy. "*I* don't even get it."

"He's a dyslexic guy," said Landon.

"Take your plates," she said, and pushed the china dishes loaded with food in their direction.

Landon tucked the bottle of Dom under one arm, then took both plates from her. Beside him, Uptown—if that was his real name—stared longingly at the food spread out along the buffet table, then seemed to jump when the music on the stereo changed, spilling Billie Eilish from the speakers.

"You know why you didn't recognize me when I was standing out by the pool?" Landon asked her.

"Because I've never met you before," she replied.

"No. It's because I'm invisible. A regular invisible man. Not a single picture of me hanging in this dump."

Behind him, Uptown swiveled his head around, as if looking to confirm this.

"My dad listens to crap music," Landon muttered. "He makes crap movies. And makes crap decisions."

She felt that last comment as a barb.

"Thanks for the grub, bub," Landon said to her, and then he skulked across the living room and out into the hall, his friend tagging along behind him like a loyal dog.

The house was an open concept, so when Maureen looked up toward the second story, she could see the boys' shapes shuffling darkly through the gloom up there, circling the hallway banister, on their way—presumably—toward Landon's bedroom.

A moment later, Maureen realized she no longer had her drink, so she went to the bar, ordered another vodka tonic—number five? number six? who could remember?—then headed back to the buffet table to frantically organize the silverware. As she did so, she glanced around to see if she could spot the woman in the black pantsuit who wore the inverted cross, but the woman was nowhere to be found.

Hours later, she awoke with a pounding headache, dehydrated from too much alcohol. Beside her, Greg, in his CPAP machine, slept with all the fanfare of the mechanically assisted. Maureen peeled the sheet from her body, tugged a silk robe over her frame, then wound down the stairs to the kitchen in the dark.

An automatic nightlight came on as she passed in front of the kitchen sink. She opened the refrigerator . . . then closed the door, opened it again, closed it again, opened it once more. *Stop it.* She took out a bottle of Evian, and was unscrewing the cap when she realized the patio lights were on at the back of the house. The pool lights, too. She went into the living room and stood before the glass slider, which stood open a few inches. It could have been left that way by one of the caterers, or even one of the guests, but some part of Maureen's brain leapt to the conclusion that it could just as easily been left that way by some intruder.

She peered through the glass and realized four things at once: that there was a man reclining on one of the patio chairs by the pool; that this man was, in fact, Landon, whom she had forgotten was even in the house; that Landon was nude, his body wet from a late-night (or early morning) swim; and that he was masturbating.

Shame enveloped her, no different than if their roles had been reversed, and she quickly backed away from the windows. In doing so, her hip knocked against the buffet table, causing its wooden legs to jump on the hardwood floor and the contents atop the table to chatter. Outside, Landon was alerted to the sound; he froze momentarily in mid-stroke, swiveling his head in the direction of the glass sliders, his wild curls slicked back from his forehead, his skin the color of marble in the moonlight.

Maureen realized she was backlit by the automated light that was glowing through the kitchen doorway, and that if Landon couldn't make out any specific details of her standing there, he could at least ascertain her silhouette.

She hurried back into the kitchen and thumbed the automatic light shut, dousing the kitchen in darkness. The only light now was coming in through the windows at the far side of the kitchen and through the living room—a combination of moonlight and the lights from the patio. She didn't dare head back upstairs in that moment—she would have had to cross in front of the sliders again in order to do that—so she just stood there in the dark, clutching the bottle of Evian in both hands, and holding her breath like a frightened child.

Waited.

Waited.

After a time, she heard the scrape of the pool chair legs across the stamped concrete patio. A moment after that, she heard the breathy whoosh of the sliding door opening wider on its track, followed by the moist tackiness of wet, bare feet on the hardwood floor. She couldn't see Landon through the kitchen doorway from where she stood, but she convinced herself that she could hear him breathing—a low, humming susurration, not unlike the sound made by his father's CPAP machine.

He didn't see me. Even with the kitchen light on, it was still too dark. He didn't see me standing there, watching what he was doing.

"Goodnight, Mom," he said from the living room, and then she heard him move coolly across the floor. When he began to climb the stairs, she could hear the tendons popping like elastic bands in his calves.

THREE

Linda had been a college professor, and she'd once written and published an academic paper on the topic of the cyclical nature of time. She'd defined it to Renney in terms she no doubt thought he might understand—namely, as the trackable repetition of events throughout the course of human history, as well as the repetitive elements in specific lives of all individuals who exist within that fabric of space and time. "Think of it this way," she explained to him. "It's as if the universe operates upon a finite set of rules, or structures, like a limited sequence of numbers, say one through five, which means that over time, the universe is bound to repeat itself. Do you see? There are only so many patterns a finite set of numbers like one through five can make, so, by definition, that same set of numbers will eventually come back around and repeat itself. Maybe it's accidental, or some fluke, or maybe it's unrealized cosmic balance at play. A cosmic echo. It's my belief," she went on, "that nature prefers the comfort of familiarity."

Renney, who had been waist deep trying to unravel a series of burglaries in West Hollywood at the time of this discussion, was admittedly only capable of grasping what his wife had attempted to relay to him in the most rudimentary fashion. He was too literal-minded—always had been—to fathom the scope, the broad strokes, the unfurling cosmic drapery, of all that Linda had been trying to impart. (And while theirs had been a good marriage, Renney would sometimes wonder if the fundamental differences in the way they thought would sometimes create a small yet not insignificant chasm between them; when the article was ultimately published, Renney had gotten it framed and had hung it on the wall of the living room as a surprise. For Linda, this gesture seemed to undermine the fundamental difference between the two of them, and while she thanked him for his thoughtfulness, Renney couldn't help feel like he'd done something improper.)

It had been years since that paper had been published, and years since Linda had attempted to explain her theory to him (and years since that old academic article had hung—briefly—in a frame on the living room wall), but now, in this moment, Bill Renney felt like some part of him—some animal part of his brain, dormant until just recently, stirred into wakefulness by whatever dim sensibility deigns to effectively rouse the animal parts of all our brains—suddenly comprehended at least a modicum of what his wife had been trying to explain to him.

Because Bill Renney suddenly found himself back in the same place he was a year ago.

A cosmic echo.

It was a gradual realization, something he didn't understand was happening until he was already in the thick of it, and by then it was too late to deny the thoughts that plagued him. There were no leads in the Gina Fortunado murder investigation, nothing he could sink his teeth into, nothing he could turn over coolly in his hands to study. There were no footprints from the perpetrator at the crime scene, no evidence of vehicular tracks from the perp's mode of transportation in the sand. There were no fingerprints, and whatever trace DNA evidence was found on the body yielded no results when run through the various databases. Moreover, Gina Fortunado's whereabouts in the handful of hours prior to her body being discovered in the high desert outside the city of Los Angeles remained a mystery for Renney, as well. There was no evidence that she had used her credit card during that period, which meant there was no location to which Renney could go pay a visit; there were no phone calls made from her cell phone during that stretch of time, either, which provided Renney with no additional leads. Her photos were plastered all over the television news as well as the internet, but no one came forward to say they had seen her the night of her murder.

A.J. Politano, whom Renney had learned had just made sergeant, was assigned to assist in the investigation. Together, they interviewed Gina's close circle of friends, to include any recent former boyfriends. After that, they expanded their questioning to include a wider selection of acquaintances—coworkers at the school where she'd taught, people she'd met on dating apps, old college friends, a former roommate. It was beginning to feel like desperation to Renney, and he wasn't buoyed in the least by Politano's enthusiasm to be working such a high-profile case.

"There was that serial shooter in Stockton a few years ago, and then there was that lunatic right here in the county last year who killed those four people," Politano said. They were technically off duty, the two of them sharing a booth in one darkened corner of the Blackbird Tavern on Bay Street, a pitcher of piss-colored beer between them. Politano had a packet of papers he was thumbing through—homicide cases in and around L.A. County that remained unsolved and, according to the newly minted sergeant, might be related to their own case. "There was also that couple in Oakland, the break-in from a few months ago, where they were both stabbed to death. Unsolved, different M.O., but I can make a call out there, see if there are any similarities that didn't make the press."

Renney sipped his beer and said nothing.

"I pulled the file on that Andressen woman from last year, too, just to bring myself up to speed," Politano went on. "I know at the time it was thought to be an isolated incident, but now that we've got a second body done up the same way, is there anything from that case you think we should revisit?"

Renney cocked an eyebrow and said, "Revisit?"

"You know," Politano said. "Re-examine, in light of this second murder." He flipped to a specific page in the packet, and Renney could see his own handwritten notes from last year's case photocopied there. "Whatever happened to that auto mechanic from Reseda? What's his name? You were looking at him as a possible suspect in the Andressen murder last year, after you cleared the husband."

"Lucas Priest. I liked him for it," Renney said. "Guy had a rap sheet longer than my arm. He felt the heat, took off soon after I talked to him. Spent months trying to find him. I've still got an open warrant on the guy."

"What about the husband himself?"

"Like you just said, I cleared him early on in the investigation," Renney said.

"Yeah, but what if that was a mistake?"

Renney cupped a hand around one ear. "Beg pardon?"

Politano dropped his eyes, and Renney was pleased to have put the kid in his place, at least for the moment. "What I meant was, what about bringing him in for questioning on this new murder?" Politano went on, a little less enthused. "At least get an idea where he was during those twenty-four hours this new girl was killed. Or maybe if we talk to him, something will click that you—that we— didn't see before. I can stop by the guy's house myself, see if he'll give a statement, come down to the station. See if he's at least got an alibi for the timeframe when this Fortunado woman was killed."

"You're pretty eager to adopt this serial killer theory."

Politano set the packet of paper face down on the tabletop. "I mean, it can't be a copycat," he said, "and it's certainly no coincidence. No one but us, the chief M.E., and the district attorney knew the specific details of how Andressen had been killed. We never put those details in the press. So, for Fortunado's body to show up in that same way, it's gotta be the same guy."

One other person knew, too, Renney thought, but did not say.

"While it's true that, in a case of a wife's murder, the husband is usually the main suspect—" Renney began.

"Because he's usually *the guy*," Politano added.

"Yeah. But serial killers have a completely different M.O. Dennis Rader didn't kill his wife."

"Who's Dennis Rader?"

"BTK," Renney said, then frowned. "I thought you were into this serial killer stuff?"

"Okay, fine, then the killer is probably not Andressen's husband," Politano went on. "Nevertheless, *whoever* it is, where do you think this guy's been all year? Usually, serial killers don't wait so long between murders. Twelve months is a long stretch. It's like a compulsion with them, right? A feeling like they can't control themselves and they have to do it."

"They make you sergeant and you're an expert now?"

"I've just been reading up on some stuff."

"Maybe the guy's been in jail for the past year on some other charge."

"Interesting. Maybe you're right."

"We get the lab results back on the adhesive used to suffocate the Fortunado girl yet?" Renney asked, by way of changing the subject.

"No, not yet." Politano picked up the pitcher and refilled Renney's beer. "You okay? You seem distracted."

"Migraine," Renney said, which wasn't wholly untrue. "Listen, it's late, I'm gonna head home," he added, which *was* untrue, and then he dug out his wallet and tossed a handful of crinkled bills on the table.

"That's too much."

"Leave a nice tip."

Truth was, there was too much going on inside Bill Renney's head for him to fine-tune his focus and start picking at loose threads, not the way Politano was doing. Anyway, there *weren't* any loose threads. Not even footprints in the sand. *There are only so many patterns a finite set of numbers like one through five can make, so, by definition, that same set will eventually come back around and repeat itself,* Linda had said. Was that what was happening now? Some blip in the seismograph of the cosmos? A repetition in the sequence of space and time? A face cut up and no footprints left behind in the sand was all Renney had a year ago, and it was all he had now. It was as if some creature had crept out of the darkness and snatched Gina Fortunado away, just as that same creature had come for Melissa Jean Andressen one year prior. Almost like magic.

Bill Renney did not believe in magic. Moreover, he knew that the type of creature that crept out of the darkness to snatch up women was always, without fail, of the human variety. So, without any other information to work off of, he began to fall back into an old pattern— one that had him, in his unmarked sedan, circumnavigating the swerving, up-and-down boulevards of Calabasas, up Malibu Canyon, north of the Ventura Freeway, spiraling, driving alone, lost in contemplation, wheels in his head at work; starting that evening after leaving A.J. Politano with a half-empty pitcher of beer at the Blackbird Tavern on Bay Street, then continuing this pattern for the next several days, dining on high caloric lunches and grease-box dinners in his car from whatever fast food establishments happened to catch his eye earlier in the day, chain smoking with the windows down, talk radio tuned to a low murmur, while gradually closing in on the suburban geography around which he drove, wheels still turning, mind still spiraling, *car* still spiraling, round and round, both mental and physical, both figurative and literal, circles upon circles upon circles, like a bird of prey strategically closing in before the strike.

He knew what he was doing on some subconscious level, although he did not allow himself to admit it until, one afternoon, he drove up the steep incline of roadway that led to a series of expensive homes perched along the crest of the canyon, each one a rambling modern construct, all steel beams and smoked black window glass and manicured lawns. He motored along the loop of this road until he found himself pulling gradually into a cul-de-sac, where one house in particular stood by itself, similarly alone, nestled behind a white stone wall and with an automated iron gate at the foot of the inclined driveway. The house stood at the summit of the cliff, nearly superimposed against a bright azure sky, surrounded by an arsenal of palm trees, pineapple guava, arrowhead fronds, blossoming birds of paradise—less a *home*, perhaps, than an accumulation of acute angles and strategically planted flora arranged to *suggest* a home. Bill Renney had been here before—had been inside that house on a number of occasions, in fact—and it had always left him feeling cold and antiseptic, the way a doctor's office might. And there was good reason for that.

From the street, and on this particular afternoon, Dr. Alan Andressen's house appeared empty. Renney knew it was impossible to know this for sure from where he sat—the windows were all tinted and if there were any vehicles on the property, they'd be behind the doors of the three-car garage—yet something needling in the back of his head assured him of this fact.

Since the discovery of Gina Fortunado's body in the desert and the subsequent late-night, frantic visit to Renney's home by the man, Dr. Alan Andressen had taken up residence in Bill Renney's mind, just as he had one year ago after the discovery of Melissa Jean Andressen's body. The past several days, Renney had been plagued by thoughts of the man, you might say, which only worsened after hearing the doctor's name on A.J. Politano's lips that one evening at the Blackbird Tavern. One night, Renney had even suffered a nightmare where Alan Andressen approached him out of the darkness, covered head to toe in bright slashes of blood (although that wasn't how he'd been in real life; there'd been surprisingly little blood on Alan in real life, Renney recalled, just a little spatter on his shirt). This nightmare version of Alan extended a hand toward Renney, and Renney could see that each of the doctor's fingers were, in fact, shiny, silver scalpel blades.

There was never any proven motive for Alan to have wanted to kill his wife.

Alan *had not* killed his wife.

So why couldn't he shake the man from his head now? Why, after all this time, were thoughts of Alan Andressen stuck in his mind like a seed between teeth?

He drove away from Alan's cold, antiseptic house that afternoon, only to find himself returning the following day. And then the day after that. And then the day after *that*. Wheels were still turning in Bill Renney's head, and he didn't like the sound of the gears. He didn't like the places to which his mind was eager to ferry him. He wondered if he should take up heavy drinking, or maybe a hobby, like woodworking or axe-throwing.

Los Angeles County Sheriff's Department released a statement later that week that did not divulge any specific details about Gina Fortunado's murder, but one that did confirm to the public that there were close similarities between the way she had been killed and the gruesome unsolved homicide of Melissa Jean Andressen, whose body was found in nearly the same location, one year prior. Media outlets thrive off sensationalism, so they wasted no time concluding that these two homicides were the work of the same unknown assailant, perhaps a budding serial killer whom these outlets were quick to dub the High Desert Killer.

Images of Melissa Jean Andressen resurfaced in the media, alongside many different photos of Gina Fortunado (provided to the news outlets by her parents, who were desperate for someone to be brought to justice for this heinous, unforgivable crime). Renney began dreaming of Melissa Jean Andressen, too, incorporating her into the same nightmares where her husband appeared with scalpel blades for fingers. Sometimes, Linda was there, resplendent in her wedding gown, her hair done up in pearl-capped pins, impossibly young, years before the cancer had begun to ravage her body. When Linda opened her mouth to speak to him, her tongue fell out, leaving a glistening, crimson contrail of blood down the front of her crisp white wedding gown.

"I've got a lead on some creepo Tinder date Fortunado had about two months ago," Politano told Renney during one of their frequent phone calls throughout the day, as Renney coasted along the hilly byways of Calabasas, Dr. Alan Andressen on the brain. "Guy's got a record, some domestic shit. I'm going to run it down. You up for a drive?"

Renney was happy to let him run it down alone and so he told him he was attending to other matters.

His mind was otherwise preoccupied.

Cosmic echo.

That night he drove out to the desert, where the moon hung fat and full amidst a saturation of stars. Coyotes watched him from beyond the road, their luminescent eyes betraying their location in the dark. His was the only vehicle on that entire stretch of roadway that night, not a single pair of headlights appearing in his rearview mirror, not a single motorist passing by in the opposite direction along that narrow strip of sand-salted asphalt. The night was mostly still, but the occasional gust of wind fired granules of sand into the glow of the sedan's headlights, and against the hood and windshield of the car in a series of soft, tap-dancing clatters.

The wind could have done away with any footprints, could have blown away any vehicular tracks in the sand. It was the same thing he'd thought one year earlier, only now he had Linda's premonitory voice murmuring inside the echo chamber of his skull: *Do you see? There are only so many patterns . . .*

Something dark shifted about in the distance, just beyond the reach of the car's headlights. Renney slowed to a stop in the middle of the road. The palms of his hands were leaking sweat on the steering wheel. He stared out the windshield and into the night, unaware that he was holding his breath, until a large mule deer came loping out of the darkness and bounded across the road: it was there and then gone in the blink of an eye. Renney barely had time to register it.

"Fuck this," he muttered aloud, spinning the steering wheel, and executing a full turn in the middle of the highway.

One afternoon, while his unmarked sedan sat idling alongside a curb in Thousand Oaks, he saw Alan come out of a coffee shop with a mocha-something in a clear plastic cup, thick as a barrel. The doctor was dressed in pleated slacks and a pressed, button-down shirt. Still way too thin, but at least more put together than he had been on the night he'd paid Renney a frantic house call.

Renney watched him climb into a brushed-silver BMW i8 and speed off into traffic. For a moment, Renney considered driving in the opposite direction and heading back downtown, but that needling sensation in the back of his mind ultimately got the better of him, and he decided to follow the good doctor instead.

Ten minutes later, Renney was easing his unmarked sedan into the cul-de-sac while Alan's BMW idled at the foot of the driveway of his cold, angular home, waiting for the automatic gate to open. Renney climbed out of his car, the engine still running, and jogged over to Alan's Beamer. He rapped a set of knuckles on the tinted glass of the driver's-side window.

The window came down only halfway, a smooth, soundless descent. Alan peered out at him from behind mirrored sunglasses. Renney didn't need to see the man's eyes to discern the stricken look on his face: the way his lips pulled tight and the muscles in his jaw clenched at the sight of him.

"Jesus, what?" Alan said. "What are you doing here? What is it now?"

"If any cops ask you to come in and give a statement, you tell them you're busy, but you'll check your schedule and get back to them," Renney said. "Then you come find me."

"Why would the police come looking for me, asking for a statement? A statement about what?"

"They won't," Renney said, although he was thinking of A.J. Politano's eagerness, and his comments about Alan. "I'm saying just in case."

"*You're* the fucking police."

"I'm just covering all the bases here."

"What bases? What the fuck do I need to know, Bill? What the hell's going on now?"

"The sheriff is going to cut through media speculation and release some details about the Fortunado girl's murder tomorrow during a press conference. They're going to release some specific details about your wife's murder, too. They won't put a name to it, but it'll be obvious what we're dealing with here once the details come out."

"What does that mean?"

"That the two murders," said Renney, "are likely connected."

The muscles in Alan's jaw tightened even further. Renney suddenly wondered what the man's eyes looked like behind the lenses of those mirrored sunglasses after all.

"You told me that wasn't the case," Alan said. "You told me it was a coincidence and that I was jumping to conclusions."

"This isn't me saying it, Alan. It's the Sheriff's Department."

"Yeah, but you're the lead investigator. They're taking into account what you say, what you think. Which means you were full of shit with me the other night at your house."

"I'm not making any determinations here, Alan. I just need to work this case. And I need you to listen to what I'm saying."

"Why would they come to *me* about this other girl?" Andressen asked.

"Because if these murders are connected, they're going to want to revisit the suspects on the books from your wife's murder, too."

"Who the fuck are 'they'?"

Politano, Renney thought. *The district attorney. Anyone with half a brain.*

"Listen," he said, ignoring the question. "Do you have an alibi for the night that Fortunado girl went missing? That would be Saturday, July twenty-seventh."

"Fuck's sake, Bill—*are you really asking me that?*"

"That's what might come up, if someone brings you in for questioning. Probably not, but maybe. Make sure you've got something solid. Do you?"

"What cops would come asking other than you? Aren't you the goddamn detective on this case?"

"I am."

"So, is this you asking me if I've got an alibi? Are we back there, Bill? Back to square one?"

"I'm not asking you anything," Renney said, which wasn't exactly the truth.

"I've got no fucking blood on my hands," Alan said.

That's not entirely true, either, and we both know it, doc, Renney thought. "I'm just letting you know what's going on," was what he decided to say. "I'm not working this thing in a vacuum."

"Un-fucking-believable. I'm calling my lawyer."

"No. Don't do anything just yet. You've got no reason to call a lawyer, because you never heard from me. You hear what I'm saying? We never had this conversation."

"Goddamn it, Bill."

"I was never here," Renney told him, and took a step back from his car.

"I think I'm going to be sick," Alan said.

The driver's-side window silently rose, and the BMW rolled slowly through the open gate, up the curled ribbon of driveway, through a thicket of palm fronds and wild orchids, and into the three-car garage.

Renney stood there for a moment, watching the house, until the garage door closed, leaving him standing there at the foot of the driveway alone. The security gate clanged shut, and the sound of it latching like a cell block door.

We've been here before.

Cosmic echo, indeed, Linda-baby.

Bill Renney lit a cigarette, got back in his car, and got the hell out of there.

—◇—

A.J. Politano called him later that night to tell him that the lead on the Tinder date was a dead end. "The guy's got a solid alibi. Been out of the country for the past month."

Renney was drinking a Coors Light, eating some cold Chinese leftovers out of the carton, and watching *Wheel of Fortune* on the living room TV. "Well, nice work running it down, anyway," he said into his cell phone, around a mouthful of lo mein noodles.

"Some prelims came back from the lab on the adhesive found around Fortunado's mouth and nose, too," Politano said. "They found traces of insecticide."

"Insecticide? What's that mean? She was poisoned?"

"No, not poisoned. Cause of death is still asphyxiation."

"Then what's with the insecticide? What's its purpose?"

"I don't know. Maybe there isn't one."

On the TV, Pat Sajak said something and the audience laughed.

"Also," continued Politano, "the sheriff dropped the news during a press conference this evening, one day ahead of schedule."

"Oh," Renney said. He was suddenly not very hungry. "I hadn't heard."

"Media will have a field day tomorrow—'L.A. County Sheriff's Department Confirms High Desert Killer On the Loose,' and some such."

"That's a bit much," said Renney.

"You know how it is," said Politano. "They've already been saying it. Only now, we've given them reason."

"Wonderful. Is that all?"

"One more thing," Politano said, then quickly added, "but don't be mad."

"Mad about what?"

"I tried tracking down that auto mechanic from Reseda who you spoke to last year—guy named Priest?"

Renney shifted in his recliner. Said, "And?"

"You were right. Looks like the guy skipped town last year, right around the time you were grilling him about Andressen. No one's seen or heard from him since. I'm talking all *year*. Pretty fucking suspicious, don't you think?"

"I doubt this guy came back into town to kill again if he was that spooked by me a year ago."

"Still, it's pretty goddamn sketchy he split town and no one's heard peep from him all year. His bills were left unpaid, he never claimed his last paycheck from the mechanic shop, and it doesn't look like he's even been accessing his bank account in all this time."

"Maybe he fell off a fucking cruise ship," Renney said.

"Yeah, maybe," said Politano. "I ran his background, too—you weren't bullshitting, he's got a rap sheet like a roll of toilet paper, Bill. I'm going to see if I can track him down."

"You're welcome to," said Renney, "but you're spinning your wheels, kid."

"Anyway, have a good night, Bill."

"Same."

He disconnected the call, then considered changing the TV channel to find a replay of the sheriff's press conference from earlier that evening. He was thinking about the mechanic—hoping he didn't come off as too dismissive about the whole thing while talking to Politano. Hoping A.J. Politano didn't dig too deep into things.

In the end, he decided to just finish his beer and go to bed, where, presumably, harsh dreams awaited his arrival.

FOUR

Maureen awoke a little after ten o'clock on the morning after the engagement party with a thumping headache seated in the left quadrant of her skull. Greg was already up—he was an early riser—but she could still smell his cologne on the sheets. She shuffled to the bathroom where she brushed her teeth, washed her face, took care of some other business, then swallowed two aspirin. After dragging a brush through her hair for an inordinate amount of time, she realized she was postponing the inevitable, and instantly felt foolish about any residual shame she might have still harbored following the incident last night where she'd seen Landon out on the pool deck.

But was it shame, or just an overall discomfort around the boy? That thought, too, had hovered around her for the remainder of the party, after Landon and his friend had vanished upstairs to eat, and then later, when Landon's friend, Uptown, had stood in the vestibule waiting for an Uber to pick him up and shuttle him off to wherever. Maureen had brought the kid a cup of coffee as he waited alone for the car, and while that kid had been a strung-out, jittery mess, sure, it had been Landon Dawson, her soon-to-be stepson, who had made her uneasy, had provoked into action some self-defense mechanism Maureen Park had heretofore not realized she'd possessed.

As she descended the staircase, she told herself it was a foolish and even unfair feeling to have: she'd only just met the boy last night, and he'd clearly been in a state—high, drunk, a combination of both—so the rational part of her brain knew she was overreacting. Greg had spoken so little to her about his son that, in her mind, the boy had taken on an almost mythical quality, like a unicorn or a dragon, so the sight of him in the flesh was akin to witnessing that fantastical creature summoned into existence before her eyes. She tried to think now of any specifics Greg might have said to her about his son in the months since she and Greg had been together, but she found she could only come up with generalities or simple platitudes—*he was a handful at times as a child* and *he's always had trouble in school and with authority* and *he's got a killer backhand on the tennis court* and *boys will be boys*. Nothing that, in Maureen's estimation, painted a very clear picture of Greg's son.

Also, something Landon had said to her last night still clung to her: the fact that there were no pictures of him anywhere in the house. Granted, there weren't pictures of *anyone*, except for the autographed headshots in Greg's home studio, but she couldn't even recall Greg ever showing her a picture of Landon on his phone.

She came into the kitchen to find Greg perspiring in his running clothes, pouring himself a mineral water in front of the open refrigerator. She glanced toward the windows over the sink, her eyes passing over every visible section of the rear patio and the pool deck, but she could not see Landon anywhere. Maybe he was an early riser like his father and had already gone out for the day.

"You feeling okay?" Greg asked, closing the refrigerator. "You were really knocking those vodka tonics back near the end there."

"I'll survive." She went to the pot of coffee on the counter, poured herself a cup. It was only lukewarm at this hour, so she nuked it in the microwave. "Where's Landon?"

Greg made some throaty noise of disapproval as he went over to the counter and began preparing one of his kale and protein shakes. "You won't see him until about two in the afternoon."

"You mean he's still asleep?"

"It's best to just let him be," Greg said, by way of an answer.

"I thought he was doing a semester in Europe after the summer? That he wouldn't be home for months."

"That," said Greg, "was the plan. But my son doesn't enjoy sticking to plans. It was an embarrassment, having him show up at the party last night looking like some drugged-out degenerate."

"I don't think anyone noticed."

"You don't think they noticed those two reprobates standing there with their bloodshot eyes and the shakes?"

"I don't think anyone was paying that close attention," she said, and realized that, in some fashion, and despite her discomfort toward the boy, she found herself defending him. "He and his friend went up to his room pretty quickly and quietly. And no one saw them for the rest of the night. Besides, it's not like the rest of our guests were stone sober around here last night, either."

"He's going to tell me he's dropped out of school again, you know," Greg said. "I'm done carrying that kid, Maureen. He causes me nothing but stress and aggravation." Greg turned and began counting on his fingers all his son's indiscretions: "It took him six years to get through undergrad, and it was all I could do to get him into law school after that. Then he drops out, says he wants to study film at USC. I pull some more strings, he does a handful of semesters, but then he says he's more interested in medical school. *Medical* school? I just laughed. Could you imagine? That son of mine has the discipline of a dog chasing squirrels—he'll run around forever and never catch anything, including his own tail. So we agreed he'd spend the summer in Europe—he needed to 'take a breath,' his words, can you imagine that, too?—but only if he'd come back and reenroll at USC. He argued for a semester abroad, and so I capitulated. It was a compromise. But that won't happen. You just wait and see—he's dropped out again, I just know it. And if he thinks he's going to lounge around here for the next year or so, he's sorely mistaken."

"Maybe you're jumping the gun," said Maureen. "Maybe he's still planning to go back to school, like he agreed to."

Greg just shook his head. He finished mixing his shake, but then only stared down at it morosely, as if suddenly disgusted by it. "You don't know him, Maur. He's always been a problem. Sometimes, I think he does stuff just to rankle me. Even if he knows he's going to suffer in the process, he'll do it just to make my life miserable."

"What about his mother? Is she still in the picture?"

"Gale? She's been done with him since he was sixteen. I don't even know where she is anymore. Arizona, I think. She hasn't spoken to either one of us in about a decade."

"I find it funny that you and I haven't talked about Landon all that much."

"You knew about him," Greg said, and she caught the defensive note in his tone.

"Yes, I knew he *existed*, Greg, and that he was in Europe, but that was about it."

"What more do you want to know? That he'd wrecked three cars before the age of eighteen? That he'd once gotten into a physical altercation with our gardener and got his two front teeth busted when he was only thirteen years old?"

Maureen took her coffee to the table and sat down.

"When he was just a little kid," Greg went on, "he used to lick doorknobs like some . . . I don't know, who the hell does that? He used to suck on pennies, too, because he liked the taste. Sometimes he'd swallow them; I know this, because there was a period when

I'd find them at the bottom of the toilet. He got kicked out of prep school for chewing on tinfoil and repeatedly disrupting the other students. He was always getting into fights. He thought coming home with a split lip and a black eye was funny."

It seemed a bombardment to Maureen, a fusillade of information that she couldn't easily digest all at once. A picture began to form in her head—a younger version of that tall, lanky, athletic-looking young man from last night, awkward in his tallness at such a young age, a face full of bruises and split lips, chipped front teeth, eyes narrowed in gleeful calculation. She found this didn't help quell her initial uneasiness about the boy, and in her mind at that very moment, she heard him once more come through the sliders in the dark, wet feet on the hardwood floor, and utter *goodnight* to her, as if he'd known she'd been there, watching him all along, and was not bothered by it in the least.

"Listen," Greg said, and his voice was more tempered now. "I don't want you to worry about any of this. What we've got going on here, you and I, has nothing to do with him."

"But he's your son, Greg . . . "

"Just keep out of his way until I can make other arrangements."

"What other arrangements?"

"Let me worry about that." He went to the blender, *whirrrrr*, then poured his shake into a tall glass. "What are you doing today?"

She thought about Landon still upstairs, a snake coiled in a dark hole, and said, "I'm going to run some errands."

"Errands? Lucinda will be here tomorrow. Have her do it."

"I think I need fresh air," she said. "It'll be nice to get out of the house. Then maybe later I'll get some writing done."

"Right," Greg said, taking a long pull of his shake. When he set it down, he had a vague green froth on his upper lip. "That reminds me. I wanted to talk to you about that."

"About what?"

"That story you were telling everyone last night," he said. "The one you're currently writing."

"Yes, I know," she said, hanging her head. "Don't tell the Hollywood vampires about my work-in-progress. I get it. I'll learn the ropes."

"That wasn't the reason I told you to stop talking about it."

She looked up at him. "Oh?"

"I've gone through two messy divorces, not to mention a host of other problems. I don't need my fiancée writing a story about two people having an affair in some seedy motel room. People will think that's how you and I got together."

Her back stiffened in her chair. "Are you being serious?"

"I just don't need that type of publicity right now, Maur."

"It's fiction, Greg. It isn't real. It's just a story. People will understand that."

"Why do you want to write about something like that, anyway?"

"It's not about the affair, exactly," she said. "It's about two people who have their sins reflected back on them in that mirror, like confronting their own consciences."

"It's tasteless," he said. "I'd like you to consider writing something else. Hell, I could get you on as a staff writer with Jeff Geboy's show. They just got picked up for another season."

"I don't want to write for TV."

"There's more money in it."

"We don't really need the money, do we?"

"I would just think you'd actually want people to see your work."

"Oh." She stood from the table, went to the counter, and dumped the remainder of her coffee down the sink. "I see."

"Come on, Maur. I'm just looking out for you."

"No," she said. "You're just looking out for yourself. I'm sorry if what I'm writing embarrasses you."

"I just want you to take the big picture into consideration," he said, and absently gesticulated as if to signify just how big the picture was. "You're not living in Wyoming anymore."

"I'm well aware," she said, and headed for the doorway.

"Where are you going?"

"To get a shower. I have errands to run."

"Maur—"

She fled.

It was at some point during the afternoon, as she meandered aimlessly from shop to shop along Magnolia, midday sun beating down on her face, that Maureen began to feel like she was being watched. It was a sensation that accosted her all at once, like a sixth sense, prompting the fine little hairs along the nape of her neck to stand at attention. Moreover, it was a sensation she thought she had been feeling for some time lately—for weeks, really. She had no reason to think this, yet there it was, a prodding certainly that sometimes tickled its way to the forefront of her brain.

She was outside a boutique, peering into the shop windows, when she felt this sensation overtake her once again; she turned and gazed up and down the boulevard, a part of her conscious mind already realizing that she was searching for Landon Dawson. It was a paranoid conceit—what would he be doing following her, anyway?—but she couldn't shake it.

She put her head down and moved swiftly up the block, careful to avoid stepping on the cracks in the sidewalk, her OCD running in the red in that moment. When she spied a coffee shop across the street, she cut a beeline in that direction, and was grateful that the door opened on an automatic hinge so that she wouldn't have to touch it. She ordered a large black coffee, then dumped a half dozen packets of sugar into it. When she turned around, she found a young man standing directly in front of her, almost too close—yes, certainly too close—and while it wasn't Landon Dawson, the appearance of this character resonated her with the same gravity as if it was.

"Uptown," she said, the young man's name—was it a name?—coming to her as if fired into her brain like a bullet from a gun.

The young man stood there in a pressed blue oxford shirt and khaki slacks, a brown braided belt twined around his waist. His hair, which had been a blondish cyclone last night when she'd met him at the party, had been wrangled into submission by a comb and some heavy product. The reddened bleariness of his eyes had been replaced by a sharp, blue gaze—so intense, in fact, that it took Maureen a moment to recognize him.

"I'm sorry," Uptown said. "I didn't mean to scare you."

"Have you been following me?"

"I'm sorry," he repeated. "I just didn't know what to do. I didn't want to go to the house."

She frowned, shook her head. "What's wrong?"

"Can we talk?"

The request caught her by surprise; nonetheless, she scanned the coffee shop and found that a booth toward the rear was empty. She nodded in the booth's direction, and without another word, Uptown skulked over to it. If she had to guess, this kid was a few years younger than Landon, perhaps appropriate post-graduate age. He dropped himself down into the booth and his hands immediately began to fidget on the tabletop.

Maureen sat opposite him, cradling her cup of coffee in both hands. She caught Uptown glancing at her engagement ring—that impossible geometric cluster of white fire on her finger, just above the knuckle, too many karats to speak of without embarrassment—then he met her eyes.

"My real name is Ross," he said. "Landon just calls me Uptown."

"Why?"

"Because I'm not from downtown, I guess." Ross hoisted one shoulder in the suggestion of a shrug. "He thinks it's funny. I don't really get it."

"Why have you been following me?"

"I needed to talk to you. Well, I needed to talk to *someone*, and I thought maybe you might be the right person."

"Okay," she said. "Let's talk."

He looked down at his hands, which were still wrestling with each other on the tabletop. He had large, clean fingers, the tips blunt, the nails small and noncommittal. "I'm not sure how to even say it, or where to start, you know?"

"Hey," she said, suddenly realizing that this kid was truly troubled by something. She reached out and placed a hand atop the two of his, steadying them. "Take a breath, and then start at the beginning."

He took a little breath, then let it out in a shuddery gust that smelled of spearmint gum. Said, "Right." Said, "Okay." Said, "You see on the news they found some dead girl all cut up in the desert outside the city a week or so ago?"

This was not where she'd expected the conversation to start. She recalled some vague news headline from a few days ago but didn't linger on it. "Yes," she said. "I remember seeing something online about it."

"I think," Ross said, and she could feel his hands begin to jitter beneath hers once more, "I mean, I think Landon had something to do with it. With what happened to that girl."

She pulled her hand from his. Said, "What?"

"He's got this book," Ross said. "He showed it to me a couple days ago, when I got back from Europe. It's like . . . I mean, it's like a scrapbook, really. It's got all these pictures of a woman whose face is cut up real bad. I mean, the pictures, they're fucking *awful*. Her, uh . . . " He brought a hand to his face, and mimed a circular motion, as if he was washing. "Her eyes had been cut out. Her nose was, like, chopped off. There were pictures of her ears, or where her ears should have been—just, like, holes on the sides of her head, all covered in dried blood and little black ants and dust from the desert. One picture had her mouth open—someone's hand was holding it open—and it looked like her tongue had been cut out, too. And then her . . . her hands . . . " He raised his own two hands and stared at them, as if puzzled by their existence at the ends of his wrists. "All of her fingers had been cut off."

"Jesus Christ," Maureen said—or, rather, heard herself say. "I don't understand—what do you mean he had these photos in a scrapbook?"

"Just that," Ross said. "Just these big glossy photos pasted into a scrapbook. I asked him where he got them, but Landon, he's . . . I mean, he never answers a direct question, you know?"

"No," she said. "I don't know. I don't know him at all."

"Right," Ross said, and he was suddenly nodding his head, appearing lost in contemplation. "Right. That's why I'm coming to you. I didn't know who else to tell. I didn't want to go to the cops—I don't like the cops—and I couldn't say anything to Landon's father. That guy scares me. But when I saw you at the party last night, I thought, well, maybe . . . "

"Did he say how he got those photos?"

"No."

"Did he say who the girl was in the photos?"

Ross shook his head.

"Did he say *anything* about it? Or did he just show it to you?"

"He said they were photos of a dead body that was discovered in desert. That's all. I hadn't seen the news about it by that point—or maybe I had, but just didn't have a reason to pay attention to it—but then I saw something about it on TV the following day. I googled it and saw that it was the body of some schoolteacher, a girl in her twenties from San Bernardino. And I thought, well, Jesus Christ, that's the *girl* . . . "

Maureen had already taken her phone from her purse and was googling the very same thing. The search results were plentiful— Gina Fortunado, twenty-six years old, a middle-school teacher from San Bernardino, California, whose body was discovered in Antelope Valley a little over a week ago. Mutilated. As she scrolled through the search results, she noticed the date the body was discovered, and a thought occurred to her.

"You were both still in Europe when this girl's body was found," she reminded him. When Ross didn't respond, she looked up from her phone and found him staring at her. One of his eyelids twitched. "What?" she said.

Ross cleared his throat, and said, "Landon's been back for weeks. He's been staying at a Motel 6 in Glendale. That's where he showed me the photos. He told me to stay behind in Europe, which I did for a while, but he came back. I only just got back a few nights ago, because I ran out of money—well, I ran out of Landon's money, or, I guess, his dad's money—and anyway, I didn't want to be in Europe alone anymore."

"Why did he come back so early and not come home?"

"Why does Landon do anything that he does?" Ross countered. "You've got to understand, Landon and I aren't exactly the best of friends. We roomed together for a while at USC, and he was weird— like, he had a hard time making friends. He's a good-looking guy, I guess, so girls flocked to him, but they never stuck around because there was always something . . . uh, I don't know . . . "

Off-putting, Maureen thought.

"... something weird about him that eventually turned them off," Ross continued. "There was one girl on campus, this really pretty brunette, and she liked Landon. I mean, yeah, there's something about how he can carry himself when he wants to, and he put it on full display in front of this girl. One night, he told me not to come back to the dorm. He gave me six hundred bucks cash and some coke and told me to crash at a motel for the night because this chick was coming over and he wanted to be alone with her, so that's what I did. Next day, I asked him how things went. He said she was a bore, that he ended the night early, and that he wouldn't be seeing her again—no, wait, he said he wouldn't be 'participating in an encore performance with her,' because that's how Landon talks—and that was that. He made it out like it was no big deal.

"Two days later, though, I saw the girl on campus. I kind of smiled and nodded at her, but she came up to me, and she was, like, furious, and she looked like she was about to cry. She pointed a finger in my face and said my roommate was a sick motherfucker—excuse my language—who should be put in jail. Everybody was staring at us—staring at *me*—as if *I* was the one who'd done something wrong. I asked her what happened, but she just stormed away. She was too upset to even tell me."

"Did you ask Landon about it?"

"No way. You don't understand—that's not the kind of thing you bring up to Landon. You only answer Landon's questions, you don't ask him questions of your own."

Maureen shook her head. "Why are you even friends with him?"

Ross hung his head and just sort of held his palms up in a soundless reply that, to Maureen, spoke volumes: *He's rich and he gives me money and drugs and pays my way to Europe and brings around the girls until the girls no longer want to come around.*

"Where is this scrapbook now?" she asked.

"With him, I guess," Ross said. "Back at the house. At *your* house. He had it in his duffel bag last night, I'm pretty sure. He took it with him when he left the motel."

Maureen's eyes drifted back toward her phone, which sat beside her coffee on the table, the screen illuminated with all the search results of the dead woman found carved to pieces in the desert a little over a week ago.

"You see why I had to say something?" Ross said. "And why it had to be you?"

"What do you want me to do about it?"

"Whatever you think you need to do. Just please do me a favor— whatever it is, you've got to leave me out of it. I don't want Landon, or Landon's dad, or the cops, or anyone else to know I saw those photos, man, or that I'm even talking to you about them. I don't want to be a part of this. I just knew I had to tell somebody."

She just stared at him, both hands wrapped around the hot cardboard tube of her coffee cup.

"Promise me," Ross said.

"All right," she said. "Okay. I promise."

This seemed to lift some invisible weight off the kid's shoulders. He leaned back in his seat and exhaled another pent-up breath— this one decidedly more sour than spearmint-flavored. "Thanks," he said, and then he slid out of the booth. He stood there awkwardly for a moment longer, his hands thrust into the pockets of his pants, as he leaned weight from one foot to the other. "I'm sorry if I scared you."

"You didn't scare me," she said.

But once he'd gone, she wondered if that was true.

FIVE

Toby Kampen had ceased being a fly. It wasn't a conscious decision, and it was not something that occurred to him instantaneously, like something un-fly-like emerging from a cocoon in a different form. It was not akin to a quickening, where in one brief heartbeat of time there is now life when, just a single heartbeat before, *whuh-whump*, there was none. Rather, it was something that dawned upon him, epiphanic, *ding ding ding*, once the transformation was already taking place.

He had been a fly for years, beating the death odds of the rest of his short-lived kin, and outlasting even the most resilient of his brethren. Never snared in a web to be fed upon, never crushed beneath the cudgel of a rolled-up magazine or newspaper. Yes, it was true: a Spider had nearly captured him when he had been very young, just out of the maggot stage, you might say, ha ha, but he'd been cunning and agile and sharp enough to finagle his way out of that morbid transaction, and fairly recently, too.

The Spider, of course, had tried to devour him—a thing possessing a bristling torso and a multiplex of glossy, obsidian eyes—and it was to his benefit that despite all the creature's arachnidal tendencies, it had, at its core, been saddled by the restrictions of a common human being. Yet, as a housefly, Toby Kampen had been able to outmaneuver the Spider, and quite deftly, seeing how he processed visual information nearly seven times more rapidly than the average human being, which was the form that the Spider most frequently took.

But—

What do you call a housefly without a house? Without a home?

How long had he been living outside of the Spider's web? Time was a struggle for him, but he'd meticulously written each day down on a slip of paper he kept in his back pocket—a series of days that culminated to four months. So: four months . . .

. . . or, as it happened, approximately one hundred twenty days into the lifecycle of a common housefly, *Musca domestica Linnaeus*, which is to say, given the average lifespan of such an insect, twenty-eight days, thirty at the very most, basically a month per lifetime, a gestational four months would account for—would *consume*—the lives of at least four common houseflies. Probably more.

A spider's web is no home for a fly, he would frequently tell himself, particularly during those first unanchored nights out there in the world, alone, as he lay curled up in an abandoned storefront doorway, or in some back alley, a sticky piece of cardboard beneath him as a bed. *To a fly, a spider's web is a dinner table, and the fly is the meal.* No love there.

So, he zigged and he zagged. Not as luminous as the firefly, not as majestic as the monarch butterfly, not as single-minded as the hornet, but rather as a workmanlike, utilitarian thing whose sole purpose was to perpetuate its own survival.

In those first few weeks as a free insect, he picked up day work with immigrants who couldn't speak the language, a congregation of flies, you might say, and he mostly kept his mouth shut to let people think he didn't know the language, either. He never made enough money to afford an apartment (and who would rent to him, anyway?), but he was able to pay monthly for a self-storage unit—*self-storage, indeed, ha ha*, and he'd laugh to himself—so at least he had four (metal) walls and a (metal) roof over his head at night. There were free public toilets and showers down at Canyon Park, so he was able to attend to his business and keep himself somewhat presentable. That worked out for a while, until an altercation brought him to the attention of the local police, who dragged him into their car, then to a jail cell downtown. After a time, he lost count of how often he'd been dragged to jail cells downtown. It was no different than his previous life, back in the web of the Spider. And in a way, those jail cells were like the Spider's web, too—a place where he was held prisoner and couldn't escape—only he was never devoured at the end of each stay. Ultimately, and without ceremony, he was repeatedly tossed back out onto the street. No one really cared what he'd done as long as some piece of paper got its stamp. Sometimes, he would have to do community service, which was fine. Other times, he was paraded in front of a shrink who orated in long, monotone soliloquies, and it was all Toby could do not to fall asleep during these tedious sessions.

The money he earned from day-laboring he kept in an old tube sock. He took whatever jobs he could get—landscaping, construction, painting and power-washing houses and businesses, and once, some loathsome fellow with a milky eye and breath like a garbage truck paid him a cool one hundred in cash to drive a rental car, no questions asked, from one part of the city to another, and just leave it there in an abandoned parking lot, the keys tucked inside the visor. He did that, and didn't think twice about it.

He began to feel good about himself. He was still a fly, of course, but a fly cunning enough to not only escape the Spider's web, but to eke out an existence among a populace of animals—people-animals—who considered him nothing more than a disease-ridden nuisance. In his own small way, it was a measure of success.

Did he ever return to the Spider's web?

No.

What kind of fly would that make him? What kind of stupid, suicidal decision would that be?

(Though what, he would sometimes wonder over those first few weeks following his escape, had ever happened to the Spider? A Spider in poor health, a family history of heart disease and diabetes, of malnutrition and an inability to hold down a job, a creature that had grown too old and too tired and too infirm to spin webs and snare prey?)

Stop. Stop. Stop. Stop. Stop.

Because flies don't generally live very long, he knew it was imperative to live life to the fullest. He rarely slept—he hated the claustrophobia of the storage unit, the oily smell of the soiled mattress he slept on, which he'd dug out of a dumpster—so he found himself buzzing around the club scene in Silver Lake, Los Feliz, Hollywood, downtown L.A. He couldn't get into most of the clubs because of the way he looked and smelled, but for every string of posh, glitzy dance clubs that lit up the boulevard, there was always some dark, dank, sewer-smelling dive just around the corner. No cover charge, cheap well drinks, outdated stripper music piped through rattling house speakers. *A fly belongs on shit.* It was not self-deprecating, but self-awareness. That was how a fly survived: by being constantly aware of its surroundings.

There was one club in downtown L.A. called The Coffin, and the only way anyone would know it was there was if someone whispered about its existence into their ear. How had he found it? Who could remember, now? No signage out front, no queue of would-be patrons snaking around the block. There was a section of rusty chain-link fence in front of the entranceway and the stink of pot smoke in the air.

But flies can get in anywhere.

A hallway of dim red lighting. The eye-watering stink of body odor. Faintly, the muted pulse of industrial music reverberating through the sheetrock—*unce, unce, unce*. A pair of iron doors sliding open—

—*zzzt zzzt zzzt*, goes the music now—

—and laid out before his compound eyes exist the writhing, undulating, spasming thoraxes, each one indistinct from the next, a pulsing mass of bodies, arms, legs, exposed midriffs and done-up, punky hair, knee-high pleather boots, javelin heels, fingernails filed to points, to claws, to razors, and glow-in-the-dark contact lenses, NASA satellite earrings, jewelry like fireworks, glimpsed tattoos, shameful, indecipherable, panty lines piped through sheer fabric skirts, hips like metronomes ticking back and forth, back and forth, *nock nock nock*, lacy bra tops exposed, glittered décolletage, errant shoulder collisions, spicy perfume, dismissive apologies, scraping barstool legs, Dentyne breath.

"Hey, there. What's your name?"

"Toby."

"Buy me a drink, Toby?"

He had the tube sock full of cash in the back pocket of his jeans, prominent as a softball. "Sure. What would you like?"

"Tequila and soda."

"Okay."

"With a lemon. A *real* lemon."

"Sure, okay," he said, although he didn't know what a drink with a fake lemon might entail.

"You're sweet," she said, and ran her fingers through his unkempt, greasy hair. "I can tell, even beneath all your crud."

"Oh," he said, and shuddered at her touch.

"Don't worry. I like crud."

She turned and smiled at him, and he got a good look at her for the first time. Saw that she had fangs. Rattlesnake teeth.

"Whoa," he said. "Are those real?"

"My tits?"

"Your teeth."

She laughed. Said, "They come out at night."

"So do I."

Her eyes were luminous, too—not the trashy, glow-in-the-dark contact lenses some of the others wore, but something more subtle, subdued, deeper in color and luminosity. In complexity, even. Firefly-like.

Toby felt something flutter in the center of his thorax.

She twirled away, insinuating herself back among the crowd, that throb and bulge of bodies, those writhing limbs and spiky hair circulating in some ritualistic demonstration on the dance floor. The bartender arrived, a rotund dude with bulldog jowls, and Toby ordered the drink.

"What kind of tequila?"

Toby considered. He knew shit-all about tequila, so he asked, "What's good?"

The bartender hoisted a gold bottle of Patrón, and Toby shrugged his shoulders. He dug the sock out of his back pocket and peeled out a few damp bills, laid them on the bar.

The bartender frowned. "Your money stinks like feet. Why don't you open a tab, pay with a credit card?"

"Why don't you mind your own fucking business?" Toby suggested.

The bartender paused. Glared at him. He was clutching the bottle of Patrón in a chokehold and his knuckles looked like the swollen knots on a tree branch. Just when Toby thought the guy might lean over and punch him square in the face, the guy broke out in a grin, exposing a mouth of too-small, yellow teeth.

"You're funny," the bartender said. "I like you."

The drink sat beside him, untouched, for an uncountable amount of time. Where was she? Where had she gone? Was she even still out there on the dance floor? Had she ever really existed in the first place? He scanned the crowd, the dim, red-tinged light not helping, smoke in the air clouding everything, searching for the lacquered purple spikes of her hair, those incandescent eyes bobbing like neutrons in that sea-soup of flailing, gyrating bodies.

Then, coming up behind him, warm breath in his ear: "My savior."

She reached over his shoulder and took the drink. He pivoted around on the barstool and watched her. Really *watched* her. He could smell her—a perfume that wasn't necessarily sweet, wasn't necessarily floral, but some dry desert offset smell that reminded him of summers in his youth before he and the Spider had moved to Central City East, and of hours spent traversing the desert canyons by himself, chasing snakes and lizards, catching the fleeting scent of dry desert flora on the hot, dry air whenever a slight breeze deigned to shuttle by. He thought of scorpions scuttling along the arid ground, of hornets nesting in the hollowed-out carapaces of sun-browned cacti.

"I wanted lemon," she said. "I wanted *real* lemon."

There was a lemon wedge in her glass, so Toby didn't know what constituted real lemon from fake lemon. He had been nursing a lukewarm Stella Artois all night, so what the fuck did he know?

He asked, "What's your name?"

She laughed in his face. Said, "Wouldn't you like to know."

"I would."

"I know *you*," she said, and those radiant eyes narrowed the slightest bit. She was beautiful. Hypnotically so. "You're a Renfield."

"What's that?"

"*Ren-field*," she said, breaking it down into two distinct syllables, heavy on the emphasis, as if this might clarify things for him. Which it didn't.

He simply said, "You're so beautiful."

She laughed again, her breath warm and fruity in his face, and said, "I'm too dangerous for you, Renfield."

"What makes you so dangerous? Those teeth?"

"I'm a bloodsucker. A child of the night. I could bite you and turn you."

"Turn me?"

"Into a creature of the night like me."

"I'm already a creature of the night," he said. Then added: "Although maybe not exactly like you."

She laughed a third time—just tossed her head back on her neck and laughed—and Toby stared at the smooth whiteness of her throat, the delicate lines of her jugular, and at those elongated incisors, curved like miniature elephant tusks, sprouting from her gum line.

"What's your real name, anyway?" she asked.

"Toby. I already told you that."

"That's a pussy name. Are you a pussy, Toby?"

"I'm a fly."

Her shimmery eyes widened. She appeared to like that answer. Said, "Oh, yeah? A fly, huh? That's something. You just buzzing around?"

"On the walls, mostly," he said. "Observing."

Slowly, she closed her mouth. Those fangs disappeared. It was like watching the curtain on a stage draw closed. Something akin to a smile overtook her face, and once again, Toby Kampen, twenty-two years old, felt that strange fluttering sensation in the center of his wiry, bristling thorax.

The lifespan of a common housefly can be summed up in heartbeats—*whuh-whump, whuh-whump, whuh-whump . . .*

"C'mere," she whispered, hot breath on his ear again, and that dry, desert flower smell engulfed him as she drew closer, closer, fine white hairs along the ridge of her jaw tingling against his own, closer, closer, sensitive as a fly, all circuits firing, slow motion now, *whuh-whump, whuh-whump*, closer, and she leaned in some more, and she opened her mouth. He felt those curled tusks graze the side of his neck. The tender, exposed meat of his throat. And there—

"Ow!"

He slapped a hand to his neck as she pulled away, laughing at him. "You bit me."

Still laughing.

And then the drink was placed back down on the top of the bar, mostly finished, and when he looked in her direction once more, the woman—whatever her name was—was gone.

"Hey!" he yelled, before he realized he was yelling. Anyway, no one heard him over the thump and pound, the *unce unce unce*, of the music. He glanced over at the bartender with the bulldog jowls, and saw he was chuckling, too. "Where'd she go?" he demanded, but the bartender wasn't having any of it.

Toby scanned the dance floor. Searching, hunting—

—as he did the next night—

—and the night after that—

—and the night after *that.*

—◇—

And at some point, he realized he had ceased being a fly. He'd become something with an agenda, and flies did not have agendas. For the first time in his life, he'd become . . .

. . . something else.

A transformation had taken place, all without him knowing or understanding, and he felt in the midst of it—chemical changes, a body rearranging. Something he didn't think would ever happen to a common housefly like him, because—

—because when he took his hand away from his throat, his fingers were tacky with blood.

PART TWO:

ONE YEAR EARLIER
or,
THE DEAD WIVES CLUB

SIX

THE MURDER OF MELISSA JEAN ANDRESSEN

I

In the days and weeks and months following Linda's death, Bill Renney had lain awake every night for hours in an otherwise empty bed, in the close, breathing dark; a slender, splinter-like column of anxiety levitating through the center of his being, sharp and uncompromising as a physical thing. It was in these hours that Renney, at his most introspective, would reflect on all the mistakes he had perpetrated throughout their twenty years of marriage—and all the ways he could have handled things differently; all the times he should have been home instead of working those long, grueling, unforgiving hours; all the small, seemingly inconsequential (at the time) moments he had let slip by when he should have been more attentive, more in the moment, more *there*—as if to catalogue these myriad shortcomings might somehow bring Linda back. Sometimes he would gather himself off the bed and, in the dark, wander to the kitchen for a beer, then sit for hours in front of the television, not really watching anything. Sometimes with the volume turned all the way down, until the initial strains of daylight fingered their way through the slatted blinds. Other times, he would sit on the front porch in the dark, watching the traffic while he smoked, and listening to the occasional dog or coyote baying at the moon.

Linda's friends suggested he see a therapist to help him cope with his grief. Renney promised he would, but he never did. Renney's own friends were just acquaintances on the job, and he never let on to the people at work that he might not be in the best mental state, for fear his supervisor might yank him off the street and prop him behind a desk. He knew he was drinking too much and sleeping too little, but he didn't care.

As luck would have it, on the first night since Linda's passing that Renney was actually able to claim a few fitful hours' sleep, he was unceremoniously awoken by the chirping of his cell phone on the nightstand beside the bed. The sun was already coming up, an unforgiving lance of early morning daylight piercing that ungodly space between the bedroom curtains, enough to cause him to shield his eyes upon waking. He rolled over and answered the phone without checking the number, some disremembered part of a dream assuring him that the call was from Linda—that there'd been a mistake, she wasn't dead, and she wanted to come back home.

The call was not from Linda.

He dressed without showering, brushed his teeth with his eyes half closed against the harsh light of the bathroom, strapped on his service weapon, then went out to his car.

Two teenage boys from Lancaster had taken a drone up into the air just before first light. Somewhere high above the marrow-colored slaloms and sun-baked plateaus of Antelope Valley, at a moment when the sun first crested the horizon to the east, the boys' drone spied something unusual on the desert floor. They brought the drone in closer for a better look, and saw that the thing on the ground was the dead body of a woman.

The desert made Bill Renney uncomfortable, ever since that snakebite in his teenage years, so he tried never to wander too far out of civilization, if he could help it. Bodies found in the desert were usually those of junkies, drug dealers, or the occasional hiker whose luck had, in some shabby form or another, run out. The officers out of Lancaster or Palmdale typically handled those calls on their own, so Renney was already feeling that this must be something different to warrant his involvement. When he arrived on the scene that morning, he saw that this hunch was correct.

A year later, Renney would reflect on the cyclical nature of time and the great cosmic echo (of course), but on this morning, and without reference to what his future held, Bill Renney stood among a handful of uniformed police officers, peering down at the mutilated corpse of a woman. The sun had broken over the horizon by this point, simmering fully in the east. There was blood baked in the sand, black and soupy as hot tar, and swarming with insects. There was blood on the woman, too—a face that was a massacre, unidentifiable even *as* a face, with clotted, bloodied sinew collected in coarse black clumps in her hair. Renney noted that the dead woman's fingers were gone from both hands, and he thought to himself, at first, *Coyotes.* Later, at the morgue, however, Renney would be informed by the medical examiner that the damage done to this woman had been perpetrated by a human being who appeared rather adept at wielding a very sharp blade. Once the body had been cleaned up a bit, the details of her mutilation became clearer: the dead woman's face had been carved up like a Halloween pumpkin. Whoever had done this to her, they had painstakingly removed the eyes, ears, nose, and even the tongue, with a precise, almost delicate sensibility. All five fingers on each hand had also been cut off, right down to the knuckles; beneath the harsh, unapologetic lights of the morgue, Bill Renney could see that no coyotes or other wildlife had been involved here, but rather some serious piece of equipment—a hefty blade or a set of industrial clippers—had seen to the removal of the dead woman's digits.

There was no ID on the body, and with the fingers missing, there was no way to quickly identify the victim. DNA was taken, but there were no matches in any of the databases. There were no scars or tattoos or any unusual piercings on the body that might assist in the identification. Moreover, whoever had perpetrated this crime had left no detectable evidence behind on the woman's body or clothing—no fingerprints or hair follicles. There were no visible tracks—either by man or machine—in the sand in the vicinity where her body was found. It was as if the woman's body had been dropped in the desert by a ghost.

"She was cut up while still alive," the medical examiner, Falmouth, told him. "Cause of death was due to a massive loss of blood."

The L.A. County Sheriff's Department issued a statement to the media about the unidentified body being found in the desert, although most of the details were kept close to the vest, including the specific way the body had been mutilated. The sheriff asked for anyone with any possible knowledge, no matter how seemingly insignificant, to come forward.

No one came forward.

Renney spoke to the two boys who'd found the body—a pair of dumbstruck teenagers who had no qualms about Renney taking the drone and the video footage into evidence; in fact, they seemed relieved to be rid of it. He canvassed the area, knocking on doors to see if anyone living out that way had noticed anything that might prove to be of any value to the case—unusual people or vehicles at strange hours of the night, things like that. But no one had seen anything. He pulled traffic camera footage from the surrounding highways and secondary roads, but nothing jumped out at him as significant.

No other state in the country boasts more unidentified bodies than California, Renney knew, and it was looking like this poor woman would be quietly and unceremoniously added to that tally.

2

Three days later, a man who identified himself as Dr. Alan Andressen, from Calabasas, California, arrived at the sheriff's station on West Temple Street to file a missing persons report on his wife, Melissa Jean Andressen. This man brought with him a glossy eight-by-ten photograph of his wife, an attractive woman in her early thirties posing as if for a glamour magazine, the collar of her white tennis shirt popped, and with a cascade of chestnut hair draped over her shoulders. Her smile was genuine, and touched her eyes. Andressen showed this photo to the officer who took his statement. On the back of the photo was the woman's name, date of birth, height and weight, and some other personal information, typed in tidy rows.

Andressen explained to the officer that he had been out of town all week, at a work conference in Phoenix. When he found himself unable to reach his wife on her cell phone for a couple of days, he became worried and flew home. His wife's car, a white Lexus LX, was in the garage when he'd arrived home, but his wife was not at the house. Her purse and cell phone were gone, too—"and she never goes anywhere without her cell phone." Andressen kept calling her phone, but it kept going straight to voicemail, as if she had the phone turned off, or maybe the battery had died. He asked his neighbors if they'd seen her, but no one had. He called his wife's friends to inquire about her whereabouts, but no one had seen Melissa Jean Andressen for days. She'd even missed a lunch date with friends and, quite unlike her, hadn't called to cancel.

The officer who had taken Alan Andressen's statement was aware of the unidentified body that had recently been discovered in the high desert, and felt that it could be a match for the doctor's missing wife. He did not say anything to Andressen about this possibility, but instead showed his supervisor the photo of Melissa Jean, which her husband had left with him.

"It's even got all her vitals on the back," said the officer. "Weirdly convenient."

"It's a headshot," said the supervisor. "Like a business card for actors and actresses. How do you not know that?"

The officer, who had transferred to Los Angeles from a small town in Idaho less than a year earlier, had never seen a headshot before. To him, headshots were what you practiced at the firing range on those silhouette targets.

"You think she could be the one we found in Antelope?"

"You never know," said the supervisor. "The hair looks about right." He dug his phone out of his pants pocket. "The detective on that case is William Renney. Here—take down this number and give him a call."

That afternoon, the officer called Renney himself during his lunch break.

3

Renney met Dr. Alan Andressen later that afternoon in the hallway of the morgue on Mission Road where, farther down the hall and behind a closed metal door, the remains of the unidentified woman were laid out nude and disfigured on a stainless-steel table, a plain white sheet covering the body from head to toe.

Renney shook the man's hand, then did what he'd been

accustomed to doing for the thirty-odd years he'd been with the L.A. County Sheriff's Department: he took quiet inventory of the man. On the surface—middle-aged, in decent shape, expensive wristwatch and clothes. Just below the surface—the faint hint of body odor barely masked by cologne, unshaven jowls, darkened pockets beneath overly alert eyes, and an overall aura of mild dislocation. The man looked like someone who'd just been shaken awake from a deep sleep.

"I won't show you the face," Renney told Andressen as they entered the room where the body was laid out on the table beneath the sheet. "Look at the hair. Look at the feet. The legs and torso, if you need to see more. Also, if you're aware of any identifiable marks that we could use to confirm—"

"I want to see her face," Andressen said.

"You can't. She's in bad shape. Like I said out in the hall, she's—"

"I want to see her face," Andressen repeated.

Renney paused a beat. His throat tightened, suddenly in need of a cigarette. Then he peeled down a section of the sheet, revealing what the assailant had done to the face of his victim. He studied Andressen's face as Andressen looked down upon a whole other face—a face that was no longer a face. There was no right way for someone to react in such a circumstance, Renney knew, so he didn't necessarily pass judgment on Andressen when, in a small voice, he uttered, "That's not a very nice thing to do to somebody."

Renney gave the man another ten seconds or so, before covering the body back up. Then he cleared his throat. Asked, "Is that your wife, Dr. Andressen?"

Andressen cleared his own throat and, in a barely audible voice, said, "Yes. That's her. That's M.J."

He then turned and wandered back out into the hallway, moving like someone trudging through a dream, a distinctive droop to the shoulders that hadn't been there a moment before, when Renney had been taking inventory of the man, and the heels of his expensive shoes squeaked on the cold tile floor.

Renney could hear him begin to wail.

4

For Christmas one year, Linda had given him a Victrola turntable and a stack of old 45s that she had found at the Goodwill. Renney, who possessed an appreciation for things older than himself, played the records frequently. After Linda's death, one record in particular—Roy Orbison's "Crying"—practically lived on the turntable. Some nights, he would drink a whole case of Coors Light while listening to the record over and over and over and over and over and over again. Other nights, he'd come awake in bed hearing that record playing in the other room, the volume at full blast, the crackle of the needle in the groove almost like the crackle of a distant forest fire. The first few times this had happened, he got out of bed and wandered into the living room, waiting for the music to dissipate as if it was just some lingering part of a dream. But he would always find the record spinning on the turntable, the strains of "Crying" coming through the speakers. He never shut it off, but would remain standing there until the song finished, his eyes filling with tears and the flesh of his face growing hot.

Once, after the song had ended, he looked across the room to find Linda sitting on the sofa in the dark. He swiped tears from his eyes and said her name aloud—"Linda-baby." He couldn't see the details of her—the features of her face, the specific contours of her body—but he knew it was her. He reached over and turned on a small lamp that stood on an end table. When the light came on, Linda was gone.

After several nights of this, he stopped getting out of bed altogether, and just lay there staring at the dark abyss above his head while Orbison sang about being left all alone by his one true love.

5

Two days after Melissa Jean Andressen's body had been identified by her husband at the morgue on Mission Road, Dr. Alan Andressen was asked to come down to the station to give a formal statement. He showed up in a stained Journey concert T-shirt and white jeans, looking like a contractor Renney might hire to redo his kitchen rather than the lauded mental health professional Renney had read about in several online magazine articles and trade journals. They sat together in a small, cement room, with a digital camera on a tripod in one corner, and a desk against one wall. Andressen did not bring a lawyer. When Renney told him their conversation was going to be recorded, Andressen merely nodded, his eyes unfocused, his hands limp in his lap.

"Before we begin," Renney said, "are you currently on any medication that might impair your responses to the questions I'm about to ask?"

Andressen's eyes hung on him. Renney, who, after three decades on the job, could spot a dilated pupil a mile away, did not contest Andressen when he said, flatly, "No."

Renney started out asking the doctor the most basic questions— who he was, what he did for a living, how long he and his wife had been married. Background info, sure, and stuff Renney had already looked up about the doctor online prior to this interview, but these questions (and their answers) also served as a baseline: he watched the way Andressen spoke, the way the muscles contracted beneath the burgeoning beard stubble of his lower face. He could see the way his nostrils flared and contracted, the reddened bleariness of his eyes, as if he'd been drinking all night (and maybe he had been), the milky ball of gunk in the corner of his left eye. When he glanced at the man's fingers, he could see they were manicured and clean, like the fingers of a surgeon. Every once in a while, he would nervously twist his wedding band around and around on his finger.

Melissa Jean Andressen did not work a nine-to-five job, but she had been involved in several charities, and was on the board of at least three nonprofit organizations that her husband could remember off the top of his head. Renney, who had spent much of yesterday scouring the internet for any information on the woman (as well as her husband), already knew this, but he nodded and listened and occasionally made a show of scribbling down some notes on a yellow legal pad as if this was the first he'd heard about such things.

"She was very altruistic," Andressen said. "She volunteered all the time. Did a lot of stuff for women and children. Especially children. We couldn't have any of our own, so . . . " He made a vague motion with his hand, but didn't complete the thought. "She wanted to be an actress, you know. That's why she came out here from the East Coast, back when she was in her twenties. I mean, she *was* an actress, although she never made it big. She was in a couple of low-budget horror movies, just bit parts, but she still went out for open calls every once in a while when the spirit struck. She liked to act, and she loved those cheap horror movies. She was actually pretty good."

"Let's talk about where you were that week," Renney said, getting down to it.

"I was at a conference in Phoenix," Andressen told him. "I rarely go to these things. I almost didn't. She said to go, to get out of town for a while."

"So it was her idea that you should go?"

"It was a mutual agreement. It was a good networking opportunity."

"Did you travel with anyone?"

"No, I flew there on my own."

"Did you know anyone else at the convention?"

"Several people. Colleagues of mine. I see them a couple times a year, mostly when they come to town."

"Could you provide a list of names of those individuals?"

Andressen nodded with numb detachment.

"When was the last time you spoke with your wife?"

"When I was in Phoenix. On the phone. The first night of the convention. She'd been having trouble with her car for a while, so I wanted to make sure everything was okay. Also, you know, just to say goodnight."

"Do you recall anything unusual from that phone call?"

"No. Nothing."

"How long were you on the phone with her?"

"Five minutes. Just a quick call home."

"When was the next time you called her?"

"The following day, around lunchtime."

"What happened when you called?"

"Nothing. She didn't answer."

"It rang or went straight to voicemail?"

"Uh, straight to voicemail. Yes."

"Did you leave a message?"

"I think I just hung up."

"No message?"

"I just figured I'd talk to her later."

"And when did you try calling her again?"

"Later that night."

"What happened with that call?"

"Nothing," Andressen said. "She didn't answer. It just went straight to voicemail again."

"What'd you do?"

"Went to dinner, then called her back when I got back to my room."

"Did you go to dinner by yourself?"

Andressen rubbed his manicured fingers along the ridges of his furrowed brow. "I went with some colleagues."

"What happened when you called later that night from your room?"

"The same thing—the call went straight to voicemail. I sent her a text, but she never responded. I think I tried calling her once more that night before going to bed."

"And the following day?" Renney asked.

"I called her repeatedly. Still no answer. Sent a bunch of texts, too, and an email. I started to get worried, so I called a few of her friends, but no one had seen her. Her friend Carla said she didn't show up for a lunch date, which was unlike M.J., so I asked Carla to drive by the house for me. She went out there, knocked on the door, but M.J. wasn't home."

"For the record, M.J. is your wife, correct?"

"Sorry. Yes. Melissa Jean. I call her M.J."

"What'd you do next?"

"After Carla said she wasn't at home?"

"Yes."

"I was worried. I left the conference and got an early flight back to L.A."

"What happened when you got to the house?"

"I saw her car was still there. No purse and no cell phone, though. No evidence of anything out of place, as far as I could tell."

"Do you keep your house locked?"

"All the time."

"Do you have an alarm system?"

"Yes."

"Was the alarm still armed when you arrived home from the airport?"

"Yes, it was."

"Has she ever not responded to your phone calls in the past?"

"No," he said, then amended: "Well, she might not answer when I call right away, if she happens to be in the middle of something, but then she always calls me back."

"Were there any marital problems between the two of you?" Renney asked.

"Us? No. We were . . . everything was good. We were good."

"Can you think of anyone who might want to do something like that to your wife?"

Some semblance of lucidity flashed across Alan Andressen's eyes; his gaze rose to meet Renney's, and there was something unwavering in that look all of a sudden. Resolute, even. Bill Renney suddenly realized he was staring at a man standing on the precipice of a great and overwhelming sense of loss, and it was only the small bursts of anger at what had been done to his wife that prevented him from jumping blindly into that grieving abyss.

"Something like *that*?" Andressen said, and there was a dry clicking sound at the back of his throat as he spoke. His tone was one of incredulity. "Who would do *that* to *anyone*?"

"I'm asking if anything comes to mind."

Andressen sighed. He leaned back in his chair, his face beet-red. "No," he said in a small voice, calming down. "Nothing comes to mind."

I warned you not to look, Renney thought, but did not say. *I warned you not to look at her face.*

"Was she having problems with anyone?" he asked instead. "Strange phone calls in the night? An argument with a friend or neighbor? Or maybe someone from one of the charities that she worked on? Things like that."

"Everyone loved my wife. And she didn't get strange phone calls in the night."

Everyone loved my wife, Renney knew, was a tell. Andressen didn't say *Everyone loved M.J.*, but *Everyone loved my wife*. Subconsciously creating distance. It was the talk of the guilty, and it caused Renney to lean forward a bit in his chair.

"What about unusual packages at the door addressed to her?" Renney went on. "People showing up that you didn't know, looking for her?"

"None of that ever happened."

"Did you both sleep in the same bed?"

Something in Andressen's posture stiffened. "What's that mean?"

"I mean, if her cell phone rang in the middle of the night, would you know about it?"

"Are you asking if she was seeing someone behind my back? Is that what you're asking?"

"Was she?"

"Fuck. No. Goddamn you."

"I don't mean to offend you. I just want to make sure I'm turning over every stone here. It's important."

"No, she wasn't seeing anyone. Yes, we slept in the same room. In the same bed. I would have heard it if her phone rang in the middle of the night. I would have known if some guy was calling her."

"Do you have people come in and out of your house?"

"What do you mean? What people?"

"Like a housekeeper or a gardener," Renney said. He'd driven by Andressen's home the day before and was thinking now about all that lush flora that decorated the property—things that were alive and verdant and required constant care, surrounding a lifeless modern house that looked as cold as a museum.

"We've got a team of guys who take care of the lawn," Andressen said. "It's some company, I can't remember the name off the top of my head. Green something."

"What about a housekeeper?"

"A woman comes on Tuesdays and Saturdays. She's worked for us for years. Gabriella."

"Could you provide me the full names and contact info for these people?"

"Yes, I can. I can do that. I can send them to you."

"Anyone else who regularly comes to the house?"

"Fuck," Andressen said, and he hung his head so low, Renney could see the thinness of his hair at the crown of his head, through which the white scalp peeked out. "No. No one who comes regularly."

"Let's talk about what you do again," Renney said, by means of redirection. "You're a psychologist, correct?"

"No, I'm a psychiatrist."

"I'm sorry. I guess I didn't realize there was a difference."

"I'm a medical doctor. I prescribe medication, diagnose mental illness."

"I see. And you work exclusively from your home?" Renney asked, although he already knew this answer.

"That's right. I've got an office on the side of the house."

"Your clients can come and go through a dedicated entrance without having to access the main house, is that correct?"

"Yeah, that's right. They can't get into the main house."

"What type of clients do you see?"

"I specialize in treating anxiety disorders, depression, adjustment disorders."

"You have no website or anything online to advertise your practice," Renney said.

"I don't need to advertise. It's mostly word of mouth."

"You do pretty well that way." It was not a question. Renney was thinking of that big, ugly, uninviting house. He'd run a property search and wasn't surprised to see that the Andressens had purchased the home three years ago for several million.

"There's a lot of anxiety and depression in Hollywood," Andressen said.

"Are your clients famous people? Hollywood types?"

"Some of them," Andressen said. "But not all. I do pro bono counseling, too. People from impoverished areas around the city. Teenagers with problems. Giving back. That sort of thing."

"That's generous of you."

Andressen made no response. The red in his face had been replaced by a paleness that made it possible for Renney to see the fine network of veins just below the surface of the man's skin.

"Did your wife ever interact with any of your patients?"

"Clients," Andressen corrected. "And no, she never had any interaction with any of them. I've always been very careful about that. I keep a clear separation between my work and my personal life."

"And these are people—these clients—with, uh . . . let's see . . . " Renney glanced down at the yellow legal pad on the edge of the desk, where he'd been scribbling the occasional note. "Anxiety disorders, you said? Depression? Stuff like that?"

"That's right."

"Do any of these clients have criminal records? Any violent tendencies?"

"None of my clients are violent," Andressen said. "Besides, I told you—none of them would have even known who my wife was."

"Not even from her movies?"

"My clients aren't the type of people to watch those movies."

Renney leaned back in his chair. "Where do these clients park when they come to the house for an appointment?"

"They park in the street. We live in a cul-de-sac."

"And how do they get to the office?"

"I buzz them in through an automated gate and they come up to the house and into the waiting room until I come get them and bring them to my office."

"You keep the door to the waiting room unlocked?"

"I unlock it remotely when I buzz them in through the gate. It's locked, otherwise."

Renney shifted in his seat. "Isn't it possible someone might have seen your wife out in the yard, or maybe leaving in her car as they're arriving?"

"Jesus Christ." Andressen dropped his face into his hands again. He stayed that way for a while, sniffling into his palms, while the tips of his ears turned a deep crimson. His shoulders hitched only once.

Renney let some time pass. He listened to the ticking of the second hand on his cheap wristwatch and the whir of the camcorder in the corner of the room. After a while, he said, "Do you have any cameras on the outside of your house?"

Andressen brought his face up out of his hands slowly. His eyes were moist, his cheeks streaked with tears. Very quietly, he said, "Yes. But they don't work."

"They don't? Why's that?"

"They stopped working about a year ago. I don't know why. I kept meaning to call someone and have the system fixed, but I never got around to it."

"You should do that," Renney said.

Andressen laughed miserably, shaking his head. Another tear trickled down the left side of his face. "Yeah, sure. I'll get right on that now."

Renney leaned forward even farther in his chair, folding his hands together between his knees. "I'd like to bring some guys from forensics over to the house, see if there's anything there that might help us narrow things down. I'd have them look over your wife's car, too. Yours, as well. The fact that the alarm was armed suggests your wife would have done that upon leaving the house, but just to be safe, I'd like to have our guys take a look around at everything. In the event something might have transpired in the home."

Andressen leaned away from Renney. He folded his arms across his chest and stared at a wastebasket on the floor beside the desk. "That's fine."

"I'd like to ask you to take a polygraph, too."

Andressen turned back and faced him. "Me?"

"Like I said, doc. I'm just trying to narrow things down."

Andressen stared at him for several moments before returning his gaze back to the wastebasket, or to maybe some undefined point in the distance of the that small, cement-block interrogation room. "You know," he said, his voice so low that Renney wondered if the camcorder was picking it up, "we had tickets to Bermuda. Our fifth wedding anniversary. In two weeks."

"I'm sorry," Renney said.

Andressen scratched at a patch of rough stubble along his neck. He still would not meet Renney's eyes.

Ticking of the wristwatch.

Whir of the video camera.

"Yeah, sure," Andressen said finally. "I'll take a polygraph. I'll take it right now."

"Great," said Renney, and then he stood from his chair.

"But first," Andressen said, "do you mind if I throw up in that wastebasket?"

6

The results of the polygraph were inconclusive. When Alan Andressen finally left the station late that afternoon, he looked like someone who'd been kept prisoner in some remote country for an undisclosed amount of time: drained, withered, dispirited. In fact, to Renney, the man looked like he had aged several years in the matter of a few hours.

Renney walked him out to the street, hands in the pockets of his chinos, jingling loose change. They did not speak. But before leaving, Andressen did something that caught Renney wholly off guard: he turned to him, grabbed and shook Renney's hand, and then he thanked him for his thoroughness.

"Just promise me," the doctor said, staring Renney dead in the eyes, "that you'll find the son of a bitch who did this to my wife."

Renney, who had broken more than his fair share of promises in his lifetime, said he would do his best.

7

What Bill Renney *did* do was his due diligence: he contacted American Airlines and found that Andressen was, indeed, on a flight to Phoenix the week his wife was murdered. Minds and Hearts was the name of the convention, and psychiatric professionals from all over the country had apparently flocked to attend. Andressen had stayed at the Hilton on Monroe Street, in downtown Phoenix, which was where the conference had been held. He pulled Andressen's credit card statements for that period and saw he'd used his Visa at that very same hotel during that week, as well as in a few other establishments throughout the city—a coffee shop, some restaurants, a bar—though he never strayed far from the hotel. He contacted hotel security and received a link to security footage from inside the hotel itself. On the night Melissa Jean Andressen was most likely murdered, her husband, Dr. Alan Andressen, was seen stepping onto an elevator in the lobby of the hotel, dressed in a shirt and tie and a nice pair of slacks, and with a portfolio tucked under one arm. Right there, on pixilated black-and-white security footage, approximately three hundred seventy-five miles from Los Angeles.

That's a five-hour car ride and about an hour and a half on a plane, though, Renney told himself, noting that the timestamp on the security footage of the doctor getting on the elevator was 5:32 p.m. A rental car would have him back in Los Angeles before midnight. A plane would get him back home even sooner. According to the Minds and Hearts conference website, the convention didn't start back up again until 8:30 the following morning, which left a window of time where Andressen could have easily traveled back and forth from Phoenix to L.A.

With this niggling disquiet in the back of his head, Renney contacted all the other airlines to see if Alan Andressen had perhaps booked another flight home during the time he was supposedly in Phoenix. He called charter companies, too. Lastly, he made some phone calls to rental car companies. But Andressen's name did not appear on any other reservation.

Renney spoke with the crew of lawn care specialists from Green Tom Thumb who maintained the lawns and flowerbeds of the Andressen house. He ran backgrounds on each of them and found that not a single person employed with that company possessed a criminal record, which, Renney thought, was unusual for such an enterprise. It was a fairly upscale outfit, though, and Renney surmised that the Andressens paid a pretty penny for that service.

He spoke, too, with the Andressens' housekeeper, Gabriella Marquardt. She was a robust, genial woman in her mid-fifties who sobbed for the entirety of their brief conversation over the tragic loss of her employer. "She was a wonderful lady," the housekeeper told him as they sat in a coffee shop in Calabasas, a large black coffee in front of Renney, a wad of damp Kleenex in front of Gabriella. "Sometimes they are not so nice, I can tell you, but that lady was as kind as they come. I just cannot *believe* what has happened to that sweet, sweet lady . . . "

At Renney's request, Andressen turned over his wife's laptop as well as his own. He gave Renney all of his passwords and he also provided a yellow sticky note with a variety of his wife's passwords on them, as well. "I'm not sure which one goes to what," Andressen explained, "but she wasn't too big on social media. If you need anything else, let me know. I'm not seeing clients for the foreseeable future, so I guess I'm just sitting around."

"I'd like to look at all of your banking and credit card statements, too," Renney said. "Any accounts you shared with your wife, as well as any accounts or credit cards you both had separately."

He expected Andressen to balk at this, to make some sort of sour expression, or at the very least suggest that now was the time he should probably consult with an attorney, but he did none of those things.

"I'll get them to you right away," Andressen promised.

8

Melissa Jean had a Facebook and an Instagram account, both of which hadn't been updated in months. The scant few messages she had received via those accounts were innocuous. Renney was able to gain access to her email, as well, but there was nothing of note in Melissa Jean Andressen's inbox—some messages from friends, from the organizations for which she volunteered, auto-generated messages about open calls for movies and TV shows in the area, and some fairly banal spam. There was the panic-stricken email from her husband, which Renney printed out for the case file, but nothing more. Her browser history was cleaner than Renney's.

At first, the cell phone company wanted Renney to submit a subpoena for Melissa Jean's records, but Andressen himself—who paid the monthly bill—made a call, and Renney had a log of phone calls and texts messages sent directly to his work email before the day was done. The last call answered was from her husband and corresponded with the first night he'd been in Phoenix. The unanswered calls from her husband were also logged, as well as unanswered calls from a few other numbers. Renney saw the text messages, too, that Andressen had told him he'd sent to her:

> trying to reach you

and

> everything ok? call me back

and

> mj answer your phone

and

> WHERE ARE YOU???

and

> im worried flying home

Renney could find nothing incriminating there, either.

No loose threads.

Only dead ends.

Motive? Sure, there was a five-hundred-thousand-dollar life insurance policy on her, but given their financial status, that was small potatoes.

What else was there? What was he missing?

Maybe it's not the husband, he started to think to himself. *The guy is on video getting on an elevator around the time his wife was most likely murdered.*

Still, the possibility that Andressen could have made the drive home then back to the conference in Phoenix with plenty of time to spare troubled him.

He received a list of names from Andressen of the colleagues who had attended the Minds and Hearts conference with him. Renney called each one and got a statement. Three of them corroborated that they'd had dinner with him that night; each one recalled the dinner ending around 8:30 that evening. This closed the window for Andressen to travel back and forth between Phoenix and Los Angeles considerably, but still didn't make it impossible.

9

A few days after Linda died, Renney sent a single text message to her phone. It said, simply:

I miss you.

It was stupid, but he stayed up for hours that night clutching his phone, wondering—even though he did not believe in such things—if by some chance she might reach out to him from beyond the grave and respond.

10

He found a handful of Melissa Jean's movies online. Her husband had been right—they were all pretty low-budget, and Renney even caught the occasional boom mic slipping into frame. Melissa Jean had small speaking roles in *Countess Depraved*, *Livid*, and a zombie flick called *They Eat Your Brains First*. In *Blood Tenant*, blink and you'd miss her—just a passing shot down a hallway as she smiled seductively at the square-jawed protagonist. The films were terrible, but Melissa Jean Andressen—credited then under her maiden name, Melissa Jean Holbrook—was young and radiant.

11

Bill Renney arrived at the Andressen home at least a full hour ahead of the forensic team. He parked in the street, hit the buzzer at the gate, then waited as the gate shuddered open to allow him to enter. He headed up the steep incline of the driveway toward the house, already sweating from his armpits and dampening his shirt in the heat of the day. He was wheezing, too. *Should really quit smoking*, which was basically an echo of what Linda had always told him. *Ah, well, maybe I should have listened*, which wouldn't have changed anything, but still. He was only halfway up the driveway when he looked up and saw a man heading in his direction, on his way to meeting him at the midway point.

It was Andressen, of course, although Renney did not recognize him at first. In the passage of just a handful of days, the doctor had lost a considerable amount of weight. He walked with a slow gait, like some lame animal, and he'd neglected to shave so that his beard was growing in sparse black patches nearly all the way down to his collarbone.

Andressen shook his hand, and it was a limp gesture, much different than the handshake the doctor had administered outside the sheriff's station. He muttered something unintelligible, then turned and skulked back toward the house. Renney came up beside him and brought him up to speed regarding the lack of any leads on his wife's computer and phone. Andressen repeatedly nodded as Renney spoke, the psychiatrist's eyes half lidded, but it looked like he was hardly listening. It seemed to take a lot of effort for him to climb all the way up the driveway to the house.

He's medicated, Renney knew. *Valium, or some antidepressant. Maybe a shot or two of whiskey, as well, judging by the smell of him.*

But it wasn't just the vague aroma of booze that clung to Andressen; he smelled unwashed, too, and looked the part. It had been just a few days since Renney had interviewed him down at the station, yet in that time, this man had become someone else entirely.

I know the feeling, Renney thought. Barely four months gone at this point, he was still mourning Linda, and often found himself in a similar state of affairs.

"I spoke to her parents again last night," Andressen said, his voice a harsh rasp. "I felt like I should check in with them. It wasn't any better than when I first told them the news. I kept putting it off, you know? A part of me hoped they'd see it on the news and I wouldn't have to tell them. Another part of me hoped they wouldn't answer their phone that first night. They live in Maine, in a cabin. That's where M.J. was from—Maine. Her father cried like a little child when I first told him."

"I'm sorry, doc."

"I cried, too. Then I took some pills, a double shot of scotch, and went to bed." He glanced at Renney, and Renney caught a good look at just how haunted the man's eyes were. "I keep feeling her in bed, you know. Right there next to me. Every night. I feel the bed move, like she's tossing around, but when I reach over to her side, she's not there. Funny thing is, when I reach over, her side of the mattress is warm. Like she'd actually been there a moment before."

Renney felt a twinge of commiseration; he'd felt a similar thing, a similar stirring, in the bed beside him in the nights soon after Linda had died. He thought, too, of Roy Orbison spontaneously calling out to him in the middle of the night from the living room, and the night when he imagined Linda sitting on the sofa, staring back at him in the dark.

"Well, fuck it, I guess," Andressen said, and ran both hands through his thinning hair.

They arrived on the porch and Renney noted the small camera mounted above the doorway. He could see the brand, SPY-X, on a label at the base of the camera, and made a mental note.

Andressen opened the front door. He stepped to one side and absently waved his hand for Renney to enter first.

The house was just as cold and uninviting on the inside as it was from the street.

Renney knew very little about art, architecture, and interior design—his appreciation for the finer things in life stopped at paintings of dogs playing poker and loafers with tassels—but he knew, without question, that he was suddenly in the presence of a certain unattainable level of wealth and sophistication—unattainable to the average person, anyway. The house was wide open, with the rear wall nothing but floor-to-ceiling windows looking out on a deck that, in turn, hung over the precipice of a vast canyon. He took in items piecemeal—a pearl-colored baby grand, a system of red sofas, a television that looked like a movie theater screen. The floors were comprised of some material that, to Renney, appeared to have been designed by NASA, and were silent beneath the soles of their shoes as they walked.

"You want a drink or something?" Andressen asked.

"Glass of water would be fine," Renney said, and he followed the doctor into a spacious kitchen. The refrigerator had a TV screen on the door and the sink faucet looked about as complicated as scuba gear. There were stacks of dirty dishes in the sink, however, and the trashcan beside the marble-topped island was overflowing with empty food containers and liquor bottles. "This is some gorgeous house, doc."

"M.J. hated it. Said it was too formal. Too un-lived-in."

"Your housekeeper quit?" he said, nodding at the overflowing trashcan.

"I told her not to come for a while."

Renney watched him go to the refrigerator, take out a bottle of Pellegrino. He didn't hand it to Renney, but set it on the marble-topped island in the middle of the room. Renney thanked him, picked up the bottle, unscrewed the cap. "I'd like to see your office and the waiting room where your clients come and go, if that's okay with you."

"Everything's okay with me," Andressen said, somewhat disjointedly. He took a clean glass down from the cupboard, and set it on the island next to Renney.

"You have a lot of parties in this place?" Renney asked, still looking around. Other than the mess in the kitchen, the place looked as homey as a mausoleum.

"No."

"Shame. Lots of space. Very nice."

"Come with me," Andressen said.

Renney left his water on the island and followed Andressen down a hallway. There were framed black-and-white glamour shots of

Melissa Jean on one wall of the hallway; on the opposite wall stood a large shelving unit packed to the gills with DVDs. Renney paused to look at the movie selection.

"Those were M.J.'s," Andressen said. "Like I said, she loved horror movies. The cheaper and cheesier, the better. She used to force me to watch them with her. Most of them are truly terrible. At the . . . at the time, I . . . " He trailed off, choking up.

If this is an act, Renney thought, *then it's a damn good one.*

"Sorry about that," Andressen said once he'd regained his composure. "Come on."

He led them to where a large oak door stood in a recessed alcove. There was a cipher lock on the door, and Renney watched as Andressen tapped in the code, not bothering to shield it from him. He heard the mechanical bolt slide, and then Andressen depressed the brass lever and they both entered the room.

Andressen's office looked different than the rest of the house: there were crowded bookshelves and lush carpeting and a desk of ornate mahogany. There were also some file cabinets, a few leather chairs piped in brass tacks, and a large abstract painting on the wall opposite the desk, which was the focal point of the room.

"That's a Pollock," Andressen said, noticing Renney admiring the painting.

"Those are expensive, aren't they?" Renney said.

Andressen made some sound that could have been affirmation, could have been a derisive dismissal of Renney's lack of sophistication.

Renney walked around the room, pausing to examine the framed degrees on the wall. An undergrad from Stanford, a medical degree from UC Berkeley. Bill Renney's highest level of education was twelfth grade, and even that had been touch and go at the time.

"I was very focused on my education," Andressen said. He was straightening some paperwork on his desk, perhaps searching for something. "I went to a year of medical school at UC Davis to be a surgeon before switching to psychiatry at Berkeley."

"Why the switch?"

"Couldn't stand the sight of blood."

It was Renney's turn to affect a sound that could have been affirmation, could have been derisive dismissal.

"After school," Andressen continued, "I was focused on my career. Tried hard to build something important, you know?"

"Looks like you did," said Renney.

"It's why I got married so late in life." Andressen paused in his shuffling of the papers and just stared down at his hands, or so it appeared to Renney, who was watching his reflection in the glass of his doctoral diploma. Then he said, "I've got all those bank records and credit card bills you asked for."

"Great, doc." Renney pointed to another door at the far end of the room. "Is that where the patients come in?"

"Clients," Andressen corrected. "Yes. It goes to the waiting room, like I told you about."

Andressen went to the door, opened it, and Renney passed through into a bland, white-walled room with cushioned chairs lining two of the four walls. It was a typical waiting area, with a magazine rack, a coffee table at its center, some droopy potted plants, and inspirational slogans hanging on the walls.

"And this door," Renney said, pointing to yet another door at the opposite end of the waiting room, "is where they come in from the outside?"

"Yes. It's locked from the outside, but you can open it from in here. So they can leave on their own accord when our time is up."

"Do you mind?"

"Go ahead."

Renney opened the door and took a step out into the bright sunshine. Winced, even. He turned and saw a buzzer where a doorbell might be. He asked about it, and Andressen said that when a client came to the door, they pressed the button, which then alerted him that they had arrived.

"It works off a remote, like a key fob on a car, so I can let them in from anywhere in the house."

Renney glanced up and saw another one of the nonfunctioning security cameras above the door.

SPY-X.

"Do you have a point of contact over at the security company who maintains these cameras?" Renney asked.

"No one specific. I just call and they hand me off to a technician."

"I'd like to speak to someone there."

"I can give you their number," Andressen said. "Also, my PIN. You'll need it to access my account."

Renney stepped back inside, closing the door behind him.

12

Renney stayed the entire time while the forensic team combed through the place. It took several hours. Restless, he walked around, admiring Melissa Jean's photos on the walls and her expansive horror movie collection, but mostly he just tried to stay out of everyone's way. At one point, he was on the phone with a technician from SPY-X, who corroborated that the system had been offline for the better part of the year. The technician confirmed that Andressen had called to report the problem, but then he had never followed up to reschedule a time for them to come out and troubleshoot the system. They had sent him a handful of emails, but had never received a response. Renney thanked the technician for his time.

Once the forensic team was done, Renney saw them out, then remained standing by himself in the spacious, echo-laden foyer of that large, cold, antiseptic house. He realized Andressen was still out on the back deck, where he had remained for the entirety of the time the forensic team had been in the house. He was leaning on the railing of the deck, gazing out over the steep drop of the canyon below while the midday sun surrendered to a hazy, yellow dusk.

Renney crossed to the far side of the house, where that wall of windows presented a vast, darkening vista, and where the lights of the city far below simmered like embers in a dying fire. He stepped outside, into the cool, foggy evening, and he thought he could smell a wildfire somewhere off in the distance.

"Everything's all finished in here," he said.

"They find anything?" Andressen asked, not looking at him.

"Doesn't really work like that. They'll run some tests at the lab on hair follicles, or any fingerprints they lifted. But no, nothing jumped out at anyone."

Andressen had both hands planted on the railing of the deck, his head slumped forward, chin resting on his chest. In Renney's thirty-odd years with the L.A. County Sheriff's Department, he had interviewed a handful of people who had later committed suicide. Looking at the way Andressen was standing there now, leaning against that railing, unresponsive, gazing down at that rocky abyss, Bill Renney realized that his own conscience was already lugging around too much weight to carry any more.

"You gonna be okay, doc?"

"Those bank records and credit card statements that you asked for are on the coffee table in the living room."

"Thanks."

The doctor slowly raised his head. He didn't turn to look at Renney, not really, but kept his gaze on the lights of the city below, each sodium pocket blinking on as night encroached. "I know I'm your only suspect. It's always the husband, right? Which means I'm worried that while you're focused on me, the guy who actually did this to my wife is getting farther and farther away. It's not your fault, Detective Renney; I understand you're just following the only potential lead you have, even though it isn't really a lead at all. But I don't want that trail to grow cold while you're busy scrutinizing me. It worries me."

Renney said nothing to that.

"I'm putting up a half-million-dollar reward for anyone who has any information about what happened to my wife," Andressen said. "I'm buying up billboards and radio ads. I'm putting stuff in the papers. Someone somewhere must know something."

"I'm not sure that's necessary, doc."

"It's no reflection on you, Detective Renney. I hope you don't think that," he said, and there was a queer sense of apology—genuine apology—in his tone that caused Renney to feel sorry for the guy; it was a thing he did not typically feel for people in his line of work, perhaps because he'd become accustomed to being the bearer of grief and had built a wall around such emotions, but he felt it now, and its arrival confounded him. "But, like I said, while you're focused on me, someone needs to be focused on my wife's killer. Anyway, I don't like sitting here, feeling helpless. It's not my style, or how I was built. At least this will make me feel like I'm doing something productive."

"You'll get all kinds of nutjobs coming out of the woodwork," Renney told him. "Your phone will be ringing off the hook day and night. Half a mil is a lot of money." It was also the amount the doctor would have received from his wife's life insurance policy, Renney noted.

"I guess that's true." Still facing the darkening vista of the valley beyond, Andressen added, "I saw on M.J.'s credit card statements she had some work done on the Lexus at some auto mechanic shop in Reseda."

"Yeah, you mentioned her car had been having trouble."

"She should have been taking it to the dealership. Back when we spoke in that interrogation room, you asked me about anything unusual that I might have noticed. M.J. taking the Lexus to some random shop in Reseda is unusual."

"All right," Renney said. "I'll look into it."

Andressen turned and stared at him, and in the waning light of day, the doctor's face was bisected directly down the middle, half in light, half in darkness. "I want to see the file you have on my wife."

"What file? The case file?"

"I want to see it all. The crime scene photos, the autopsy report. I want to see the names of anyone else who's jumped out at you as even remotely suspicious. Everything you have, I want to see it."

"I can't share that stuff with you, doc."

"She was my wife," Andressen said. "You can't stop me from seeing those things."

"It's an open investigation. I can't do that."

"I'd threaten to hire an attorney who would insist you share that stuff with me, but I don't want to distract you from the real issue even more than you already are. Just think about what I'm asking. Please."

The bleat of a distant car horn.

The cawing of a nearby crow.

"You must know other shrinks, right, Alan?" he said, realizing it was the first time he'd referenced the man by his first name—be it on his lips or in his mind. It seemed to take hold from that moment on.

Alan just stared at him while the dark of night bled across his face in small increments. The world seemed to move like a cagey, living thing.

"Maybe you should talk to one," Renney continued, "because you don't look so good."

"Yeah?" Alan said, and Renney could feel the man studying him. "You don't look so good, either."

Renney suddenly felt like he was on full display. And he didn't like that feeling one bit.

He left Alan on the balcony, but he didn't feel good about it.

13

In the desperate hours of some random evening—perhaps a Saturday night, perhaps in the dwindling dusk of some indiscriminate Tuesday—Bill Renney sat by himself at a table for two at a restaurant that had once been a dive bar called Lucky Larry's. Now, under new management, Lucky Larry's had become a slightly more upscale joint called Café Oleander. He was a cheeseburger and domestic beer kind of guy, not a *foie gras* kind of guy, whatever the hell that was, but this had been his and Linda's place once, so it became tradition—or just a plangent longing—that saw him returning here once a week after Linda's death.

A tumor tucked almost discreetly—at first, anyway—within the delicate folds of his wife's brain tissue, they hadn't even known she'd had it. When she lost feeling in the fingertips of her left hand, there had been a series of scans and MRIs, and sure enough, there it was—a nefarious little white-hot splotch on a lighted screen smack-dab in the center of her brain. Three months later, Linda was dead. It could have been worse, he would sometimes rationalize to himself;

she could have suffered for longer, maybe even years, so perhaps there was some good in how quickly she went. But for Renney, it was like a sudden amputation. It seemed he had hardly begun to digest the cancer diagnosis, and he was already picking out an urn.

On the table in front of him was the Andressen case file. He kept rereading the autopsy report, as if that might clue him in to something he'd previously overlooked; he kept reading the transcript of her husband's interview over and over as well, and finding that with each reread, he was growing more and more sympathetic toward the man. *The Dead Wives Club*, Renney thought morbidly. *Ah, shit*, and then he closed the file and set it aside.

He had finished his meal and was halfway through his third bottle of Coors Light when the tinkling of female laughter caught his attention—caught it because women did not generally come in here, at least under the old ownership, but more so because he thought he recognized one laugh in particular among that rising, high-pitched orchestration.

He looked across the bar to where a group of women sat having drinks in a semicircular booth in one corner. He had turned fifty the year before, but his uncorrected vision was still pretty good, so he had no difficulty picking Linda out among them, even in the dim lighting of the restaurant.

He nearly knocked his beer bottle over in his attempt to bolt up out of his chair.

He approached the table of women, his body simultaneously hot and cold, his muscles vibrating, a runnel of sweat trickling down the left side of his temple. He wasn't an overly large man, although he had gained some belly weight in recent months due to stress and grief, but he must have approached with an air of predation, because all the women went silent at the same time. Their heads all turned in his direction as his shadow fell upon their table.

Linda, of course, was not among them.

"I'm sorry," he said, raising his hands to show no ill will. He was suddenly mortified. "I thought I recognized someone. I'm sorry. I'm sorry."

The eyes on him. That cool glister of sweat beading down the side of his face. A feeling like some part of space and time had been shaken, like a box of jigsaw puzzle pieces, where, in one moment and by pure happenstance, an image formed even when it shouldn't have.

There are only so many patterns a finite set of numbers like one through five can make, so, by definition, that same set of numbers will eventually come back around and repeat itself...

He returned to his table and sat heavily in his chair. Finished off the beer in two hearty gulps, then flagged down the waitress for another. It was then that he heard his cell phone chime with an incoming email. He picked it up, checked the screen, and saw it was a message regarding the phone calls Alan had made to his wife while in Phoenix.

14

According to the information collected from a series of cell towers, all of Alan's phone calls to his wife during that forty-eight-hour period when she'd vanished and was likely murdered were made from Phoenix, Arizona. Which meant Alan couldn't have been back in Los Angeles that night.

He wasn't the killer.

15

The sizzle-pop of a needle in the groove.

The heartbeat *rump-a-bump-bump* of muted drums.

The shimmery strum of an acoustic guitar.

And the rich, velvet crooning coming from the living room in the middle of the night.

Renney opened his eyes but didn't get out of bed. Instead, he listened to the song play in its entirety, until that last final, heartfelt (and deliberately off-key?) note gave way to a fizz of static coming through the turntable's speakers.

Sizzle-POP.

Sizzle-POP.

When he got out of bed and went into the living room, he saw Linda sitting in the recliner, her dark shape silhouetted against the moonlight coming through the window.

He said her name, but it came out in an almost inaudible whisper: the rasp of a palm across rough fabric. It melded perfectly with the sizzle-pop of the record player on the other side of the room.

The dark shape that was Linda tilted her head gently to one side, the way she would sometimes do when she was lost in concentration. Or when she had figured something out and was waiting for her husband to catch up.

"What?" he said. "What is it?"

She held something in her hands, too, he saw—a sheet of paper illuminated by the moonlight coming through the window, so bright it looked nearly spectral.

The TV winked on, dousing the living room in a cool, static-blue light. It took a moment for the image on the screen to resolve, and once it did, it took Renney a few moments more to understand what he was looking at.

It was a view of the desert floor, filmed from some great height. At dawn, if he had to guess, judging by the quality of the light. Whatever camera was filming this, it moved swiftly through the atmosphere, unimpeded, catching the elongating shadows of cacti and the occasional flit of wildlife rushing to keep in the shadows as daylight encroached. He saw the gullies and dry ravines, the graying tufts of sagebrush motionless in the still, morning air. And then there she was, Melissa Jean Andressen, the dead woman, a sky-view that showed the brokenness of her, the clear and unquestioning absence of life. He realized he was staring at the drone footage the two boys from Palmdale had taken, although how it had wound up here on his television screen—and *was* it here?—was beyond him.

"What?" he said, turning back to the dark shape that was Linda seated in the recliner. "Am I missing something?"

Maybe you've already missed it.

"I don't understand, Lin," he said.

There was no further response—not from inside his head, not from the shape that was his dead wife in the recliner. After a moment, she set the sheet of paper down on the coffee table, then got up from the recliner and went down the hall.

"Lin, wait . . . "

Renney pursued her, but when he turned the corner, she was not there.

And then the room went dark as the TV blinked off.

Linda, please . . .

He stood there for a moment in the dark, his heart galloping in his chest, a cool ball of sweat rolling down the center of his back. He went to the coffee table and picked up the sheet of paper that Linda had been holding. It was a page from Andressen's credit card statement.

Maybe you've already missed it . . .

He jumped when the Roy Orbison record began playing again, that opening drumbeat, *rump-a-bump-bump*, matching the rhythm of his heart.

And if all of this actually happened, Bill Renney would convince himself upon waking that it had been nothing more than a vivid dream.

16

"Can I ask you something?" Alan said.

"Shoot, doc."

It was evening, and they were at Alan's house. Alan was seated at the dining table, a laptop in front of him, his face a pale blue in the glow from the screen. Renney had wanted him to review a series of his wife's emails and some phone numbers from her cell phone that he had compiled to see if anything jumped out at him as suspicious. There was a bottle of pinot noir opened on the table, too, but only a single wineglass. Renney was standing at the far side of the room, a glass of ice water in one beefy paw.

"You were married," Alan said. He glanced up at Renney from the far end of the long, marble-white table. "But not anymore. Something happened to your wife."

The comment knocked something loose inside Renney. Not only had he not been expecting it, but he'd never said a word to Alan about his personal life. How the man had arrived at such a conclusion left Renney momentarily speechless. Not to mention he'd just been daydreaming about Linda while he stood here, clutching his glass of water.

"You work late hours," Alan concluded, not waiting for a response. "You've got a wedding ring on, but you never check your phone for messages. Which means there's no one waiting for you at home. Do I have that right?"

"Pretty astute," Renney said.

"It's in my job description."

Mine, too, Renney thought.

"You could be divorced," Alan continued, "and still wear the ring. Lots of people do. But I don't sense that about you. Meaning, you're not the kind of guy who'd hang on to someone who didn't want them hanging on. You're not . . . desperate like that."

"I appreciate the positive character analysis," Renney said, a hotness prickling along the nape of his neck. It wasn't really an acknowledgment, wasn't really anything. He just didn't like feeling upended.

"Your wife has passed," Alan said, "and I'd guess it was fairly recent, judging by . . . well, just judging."

"What does that mean? Judging by what?"

"It's like looking in a mirror," Alan said. "I'm exactly where you are right now. Or, well, maybe you're slightly ahead of me down that path. Grief, I mean." He nodded at Renney, and said, "You've been wearing the same slacks the past two times I saw you. Shirts are always wrinkled—no offense. You've got beard scruff like Velcro, although I'm not one to criticize at the moment. But mostly, it's in your eyes. I look at you and I can just tell."

Renney cleared his throat, and heard something click. Said, "She's been dead nearly five months now. Glioblastoma."

"Was it quick?" Alan asked, and Renney could tell by the way he asked the question—the tone of his voice, perhaps, or maybe the narrowing of his eyes—that he probably already knew the answer. He was a doctor, after all.

"Went from nothing to her being dead in three months," Renney said.

Alan nodded. His dark eyes hung on Renney from across the room. "Quick enough that she didn't have to suffer too much," he said, "but enough time for you to get some things in order, I'd assume. The both of you. To prepare. You were probably by her side when she passed, too, I'd guess. To say goodbye."

Renney had been: right there in a sterile white hospital room at Valley Presbyterian, clutching Linda's cold, frail hand, while he watched her sink down into herself and turn gray and stop breathing. She'd been blind and deaf by then, and had no feeling in her hands, but he had hope whenever those weak, bony fingers would tighten ever so slightly around his own. He'd stayed for a while after that, still holding her hand, as his teardrops fell onto the meaty part of his thumb, the bony part of her thumb. Their thumbs.

"I'm sure there were terrible moments there," Alan went on. "But I'd bet there were some wonderful, tender moments, too. An understanding that your two souls, intertwined, were now separating."

"I'm not much for that kind of talk, doc," Renney said, and he hated that he heard his voice quake. He was thinking now of the Roy Orbison record that sometimes played spontaneously in the night. Perhaps if he took it off the turntable it wouldn't—

"I'm not speaking metaphorically, or even spiritually, Bill," Alan said, and Renney noted it was the first time the doctor had addressed him by his first name. Alan sat back in his chair, and Renney was suddenly thinking of those horrific crime-scene photos of Alan's dead wife tucked discreetly in the case file that was, in this very moment, in Renney's briefcase on the floor at his feet: a morbid collection of glossy eight-by-tens that lay in stark juxtaposition to the framed glamour shots decorating the walls of the house.

"Then what are you saying?" Renney asked.

"I'm saying you had a chance to *prepare*," Alan said. "You had an opportunity, however morose, to say goodbye."

Renney laughed. "Morose?" He was thinking of that frail hand with the teardrop on it. The iciness of that palm and the stiffness of those fingers—fingers that could no longer feel. He was thinking, too, of the wedding photo on the wall in their home, Linda laughing and looking lively and bright. The delicate contours of her collarbones. *Collarbones,* he thought now, *are so goddamn beautiful.*

"Did you ever consider killing yourself?" Alan asked.

"No," Renney lied.

"Really? Because I've thought about it. Not right after it happened, not even after I saw her body in the morgue. It was days later, and for some reason it occurred to me that I could just jump over the railing of the back deck and fall straight down to the bottom of the canyon."

"But you don't think that way anymore," Renney said. It came out as a statement, as if he was forcing Alan to agree. An old cop trick he was helpless to shake.

"No, not anymore. It was just a fleeting thought. Besides, I've always been a man fueled by his work." He glanced down at the laptop in front of him. "And you and I have got some work to do, Bill."

Alan got up from the table and went across the kitchen. From one cupboard, he got down a second wineglass. He brought it back to the table, poured Renney some wine, then sat back down without saying another word.

Renney looked at his watch. Thought his fish might be hungry. Felt his heart hurting a little bit. Said, "I should probably go . . . "

"When was the last time you slept through the night?"

Renney laughed, though there was little humor in it.

"Funny?" Alan asked, his eyebrows arched.

"I can't remember the last time I've slept through the night, doc," Renney confessed. Thinking of drums going *rump-a-bump-bump.* Thinking of Linda sitting in the recliner or on the sofa in the dark of the living room.

"I can give you something for that," Alan said, and before Renney could respond, he was up and out of his chair again.

"Hey," Renney called. "Come on, doc. No need."

Alan vanished down the long, dark corridor toward his home office. Maybe he was only gone for less than a minute, but to Renney, standing there sweating in his blazer and dress shirt, gripping that perspiring glass of ice water, it felt like an eternity.

When Alan returned, he was carrying an orange plastic vial of pills. He set them down on the table, right beside the glass of wine he'd poured for Renney, then leveraged himself back down in his own seat again.

"Thanks, doc, but I don't need your narcotics."

"They're not for you," Alan said. He drained his wineglass, then poured some more from the bottle.

"Yeah? Who're they for?"

"They're for me," he said. "You take them, get a good night's sleep, and maybe you'll be able to focus on who killed my wife."

"I don't . . . " Renney began, but then the sentence—whatever it would have been—dried up on his tongue. He was gazing across the room at Alan, and could feel the man's dark-eyed stare piercing straight through him.

"Some monster cut her up," Alan said. He was staring at the laptop screen again, only this time tears were trembling in his eyes. "I didn't have a chance to say goodbye to her. I didn't have a chance to get my shit in order." He looked up at Renney, and one of those tears slipped free, and cascaded down the swell of Alan's left cheek. It got snared in the stubble of his beard. "You need to find that monster, Bill. You need to find him, or I don't know what I'm going to do with myself."

Renney sighed. He set his glass of water on the table, then picked up his briefcase. Alan's eyes hung on him from the far end of the dining room. Renney took the case file from the briefcase and set it down on the table.

"It'll bother you. At the very least, it'll give you nightmares. I don't know why you'd want to look at this stuff, anyway."

"I'm having nightmares as it is," Alan said. "I've never been one to just *sit tight*. Looking through that stuff will let me feel like I'm accomplishing something. I'll approach it clinically, so I'm detached. Yet it keeps my mind active, and off . . . well, other things." He took a sip of his wine, nodded at the case file, and added, "Besides, I might pick up something in all of this that you've overlooked."

Renney couldn't help it: he chuckled, even though he knew Alan had not been making a joke.

17

He hadn't let Alan see the entire case file, of course—he'd purged it of sensitive material, such as the inconclusive findings of the polygraph, and he'd taken out most of his notes about Alan, including the early reports when he'd misprinted Alan's last name as *Anderson* instead of *Andressen*. The crime-scene photos gave away no trade secrets, only the gory details of what had happened to his wife, and while Renney didn't think it was such a good idea for Alan to dwell on such horrific details, he had ultimately felt the need to acquiesce. Things had changed between them ever since Renney had received that email about Alan's phone calls, which gave him a solid alibi and ruled him out as a suspect in his wife's murder. Now, he and Alan were just two sad members of the Dead Wives Club, and nothing more.

Also: the pills helped. Even when Roy started crooning from the living room, the pills helped. And he silently thanked the good doctor.

18

During that same week, a thirty-four-year-old auto mechanic named Lucas Priest was arrested for attempted kidnapping and assault. The victim in question was not a child, but a married woman of Priest's age, named Rachael St. Claire. As St. Claire recounted to the arresting officers, she had dropped her car off at the mechanic's shop for what she'd anticipated being a routine oil change, but was quickly notified by the mechanic—Priest—that her vehicle, a 2015 Chevy Equinox, had a host of problems.

"He told me there was something wrong with the brakes," she told the police. "He said it was something that needed to be addressed right away, that it was dangerous, a safety issue, and that he couldn't legally let me drive off until the problem was corrected. He said it wouldn't be safe, and that the brakes would fail if I tried to drive it home. He made me scared to drive the car."

She had been to that particular mechanic shop a number of times in the past, and had developed a rapport with Priest. She trusted him, and as far as she was aware, he had never overcharged her for work, nor tried to get her to pay for something that wasn't necessary. She had no reason to question him on this day, and in fact felt a sense of relief that Priest had discovered the problem before something serious had happened. (She had two young kids, and was constantly chauffeuring them here and there in the Equinox; it was a blessing, she'd thought, that something tragic hadn't happened already. And Priest had agreed with that sentiment.)

The problem was, Priest wouldn't be able to get to the vehicle until the following morning. It was nearly five o'clock, and guys were already clocking out for the day. Priest himself had already turned off the lighted OPEN sign in the window. In other words, she would need to leave the vehicle here overnight and find a ride home.

Her husband was out of town on business and the few friends she'd called to come pick her up did not answer their phones. She had just opened the Uber app on her phone when Priest came up beside her, making a show of jangling his car keys.

"You live on DuPont, don't you?" he asked her.

She said she did, then asked him how he knew that.

Lucas Priest laughed. He was a good-looking guy, classically rugged, with his chestnut hair pulled into a ponytail, and a week's worth of beard scruff with just the slightest hint of white at the sideburns. "It's in our system," he said. "That's how we spam you with coupons in the mail. Anyway, I'm just a few blocks up from you, on Rosemont. I'm taking off now and can give you a ride if you want, no problemo."

"Well," she said, drawing out the word, stretching those *l*s, and making a show of staring at her phone. She didn't know this guy, not really, but was there really any harm? She had been coming here for years. Once, while she'd waited in one of the uncomfortable molded plastic chairs in the waiting room, he'd even brought her a bottle of orange soda from the soda machine. "I guess that would be okay."

He drove a cherry-red Trans Am, what Rachael thought of as a real meathead's car, but then she silently chastised herself for being so judgmental. He'd been nice enough to offer her a ride home, after all.

The interior of the car smelled clean. A string of wooden rosary beads hung from the rearview mirror, and there was a small rectangular photo of two young children clipped to the visor above the steering wheel.

"Are those your kids?" she asked him, pointing at the photo.

Priest cranked the ignition and the engine growled to life.

"My niece and nephew," he said. "My brother's kids. They live in St. Louis. They're the best."

They pulled out into the street and headed toward the freeway. Rachael buckled her seatbelt, but she noted Priest did not wear his. She took inventory of him then—she admitted this much to the police after the fact—appraising the bulge of his biceps, the tattoos down his arms, the heady musk of his skin beneath his cologne. He had the chronically black, grease-encrusted fingernails of a career wrench jockey, but Rachael realized that she did not find that off-putting.

"How much do you think it's going to cost?" she asked him as they drove. "The car, I mean."

Priest scratched his forehead with a thumbnail. He was squinting at the glare of the setting sun coming through the Trans Am's windshield. "Won't really now until I take it apart and get in there."

She sighed. That sounded expensive. "I guess I'm just glad you found it."

"Do you have someplace you need to be tonight?" he asked her. He turned and looked at her, and she saw that his eyes were ice blue.

She had a million places she *should* be—picking up fresh vegetables and maybe a piece of salmon from the grocery store for dinner, grabbing the dry cleaning before they closed at seven, dropping off the check at the girls' dance studio which she'd meant to do earlier that day but hadn't gotten around to it. But instead of saying any of those things, she said, "What do you mean?"

"Ever been to the Sly Fox? It's on Lombard. They make a mean margarita."

She said, simply, "Oh."

"Been a long week, is all," he said. "You *do* drink, don't you?"

She laughed at him.

He took a turn that was not in the direction of her neighborhood. She wanted to say something at that point, but didn't want to sound like a bitch.

"You got a boyfriend?"

"I've got a husband." As if the wedding band glinting on her finger in the fading sunlight wasn't a clear giveaway.

"Hey, I'm sorry. I didn't mean anything by it. I just thought one drink wouldn't hurt."

A notion accosted her then, one she would admit to herself later that she wasn't terribly proud of—the fact that Randall was away on business and the girls were spending the weekend with Randall's parents in Anaheim.

She glanced in the back seat of the car. There was a small stack of library books back there—Voltaire, Thoreau's *Walden*, Mary Shelley's *Frankenstein*, among some others she was unfamiliar with but which looked just as dense. She'd been an English major at Irvine about a million and a half years ago.

"You've read those books?" she asked.

"Trying," Priest said. "I'll admit, they're a little dry. And I've never been a good reader; my mind wanders. But I do read a lot." He glanced at her. "You surprised?"

"No, no, I'm sorry. That's not what I meant."

"It's just that I never went to college, so I'm, you know, trying to better myself, I guess."

There was a self-consciousness about him as he spoke that Rachael found endearing. She wouldn't have expected that from a man who drove a Trans Am and had a tattoo of a topless hula dancer on his right bicep.

Quit being so goddamn judgmental, she chided herself.

"Tell you what," Priest said. "I can't make any promises about the cost of the parts, but as far as labor goes, I'll do the whole job for thirteen bucks."

Rachael laughed. Said, "Thirteen bucks? That's awfully specific. Do you have to pay a parking ticket or something?"

"It's the cost of a margarita at the Sly Fox," he said, and pointed beyond the windshield to the pub right there on the corner. The sign above the entryway showed a cartoon fox with drunken spirals for eyes hoisting a foaming pint of beer.

"He doesn't look so sly," Rachael commented.

"What do you say?"

I should tell him to take me straight home, she thought. Instead, she said, "One drink won't kill me. Besides, I can't beat thirteen bucks on labor."

"Don't start spreading that around town, I'll go broke," he said, and pulled into the pub's parking lot.

At the bar, she sat on a swiveling chrome stool with a cushioned bottom, like one you'd find in a 1950s soda shop. Priest remained standing beside her, one elbow on the bar. By the time she was halfway through her first margarita, she decided that, yes, this man was extremely attractive. She also decided that she would finish the drink, pay the bill, and have him drive her straight home. Anything beyond that, and she knew she was courting trouble.

Randall had had an affair. It had been soon after Ellen, their second child, had been born. He'd gotten caught when Rachael had discovered a hotel receipt in his pants pocket. She'd confronted him about it, he'd quickly admitted what he'd done, and more than just a little bit of chaos had ensued. But they had gotten over it, with a little help from therapy (and a lot of help from Prozac).

Yet before she had finished her first margarita, Priest was ordering another round.

"The price of labor seems to have gone up," she commented.

"This one's my treat."

The margaritas arrived with a couple shots of tequila on the side.

"Jesus, no," Rachael said. "I can't. My head will spin off."

"It's Friday," Priest said. Then he lowered his voice, and added, "Things can come off."

Jesus Christ, Rachael thought. A strange sort of giddiness was slowly pervading the whole of her body.

At one point, he went in to kiss her.

She stopped him with a hand against his chest.

"Not a good idea," she told him.

"Can't blame a guy for trying," he said.

When the bill came, Priest paid the whole thing. Rachael thought she had blown the deal by rebuking his kiss, but that was probably for the best. Besides, she wasn't in the business of whoring herself out for discount auto repairs.

She stumbled a little as she climbed down from the barstool.

It was dark when they got back into Priest's car. What time was it, anyway? How long had they been in that place? She didn't know.

That growl of the engine, and then they were coasting through a narrow street flanked on either side by bars and boutiques.

"There's a place up ahead we can go," Priest suggested. He did not elaborate.

"No. I need to get home. It's late."

"Not really."

"Late for me."

Those margaritas had been strong, and the shot of tequila hadn't helped. Her head *was* spinning.

"You on FetLife?" he asked.

"I don't know what that is," she said.

"Right," he said, and now it was his turn to draw out the word—
Riiiiiight.

They took a turn that, even in her current semi-drunk state,
Rachael knew was taking them in the opposite direction from
where they needed to be. True, there was less traffic on these side
streets, so maybe he knew a better way to go. Still, she suddenly felt
uncomfortable. Maybe this had been a bad idea after all.

"I don't want to sound ungrateful—" she began, but he quickly
cut her off.

"I find you extremely attractive, Rachael."

He glanced at her, and something in the atmosphere of the car
had decidedly shifted. She drew her knees closer together.

"I think we're going the wrong way," she said, shifting about in
her seat.

Priest laughed, and she saw that his teeth were perfectly straight,
perfectly white. He was handsome, yes, but she no longer wanted to
be in this car with him.

"This isn't the way home," she said.

"I thought we'd take a drive."

"I don't want to take a drive. I need to get home."

"It's a nice evening."

"You're making me uncomfortable," she said, not caring if she
sounded like the biggest, most ungrateful bitch in the world now.
"Could you please pull over and let me out?"

The Trans Am slowed, and for a moment, she thought he was
going to pull up to the curb and let her out. Instead, he coasted
through an intersection, trailing a banner of black exhaust that
Rachael could see in the car's sideview mirror even in the dark.

"Goddamn it, Rachael, you're so fucking sexy," he said. And then
he reached over—

—and placed his hand on her thigh.

Squeezed.

"Hey," she said, and pulled his hand away.

Priest laughed. Asked, "You smoke?"

"Let me out."

"Check the glove box."

"I don't want to check the glove box. I want you to let me out of this car. Or I'll call the police." She said this automatically, even before she realized that her cell phone was in her purse, and she could do that very thing. She reached into her purse, pulled out her phone, and brandished it like some kind of weapon.

Priest turned and stared at her. His lecherous smirk was gone, his face now emotionless.

That's the real him, Rachael had time to think, and the thought chilled her. *Everything until after the bar was an act. Was a trap.*

"I was just trying to be nice," Priest said flatly, still staring at her. A car blared its horn as they cruised through another intersection. "I was just trying to be friendly. Just like when you come in with your car. You're always friendly. You're always flirting."

"Just let me out of the car please."

Priest effortlessly plucked the phone from her hand and tossed it into the back seat.

"Hey!"

"Calm down," he said, finally—blessedly—returning his eyes to the road. "I'll pull over and let you out. Just give me a sec. We're in the middle of the street. I don't want you getting creamed by a bus."

"Pull over *now*."

Another turn.

Sped up.

"Hey—"

Another turn.

And then he was gliding across the road and into what looked to Rachael St. Claire like an empty parking lot, poorly lit and in the middle of nowhere. The ground was cracked, uneven asphalt, and there were tall, sinewy stalks of grass sprouting from the cracks. A chain-link fence surrounded the lot, and at the far end, she could see a tow truck and a series of cars up on blocks. There was a brick building to their right, the windows boarded up, a slogan in haphazard neon spray paint along the facade—REPENT ALL DAUGHTERS AND SONS.

The car jerked to a stop.

Priest slammed it into Park but did not shut down the engine.

Rachael groped for the door handle, but the door wouldn't open. It was locked, and for some reason, her mind couldn't figure out how to *unlock* it.

"You know, you come around wearing your tight fucking clothes and wag your ass around so you can get a discount on fuckin' brake pads or whatever, and now you're playing hardball. Real fucking classy, lady."

And then he leaned toward her, a wall of him, a tidal wave of him. A hand groped her left breast, his prickly cheek pressing against the crook of her neck. When she felt his hot breath against her clavicle, she screamed.

"Maybe—" he began, but she didn't let him finish.

She struck him across the face with her house keys.

He drew back, clutching a cheek.

Something clicked in her head, or maybe it was the sound of the door lock, because she was suddenly swinging the passenger door of the Trans Am wide open and bolting out into the warm, buggy night, cork-sole espadrilles pounding against the asphalt of the parking lot, legs pumping, something like a shriek or a groan or a whimper scrambling up the narrowing channel of her throat.

She ran into the street, hooked a right, then kept running for several more blocks. When her adrenaline finally waned and exhaustion took over, she slowed to a gallop, a trot, and ultimately some zombie-like shamble. She didn't know where she was, had drank too much tequila, and felt on the cusp of hysterics. She still had her purse, but her phone was in the back seat of the son of a bitch's car.

Once she got herself under control, she saw a Walgreens on the corner of the next block. She went inside, begged to use their phone, and then called the police.

Bill Renney learned about this incident the way most cops learn most things: by pure dumb luck. He'd overheard the two arresting officers discussing the case at the stationhouse, and when they mentioned the mechanic's shop in Reseda, Renney—who had been passing down the hallway with an egg salad sandwich wrapped in cellophane in one hand, a can of Diet Coke in the other—paused and poked his head into the break room. He asked to see the file on the guy they'd arrested, Lucas Priest, and one of the officers gave him the case number.

"Guy's already out on bail," the officer told him.

"Isn't that always the case," Renney replied.

19

Lucas Priest wore a bright red gash along the left side of his face from where Rachael St. Claire's house keys had dug a channel through his flesh. Aside from that, the guy was handsome, no doubt about it, like some actor in a daytime soap. He was in good physical shape, too, with hands as big as catcher's mitts, bulging biceps, and a pair of well-defined pectorals beneath the canvas work shirt he wore. He possessed the tapered, sturdy waist of a bodybuilder.

Renney approached Priest in one of the garage bays at the shop in Reseda, flashed him his badge, then asked, "Is there a place around here we can talk in private?"

"My lawyer said not to talk to nobody about what that woman is saying I did," Priest said. "Which is bullshit, by the way."

"This isn't about her," Renney said.

The muscles in Priest's face appeared to tighten. Renney couldn't yet tell if this guy was just some lunkhead or if he actually had half a brain, so he reserved his judgment for the time being.

"What's it about, then?" Priest asked.

Renney shrugged, then made a show of glancing around at some of Priest's coworkers who were within earshot. "Probably best we talk in private."

Priest tugged a rag from the rear pocket of his pants, wiped the grease from his hands, then tossed the rag on a nearby workbench. In the next bay over, Renney heard the *ssssst* of an air compressor, then someone dropped a wrench and cursed.

"Yeah, all right," Priest said, ducking beneath the tires of a sports car raised on a hydraulic lift. "There's an office back here."

The office was a cramped shoebox, water cooler in one corner, hotplate in another, and a *Penthouse* calendar on the wall. There was an aluminum desk in the center of the room, a couple of metal folding chairs crowded around it. Priest sat behind the desk while Renney eased himself down in the chair opposite him. Renney dug his phone from the inner pocket of his sports coat but didn't punch in the code just yet. Just held it in one hand.

"Been working here long?" he asked Priest.

"Seven years."

"You the manager?"

"Assistant manager. What's this all about?"

Renney punched in the code to his phone, then scrolled to a

particular photo. He handed the phone over to Priest, who took it somewhat reluctantly.

"Recognize that woman?"

Priest shook his head and thrust the phone back toward Renney.

"No, no, take a closer look," Renney said. "Please. I wanna make sure."

"Make sure of what?"

"Make sure you recognize her."

"I don't."

"Maybe you'd recognize her name? Melissa Jean Andressen?"

"Don't know her." He handed Renney back his phone.

Renney slipped the phone back into the inner pocket of his sports coat, then removed a few folded slips of paper from that same pocket. One was a page from Melissa Jean's credit card statement, the one Linda had been holding in Renney's dream. He unfolded it now, pretended to study it for perhaps a second or two, then slid it across the desk to Priest.

"She was here getting work done on her car last month," Renney said. "There's the charge right there on her credit card."

Priest leaned back in his metal folding chair. His eyes, which had looked as blue as Caribbean water back in the garage bay, had now darkened to the color of pewter. He didn't bother looking at the credit card statement. "I don't know everyone who comes in and out of this place."

"Oh, I'm sure, I'm sure. But you *do* know her," Renney said, and laid down another slip of paper on the desk. It was an invoice for the work done on Melissa Jean's car. Renney pointed to the signature line. "That's your John Hancock right there, isn't it? Easy enough to read."

Priest just glared at him from behind the desk.

"You didn't even really look at her photo," Renney told him.

"Which tells me you absolutely know who she is."

Priest leaned forward. He folded his hands atop the desk, and said, "So what's this chick's complaint about me?"

Renney gathered up the papers, refolded them, and tucked them back into the inner pocket of his sports coat. He coughed once into a fist, then said, "No complaint. This woman was murdered last month."

Something went slack in Lucas Priest's face. "What?"

"Her picture's been all over the news. What's the matter, you don't watch the news, Luke?"

Priest's hands slowly drew back from the desktop until they fell into his lap.

"Someone cut her up pretty bad, dumped her body in the desert outside the city," Renney went on, watching Priest's face. "Last charge on her card before she disappeared was from this place, with your signature on that invoice I showed you."

"So this is, what?" Priest asked. "A murder investigation?"

"You wanna see her picture again? See if it refreshes your memory?"

"No," Priest said. "I don't need to see her picture again. I told you, I don't know everyone who comes into this place. You think I remember every person's car I work on?"

"Her husband said it was unusual for her to have come to this garage instead of going to a dealership. I'm thinking maybe you knew her, cut her a break? Maybe you two were friends or something?"

"I didn't know her. And if you're suggesting I had something to do with what happened to—"

Renney raised his hands, shook his head. "Whoa. I'm not suggesting that at all, Luke. You misunderstand. I'm not here looking for a *suspect*, I'm here looking for a *witness*. This is the last location I can place Mrs. Andressen before she died, and like I said,

I've got your signature on that final invoice. You're the last guy who's seen her before she was killed, far as I can tell. So I'm here asking for some assistance from you. Anything you remember about her that might be helpful. Maybe you overheard her making a phone call, or maybe she had someone with her that day she came in here with her car, maybe someone to give her a ride. Anything like that."

He saw something change in Priest's eyes following that comment—a narrowing not so much of the man's eyelids but of the eyes themselves, as if he were capable of drawing them deeper into their ocular cavities.

She was in your car, wasn't she? Renney had time to think.

"Really," Renney continued, "anything you can remember might be helpful. It also might help you with that other issue from last week—the one we're not supposed to talk about—when a judge sees how agreeable you were to help me today."

It was the wrong tactic: he watched as Priest's body tightened, and the man drew his big arms around himself somewhat subconsciously. The mention of what had happened with the St. Claire woman last week had only reminded Lucas Priest of the trouble he was currently in.

"What I'm saying," Renney pressed, leaning forward, trying to salvage this, "is that maybe we can help each other."

Priest seemed to consider this for a moment.

Come on, you bastard, Renney thought. *Take the bait.*

"Sorry," Priest said. "I wish I could help you, but I don't remember anything about her."

20

Back at the station, Renney ran a background check on Lucas Priest, which revealed a laundry list of DUIs, minor drug charges, and one physical altercation with a police officer while resisting arrest. The guy also had quite a history of domestic violence and assaults against women. The kidnapping and assault charges resulting from the Rachael St. Claire incident last week seemed right at home on Lucas Priest's rap sheet.

It was a check he should have done *before* hitting up Priest, but he'd had another rough night the night before and hadn't been thinking straight the following morning—more Orbison on the turntable and a glimpse of Linda ghosting about the darkened house; he'd risen from bed and followed her down the hall, her body an amorphous shape until she passed through a panel of slanted moonlight coming through the side window. When she turned to face him, he saw the skeletal look of her, just as she'd looked in the days before her death. Something in Renney's throat had tightened. When he reached a hand out in her direction, perhaps to touch her, Linda's body dispersed into tendrils of black smoke. Later, he'd woken on the floor in the hallway, his head pounding as if with a hangover.

He knew his mind wasn't fully engaged; he felt like an engine running on fumes.

This guy fits the bill, he thought, going over Priest's criminal history. *This guy is trouble.*

He made some phone calls.

The women who dared speak with Renney about Lucas Priest all sang a similar tune: the guy was an abusive asshole, full stop. One woman, whom Priest had dated for a few months a year or so ago, relayed how she'd wound up in the hospital with a fractured eye socket and a broken wrist after an argument with Priest had turned physically violent. "That's the thing," the woman said over the phone to Renney, her voice a harsh, smoker's rasp. "*Every* argument with that son of a bitch turned violent. He couldn't help himself. He's a fucking monster."

Another woman confided over the phone: "He drugged me. Rohypnol. I couldn't prove it and I never pressed charges, but it was rape, plain as day."

There had been no evidence of Rohypnol nor any other narcotics in Melissa Jean's toxicology report, but Renney didn't know if that meant her assailant hadn't used it or a similar drug to knock her out. He recalled what Falmouth, the medical examiner, had told him following Melissa Jean's autopsy—*She had been cut up while still alive.* Falmouth had also explained that there'd been no evidence to show she had struggled with her assailant, which likely meant she'd been rendered incapacitated while her assailant had mutilated and ultimately murdered her.

Incapacitated, he thought. *Drugged, in other words.*

Bill Renney felt things coming into sharp relief.

He called Falmouth and asked if Melissa Jean's killer could have dosed her with Rohypnol and have it not show up in the post-mortem toxicology.

"Not likely," Falmouth said. "We'd be able to detect it up to sixty hours after ingestion."

"Shit," Renney said.

"But GHB, on the other hand," Falmouth went on, "dissipates quickly. It would have a similar effect as Rohypnol—it's also a date rape drug—but it's difficult to detect as a foreign substance, since trace amounts of gamma hydroxybutyrate are produced endogenously in various tissues throughout the body, including the brain."

"Yeah? So, you're saying the killer could have dosed her with GHB to knock her unconscious, and it might not show up on the toxicology?"

"Or show up in such a minute amount that it wouldn't—it *didn't*—raise any flags," Falmouth explained.

He couldn't help himself, the woman had said over the phone. *He's a fucking monster.*

The following day, Renney received a phone call from one of the officers who had arrested Priest last week for the assault on Rachael St. Claire. "You're the guy working the Andressen homicide, right?"

Renney said, "Right."

"We impounded Priest's vehicle and found some hair fibers. DNA matches your victim."

Renney, who was having a sandwich at Rosa's on Jackson Street, spat a lump of roast beef and horseradish into a paper napkin. Into the phone, he said, "A match?" As if he'd misunderstood.

"Got the report right here," the officer said. "I can email it to you. Near perfect match for a Melissa Jean Andressen, deceased."

Son of a bitch, I got you, Renney thought.

"Send the report over now," he told the officer.

21

He saw one of Alan's billboards along the 101 later that evening. The giant image of Melissa Jean loomed above an archipelago of low, sand-colored buildings, and the sight of it—of *her*—nearly caused Renney to rear-end the guy in front of him. It was the same photo that had been circulating throughout the media—Melissa Jean in a white tennis shirt, collar popped, hair a dark, luxurious cascade like twin waterfalls down the sides of her unblemished, heart-shaped face. Beneath her photo, it said, REWARD FOR ANY INFORMATION THAT LEADS TO THE CAPTURE OF HER KILLER: $500,000. And below that was a phone number.

22

"Arrest him, goddamn it!" Alan shouted.

"I can't do that just yet," Renney said. "There's not enough probable cause for a warrant."

"How can that *be*? You can't make a phone call, get someone to do something? I'll call the fucking district attorney myself!"

"If he's our guy, we only get one shot at him. Let me run this down and build a case against him. It's going to take time. If I arrest him now based solely on a strand of your wife's hair being in his car, then the clock starts ticking, and I gotta find additional evidence to keep him behind bars."

"Priest," Alan said, as if tasting the name. His hands were trembling and his eyes were glassy with tears that had not yet fallen. "Lucas Priest."

They were in Alan's dining room, a long sheet of paper from an industrial roll stretched out from one end of the dining room table to the other. Alan had been making a timeline of events on it with a thick black Sharpie when Renney arrived, little hash marks with specific dates and times that corresponded to where his wife had been in the days leading up to her death, cobbled together from phone records, credit card statements, and random other circumstantial evidence. Like Renney, whose mind was similarly restless, Alan had been attempting to build his own case.

He tore the sheet of paper down the middle now, then dropped down in a chair. He hung his head, pressed his face against the palms of his hands. His shoulders shook.

Renney was seated at the far end of the table, a cup of black coffee in front of him. There was a bottle of scotch at Alan's end of the table, an empty lowball glass beside it, and Renney wondered how many drinks Alan had had before Renney had arrived.

Maybe this was a mistake, he thought, watching Alan weep silently into his hands at the far end of the table. *Maybe I've lost perspective on this thing and should have just kept my big mouth shut.*

He had mentioned to Alan the incident with Rachael St. Claire that had put Priest on his radar, as well as the telephone conversations he'd had with some of Priest's ex-girlfriends, all of whom painted Priest as a violent, unhinged abuser. He also told Alan about his conversation with Priest at the auto shop in Reseda, where Priest had denied knowing Melissa Jean, followed by the phone call he'd received about the DNA match to the hair found in Priest's Trans Am.

Had it been the billboard that convinced him to say something to Alan? The medication Alan had given him to help him sleep through the night and, for the most part, keep the nightmares at bay? Or had it just been their shared grief—these two hopeless members of the Dead Wives Club? This bastardized version of a friendship?

"What about a search warrant for Priest's place?" Alan suggested. His voice was muffled because he still had his face buried in his hands. "See if there's any evidence that M.J. had been . . . I don't know . . . taken there?"

Renney shook his head. "I'd still need probable cause for a warrant. A judge will say I've got no reason to believe your wife was in his place."

Alan peered up at him from over the tips of his fingers. His eyes were messy and red. "How the fuck isn't her hair in his car probable cause?"

Truth was, Renney thought he *might* be able to get an arrest warrant on that—it was flimsy, but possible, depending on the judge—but once Priest was arrested then the clock would start, just as he'd said to Alan, and he had nothing else to go on to link Lucas Priest to Melissa Jean's murder. He would need something stronger—something more conclusive—to keep the son of a bitch behind bars.

"You just have to trust me on this, doc," Renney told him. "I'm working through it."

"How much jail time is he looking at if he's convicted of the charges against him in the incident from last week?" Alan asked.

Renney shifted uncomfortably in his chair. He took a long pull on his coffee, then cleared his throat. "The St. Claire woman isn't pursuing the issue," he told Alan. "She's dropping the charges."

"*What?*"

"She's married and she doesn't want this stuff coming out," Renney explained. "But listen, that doesn't mean—"

"Jesus *fuck!*"

"—that doesn't mean the whole thing goes away. He's got a whole rap sheet of this kind of behavior. He'll still have to face a judge."

"And then what? He sits in a jail cell for thirty days until they cut him loose?"

"If so, then that gives me thirty days to keep digging and try to make the case."

"Why," Alan said, planting two fists down on the dining room table, "did M.J. go to that auto shop in the first place? That's what keeps bugging me. That's what keeps whirling around inside my head. She was supposed to go to the dealership. She *told* me she was going to the dealership."

A spark of something came to light inside the dark, flustered walls of Bill Renney's skull—a spark of something he didn't altogether like, but something that made logical sense nonetheless. He wondered if Alan had caught a glimpse of that spark, too—if Renney had said too much, causing Alan's mind to make the leap from his one unanswered question to one possible answer.

"The 'why' isn't even the important part right now," Renney said. He was trying to mitigate the situation, to derail the train of thought he could see Alan was on just by looking into the man's eyes. "It could just be a confluence of circumstances."

"A guy like that is a predator," Alan said, ignoring him. He was examining the timeline on the unrolled sheet of paper before him on the table, torn down the middle and crumpled. "He's sharp. He's slick. That's how the mind of someone like that works, Bill. I'm telling you: that's how people like Priest think."

Alan smoothed out the crumpled sheet of paper, uncapped a Sharpie, and circled the words AUTO MECHANIC SHOP – RESEDA, which he'd previously printed on the timeline.

"I knew something was off," he went on, musing more to himself now than to Renney. "I knew something was . . . that something was just . . . "

He trailed off.

This was a mistake, Renney thought again. He'd fallen into the habit of sharing information with Alan, because he'd felt sorry for the guy and because they shared a commonality as two members of the Dead Wives Club, true. But now he feared he had gone too far. He should have kept his mouth shut about Priest, should have worked it out on his own just like any other case. Why was his head so fucked up this time around? Why did he not feel like the old Bill Renney?

Because I'm not, he thought. *Because I haven't been for the past five months, not since Linda died. I told Alan that it could just be a confluence of circumstances that saw his wife arrive at that auto shop in Reseda, but isn't it true it's also a confluence of circumstances that has dropped me in the middle of this investigation during a period of mourning, of grief? At a time when I'm imagining records playing by themselves in my living room and my dead wife seated in my recliner? At the lowest, most aggrieved time in my entire life?*

"What's the next step?" Alan asked. He was staring at Renney with those red, watery eyes.

"I'm going to pay Priest another visit," Renney said. "See how he explains your wife's hair in his car."

"You think he did it, Bill?" Alan asked. "You think this guy Priest killed my wife?"

"Doc, I think you need to let me—"

"Just fucking answer me, man. I'm begging you. Do you think he killed my wife?"

Bill Renney said, "Yes."

Alan stood up and migrated over to the kitchen sink. The water was running from the tap, but he did not appear to be doing anything with it; he merely stood there, hands on either side of the sink, head down again, shoulders slumped. It was then that Renney realized he was using the sound of the running water to cover up the sounds of his anguish.

Renney rose from his chair. "I'll let myself out, doc."

Alan did not respond. He did not act as if he'd heard Renney at all.

This was a mistake, Renney thought again, kept thinking it, powerless not to think it, as he went down the hall to the front door, footfalls resounding throughout that enormous echo chamber of a house. *I've crossed a line here and I wish I could take it back. This will only cause problems.*

He didn't realize in that moment just how right he was.

23

It was as if Lucas Priest expected him to return.

"You wanna use that office again," Priest said as Renney ambled over to him from across the parking lot, and it was not a question. Priest was smoking a cigarette, his grease-covered fingers leaving black smudges on the white filter. Maybe he'd just arrived at work, because he wasn't wearing his work shirt but an Urban Outfitters flannel with the sleeves cut off. There was a ball of keys on his belt the size of a yo-yo.

"Probably best," Renney said.

Priest finished his smoke, tossed the butt to the pavement, then led Renney back through the lobby of the mechanic shop and into that cramped, shoebox-shaped office again.

"That St. Claire woman dropped those charges against you," Renney said, sitting down in the metal folding chair in front of the desk.

"Because it didn't happen," Priest said, claiming his chair behind the desk. "Just like I told you."

Renney waved a dismissive hand in the air. "Women get confused. They have a couple of drinks, next thing you know their imaginations start running wild." It was a comment for which Linda would have jabbed him good and hard in the ribs, even though she would have known it to be a ruse.

"So what's this about now?" Priest asked.

"I need to ask you about the Andressen woman again, Lucas. And this time, I want you to think long and hard before you answer. Playtime is over."

"So ask," Priest said.

"I want you," Renney said, "to tell me exactly how you knew Melissa Jean Andressen."

"I've already told—"

"No bullshit," Renney said, cutting him off. "Clearly I'm back here because I know more than you think I do. So don't make this worse on yourself."

Priest turned away from Renney. He chewed for a moment on his lower lip. His eyes gleamed like bright blue sea glass. No doubt he was trying to figure out if Renney really did have something on him, or if he was just bullshitting. Finally, he relented. "Yeah, I knew her, okay? But I didn't fucking kill her, if that's why you're here. I mean, Jesus Christ, I'm no murderer. But, yeah, okay? I knew who she was when you showed me that picture."

"Good," Renney said. "How did you know her? And I don't mean from her coming here to get her alignment done."

"Well, that *is* kinda how I knew her. I was driving into work one morning and saw her car on the side of the road, hood up, the engine steaming. She was standing there on her phone. I pulled over, took a look at it. Couldn't get it running, but called and had a truck come and tow it to the shop."

"Chivalrous of you."

"She looked good, you know?"

"She didn't ask to have it towed to the dealership?"

"I mean, I'm a nice guy, but I'm not doing charity work. Besides, I said I would cut her a break."

"I'm not so sure money was a concern of hers. Was there something else going on?"

Lucas Priest turned his head to one side again and laughed silently—more of a hitch of his chest and a buck of his head than an actual laugh.

"Is that a yes?" Renney asked.

"Listen, man. It was no big deal. She was bubble gum. That's all."

"What's that mean? Bubble gum?"

"You know," Priest said. "Chew it awhile until it loses flavor, then toss it in the trash."

What a stellar human being, Renney thought.

"You saying you had sex with her?"

Priest folded his thick, tattooed arms across his chest and leaned so far back in his chair, the back of his head nearly pressed up against the *Penthouse* calendar. "Listen, man. Don't make me out to be some misogynist. Women come in here all the time. Sometimes you can just look at somebody and know who's down."

"Down?"

"To *fuck*," Priest said.

"You didn't answer my question. Did you have sex with Melissa Jean?"

"No."

"You sure about that?"

"Yeah. I'm sure about that."

"When was the last time you saw her?"

"I have no idea when that was."

"The date on the invoice from this place is the day before she was killed. Did you go out with her that night?"

"We went out for a drink while her car was being worked on."

"Where'd you go?"

"Place on Lombard. Sly Fox."

"How'd you get there?"

"In my car."

"How'd you get her to go with you?"

"I turned on the fucking charm."

"I have no doubt," Renney said. "But specifically, how'd you get her to go with you?"

"I said she looked familiar, asked if she was an actress."

"You'd seen her movies?"

"Fuck, no."

"Then how'd you know she was an actress?"

"Every chick in this town's an actress."

"What happened when you went for drinks?"

"Nothing. Just drinks."

"What was she drinking?"

"Margaritas."

"You get physical with her?"

"What do you mean? Did I hit her? No fucking way."

"I meant romantic."

"Oh. Well, I put the moves on her when we got back in my car, thought she was receptive at first, but then I guess she changed her mind because she wasn't having any of it. So I took her back here to the shop. Her car was fixed by then, she paid, then got in her car and left. And that was the one and only time I saw her."

That would explain the hair in his car, Renney thought. He was trying to decide what he wanted to believe.

"Was there any argument or disagreement when you got back in your car and you, to use your term, put the moves on her?"

"No. I thought maybe she'd be up for it, but she wasn't. I guess she got an attack of conscience. I don't have time for that shit."

"You sure there wasn't any type of altercation?"

"Look, man, I know what you're getting at. I didn't take advantage of that drunk bitch from last week or whenever, which is why she dropped those charges, and I didn't take advantage of this chick, either. There ain't nothing against the law about having sex with women, even if they're married or whatever."

There's certainly something against the law about fracturing a woman's eye socket and wrist, he thought, but had the good sense not to say. *There's certainly something against the law about drugging women so you can fuck them while they're unconscious.*

"And I certainly didn't fucking kill her," Priest added.

Renney sighed. Leaned back in his chair until the metal legs creaked. Said, "I believe you, Luke."

"It's Lucas," Priest groused.

"I believe you, Lucas. I think it all played out exactly as you say. Will you do me one favor, though?"

Priest shifted uncomfortably in his chair.

"Will you come with me to the police station and take a

polygraph?" Renney asked. "Just to prove this story as fact."

Priest unfolded his arms and stood up.

"I think I'm done talking about this," he said.

24

In the days that followed, Renney avoided Alan's phone calls and text messages. Alan left voicemails of increasing agitation—

"Where the hell *are* you, Bill? What's going *on*? I need to fucking *hear* from you, goddamn it . . . "

—and one in the middle of the night that was practically unintelligible. A thing had taken hold between the two of them and Renney was now desperate to shake it loose.

25

After working late one night, Renney arrived home and pulled into his driveway, a pepperoni and mushroom pizza from Giovanni's on the passenger seat. As he got out of his car, he noticed a man crossing the darkened street toward him. Renney recognized the vehicle parked along the curb—a silver BMW i8—and then the man passed beneath a nearby lamppost and Renney was suddenly no longer hungry for that pizza.

"Alan, what are you doing here?"

Alan stopped at the foot of Renney's driveway, so suddenly it was as if there was an invisible barrier there preventing him from going any farther. "I've been trying to reach you. I've been calling, been texting—"

"I know," Renney said. "I got your messages."

"Why didn't you call me back? What's been going on, Bill? Did you talk to that son of a bitch mechanic again? What'd he say?"

"Alan—"

"What'd he say about my wife's fucking *hair* in his goddamn *car*?"

"I think," Renney said, his voice calm and deliberate, "that I need to handle this on my own from now on, Alan."

Alan shook his head. "What does that mean?"

"It means we've blurred the lines here. *I've* blurred the lines. I apologize for that, Alan, but I need to get back to work on this case. And you need to go home and get back to living."

"What the hell are you talking about, Bill? Jesus Christ, what did he *say*?"

"You need to go—"

"I want you to arrest the motherfucker! I want him in fucking jail!"

"Lower your voice," Renney said.

Alan Andressen's hands began to tremble at his sides. He cocked his head at a slight angle so that the tears in his eyes glittered beneath the glow of the streetlamp. He looked like he wanted to say something more but did not possess the power to do it.

"Go home, Alan," Renney said—still calm, though he was sweating through his shirt now. "I'll be in touch with any news, once I have it. That's the most I can do from here. Do you understand?"

They stood there a moment longer, staring at each other, while the pizza box grew hot against Renney's palm.

"Do you understand, Alan?"

Alan said nothing.

Renney turned, went up the porch steps, and slipped quietly into the house. He kept the lights off as he went to the kitchen and dumped the pizza box on the table. He tossed his keys with a jangle into the little ceramic bowl that sat on the half wall. Then he went back out into the living room and, with the lights still off, peered out into the street.

Alan was still standing there at the foot of the driveway. He was still staring at the place Bill Renney had been standing moments ago.

"I fucked this up real good, didn't I, Lin?" He didn't realize that he'd spoken the words aloud.

Renney went to the bathroom, washed his face and hands, and peeled off his sweat-dampened shirt. The Smith & Wesson poked at a forty-five-degree angle along his hip due to the extra weight he'd put on since Linda's death.

Fucked it up real good . . .

When he went back out into the living room and stared through the front windows, he saw that Alan Andressen and his BMW were gone.

26

Two nights later, Bill Renney was awoken by the shrill ringing of his cell phone. He had been in the throes of a terrible dream, where a shapeless *thing* had him bound by chains and was systematically amputating pieces of his body with the shiny, razor-sharp blade of an enormous scalpel. He groped for the phone and pressed it to his ear without checking the caller ID. His mind was still groggy from sleep, his body coated in sweat from the nightmare.

Muffled noises on the other end of the phone.

Renney muttered, "H'lo?"

"Bill." Then again, with a touch more urgency: "*Bill.*"

He glanced at the number on the screen and saw that it was Alan. "Alan, what's wrong?" he asked, sitting up against the headboard.

"Jesus, Bill. Jesus Christ. *Fuck.*"

"What's going on, Alan?" Renney asked. He pictured the doc leaning over the railing at the back of his house, the drop below unfathomable in the darkness of the night, the phone pressed to his ear, half his face lighted by the LED screen. Thought of him saying, *Because I've thought about it. Not right after it happened, not even after I saw her body in the morgue. It was days later, and for some reason it occurred to me that I could just jump over the railing of the back deck and fall straight down to the bottom of the canyon.* "Alan, are you there? Are you okay?"

Several seconds passed before Alan responded.

"I've done something," he breathed into the phone. His voice was shaky, and he sounded very unlike himself. "I need help, Bill. I need your help."

"Calm down," Renney said, switching on the lamp beside the bed, then wincing at the brightness of it. "Where are you?"

"Please, Bill . . . "

"Tell me where you are."

Alan took a deep breath, and said, "There's a church . . . "

27

Ninety minutes later, the headlights of Renney's unmarked sedan were carving a trench through the weighty darkness of the desert highway. He crossed the Los Angeles County line, the night sky above fecund with stars. The moon was a grinning skull behind a wisp of threadbare clouds. When he came upon the unnamed, un-numbered stretch of dirt roadway that veered off even deeper into the desert, he took it, and drove a while longer. He was familiar with the old church, knew it had appeared in a handful of movies over the years, but also knew that at this hour and in the dark he risked driving right passed it without realizing, so he slowed the sedan to a crawl.

After a time, it appeared in the distance: an abandoned, Spanish-style chapel, looking like a miniature Alamo. There was an empty stone tower where a bell had once hung, and a pair of wooden doors beneath a corrugated-tin overhang. The whole building was the color of the earth, and indeed looked like something that might have risen straight up through it, as opposed to having been constructed upon it by man.

Renney turned the steering wheel, cutting the sedan's headlights across the church and the bristling Joshua trees beside it—things that appeared, at this time of night, to be clawing their way out of the ground.

Alan Andressen stood in the glow of the car's headlights. He was standing in a patch of shadow between the Joshua trees and the bone-colored hide of the chapel. As the sedan's headlights fell upon him, he raised an arm to shield the glare from his eyes.

There was a small amount blood on his shirt in a rough, spattered arc.

You dumb fool, said a voice at the back of Bill Renney's head. The voice was not chastising Alan, he knew, but Renney himself. *You big, dumb, careless fool. See what you've done?* And there was no denying it: this was his fault.

Renney put the car in Park but kept the engine running. He stepped out into a cloud of desert dust. On the other side of that dust cloud, Alan stood, looking like someone—like something—summoned from a dream. Something was wrong with his face.

"Where is he?" Renney asked.

"Over there," Alan said, his voice low and hardly audible over the hum of the sedan's engine. With one shaky hand, he pointed beyond the chapel and toward some indeterminable spot in the pitch blackness of the desert.

"Fuck," Renney said. His mind was reeling.

"I just . . . I didn't know what the fuck to do, Bill," Alan said. He took a step closer to him, passing through the dissipating cloud of dust. That streak of blood across his polo shirt looked as black as roofing tar.

Renney leaned into the car, shut down the engine, switched off the headlights. Then reached over to the glove compartment and opened it. A hefty black Maglite rolled into his open hand. The flashlight's shaft felt cold as ice in the sweaty pocket of his palm.

When he climbed back out of the car, he was startled to find Alan standing just a few feet from him. The man's eyes were wide and staring, and his face, except for where the brownish dust had collected within the damp patches below his eyes, was the color of the moon. The left side of his jaw was swollen and there was a bloody split in his lower lip.

"Show me where," Renney said, clicking on the Maglite.

Alan led him around the chapel, to where the desert floor lay unfurled in an endless black carpet straight out to infinity. Renney kept the flashlight trained on the ground, wary of snakes, as he followed.

"I keep seeing things out here," Alan said. "Feel like there's been a pair of eyes on me, watching me from some great distance, like those mesas over there. Christ, Bill, I'm losing my fucking mind."

"Tell me what happened," Renney said.

They walked several more yards in silence.

"Alan," he said, prompting the doctor.

Alan glanced over at Renney, that waxen, moon-white face nearly luminescent. There was a small pinpoint of blood high on Alan's left cheekbone, just above the swollen section of his jaw, perfect as a jewel. His eyes glittered with tears. "I didn't mean to do it," he said. His voice shook. "It just . . . it just *happened*. So fast. It was like I was watching someone else do it. But it wasn't . . . wasn't *wrong*, you know? Because when I saw him, I just *knew*."

"Knew what?" Renney asked, but he thought he already knew.

"It was something you said at my house, Bill. Maybe you didn't even realize what you were saying at the time."

But Renney thought he did.

"It was when you said the St. Claire woman was dropping the charges but that Priest would still have to face a judge. You said he had a history—a whole 'rap sheet,' remember?—of this type of behavior. Of picking up women, getting them drunk, maybe charming their pants off. A modus operandi. Isn't that what you law enforcement guys call it?"

You big, dumb fool, Renney thought again, a sinking feeling in his gut.

"So, tonight I drove out to that mechanic's shop in Reseda and waited in my car across the street for the place to close. When I saw Priest come out, I just *knew*—I just *knew* he'd killed M.J. And I also wondered what *else* he'd done to her. What else might have . . . have . . . " He paused in his stride, his head slung low on his neck. He was a few paces ahead of Renney so Renney couldn't see his face, but he thought he might be weeping. His body swayed, insubstantial as a scarecrow. It looked like he might fall over, but he didn't. After a moment of just standing there, Alan muttered, "You know what I'm saying, Bill?"

Renney didn't respond to that. He knew what Alan was saying, all right.

Alan turned, and Renney could see that he'd been right: the man was a mess, fresh tears cutting slick tracks through the dust on Alan's face. He felt pity for the man in that moment, but more than that: he felt responsible.

You big, dumb fool.

Renney nodded for Alan to keep walking. Alan returned the nod—a detached, automatic gesture, void of emotion—and then proceeded to creep farther into the darkness while he finished his story.

"I drove my car up alongside the shop, where he was standing, smoking a cigarette. I wanted to do it right then and there, swear to God, I was so fucking angry, Bill. But I also knew I needed to hear him *say* it. So I got out and apologized because I knew they'd just closed for the night, but said my engine was making a funny sound, a *click click click*, and if I popped the hood could he have a look? I said I'd pay him for his time, and showed him I had the cash on me. Hundred-dollar bill. I started to feel sick to my stomach. I still do. Not because I was nervous, but because I wanted to hear him *say* it and then *kill* the son of a bitch . . . "

Up ahead, Alan's silver BMW materialized out of the darkness. They were walking toward it. Renney could see that the trunk was open.

"While he was checking out the engine," Alan continued, "I jabbed him in the neck with a syringe of propofol."

"What's propofol?"

"A sedative. It's strong. He just sort of jumped, like he'd been stung by a bee. Slapped a hand to his neck, then banged the back of his head on the hood of my car as he stood up. The dose I gave him knocked him out in under sixty seconds. Before he hit the ground, he just stood there staring at me, this confused look on his face." Alan laughed humorlessly, a miserable sound that could have been a sob. "You know what I didn't take into account, Bill? Just how fucking *heavy* he was. All muscle."

Alan's repeated use of his first name was making Renney uncomfortable. It was as if they were conspirators in this, members of the Dead Wives Club colluding under the cover of night.

Is that so far from the truth? the voice in the back of Renney's head spoke up again. He thought it sounded very much like Linda's. *You were careless, lost in your own grief, and you let too much information pass through your lips to this man, who was also lost in his own grief. You let your own grief and your pity for this man cloud your judgment, you big, dumb fool.*

"Still," Alan went on, "I somehow managed to get him into the trunk of my car. And then I drove him all the way out here."

As he said this, they reached Alan's BMW. The trunk was open, but it was empty, except for a shovel, a pickaxe, some rope, and a spare tire. Renney could see no signs of Lucas Priest anywhere.

"So where is he?" Renney asked.

Alan nodded his head at a patch of darkness. "Right over there."

Renney repositioned the flashlight until it shone on a tangle of limbs lying in a heap on the desert floor, just a few yards away.

He walked slowly over to Priest's body. In the glow of the flashlight, the body was a moving, shifting canvas of shadow and light. He directed the beam toward Priest's face, only to find that the face was awash in blood. Priest's head had been smashed in, the scalp split. Jagged bits of skull poked through like shark's teeth. There was blood everywhere.

A few feet away from the body was a crowbar. Renney redirected the beam and saw the curved end of the tool covered in blood and clumps of Lucas Priest's hair.

"He was conscious by the time I opened the trunk," Alan said, coming up behind Renney. "He came at me. I had a crowbar and I struck his arms, but he still managed to hit me across the face. Then I took a swing and struck his left knee. I actually heard the kneecap pop. He went down then, all the fight sucked out of him."

Renney brought he flashlight back around to what remained of Priest's face. "And then you just kept swinging," he said.

"No," Alan said. "I showed him pictures of me and M.J. on my phone. I showed him the tickets to Bermuda I'd purchased for our anniversary. I told him to tell me what he did to my wife."

"And what'd he say?"

Alan shook his head, pressed his fingers to his eyes. "I can't be sure now. Everything's a blur."

"Try to remember."

"I asked if he killed her," Alan said, his voice shaking, threatening to break apart, "but he said no, told me to go fuck myself, said he only . . . only picked her up, took her out for drinks, hit on her . . . that he . . . he didn't . . . but then I *think* he started to say it . . . "

A clean, scentless breeze shuttled through the desert. Renney turned his head to keep the grains of sand from getting in his eyes.

"But I didn't need to hear him say it, Bill," Alan went on. "I thought I did, but in the end, I didn't. I know what he did to her. One look at him and I could just tell. Just like when I asked you if you thought he'd killed her. Do you remember what you said to me?"

Renney said nothing.

He remembered.

"You said *yes*, Bill. You said *yes*." He stared at his shaking hands. "It was like I went into a blind rage. Swinging that crowbar, over and over, until it was done." His eyes ticked back at Renney. Like some suddenly remembered thought, he repeated, "You said *yes*."

Then Alan dropped to his knees and sobbed like a child.

28

There are places in the desert where things can be hidden and never found.

29

When it was done, their bodies aching from the labor of it and their clothing cruddy with sweat and grime, they walked together in silence back to Alan's car. They were far from the unpaved road and from any vestige of civilization, but Renney felt in his bones that there was really no place on this planet so remote, so distant, as to obscure the inexcusable and calamitous nature of man.

30

The sun had just started to rise by the time Renney got home. Linda was sitting in the recliner and Roy Orbison was playing on the record player. Exhausted, Renney just stood there staring at his dead wife. He wondered if he wasn't losing his goddamn mind.

What'd you do tonight, Bill? Linda asked.

"What I had to," he said, and then he went down the hall to his bedroom, where he collapsed on his bed.

PART THREE:

HOLLYWOOD VAMPIRES

SEVEN

The conversation at the coffee shop with Landon's friend Ross had left Maureen unnerved, but once she had a few moments to herself to digest what she'd just been told, she began to wonder if it all wasn't some put-on at her expense. Was Landon Dawson hazing his soon-to-be stepmother with some elaborate prank? The notion seemed childish, but Landon seemed just peculiar enough to find something like this humorous, or so it seemed to her. Moreover, Uptown—Ross—seemed like the type of guy who'd reluctantly go along with whatever the alpha male put him up to. So, instead of worrying herself over such nonsense, she got into her car—buckled and unbuckled the rear seatbelts three times each before doing the same with her own—and decided to see if there was even a Motel 6 out in Glendale.

There was—the GPS on her phone pulled it up without incident, right there on East Colorado Street—but that still didn't mean what Ross had told her had been the truth. She drove out there, found the place, pulled into the parking lot. The building was surrounded by telephone poles and power lines, some chairs on empty balconies with wrought-iron railings. The scant few cars parked in the lot looked like they belonged to drug runners, with fat rear tires and blackened windows.

She pulled into a spot but left the car running. She was already lambasting herself for being such an easy mark, but the writer in her recognized an inkling of authenticity in Ross's story. He might be some pushover lackey who'd blindly do Landon Dawson's bidding, but the kid didn't strike her as an actor, and he'd been legitimately upset back at the coffee shop.

This is silly, she thought. *I should just go home.*

Instead, she shut down the car, unbuckled then re-buckled her seatbelt several times—

Goddamn it, calm yourself.

—and then climbed out into a mid-afternoon with a heat index somewhere near the low nineties. She could hear car horns and stereos blasting down East Colorado, and somewhere nearby a woman was shouting at someone in a language Maureen could not readily identify.

Her nerves felt frayed, and her compulsivity was running in the red: she kept her eyes on the ground as she walked across the parking lot, deliberately avoiding cracks in the blacktop, moving in a straight line, and holding her breath every time she stepped over a painted yellow line marking the perimeter of a parking space.

The motel lobby was shabby and smelled of body odor. A man in a bowling shirt sat behind the front desk, slouched in a chair, watching some video on his phone. He did not look up at her when she approached the desk until she audibly cleared her throat.

"Sorry to bother you," she said, "but could you tell me if my son has been staying here?"

The man's face was expressionless, with one eye cast outward like some strange, deep-sea fish, while his other eye took her in almost ravenously. "Who's your son?" he asked.

"His name is Landon Dawson."

"No one by that name been here, lady."

"Maybe he used a different name," she said.

"You got a picture?"

"Sorry, I don't."

"You don't got no picture of your own son?"

"Sorry, no," she said, but then realized the surreality of her situation; she took out her phone and googled Landon. She was surprised to find very few photos that weren't actually of Greg, but there was one from some Hollywood premiere with Landon standing slightly behind his father. She enlarged the photo on her phone so that it was only Landon's face then showed it to the man.

The man glanced at the image on her phone, then hoisted himself with great effort out of his chair. He wore a bowling shirt and a bunch of beaded necklaces around his neck, and they all clattered together as he rose, like some ancient percussion instrument. He set both meaty paws on the counter and said, "Fifty bucks."

"For what?"

"For information," he said, and then he pointed to a sign that hung on the wall behind the desk—PARKING LOT FOR RESIDENTS ONLY.

"That's not what the sign says," Maureen informed him.

"*Cincuenta dólares.*"

She dug fifty dollars out of her purse and placed it on the desktop, careful to withdraw her hand before one of the man's meaty paws made contact with it while going for the money.

"Well?" she said.

"Yeah, that kid stayed here for a bit. He checked out . . . I think, yesterday? Day before? I don't remember."

"You're serious?" she said. "He was really here?"

The man folded the fifty and tucked it into the breast pocket of his bowling shirt. Then he gathered up his phone and eased himself back down into his chair. Either the chair cushion or the man himself released a trumpeting burst of air.

"Thank you," Maureen said, and hurried back out into the parking lot.

She arrived home to a quiet house, which gave the false impression that no one was home. When she went into the living room, she could see Landon lounging out by the pool, catching some sun. Unlike the night before, he at least wore a bathing suit now— turquoise Speedos that looked two sizes too small—and had a pair of aviator glasses on his face. His body was beaded with water and appeared to radiate beneath the glow of the midday sun.

She went upstairs and stood for a ridiculous amount of time outside Landon's closed bedroom door. She had been living in this house with Greg since the spring, but this door had always remained closed. And not just closed, but locked. She had asked Greg about it once, and he had commented that the house had plenty of rooms, so why was she worrying about his son's bedroom? Once, she'd even asked Lucinda if she had a key to get in there to clean, but Lucinda had just fervently shaken her head and, in her broken English, confided that she *never* went into *Señor* Landon's room.

She tried the knob now and was surprised to find that it turned.

She possessed no ability to imagine what Landon's bedroom might look like—she didn't know the boy well enough to summon an image to her mind—but was surprised nonetheless when she opened the door and stepped inside.

The bedroom was spotless. The carpet was a deep, lush burgundy, which matched the bedspread on the neatly made bed. There was a wooden valet stand beside the bed, the navy-blue blazer Landon had been wearing the night before now hanging tidily from it. A simple desk was set against a rank of windows, a pristine ink blotter and a gooseneck lamp the only items on top. There were some bookshelves beside the desk, housing thick, leather-bound volumes that looked like either medical or legal books. Every wall was bare—not a single photo, poster, or shelf in the place. Just barren white walls, much like a hospital room.

A pair of cordovan loafers sat on the floor in front of the closet, the doors of which stood partway open. The duffel bag Landon had been carrying last night when he'd arrived unannounced at the engagement party was on the floor of the closet. It was a simple black gym bag with white piping and some logo on the side. As she stared at it, Ross's voice floated back to her: *He had it in his duffel bag last night, I'm pretty sure. He took it with him when he checked out of the motel.*

"Are you lost?"

Maureen cried out, and whirled around to find Landon standing in the doorway. She'd been so startled that she pressed a hand to her breast and could feel her heart strumming against the wall of her chest.

"It's a big house," Landon said, "and you're new around here, so I can see how you might wind up in the wrong place."

"I was just coming to see if you wanted some lunch," she said.

"Are you a good cook?"

"I make a mean grilled cheese."

He stepped into the room, towel over one shoulder, his body still wet from the pool. His feet left behind damp boomerangs on the burgundy carpet.

"So what am I supposed to call you?"

"You can call me Maureen."

He grunted. "Can I ask you something?"

"Of course."

"Why are you marrying Greg?"

His use of his father's name gave her pause. Then she said, "Because I love him."

"Well, that all happened pretty quickly." He yanked the towel off his shoulder and tossed it over the back of the desk chair. His thin, pale frame looked like something intricately carved from a block of marble, or maybe soap. There was a narrow strip of dark hair climbing from the waistband of his Speedos to his bellybutton. "You only met this past spring, is what I mean. Isn't that right? And Greg, he doesn't exactly have the most pristine track record when it comes to marriages."

"Well, I appreciate your concern, Landon, but your father and I are—"

"He's not as rich as he says he is, by the way. I hope you realize that. I think you should know."

She sighed. Said, "I'm not marrying him for his money, if that's what you're worried about."

"Oh, no," he replied, holding up both hands as if in surrender. "Me? I'm not worried about anything. It's just that Greg likes to wear a false face. It's second nature to him. It's part of living in this town."

"Well, I appreciate you looking out for me," she said, and then she moved around him toward the door.

"I read your book, you know," he called after her.

She stopped in the doorway, turned back around. "Did you?" she said, already not believing him. "Doing your homework on me?"

"Something like that."

"Must've been hard to find," she said. "It's been out of print for a while."

"They're pretty cheap on eBay."

"Well, don't keep me on pins and needles. What's your verdict?"

"That it reads like a first novel," he said. He sauntered over to the closet, opened the doors the rest of the way. That duffel bag was right there on the floor, beneath a file of white dress shirts, dark blazers and slacks, and a rack of neckties. "Of course, it's your *only* novel, so it should probably read like a last novel, too, which doesn't come across as favorable when you consider it in that way."

"That's very astute, I suppose."

"But don't get me wrong," he said, taking down a white cotton dress shirt from the closet, and examining it at arm's length. "I rather enjoyed it. That scene at the end of part two? What that guy does to the other guy with that crowbar? I must have read that scene a dozen times. Just over and over."

"Critics said it was excessive and gratuitous."

"Oh, it absolutely was. No question. That's why I liked it so much." He slipped one arm into a sleeve of the shirt, and then the other. "The rest of the book is very tame. It's a safe novel, Maureen, and I can tell you were young and safe when you wrote it. But I think that's why that crowbar scene really got to me, you know? It's just this intense snapshot of horror smack in the middle of . . . well, let's face it: some pretty mundane writing."

"You've really given this a lot of thought."

"It made me curious what you were working on now. I hope you don't mind, but I read a few pages of your latest."

She blinked, shook her head. "You did *what*?"

"Hey," he said, and held a hand out toward her, a soft but uncompromising smile suddenly on his face. "It wasn't on purpose. I mean, I didn't go in there with the *intention* of reading it. But your laptop was on and the pages were right up there on the screen, so I thought what the hell, and I just glanced at them. That's really all it was—just a harmless glance."

He must have sensed her discomfort—the feeling that she'd somehow been violated by this kid right here in her own home— because he lowered his hand and that kiss-my-ass grin vanished quickly from his lips.

A million responses shuttled through her head. In the end, she said, "This is your house, so I suppose you can go wherever you like in it, which includes the room where I write. But what's on my laptop is private, and I'd appreciate you respecting that privacy in the future." She added, "Please," then immediately felt as though she'd wilted a bit in doing so.

"Don't you even want to hear my thoughts?"

She shook her head. "Not really."

"Because I think what you're writing now is really good. At first I thought you were writing another love story, but there's no love in there at all, is there? Those two are just down to fuck. And then there's this weird religious altar in the motel room? You've got me intrigued."

He took a step toward her, the cotton shirt on but unbuttoned, and Maureen suddenly noticed that the front of Landon's Speedos had gotten tighter, and that there was more of him there than there had been a moment ago.

"You've only known him for a handful of months," he said, still moving closer. "Maybe you love him, maybe you don't. But you certainly don't *know* him. And it makes me wonder why this marriage thing is happening so quickly."

"I *do* love him," she said, and hated that it sounded weak, sounded like she was trying to convince this kid and herself at the same time.

"What I'm saying is, what dark secret are you trying to escape by wearing my father's life as a mask to cover it up?"

"Stop walking toward me," she said, and held up a hand.

Landon paused, midstride.

"You're too young and pretty for my dad," he said, and suddenly his face—those angular jowls, those piercing dark eyes beneath a pronounced ridge of brow—grew deadly serious. "Also, you have no idea what the hell you're getting yourself involved with."

She stared at him, eyes hard, arms hugging herself. Then, without wishing to engage with him further, she turned and left.

—change, or at least the *image* in the mirror changes. She stands there in the dimness of the motel room, naked, her body slick with sweat, and sees her lover's dark form on the bed, a jumble of limbs twisted about a ghostly whip of damp sheet, his chest slowly rising and falling as he sleeps. A second figure is there now, but only in the glass of the altar vanity, because when she looks over her shoulder and across the motel room, there is only her lover on the bed, just where she left him, but when she looks back at the mirror, that additional figure is still there: stark and undeniable and standing motionless in the corner of the motel room beside the bed. The lights are off and the blackout curtains are drawn so that the room is wholly dark—they hadn't wanted to look at the altar vanity while making love—but her eyes have grown accustomed now, and there is no denying this third human being standing in this seedy motel room with them, if only on the mirror side of things.

The woman steps closer to the glass and even reaches out a hand. The tips of her fingers press coolly against the mirror. This action seems to beckon the mysterious figure to edge closer. He does not move tentatively, but with some predatory—and admittedly frightening—authority. She can see that he is tall, the shape of his body that of an athlete. She sees, too, that he is nude—that the dark shape of him hints at a hairless, sculpted chest, a smooth abdomen, a shadowed, secretive thatch at his groin that she can't quite make out.

It's all she can do not to turn her head and see if this stranger is actually in the room (she knows he isn't), but is too afraid to move. Also, a part of her just doesn't want to take her eyes off him as he closes the distance between them.

His dark shape comes up directly behind her own reflection. He is nearly a foot taller than she is, and their conjoined reflections look like some totemic sculpture, a thing with multiple heads and too many limbs.

She cannot make out any details of this man's face.

In the mirror, he raises a hand and slowly places it on one of the woman's bare shoulders.

She feels it in real life, and cries out.

Like some choreographed dance, Landon was dressed and out of the house five minutes before Greg's Escalade pulled into the driveway. She'd avoided Landon for the remainder of the day, hiding in her writing room but unable to get any writing done. She checked her laptop, and saw, when the screensaver cleared, that her manuscript was right there. Had she really left it up or had Landon come in here and gone through her files? And why, anyway? Just to mess with her head? He was too old to be bitter about Greg replacing his mother with someone new. Besides, Greg had had two wives between them. Whatever the reason, that sense of violation persisted, so she'd taken a Jodi Picoult book down from the bookshelf and zoned out for a few hours, pretending to read.

Greg was in a good mood—the last bit of funding for the production had come through—and he insisted on whisking Maureen away to a fancy dinner. She wasn't in the mood, but acquiesced nonetheless, and went upstairs to find something nice to wear.

At the top of the stairs, she peered across the second-floor landing and at Landon's closed bedroom door. Downstairs, she could hear Greg dumping ice cubes into a glass. He was flying so high he was literally humming to himself.

She went down the hall and approached Landon's bedroom door. She felt abruptly foolish, much as she had in the parking lot of the

Motel 6 in Glendale; like she was chasing a set of perceived clues that, in actuality, added up to nothing.

She pushed open the door and entered the room. The vague hint of cologne—something of the sandalwood variety—hung in the air. She crossed the room, bare feet whisking along the lush burgundy carpet, and went directly to the closet. She pulled open the double doors and turned on the closet light.

She'd expected Landon's duffel bag to be gone, but it was still right there, on the floor beneath his dress shirts and blazers.

She dropped to her knees and unzipped the bag . . . then zippered it back up. Unzipped, zippered, unzipped, zippered. *Calm yourself, girl.* Unzipped, and spread it open.

A profusion of balled-up gym socks lay on top, startling white snowballs of socks. She brushed them out of the way, but realized they all moved with some unexpected weight to them. She unrolled one of the socks, felt something bulging at the toe. She shook it out into the palm of her hand and saw it was a small bag of multicolored pills. She couldn't identify any of them, nor did she suspect they were legal—not hidden in a tube sock like that—so she dumped them back inside the sock and rolled it back up. She looked in another sock and found a baggie of cocaine. A third contained a Ziploc bag of weed.

Beneath the socks was a paperback copy of her novel. She took it out, thumbed through the pages, and was a bit chagrined to find that Landon had annotated nearly every page in cramped, spidery handwriting. Some passages had been underlined while others had been crossed out completely. Some words were circled, though there was no reason given for why. She landed on one pages and read some of the annotations—

> juvenile depiction of sense of love
> overworked similes

uses em dashes where colons would be more appropriate (though it does infuse a sense of abruptness that may or may not be deliberate by the author)

nice description of a nipple

She turned the book over and saw that someone had poked holes through the eyes of her author photo.

There was one more item at the bottom of the duffel bag—another book whose dimensions were just slightly larger than her own novel. A scrapbook with a tufted fabric cover. A small plastic window sat in the center of the cover, one word printed behind the plastic of that window:

MEMORIES

She brushed the remaining socks off the scrapbook and then eased it out of the duffel bag.

Her eyes had been cut out. Her nose was, like, chopped off. There were pictures of her ears, or where her ears should have been—just, like, holes on the sides of her head, all covered in dried blood and little black ants and dust from the desert.

Did she really want to open this book? Prank or no prank, did she really want to see those photos, even if they were fakes, done up by some Hollywood special effects guru?

I might open this scrapbook and find a note that says, simply, "Gotcha!"

But she didn't think that would be the case.

She opened the scrapbook to the first page.

"You haven't touched your steak," said Greg.

They were seated at a small, candlelit table at Greg's favorite steakhouse on Melrose, a bottle of Chateau Lafite Rothschild between them, a thick cut of sirloin in the center of Maureen's plate.

"In fact," Greg went on, "you haven't eaten anything since the food arrived. Are you feeling okay?"

"I think I'm going to be sick," she said, jumping up from the table and hurrying off to the restroom.

EIGHT

Toby Kampen, the Human Fly, had cultivated a mission. Since having met the woman with the vampire teeth, he'd returned to The Coffin every night with an almost religious fortitude, sitting by himself at the bar while nursing a solitary drink for the entire evening. Sometimes the crowd was heavy—bodies dancing through the smoke-machine fog, squirming on the dance floor, a collaboration of arms and legs and glimpsed torsos—but other nights, the crowd was so thin, it couldn't fairly be *called* a crowd. Toby felt uncomfortable on those nights, when it was just a few other stragglers and himself in the place, because it made him feel like a liar and a standout and someone destined to be called out for not belonging. He began to worry that the woman would never return to this place, that she had fled for fresher parts of the city, parts where Toby, as a fly, would not be as welcome.

He had written one word in permanent marker on his arm, RENFIELD, which he ultimately googled at one of the free computers at the local library (his cell phone was dead). Turned out, it was the name of a character from the novel *Dracula*, which Toby had never read. He stole a copy of the book from the library, and in the evenings, as he waited on his barstool in one smoky, bleak corner of The Coffin, night after night, for the woman to return, he began to read.

Renfield, as it turned out, was a deranged lunatic who resided in an asylum. He was also a fanatical devotee of Count Dracula, and had acted as the count's familiar in order to bring about the turning of Mina Harker. In exchange, Dracula provided Renfield with an unending supply of insects to eat, the life force of which Renfield believed would grant him immortality. When Toby arrived at that particular passage in the novel, he felt the world around him narrow to a pinpoint of clarity. How could the mysterious woman with the vampire fangs intuit such things about him? Had she sought him out of the crowd that night because she sensed some . . . *familiarity* . . . in him? Had she bitten his neck not to frighten or even turn him, but to pass along to him some measure of understanding, of commiseration, of sameness?

Excitement trilled through him like a live wire.

Then, one night, he happened to look up from the book to see her familiar shape misting toward him through the smoke, arms above her head in some Egyptian pose, hips swinging like a metronome to the music. She wore a cropped black tank top, dark denim shorts cut high at the crotch, and dense fishnet stockings. Her black leather heels looked like lawn darts. Against all that black, her skin shimmered like porcelain.

She arrived at the bar, just a barstool away from where Toby was sitting, and leaned forward to kiss the female bartender on the mouth. They shared some secret joke—something Toby couldn't hear over the thumping of industrial music—and then a drink materialized on the top of the bar, a wedge of citrus fruit curled about the rim. Toby watched as the woman picked up the drink and turned slightly to survey the club. She sipped demurely from a too-thin straw. Toby drank her in: the pale, angelic quality to her face; the cluster of earrings along the outer rim of an ear; a tiny diamond stud in her nose. Her hair was swept back from her temples, so severely Toby could see the white streaks of her scalp, and pinned back in a ponytail that sparkled with glitter. He watched her hands, too—the black nail polish, the silver bracelets, the intricate veining of tattoos creeping like ivy on the insides of her pale white arms.

Toby said, "Hello."

The music went *unce unce unce ZAT, unce unce unce ZAT.*

She was scanning the crowd, oblivious to him. Had she come here with someone?

He got up from his stool and slid closer to her down the bar. Said, "Hello."

She actually jumped, as if he'd startled her. He had grown accustomed to such reactions—Toby Kampen had spent the majority of his brief adult life startling people—but coming from her, it seemed almost an affront, like she was breaking some unspoken protocol.

"Do I know you?" she said, and he caught a glimpse of those elongated incisors curling from her upper gum line.

"It's me," he said. And when she said that she did not recognize him, he added, "You bit my neck a couple weeks ago." He tipped his head to one side, exposing the section of neck—unmarred, of course—where she'd playfully laid those fangs.

"You'll have to be more specific," she told him.

"Renfield," he said, and then he held up the copy of *Dracula* he had been reading.

She glanced at the book, then back up at his face. It was hard to judge just how big or small her eyes were—and Toby was a student of eyes, was a student of all sensory vehicles—because she wore so much makeup, maybe even false eyelashes. Still, she was the most stunning creature Toby Kampen had ever laid eyes on.

It wasn't quite a smile that broke across her lips, more like some sly, calculated grin mixed with a bit of a snarl. Animalistic, whatever it was. Excitement once more shrilled through him, straight from the core of his body and zipping right down to the tips of his extremities. He suddenly felt lightheaded.

"Right," she said. "I *do* remember you. You had a pussy name."

"Not anymore," he said, and patted the novel with one hand.

Her eyes narrowed the slightest bit. She asked if he owned a car.

"Uh, no. I don't."

"That's too bad," she told him. "I could really use a car tonight."

"Where did you want to go?"

She didn't answer him; she took another sip from the too-thin straw, her painted eyes surveying the dancers on the dance floor.

She's on the hunt, Toby thought. *She's searching for her Mina Harker.*

Still gazing at the dancers, she reached over and gripped him about one wrist. Her fingers were strong, the black-painted nails biting into the tender flesh. She leaned closer to him—close enough so he could smell the mix of perfume and sweat on her skin—and he instantly felt himself swell inside his jeans.

"You should get a car," she said. It was her profile he was watching, as she watched the dancers. A single hooked incisor. "And you should shower and get fresh clothes because you smell like death."

She released the grip on his wrist, finished her drink, then set the empty glass on the bar top. As Toby stared at her, she positioned her hands above her head once more in that mimicry of Egyptian dance—

"Wait!" he yelled at her. Actually reached out toward her.

—but she ignored him, her hips clocking back and forth as she pushed away from the bar and swam into the sea of undulating bodies on the dance floor.

Once unce unce ZAT, unce unce unce ZAT.

He abandoned his book and pursued her onto the dance floor, moving like some lame beast among a herd of graceful gazelles, or like an injured fly desperate to take off with only one functional wing.

He saw those hands in the air above her head, cleaving through the dancers like a dorsal fin, and he followed them. Someone slammed against him, a rock-hard shoulder against his solar plexus, knocking the wind out of his lungs. When he bent forward, someone else elbowed him across the jaw. Some part of his brain laughed—this was nearly comical, wasn't it?—yet that quiet humor was overshadowed by a rising sense of panic within him. For whatever reason, he was desperate not to let the woman get away from him this time.

But there were too many bodies. There was too much smoke. The music was beginning to infuriate his ears (and he'd always had sensitive ears, especially as a child). By the time he clawed his way to the opposite end of the dance floor, he had lost sight of those dorsal-fin hands, had lost sight of her wholly and completely.

Was it a game?

Was it a test?

She was no longer in the club, at least from what Toby could see. He turned and saw the lighted red EXIT sign, a push bar instead of a handle on the door. He drove his weight into it—

—and came skittering out in a trash-strewn alleyway behind the club.

To his left was a black pit of brick, chain-link fencing, and iron bars on windows. To his right, he could glimpse a section of the street—cars zipping by, some neon signs in a shop window, a traffic light about to turn blood-red.

After a moment, he cast his glance straight up at the night sky. Not so sure what he expected to see in that direction, other than a full moon obfuscated by a parade of gray, wispy clouds. He stood there staring at the sky until he lost all concept of time, which wasn't unusual for him.

Vanish, he thought, and suddenly realized he had left the copy of *Dracula* back at the bar.

—◇—

You should get a car.

A plan had been set into motion, or so it felt to him the following morning. He awoke in the stuffy confines of his self-storage locker, grimy with night-sweat, reeking like the alley he'd found himself in at the conclusion of last night's chase. Flies swarmed around his face and buzzed listlessly from the strips of flypaper he'd hung from the ceiling of the storage unit. She might be a vampire, but Toby Kampen knew what it was like to exist inside a coffin.

You should get a car.

He'd spent the past . . . how many months now? . . . performing the magic act of extricating himself from the Spider's web, only to arrive at the bitter conclusion that perhaps his extrication had been premature. Other things had happened. Other things were at hand now. Like R.M. Renfield, he had been given instruction, and he intended to follow it. No matter what the consequences.

You should get a car.

He would just have to be careful.

The Spider lived in an apartment in Central City East. Toby took the Metro B Line toward Pershing Square, then walked the remainder of the way—about half a mile—to the slum-ridden, urban quarters where he had spent the majority of his adolescent life. Spiders generally built their webs in places of high traffic, to ensure the maximum number of wayward insects would ultimately become trapped, and Toby Kampen's Spider was no different: the apartment on Chamber Street looked down upon a street bustling with the indigent, flea-ridden countenances of the sunburned homeless. Rats ruled, and they made no qualms about skittering back and forth across the street, from swill heap to swill heap, in broad daylight. *Brazen fuckers*, the Spider had frequently said of the rats in moments when her ire was raised.

It had long been Toby's opinion that only the most foolish of flies returns to the web once they'd managed to escape, but on this morning, he felt he had no other choice. *You should get a car*, the vampire girl had told him. Also: *You should shower and get fresh clothes because you smell like death.* Perhaps an asylum was befitting of R.M. Renfield, but even in that godforsaken place, the poor bastard had most likely been able to wash up from time to time.

Things have to change if this is going to work, he told himself as he slipped down the narrow passageway between two apartment buildings, where a wrought-iron gate hung partway open, and where some dog barked its fucking head off at the morning sun. *I'll have to be cautious and cunning if it's going to work, but I've been given instruction, and I must comply.* This, he suddenly realized, was his lot in life.

Finally.

The iron gate shrieked when he pushed it open—*Oh, I remember that sound, and I hate it*—and when he stepped through, the soles of his Converse crunched on shards of broken glass, grinding them into the pavement. He took a set of concrete steps up to the second floor of the building, then wound around an outdoor walkway that overlooked the parking lot. He caught a whiff of human excrement and absently wondered if it was him.

This building had been home since Toby had been a teenager. Prior to that, he and the Spider had lived in a small tract house in Palmdale with a satellite dish on the roof, where their property stretched out to the dune-flat horizon, and where their neighbors were the cactus wrens and red-tailed hawks, the scorpions and king snakes and coachwhips, the screeching, ominous buzzards and the steely-eyed, tufted-tailed coyotes that crept out at dusk in search of food. He had spent his youth out there among those things, studying insects and lizards alike, his forehead blistering with sweat, his bare knees scuffed and abraded from kneeling on the hot, grainy sand where he would remain crouched for hours watching some dead thing being devoured by a flood of nondescript insects. There had been an older boy in the area, a bully, really, who was sometimes Toby's friend, and they would often walk the desert together, turning over large rocks to see what wildlife they'd find underneath. This boy's name was Donald, and to this day, Toby could still picture Donald's brushfire-orange hair, his freckled face as round as a pie tin, and the kiln-baked redness of the larger boy's upper arms in the dead of summer. Donald's breath always smelled of puke and his T-shirts were always drenched in sweat. Donald's nickname for Toby had been Dumbo, and the older boy would chant the name sometimes as he threw rocks at him, or when he would bully Toby to drop his shorts and sit bare-ass on an anthill—*Don't be chicken shit, Dumbo!* Donald also took great delight in grabbing Toby from behind, gathering him up in a chokehold, and squeezing him about the neck until he lost consciousness; Toby would frequently come to on the ground, staring at the sun, the crotch of his shorts wet, and Donald—the sometimes-friend/sometimes-bully—having fled no doubt upon a peal of giddy laughter. Back then, the Spider's increasing health concerns, which were legion, had seen to it that she could no longer work, and soon, the bank had come calling for the little square tract house with the satellite dish on the roof in Palmdale. And so, they had moved.

Here, in Apartment 218, their neighbors had been rats and roaches and all manner of indigent zombies roving up and down Chamber Street at all hours of the night. There were no puke-breath bullies pouncing on his back and snatching him up in a chokehold, true, but there were other dangers lurking in the streets and alleyways that Toby, even at a young age, was keen to keep away from . . . for a while, anyway.

Trouble did find him. Or, rather, *he* had found *it*. His teenage years were plagued by bad decisions and increasingly criminal behavior—vandalism and shoplifting, mostly. At first, anyway. There'd been an incident with a neighbor's son when he was twelve that had been awkward, with all parties agreeing it was best left forgotten; there had been an incident the following year with a female classmate that had not been as easily forgotten, and that was where some real troubled had started. (Even now, he didn't like to think about those things.) As he'd gotten older, he found that *things* had a tendency of slipping away from him—*things* such as a firm grasp of right and wrong, of reality versus fantasy. Of responsibility and culpability. Of time, too—a sense that, sometimes, the past, future, and present were interchangeable, or merely jumbled up in a way that allowed everything to happen all at once. It often confused him. It was in those years that he first became aware of the Spider nestled silently within the skin-suit of his mother. Terrified of it at first, yet keen enough to realize that he, too, was something other—

(a fly!)

—and equally adept at obfuscation.

Did he really want to do this? Did he really want to crawl back into the Spider's web?

No.

But—

(you should get a car)

—things needed to change.

He took a deep breath, then knocked on the apartment door.

There was no sound at first, except the shush of traffic across the courtyard, and some damn fool relentlessly ringing a bicycle bell. But then his fly sense honed in on a subtler sound—more of a dislocation in the atmosphere than an actual *sound*, to be honest—and he felt the hairs along his arms stiffen. There was one large window to the left of the door, covered in a filthy vinyl shade the color of bone; Toby saw that shade ripple now, as if in anticipation of some momentous occurrence, and then a section of it near the bottom of the sill peeled away. A triangle of darkness appeared behind the shade, and for a split second, Toby glimpsed a set of blunt, white fingers. In that moment, he pictured the owner of those fingers not as a Spider, but as a single flickering flame: blue at the base, with a dancing orange crown.

Stop. Stop. Stop. Stop. Stop. Stop.

He shuddered, felt something hitch at the base of his throat, but forced himself not to flee.

The bolts on the inside of the door cranked. A chain rattled. The knob twisted with an audible squeal.

"*TOBEEEEE!*"

His name, stretched to impossible lengths, came wailing out from behind the door before it was fully open. Borne on that wail: a fluster of meaty arms and a face as round as a globe. He stood there motionless and allowed himself to be swallowed up by the Spider's embrace. He felt her blunt, peg-like fingers press against his spinal column, her head with its nest of short, bronze hair thrust against his breastbone. She reeked of liniment oil and baby powder, which Toby knew was merely a facade used to mask her true nature. There was no fooling him on that score.

"Toby, honey, where have you *been*?" she wept against his chest. Then she pulled away from him, clamping her cool hands on either side of his sweaty face. She stared at him with pearly gray eyes already spilling tears down the bulwark of her face. "I've been so *worried*, so *petrified*, that something terrible had happened to you!

I've spoken to the police over and over and over again, Toby, but no one could tell me *anything!*"

"I'm right here, Mom," he told the Spider. "You can quit crying already."

"Oh, Toby! *TOBEEEEE!*"

She clutched him tighter, one narrow cheekbone driving into the bony notch at the center of his ribcage.

A few apartments down, a man in a stained white undershirt and thick, black-framed glasses poked his head out of the door and stared at them. Toby scowled at the man, which caused him to vanish back into his apartment.

"Come on, Mom. Cut it out. Let's go inside."

"My baby," she said, reaching up for his face again. He turned his head, but she was adept at catching him—she was a Spider, after all—and she pressed those cool, flat hands against his cheeks again. "My baby boy," she said, "you smell so bad and look so terrible," and then she brought his face down to hers so that she could kiss the soiled dimple at his chin.

He had only been gone a handful of months (according to the folded bit of paper with the hash marks he'd used to help keep track of time), yet for some reason, he expected the apartment to look different: broken, somehow, as if the walls had been held together with his own bodily excretions or, like a bird constructing a nest, with saliva and tenacity, only to crumble and come apart in the wake of his hasty departure. But the place was still standing, and none the worse for his absence. The walls were still meticulously decorated with the Spider's bric-a-brac—porcelain animal figurines, religious iconography, countless black-and-white photos in tiny brass frames of family members Toby had never known. They say the olfactory sense is the one linked closest to memory, and the smell of the place—that eye-watering, antiseptic conglomeration of Lysol, detergent, and eucalyptus—shuttled him straight back into the past, and the countless hours he had spent molting and shedding and squirming in this claustrophobic prison.

The Spider hovered around him, poking and prodding him to assess the consistency of him as a meal.

"You've gotten so thin! Toby, it pains my eyes! Where have you *been*? What have you been *doing*?"

He ignored her, wandering into the tiny kitchenette where a set of sheer floral curtains hung over a window outfitted in metal bars. The Spider had a habit of laying out dishes on the table first thing every morning, and he saw that this morning was no different, except that he was surprised to find she was still setting out two plates, two drinking glasses, two sets of utensils. He understood this sight should have registered within him at least a modicum of grief, but instead, he found himself feeling nothing but pity for the Spider.

"Are you hungry, Toby? Let me cook for you."

He *was* hungry, though he did not say so. Instead, he pulled out his chair and dropped soundlessly onto it. His back and shoulders ached from sleeping on that shitty mattress on the floor of the storage unit for months—and had it really been months?—and his whole body felt itchy with grime. It was as if those aches and itchiness were only just now making themselves apparent, now that he was back in this place—a place that had judged him so harshly.

The Spider scurried to the refrigerator, and began piling food onto the countertop—a carton of eggs, a carton of whole milk, a loaf of white bread, a packet of bacon nearly the size of a two-by-four. She wrangled a pan out from beneath the counter, set it on the stove, and the burner went *tick tick tick* before a dull blue flame blossomed from the grate. Then it was back to the fridge, where she retrieved a brick of butter. She sectioned it into thirds with a butter knife, then knocked a third of it into the pan, where it sizzled angrily.

On the wall of the kitchen hung a calendar. Toby noted that it had not been changed since he'd disappeared, as if the Spider had been trapped in some sort of stasis awaiting his return. He stared at the calendar's grid of boxes, nearly every one full of the Spider's precise yet somehow agitated handwriting, each notation either having to do with her medical appointments—they were plentiful —or something to do with *him*: court appearances, psychiatric appointments, court-appointed community service, innumerable medication refills, running errands for the apartment complex's maintenance man, Mr. Zebka. On every Tuesday and Thursday, the Spider had written *Toby walks the dog*, even though Toby hadn't walked the neighbors' dogs for money since he'd been fourteen.

The pan slamming down on the stovetop caused him to jump in his seat. He swiveled his head and saw the Spider gripping the handle so tightly, her knuckles had turned white. As he stared, she lifted and slammed it down again, speckling the backsplash and countertop with sizzling butter. Another slam down with the pan and Toby watched a glob of butter strike the Spider's left forearm before dropping to the floor, leaving a dime-sized red mark on her flesh.

Her back to him, the Spider hung her head. She appeared to most people as a short, stocky woman with batwing flaps of loose skin hanging from her upper arms. Her age was more in line with a grandmother than a mother, something that Toby had always been self-conscious about when he'd been younger. Now, of course, it didn't matter.

He said nothing as he watched the Spider's shoulders throb up and down. He knew she was sobbing even though she made no sound. Not for the first time, he wondered if it was painful to conceal an enormous, bristling, eight-legged arachnidan frame beneath the fragile, paper-thin exterior of an elderly woman.

"You *stink*, Toby," she said—no, she *wailed*—not looking at him. "Maybe you've been living in a sewer. I don't know. But that stench does not belong in this home."

He *did* stink; he couldn't argue with her on that score.

She turned and looked at him. Instead of sobbing, her face was an angry red mask, where the fury just below the surface was threatening to split her at the seams. He wondered, absently, what she would look like if that actually happened—what she would look like in her true form.

I know what you are, he did not say. *I've known for a long time, now. And just because I've come back, you think you can begin to feed off me again, but what you don't know is I'm on to you, Spider, and I've come prepared. And with a mission.*

"Go take a shower," the Spider said, and the anger seething within her caused her teeth to clench. "Wash that filth from your body. And when you're done, take the towels straight out to the trash. Your clothes, too. You've got all fresh things still in your bedroom. There'll be no getting that stink out." When he didn't respond, she took a step toward him, reaching for his ear, blunt fingers suddenly pincer-sharp, shouting, "Do you *hear*? Do you *hear*?"

He casually swatted her hand away, then stood up. The fly wanted to fly, which is what flies do, but that hazy, smoky image of the woman with the vampire fangs interjected, her face more powerful than the Spider's, eyes like polished obsidian, black lipstick stretching to reveal her true nature.

See? Toby thought, and he actually grinned to himself, as if having just received some long-awaited validation. *Everyone wears a mask to hide their true form. The Spider, the Human Fly . . . the Vampire . . .*

The Spider must have thought the grin was for her; she took a step back from him, the small of her spine prodding the handle of the frying pan, and sending it sliding across the stovetop. Toby had a brief image of the Spider's housedress catching fire in the burner flame, but of course that didn't happen.

"I love you, Toby," said the Spider. A switch had been flipped; she was back to the whimpering, teary-eyed, doughy thing she had been at the front door. "You know that I do. I'm just looking out for you, my little boy. I'm just so *worried* about you. All the time."

Toby said nothing. He moved around the cramped little kitchenette, careful not to brush against the Spider's clean housecoat and risk setting her off again, then skulked down the hall toward the bathroom.

No lie: a proper shower felt good. He stared down at his feet and watched the grime peel away from his thighs and shins, watched the black, soupy water swirl and chug down the drain. He must have remained under that tepid spray for nearly an hour, it felt so good. When he was done, he stepped from the stall and swiped a hand across the steam on the mirror above the sink.

He was perturbed by what he saw there in the glass.

Clean: yes. Healthy in appearance: most certainly. But it was also a regression, a fly having capitulated to the enchantment of the Spider. He was a young boy again, in the years he and the Spider had relocated from the dusty but pleasant single-family home in Palmdale to this garbage dump section of the city. Had time skipped backward again?

Who am I, really? What do I look like inside? Behind this mask?

When he was just a little boy, he had saved up his money and purchased a Polaroid camera. For the next several years, he would take a single picture of himself at the start of the day—a selfie before cell phones. These photos accumulated, and he kept them in a shoebox on the top shelf of his closet—perhaps a thousand selfies, maybe more, of Toby Kampen's bland, glum face staring at the camera. He did this because he could feel the change coming upon him even back then—from boy to fly—and he knew that the metamorphosis, the transmogrification, needed to be documented. He needed to compare one photo with the next in order to see that the transformation, however slow, however subtle, was taking place. It was akin to watching a plant grow, or the drifting of clouds across the sky—things you couldn't rightly see with the naked eye, but things that could be *documented* and *preserved* with the proper equipment. Meaning: where did he come from? Who was he *really*? He had asked the Spider on many occasions who his father was. The answer varied with each asking—*he was a louse not worth speaking of* to *he was a saint who passed too quickly* to *he was a man from another world who arrived on a floating pie tin* to *he was something terrible and strange and of biblical proportions and your birth was every bit as divine as the birth of Christ, and I screamed for hours, Toby, for hours.*

The Spider, of course, was crazy—even as a child, Toby never believed any of that nonsense—and so he'd just quit asking.

A gentle rapping on the bathroom door.

"Toby? Did you fall in, sweetheart? Breakfast is on the table."

"Be out in a minute," he said, then held his breath. He glanced down and saw the stocky silhouettes of her feet remaining on the other side of the bathroom door. Unmoving.

You won't snare me.

Waited.

Waited.

The Spider's feet slowly receded, and Toby could hear the creaking floor as the massive arachnid retreated back toward the kitchenette.

Toby wrapped a clean towel around his waist. He dumped his soiled clothes and wet, dirty towel into the trash pail beside the toilet, then crept back out into the hall on a gust of steam.

His bedroom had remained untouched: the black walls, hardcore band posters, rubber monster masks on white foam heads. There was a terrarium of Venus flytraps on the sill of the window, surrounded by the molted skins of snakes and lizards, rattlesnake rattlers, a container of Mexican jumping beans, each bean hollowed out after the moth larva had escaped. His dirty clothes were in a heap on the floor exactly where he'd left them months ago, a sleeve of clean ones hanging just beyond the open closet door. He had his REGULAR CLOTHES, which consisted of cargo shorts and threadbare jeans, ratty T-shirts with gratuitous slogans, grimy Converse sneakers. And then he had his RESPECTABLE CLOTHES, which he wore to court appearances, doctor visits, psychiatry appointments. These were the collared shirts and khaki pants, a pair of dress shoes two sizes too big that the Spider had picked up at Goodwill. A regular man might have felt uncomfortable in clothes like these, feeling like some carnival act dressed up and marched out onto a stage, but much like the Spider herself, Toby Kampen, the Human Fly, was proficient at concealing his true nature, and he did it with aplomb.

He went now to the closet. Comic books and fast food wrappers littered the closet floor; he brushed those aside until he located a simple, unadorned cardboard box. A strip of masking tape held the flaps closed, and it did not appear as if the Spider had tampered with it in his absence. He stripped the tape away and pulled open the flaps of the box. He had no awareness that he was holding his breath.

THE WONDERFUL THING was still inside.

Just seeing it there filled Toby with a queer stirring that fluttered about inside his ribcage: a thousand flies humming to life inside him. It was such a tactile, *literal* feeling, he believed that if he opened his mouth wide enough in that moment, those countless flies would come bursting from his throat and swirl in a black whirlwind throughout his bedroom.

He closed the flaps of the box then ran the strip of masking tape back across it. Then he dressed quickly in a pair of cargo shorts and a Broken Hope T-shirt that he'd scooped up from the dirty pile.

Out in the hall, he removed the lid off a decorative urn that stood on a small table flanked by ceramic religious figurines, and dipped his hand inside. He snatched a wad of bills from the bottom of the urn, stuffed them in one pocket, then returned to the kitchen.

"Well, now," said the Spider, grinning from ear to ear. She came to him, pressed those cool and steady hands against the sides of his face, holding him in her tractor-beam stare. "There's my little boy again."

He dipped his head and somehow maneuvered out of the Spider's grasp. He saw the food on both plates—steaming heaps of scrambled eggs, buttered toast, crispy planks of bacon, two small bowls of fresh fruit, two full glasses of milk so white it hurt his eyes to look at it—and felt his stomach clench with hunger. He couldn't remember the last time he'd had a proper meal. Probably not since he'd left this place.

Because she's fattening me up, he thought. *If I feed, then* she *can feed.* But right now, he was too ravenous to care.

"I'm going to phone the police, let them know you've returned, safe and sound."

"They don't care, Mom."

But she ignored him, and went to the phone, anyway. It was an ancient rotary phone, mustard yellow, that had hung on the wall for as long as Toby could remember. The Spider abhorred all modern technology—they had no microwave (cancer), she owned no cell phone (brain tumors), and refused to pay for cable television (subliminal signals pumped into your home from the government)—and that shitty rotary phone had become synonymous with everything that was fucked up and upside down in their lives. As a child, he had watched her on that phone, talking with her distant and never-seen friends for hours—talking about *him*. She'd pace the kitchen, weaving that phone cord back and forth, a sickening yellow web in the center of which resided the Spider.

He watched her pick up the phone now, saw one plump finger dive into each rotary hole, dial the emergency line for the police. She pressed the receiver to her nest of dyed orange clown hair, then stepped out into the hall. He blocked out whatever she was saying out there—the fucking police wouldn't give a shit that her adult son had finally come back home—and instead he dumped himself in his chair and proceeded to shovel forkfuls of steaming scrambled egg into his mouth.

"Well, fuck them proper," the Spider said once she'd returned to the kitchen. She hung up the receiver, then folded her hands across her chest as she turned and looked at him. Something like a smile stretched the boundaries of her spidery mandibles. "That's right," she said, pleased. "Eat, Toby. Eat it all up. You've lost too much weight out there in the world, and it hurts my eyes to see you so thin."

"If the eye offends thee, pluck it out," he said around a mouthful of egg.

"Don't be flippant with the Scripture, boy."

He averted his eyes, then hated himself for feeling like a miserable child again so easily in her presence.

The Spider sat opposite him at the table. She picked up her fork, but merely readjusted the food around in her plate. She fed off *him*; food on her plate was merely a pretense, and they both knew it.

"Tell me," she said. "Where have you been?"

"I got a place downtown."

"A *place*? Like, a place to *live*?"

He said nothing, just kept steam-shoveling that food into his craw.

"You never even said goodbye," said the Spider. "Didn't even leave a note. I didn't know what had happened to you. I called the police so many times they told me to stop calling. They said you were an adult and could do as you pleased."

"They're right, Mom."

"Well, they don't know you the way I do. I know you need your mother. I know you need . . . well, looking after."

"I don't need looking after. I've been doing just fine."

"*Fine*? Because you have a 'place downtown'? You have no money. Do you even have a job?"

"Cool it, Mom."

"No, I won't 'cool it, Mom.' Tell me, Toby—*what do you have*? Nothing. That's what."

He closed his eyes and exhaled audibly through flared nostrils.

"You look like a bum." Her voice was abruptly sharp enough to freeze the fork halfway to his lips. "You look like someone who's been sleeping in a gutter."

"Point is," he said, his fork still hovering in the space between his plate and his mouth, "I can do what I want. It's my life."

"Is it?" She cocked an eyebrow at him. Hers was a perfectly round, perfectly white face, but her eyebrows (as well as her short-cropped hair) were a disconcerting shade of orange. Clown-like. "I don't suppose you've kept up on your medication."

He grunted, which approximated to a non-answer.

"Or any of your scheduled appointments," she added.

He set his fork down in his plate. "I've completed all my court-appointed mandates and I don't need to see a shrink anymore. That part of my life is behind me."

"Then tell me," she said, leaning incrementally closer to him from across the small kitchen table. "What part of your life are you in right now?"

He considered this, and in truth, it was tough to hide the grin that wanted to break out across his face.

"I'm going to need the car for a while," he told her.

NINE

A.J. Politano called Renney on a Saturday. Said, "You need to come in and have a look at something, Bill."

Renney, who had spent the past two hours of his day off cleaning his fish tank, said he'd grab a shower and head right in.

He arrived at the police station a little after one. He hadn't ingested anything all day except two cups of tar-black Folger's, so he'd stopped at an In-N-Out Burger where he picked up a Combo #2 and a strawberry shake. He devoured the food, with more than just a modicum of self-loathing, in his car.

Politano was in the media center when Renney arrived, which was a reconstituted storage room that housed a bunch of standalone computers, TVs, and various recording and viewing devices. Renney eyed Politano's lunch which sat atop a wooden stool nearby—a bland-looking salad in a Tupperware container—then glanced around for a trashcan where he could hastily deposit what remained of his strawberry shake.

Politano was seated before a computer screen, but stood quickly from his chair at the sound of Renney coming into the room. "Listen," he said, and Renney quickly noted the apologetic tone to the younger officer's voice. "I know you, Bill. Promise me you won't get pissy about this, okay?"

"What are you talking about?"

"I've been going back through the cold case on that Andressen woman from last year, seeing if I could connect any dots to the Fortunado murder—"

Renney shook his head.

"—and I think I found something."

"Yeah? What do you think you found?"

"Have a look."

Politano dragged a second chair in front of the computer. Renney came around and sat in it, setting his milkshake on the stool beside Politano's salad. Politano tapped the keyboard and an image filled the screen—one that Renney had seen before.

"It's the security footage from the Hilton in Phoenix," Politano explained. "It's where Andressen's husband, the psychiatrist, was staying the week she was murdered."

"Yes, I know what it is."

On the computer screen was the bank of elevators in the hotel lobby. The screen was paused, with a date and time in a digital readout in the upper right-hand corner of the screen. The few people on the screen were frozen in motion, partially blurred.

"When I un-pause," Politano said, "you'll see the doors open and then Dr. Andressen will get on."

"I know," Renney repeated. "Just get to the point."

"I want you to watch. Tell me what you see. Tell me *if* you see it."

"See what?"

"Just watch."

Politano hit the space bar and the video resumed. It had been roughly a year since Renney had viewed this footage, and he couldn't for the life of him figure out what had gotten Politano so excited, but he kept his mouth shut and watched. After about twenty seconds, Alan appeared on the screen. He was dressed in business casual attire and was carrying a black portfolio under one arm. Renney watched as he pressed the call button. When the elevator arrived and the doors opened, he and two other men got on. Before the doors shut, a woman rushed on, and then the doors closed.

Politano poked the space bar and froze the video. "Well?" he said.

"Well what?"

"Did you see anything?"

"Goddamn it, just tell me what the hell I'm supposed to see."

"Two things, actually. Here—watch it again. I'll zoom in this time."

"Zoom in on *what*?"

Politano didn't respond, except to replay the footage. When Alan arrived on-screen, Politano zoomed in on the doctor's right hand—the one clutching the portfolio. Renney folded his arms, agitated . . . but then a memory lit up at the forefront of Renney's mind. A memory from a year ago, back when Alan had sat across from him in the interrogation room while Renney plugged him full of questions. How Alan's face had been red and blotchy and how he'd sobbed.

How he'd twisted that wedding ring around on his finger . . .

Renney sat up straighter in his chair. "He's not wearing his wedding ring," he said.

"That's number one," Politano said. "Now wait for number two."

Once again, the elevator doors opened and Alan got on, along with two other men. He made no eye contact with the men, but when the woman hurried onto the elevator, Renney saw one corner of Alan's mouth tick upward in some semblance of a grin. The woman sidled right up beside him, and just before the elevator doors closed—

"Son of a bitch," Renney muttered.

—he saw the woman rub the back of her hand against Alan's.

Politano hit the space bar again, and the video froze. "I mean, I'm no expert on infidelity," Politano said, "but if I had to lob a guess in the dark—"

"That's hardly proof of infidelity."

"The missing ring? The smirk when she gets on the elevator? There's more than enough room in there, but she's practically pressed up against him."

"Pretty flimsy," Renney said. "Still, even if you're right, what does this mean? The guy's a creep? Is this all you got?"

"Did it ever come up when you interviewed him?"

"No."

"It could be motive."

"Plenty of guys fuck around on their wives. Doesn't mean they wanna kill 'em."

"Look," Politano said, gathering up his salad off the stool (and nearly knocking over Renney's milkshake in the process). "I'm not saying this is hard evidence. Far from it. But it's *something*, right? We can go to him, ask him about it. Find out who the woman is, ask *her* some questions. Pull at the threads, just like you say, right?" He shoveled a forkful of lettuce into his mouth.

"The guy called his wife repeatedly from Phoenix," Renney said. "Cell phone towers show he was making the calls from there, in Phoenix, when she was likely being killed here in California."

"Did he leave voicemails?"

Renney thought back. "No. No voicemails. Just called and hung up. Some text messages, too."

"Right."

"Right, what?"

"What if it was the girlfriend making the phone calls?"

Renney laughed. Said, "Ah, come on."

"Think about it," Politano went on. "He leaves his phone with his girlfriend, and she keeps making calls and sending texts while he's back here in L.A."

He patted A.J. Politano on the shoulder as the man tried to wedge another forkful of salad into his mouth. Said, "You've been watching too many true crime shows on Netflix."

Yet Renney's insides suddenly felt cold.

He went that night to Alan's house. Lights were on in the large, floor-to-ceiling windows, a muted yellow haze behind the smoked glass. He drove up to the gate and hit the buzzer. Waited. Up the hill, he could see someone—Alan—shifting about within a frame of muddled light. Peering out at him idling out here in the dark.

If he doesn't let me in, I'll climb the fucking fence, he thought. He was angry at having missed those details in the hotel security footage, angrier still for Alan to have kept this information about the woman a secret from him last year as they meticulously combed through the details of the investigation. He thought of the large spool of paper upon which Alan had painstakingly documented the timeline of events leading up to his wife's death, the billboards he'd taken out along the freeways, the look on Alan's drawn, anguished face as he stared blankly out over the canyon in what appeared to be some dark contemplation. He kept replaying, too, the scene in the desert as they both stood looking down at Lucas Priest's crushed and bloodied skull, and Alan dropping to his knees and sobbing.

The day after they'd buried Lucas Priest's body in the desert, Renney had driven out to the Sly Fox on Lombard Street and asked to see the security footage from the night of Melissa Jean's murder. The owner, a retired police officer, was happy to comply. In a small office behind the bar, Renney sat hunched in front of a monitor and watched Lucas Priest and Melissa Jean Andressen seated at the bar drinking margaritas. She was beautiful in everyday life, he realized, just as she was in the glamour shots that adorned the walls of her home. She was also wearing the clothes she would be murdered in, Renney noted. In the video, Priest leaned close to her several times, spoke inaudibly into her hair, and kept putting his hand on her shoulder. She laughed at some of the things he said. She didn't seem to mind his hand on her shoulder. Once or twice, she leaned her head over toward him. Could there be something more to their relationship than what Priest had told him? Renney couldn't tell.

When he'd asked the owner what his assessment was of the couple, the guy admitted that he hardly remembered them coming into the place. "But I certainly don't remember any, you know, problems between them," he'd said. "No fights or nothing, is what I mean. This that chick whose body was dumped in the desert? It ain't the husband who did it?"

The day after that, Renney took the footage and the DNA results of the hair found in Priest's car to the district attorney's office. In less than forty-eight hours, he was granted an arrest warrant for Lucas Priest.

He did it to cover his ass: securing that footage and the arrest warrant was what any cop worth their salt would have done. He even made stops by Priest's apartment and repeatedly dropped in at the mechanic shop in Reseda to show that he was looking for Priest. When he asked the manager where Priest had gone, the guy said he had no idea, that Priest had just vanished without notice, then intimated that Priest often took off with some random chick for days at a time, particularly if the chick had money.

Renney felt haunted by this recollection now. True, the world was no worse for wear with a piece of human garbage like Priest out of the picture, but had Renney been thinking more clearheaded back then, he would have retrieved that footage immediately after his second conversation with Priest, and would have been granted a warrant for the guy's arrest before Alan had done what he did.

He felt sick thinking of that now.

The gate shuddered open.

Renney drove up the long, twisting driveway, noting even in the dark how the plants and trees on either side had been left to fend for themselves. The gardens looked untamed and overgrown. Beyond, the house loomed against the night sky, an angular box whose roof pitched at an unsettling forty-five-degree angle.

The front door came open, spilling a panel of silvery light onto the porch, even before Renney shut down the car's engine.

"You know, my stomach ties up in knots every time I see you coming," Alan said, as Renney walked up the slate steps toward the front door.

"We need to talk."

Without a word, Alan receded back into the house. Renney let himself in, closing the door behind him; the sound of it shutting echoed across the enormous, empty foyer, loud as a gunshot. He recalled something Alan had said last year, when Renney had first come to the house: *M.J. hated it. Said it was too formal. Too un-lived-in.*

There was classical music playing on the stereo, a bottle of cabernet and an assortment of paperwork on the coffee table down in the sunken living room. It had been approximately a year since Renney had been in this house, and with the exception that the place was now nearly spotless, it seemed that nothing had changed. It *was* un-lived-in: a person could only *subsist* in a place like this, not *live*.

"Grab a glass from the cupboard, if you want," Alan said as he sank down into the living room. He was in socks, a pair of old trousers, a UC Berkeley T-shirt. There was a ballpoint pen tucked behind one ear.

Renney stood on the landing and watched as Alan sat on the long, red, leather sofa. He plucked the pen from behind his ear, jotted some notes on one of the papers spread out across the coffee table, then tossed the pen down. He leaned back against the sofa in an exasperated huff. Ran his hands down the length of his weary face. Said, "I'm thinking of calling it quits. Selling this place, maybe moving up north and out to the coast."

"What about your patients?"

"Clients. I've already started referring some of them out. And some never came back when I took that break last year. Right now, I'm only handling a small pool of pro bonos." He sighed. "Fuck. Maybe I'll take up pickleball." He glanced up at Renney, as if just realizing he was there. "What are you doing here, anyway?"

"Were you having an affair with a woman in Phoenix last year?"

Alan's mouth dropped open, but he didn't say anything. Renney didn't need him to: he could see the truth of it flash across the man's face, valid as a confession.

"Bill, what are you talking ab—"

"Brunette, maybe in her late twenties, if I had to guess," Renney said.

Alan shifted on the sofa, perceptively uncomfortable.

"Where does she live, Alan? Maybe up north and out on the coast?"

"No, that's—"

"How long have you been seeing her?"

Alan shook his head. The expression on his face was one of misery. "You've got it wrong, Bill."

"Yeah? Then tell me what's right."

"She was someone I met at the convention. She'd read some articles I'd published and we went to dinner."

"Not just dinner," Renney said.

Alan expelled a shuddery breath. "No, not just dinner."

"What's her name?"

"Celia something." Alan motioned with one hand in the approximate direction of his office at the rear of the house. "I'm sure I have it on the convention roster somewhere."

"Did she know you were married?"

"I told her M.J. and I were separated."

"When was the last time you spoke to her?"

"The night I left Phoenix to come back home."

"The night you were texting and calling your wife's phone," Renney said, putting it in different terms. "You're so panicked about your wife, yet you still go to bed with this Celia woman."

"Not that night. We slept together the first night of the conference. Once I started worrying about M.J., that was all I thought about. When I decided to leave the conference early to come back home, I saw Celia in the hotel lobby. I told her something came up, said goodbye, and that was it."

"And you haven't spoken to her since?"

"No, Bill, I haven't. It was a one-night stand and I'm not particularly proud of it, okay? What's this about, anyway? You just want to hear me admit what a shit I am? Where's this going? How'd you even find out about this?"

"Why didn't you tell me about her before?"

"When? Last year? When you were investigating me for my wife's murder?"

An admittedly childish thought occurred to Renney in that moment: that he, too, had been cheated by Alan Andressen.

"Things are different this time around," Renney told him. "I've got a partner on this and he's under the impression that maybe you left your cell phone with that woman so she could call your wife's phone from Phoenix."

Alan frowned. "What? Why the hell would I do that?"

"You're a smart guy, doc. You know what I'm getting at."

"You're getting at asking me if I killed my wife," Alan said. The misery on his face had transitioned to a simmering, red anger. "Is that where we are now, Bill? Full circle, back to the beginning?"

"I'm not asking you anything, doc. Like I said, I'm not working in a vacuum anymore. This other guy, he's on the phone with that woman right now, following up on his hunch."

"Celia? Right now? Jesus Christ, Bill, I wish he wouldn't."

"Yeah? How come?"

"Because it's embarrassing as hell. And because I've already been put through the ringer once on this." He stood, hands on his hips. He looked momentarily flustered, but then he leveled his gaze on Renney. Sweat glistened along his forehead. "My marriage wasn't perfect. I made mistakes. But that doesn't mean I didn't love my wife. And I certainly didn't fucking kill her."

"You should have told me about this other woman last year."

"I didn't because I felt like shit about it."

"What's this Celia woman gonna tell us?"

"The same thing I just told you: that it was a one-time thing. Christ, Bill. Is this really you asking me this?"

"I'm just letting you know how it is," Renney said. "And if there's anything else I need to know, you better tell me now."

"There's nothing," Alan said. He turned away from Renney and stared out at the darkness beyond the wall of windows that looked out upon the canyon.

Sweaty and uncomfortable, feeling itchy in his skin, Renney turned and walked back down the hall toward the front door. His footfalls echoed off the oddly angled ceiling and reverberated in the foyer. The moment he stepped outside, he was grateful for the fresh air and the slight breeze.

He got into his car and was rolling slowly down the hill when his cell phone chirped.

"This is Renney."

"Bill, it's Politano. I just got off the phone with the woman from Phoenix. Her name's Celia Davens and she lives in Utah. She said she met Andressen at the conference, they had a few drinks, then wound up in bed. She said she hasn't talked to him since and didn't even know he was married until she saw the news about his wife. She said it fucked her head up pretty good back then. Bottom line is you were right, Bill—she says she didn't make any phone calls for him and I believe her."

"Andressen said the same thing," Renney said. "I'm just leaving his residence now."

"Well, it was worth a shot. Sorry for wasting your time. Have a good night."

Renney disconnected the call.

He felt sick to his stomach.

TEN

Toby Kampen, a Human Fly in transition, now had a set of wheels at his disposal. It was the Spider's champagne-colored Lincoln Town Car, a thing nearly the same age as Toby himself and with almost two hundred thousand miles on the odometer, which was sometimes how Toby felt. It was kept in a numbered parking space behind the apartment complex, tucked in between Mr. Zebka's white panel van and a rust-colored Honda with no hubcaps. A lightning bolt crack bisected the Lincoln's front windshield, and the passenger-side mirror was missing (perhaps the rust-colored Honda had knocked it off while attempting to park). The Lincoln's tires were bald and in need of air, and Toby noticed that the registration sticker on the license plate was four years out of date, but it was now *his*.

You should get a car.

And now he had one.

Of course, there were stipulations. The Spider would allow him to use the car as much as he wanted—she rarely used it now herself, except for traveling to and from her doctors' visits—and in return, he would agree to get back on his medication and to find a part-time job. So he lied and told her he already had a job working nights at the self-storage garage (where he'd previously been living), which allowed him to be out for all hours of the night without raising any of the Spider's suspicion as to what he was up to; as for the medication, he made a show of popping the pills in his mouth every morning while she looked on, dry swallowing them, showing her his empty mouth and the underside of his tongue. Minutes later, he would cough them back up in the trash-strewn alleyway behind the apartment building.

He felt emasculated having to agree to these terms, but understood it was necessary to get what he wanted. Toby knew the Spider still saw him as a kid, and at twenty-two years old, Toby was not lacking in self-awareness—he understood that his head worked a little differently than most people's, and that he had a difficult time fitting in, always the chronic outsider. He also understood that the Spider did not operate like most people, either (and was probably the reason Toby was so fucked up). One moment she was fussing and caressing and fretting over his every need; at other times, it was as if the smallest infraction on Toby's part would awaken the Spider within the mother-suit, and that terrible creature would rupture straight through the fabric of that false human flesh, splitting the mother-suit down the middle with a sound like tearing burlap, until it was there, right there, multi-limbed and obsidian-eyed, black, bristling hair as thick as porcupine quills, fang-tipped chelicerae dripping snot-like venom onto the floor of the tiny Chamber Street apartment. He could have argued the terms of her agreement, but he knew that would also risk rousing the true Spider, and so he'd quietly acquiesced.

None of that mattered tonight, however.

There were other things on his mind.

He guessed it had been a little over a week since his second run-in with the vampire girl from The Coffin nightclub, but his unreliable sense of time told him not to trust that estimation. He had returned to the club—this time, with the car—every night since, desperate to seek her out yet again, and to show her that he had followed through with her request. No, the twenty-year-old Town Car wasn't exactly a Ferrari or even a Cadillac, but she hadn't been specific with her instruction—she'd merely told him to *get a car*, and Toby had.

Countless nights in a row prowling up and down the streets in the Town Car for a glimpse of her. Countless nights skulking through the dark, misty, body-soup atmosphere of The Coffin, nursing a single room-temperature beer the entire evening, eyes on the prowl, his housefly senses on full alert. Would her hair be lacquered purple spikes like that first night, or pulled back into that severe schoolgirl ponytail from last week? Countless nights in a row without a single glimpse of her, yet Toby did not grow discouraged. And really, it wasn't a matter of *him* finding *her*. She had sent him on a mission and he had returned successful; *she* would find *him* when the time was right.

A set of long fingernails gently grazed his shoulder.

"*Renfield . . .*"

He spun around on his barstool, expecting to find nothing but diaphanous smoke in the dark corner at his back. Yet there she was—a thing that had materialized straight out of the gloom, her skin like white satin, the pupils of her eyes aglow with a dim, yellow fire. The left side of her head was shaved now, the right side a waterfall of black, inky hair. She ghosted toward him, those long, black fingernails skittering across the upper part of his back.

"You keep coming back," she said, bringing her mouth very close to his ear—for him to hear her over the pounding industrial music, or perhaps to merely tantalize him for a moment. "I saw you sitting here last night, right on this very stool. And the night before that, too."

"You were here?" he said. "I didn't see you. I looked for you all night. I've been looking for you all week."

She drew the beer bottle out of his hand, peered distastefully at the sudsy backwash at the bottom of the bottle, then set it on the bar top.

"Let me buy you a drink," he said, already digging cash out of the pocket of his cargo shorts. He'd made off with over two hundred dollars in cash from the Spider's decorative urn and he was suddenly eager to spend it. "Tequila and soda. With real lemon. Right?"

There was a black swipe of paint across the woman's eyes, like a raccoon's mask. The eyes within that mask narrowed, the dull yellow lights of her pupils holding steady. She was studying him. Ordinarily, this would have made him feel self-conscious. But for some reason, he didn't mind her scrutinizing him—felt something stir about in the front of his cargo shorts at the thought of it, in fact.

"You're clean," she said finally. And for a moment, Toby thought she was imparting some magical spell over him. But then she said, "Your clothes. Your skin. Your hair. You no longer smell like death, Renfield."

He had been staying at the Spider's den on Chamber Street ever since he had returned for the car, sleeping during the day, showering and eating there, the Spider laundering his clothes. For those hours, he was that trapped and helpless fly again; it wasn't until nighttime, when the Spider thought he was off at work, that the Human Fly transformed into Renfield, Eater of Flies, and the world began once more to make sense.

"The world makes sense," he blurted, and then immediately realized he was speaking his thoughts aloud.

The woman's black-painted lips pulled apart in a smile. Toby could see her fangs.

"I have a car," he told her.

"Big boy," she said.

"Don't you remember? You asked me to get a car. Told me to."

"That's good of you, Renfield."

"It's parked down the street."

"That will be good for later," she said, bringing those lips close to his ear again. Toby could smell her—a mixture of perfume and the titillating aroma of her perspiration. She was wearing a black, formfitting tube top, and this close, Toby could see a sheen of sweat shimmering across her shoulders like glitter. She was as bright and sparkling as a disco ball wrapped in people skin. "Yes, Renfield, get me that drink. Then I want you to stay seated here while you watch me on the dance floor. Will you do that for me?"

"Yes," Toby said. He was nodding emphatically. "Yes, I'll do that for you. Whatever you say."

(whatever you say, master)

"Good," she said . . .

. . . and then there was a sudden sting as she bit his left earlobe.

Toby jerked back, slapping a hand to his wounded ear. He could feel the place where she'd bitten him, didn't have to look at his fingers to know she'd drawn blood. He kept his eyes locked on hers—he was powerless to look away, in fact—and she was still grinning at him, those elongated incisors practically glowing beneath the dance-floor lights.

He watched her drift back out onto the floor of bodies, white legs wrapped in fishnets, a denim skirt slung low on one hip, a panel of luminescent belly repeatedly winking at him, winking at him, winking at him.

He ordered her drink quickly, terrified that he'd turn back around to find her gone again. But no—she was still out there, arms above her head now, delicate divots of her armpits, intricate and indecipherable tattoos crawling up and down the length of those otherwise pale arms, silver bracelets a-shimmer with the dance-floor lights. Sometimes it seemed like she was at one with the roiling, undulating smoke; other times, it was as if she *was* the smoke.

He wanted desperately to breathe her in.

She did vanish from him for a while—there on the dance floor one second, gone the next—and this incited a rattle of anxiety to quake through him. She was adept at disappearing, but Toby, a lifelong horror-movie fan, and a recent consumer of Bram Stoker's novel *Dracula* (well, most of it, anyway), knew that vampires could vanish in a puff of smoke at will. He tried not to let this bother him, and he continued to do as he'd been instructed—to sit on the stool and not move.

When she appeared on the dance floor again, she was not alone. A woman with a shaved head and gauges in her ears was writhing up against her, so close that Toby had difficulty discerning whose hands belonged to whom. Fishnet legs against this hairless woman's tight white jeans, black and white, the two of them, like a photo negative of each other. Something about the way they moved together made Toby nervous; he finished the backwash at the bottom of his beer bottle, then took a gulp of the drink he'd ordered for—

What was her name?

He didn't know.

The drink tasted like turpentine and he winced as it hit the back of his throat. It seared its way down the quivering channel of his throat.

He watched, for a while longer, the luminous yellow pinpoints of her eyes as she writhed and twisted out there on the dance floor. At one point, the hairless woman leaned against the shaved side of the vampire woman's head and spoke something into her ear. The yellow lights in the vampire's eyes appeared to momentarily intensify, although Toby conceded that could have just been reflection from the dance-floor lights. Then they were both making their way toward him through the crowd, hand in hand.

"You said you have a car," she said to him.

His eyes volleyed from her to the bald-headed woman, who was grinning at him lasciviously. "Yeah," he said. "It's parked just a few blocks away."

"Let's go," she said.

"Where are we going?" he asked from the driver's seat.

"Just drive around awhile," she responded.

Both women were in the back seat of the Lincoln. They were dark and formless back there, a pair of heads that occasionally occluded the rear windshield when they came together. Whenever he'd drive through a traffic light, he'd glance up at the rearview mirror to observe the bands of streetlights wash across their bodies, film in a projector, and he could feel his skin prickle and the greasy bulbs of sweat wringing out of the pores along his forehead.

"What's your name?" he asked after a time.

There was some muted laughter, a coarse rustle of fabric, and then the bald-headed woman said, "Michaund."

"I meant you," Toby said, catching the vampire woman's yellow stare in the smudgy glass of the rearview mirror.

The vampire only grinned. And even though he could not see those elongated fangs with any clarity from where he sat in the dark of that car, he recalled how she had bitten his ear earlier, and had nipped his neck with them on the first night he'd met her. How she had drawn pinpoints of blood.

"Take a left at the next light," Michaund said. Hers was a husky, smoker's voice.

Toby abhorred the notion of cigarettes.

At the next intersection, he took a left, then motored slowly down the boulevard while awaiting further instruction. When none came, he said, "Where next?"

"Keep going," Michaund said. "All the way."

He kept going.

All the way.

After a while, the busy club streets and neon lights denigrated to industrial warehouses and power stations, empty car lots and homeless shelters. The streetlights flickered and NO TRESPASSING signs were in abundance. They had been driving for a while now and he was unfamiliar with this part of the city. In fact, it didn't appear that they were even *in* the city anymore, although that couldn't be true.

The vampire has magicked us away to some alternate plane of existence, he thought to himself. It was supposed to be humorous, something that might bring a smile to his lips, but once he'd thought it, he found he was chilled by the notion.

"Turn here," said Michaund.

He couldn't see a place to turn.

"Here here here," she repeated, urgently.

Then he saw it: a narrow strip of potholed roadway woven between another industrial park and a brick warehouse that looked fire-scarred and abandoned. He glimpsed snippets of graffiti sprayed along the exterior of the warehouse, partially illuminated within the glow of nearby sodium light—KILL ALL RAGERS and GAS HEAD LIVES and something that looked like an elaborate, multicolored flower, or maybe it was some psychedelic wheel. Toby couldn't be sure.

They were whispering to each other in the back seat. When Toby glanced up at the rearview mirror again, he saw their heads—their faces—pressed very close together. Their commingled breath was fogging up the car's windows. A pang of jealousy tremored through him.

"Do you have any money?" Michaund asked. And when Toby didn't answer—had she been talking to *him*?—she asked again, leaning forward so that he could feel her warm, alcohol-scented breath against the sweaty nape of his neck: "Hey. You have any money, fella?"

He thought about lying to her, but when he opened his mouth to do so, he felt—or imagined he felt—the vampire's fire-yellow eyes boring twin beams of burning light into the back of his head. He said, "Yeah, I've got a little money."

"Great. There's a motel at the end of the next block. Ain't much to look at, but it's real cheap and it's got a roof and four walls. Park there and get us a room."

A motel? Here? He could see no evidence of one. Anyway, who in their right mind would stay in this section of town? Yet as he passed through the next intersection and drove a block farther, he could see the rundown saltbox building with a crackling neon sign behind a sheet of window glass that said VACANCY.

This motel made the apartment complex on Chamber Street look like a palace—it was a squat, ugly building where the rooms all faced the parking lot, and there were bars on all the windows. The scant few cars in the lot looked like they had been there for ages, and likely were no longer capable of movement.

The women in the back seat must have sensed his apprehension as he slowed the Town Car to a crawl in the street parallel to the parking lot, because the vampire herself now brought her mouth very close to his ear, and said, "Are you afraid of something, Renfield?"

His sweaty hands tightened their grip on the steering wheel.

"No," he said. "No way."

"Pull into the lot and get us a room."

And it was as if he had no choice in the matter.

"What's that thing on the dashboard?" she asked.

It was one of the Spider's plaster statuettes, this one depicting Jesus, dead, splayed out across Mary's lap. It was stuck to the center of the dashboard with some epoxy.

Before he could cobble together a response, the vampire said, "Get rid of it."

"Why?"

"Because it's offensive to my nature. And never ask me 'why' when I tell you to do something."

Toby pulled into the parking lot and slid into a space close to the smoky window with the VACANCY sign in the glass. He wiggled the statuette back and forth until it came free, a section of the vinyl dashboard coming with it. He could see bone-colored foam in the hole left behind on the dash.

"We'll only need an hour," the vampire said.

"You can do that?" he asked.

"Just tell them that's all we need. You have to pay in cash."

"Okay."

He climbed out of the car, stuffing the Spider's statuette into the pocket of his cargo shorts, and hurried into the small, fish-tank lobby of the motel. A large man in a ribbed, sleeveless shirt sat on a stool inside a metal cage. Toby gave the man the vampire's instructions—just an hour—and then he passed a pocketful of damp bills through a slot in the metal cage. Wordlessly, the man handed him his change and a metal key dangling from a plastic fob, A1 printed on it. The man's fingers were as thick as plantains.

When he went back outside, he saw the two women already standing beneath the glow of the solitary lamppost on the edge of the motel's property. They looked like hookers, he thought, in their skimpy club clothes. They were holding hands and watching him with an eagerness that was nearly palpable.

He handed the key over to Michaund, who glanced at the room number, then cried out, "A1! Steak sauce, baby!" into the night.

The room was tiny, and smelled of urine. There was a single queen bed in the center of the room, no headboard, no framed prints on the plain, alabaster walls. The carpeting looked like it was made from some crude, fire-retardant substance, and there were too many stains of varying colors and sizes—both on the carpet and on the bedspread—for Toby to count.

The stains did not appear problematic for Michaund: she flopped backward onto the mattress, her body sinking more than it should have, bedsprings squealing. Toby looked past her, to where a rickety wooden vanity stood beside the bed, its mirror cloudy with countless finger- and handprints. There was an open box of Trojans on the vanity's shelf.

The vampire watched Michaund from across the room. She was swaying back and forth, hips like clockwork, the same as she had been doing back on the dance floor at the club. Toby could see her better in the light of the motel room—could see just how pale her skin was, but also the smattering of faint freckles along her shoulders and upper arms. Her fingernails weren't black, he realized, but a dark purple. The makeup she wore on her face—that black raccoon mask across her eyes and the black lipstick—looked somehow less seductive and almost juvenile in the bright, garish light of the motel room.

One thing hadn't changed regarding her appearance: she still looked ageless.

Of course she is, Toby told himself.

"Hey," Toby said, sliding over to her. Studied the lines of her face, her cheekbones, the perfect denouement of her chin. There were sparkles in the lock of dark hair running down the right side of her face, and along the swell of her cheekbone, the slope of her neck and upper chest, making it appear as if she was comprised of tiny fractals of light. "Hey," he repeated. "I don't know your name."

"Sure you do, Renfield," she said, not looking at him. She was watching Michaund writhing around on the filthy bedspread. "You know me."

"You never told me your—"

She turned abruptly and went into the bathroom. He heard the light snick on, glimpsed a wall of busted brown tiles and a toilet whose seat looked perceptibly lopsided. The vampire leaned forward, leaving Toby a view of only her ass and legs framed in the bathroom doorway. He heard the shower chug on, water splash down into the tub. When the vampire returned in full view, she said, "Michaund," once more, then peeled off her tube top.

A funny sensation not unlike going down too fast in an elevator overtook Toby. He watched as the vampire tossed her tube top on the bed beside Michaund, unable to peel his eyes from her breasts. They were pale, smooth, and not overlarge, with a pair of small, pink nipples, clearly aroused. When she turned the slightest bit, Toby saw a tattoo on the outer rim of her left breast, a little black design, although he couldn't make out what it was from where he stood. He simply stared at her—at her *breasts*—as steam rolled out of the bathroom and filtered into the room, much like the smoke on the dance floor of the club.

Something is going to happen, he thought, that sensation of falling too fast ratcheting up so that he was now beginning to sweat profusely. *No—something* is *happening. It's like a crackle of static electricity in the air that I can feel . . .*

Michaund sat up on the bed. She was not very pretty, Toby decided, and the shaved head did not help matters: her eyes looked too far apart, her nose too wide. There was something masculine about her hands that turned Toby off.

Michaund stood, removed her own shirt. Her breasts were heavy and sagging within the confines of her purple silk bra. She wasn't as white-skinned as the vampire, but her breasts were pale enough so that Toby could make out a tract of blue veins just below the surface of her flesh.

Michaund sauntered across the room toward the open bathroom door. In a cloud of steam, the women embraced. They kissed, open-mouthed. Michaund put her head back on her neck and the vampire kissed and licked her way down, leaving smears of black lipstick along her throat.

Toby Kampen was suddenly aware that he was standing there with a full erection straining against the fabric of his cargo shorts. Ashamed, he brought both hands down to conceal his embarrassment. His body was swampy with sweat, his heart was trampolining in his chest . . . and a part of him knew that *sometimes*, when he'd been off his medication for a while (which he had been), the concept of *reality* became murky. He began to wonder if he was, in fact, standing here with these two women at all. He began to wonder if maybe he was standing here all alone, imagining this scene unfurling before him, some dark and desperate desire deeply seeded in his subconscious. Maybe he was even back at the Spider's den right now, asleep and dreaming in his childhood bed. Or squirming on the sodden, filthy mattress on the floor of the self-storage garage.

The vampire removed her lips from Michaund's throat. She looked across the room at Toby, her pupils no longer those dim pinpoints of golden light, but black and bottomless as the deepest regions of space. "Wait right here," she instructed him. "No matter what you hear in this bathroom, do *not* come in. Do you understand, Renfield?"

"I understand," he said, struggling to mask his erection while at the same time trying not to bring attention to it. "Yes, I understand."

Her smile was impossibly wide. Those fangs gleamed, a color slightly off from the rest of her teeth.

She took Michaund's hand and led her farther into the bathroom. Michaund went willingly—eagerly—and shut the door behind them.

—◇—

Time was his enemy, so Toby couldn't be sure how long they stayed in there. He heard some laughter and some other sounds—an occasionally banging or thumping sound, too—although nothing was very clear over the rush of the shower. Steam billowed out from beneath the door. At one point, he crept over to the door, his erection fierce and painful in his shorts, and pressed an ear to it. He could hear them moving around in there, could hear one of them (or both of them) moan with what sounded like pleasure from time to time. And then those sounds stopped, replaced by an urgent knocking. It sounded like the toilet tank rhythmically banging against the tiled wall.

He couldn't help it—that sensation of falling reached such velocity that Toby bent at the waist and felt himself ejaculate in his shorts. That momentary spasm of pleasure was quickly replaced by a shame that burned across his skin like fire. The Spider's round, disapproving face appeared before his own, and the indignity that came with it was tantamount to physical torture.

He would go in the bathroom and clean up, once the women had come out. For now, however, he would have to suffer with that cooling, sticky embarrassment against his inner thigh, turning to gel in the wiry nest of his pubic hair.

He realized then that he still had his mother's religious figurine in his pocket. The sin of such a thing—keeping it in his pants after what he'd just *done*—was unfathomable. He quickly removed the item and examined it for any . . . well, any excreted embarrassment. It looked okay.

Get rid of it, she'd said.

He went over to the mirrored vanity and placed the statuette on the wooden shelf. On the opposite side of the shelf from the box of condoms.

When the bathroom door finally cracked open, Toby was seated like a good and patient—

(housefly)

—boy on the edge of the filthy bed, hands in his lap to cover up the stain.

The vampire slipped out through the meager crack in the door upon a cloud of steam. Her hair was a mess, and her pale, slender torso was striated with reddish finger marks. Her makeup was smudged, her black lipstick smeared across the lower half of her face. There were bruises—*hickeys*—on her neck. She still wore her denim skirt, but it was unzipped along the left thigh, where Toby caught a glimpse of the sheer white panties she wore underneath.

She was holding a small plastic bag with some white powder in it.

"Are you okay?" he asked her. He kept glancing at the partway open bathroom door, wondering why Michaund hadn't come out, too. The shower was still running in there, the room filling up with steam.

"Why wouldn't I be okay?"

"I don't know. I was just worried about you."

"I'm not sure 'worry' was your primary emotion," she said, noticing the stain on the front of his shorts.

Ashamed, he repositioned himself on the bed but did not stand up.

The vampire took her tube top from the bed. As she tugged it on, Toby got a better look at the tattoo along the outside of her left breast—a simple black inked image of a fist. She straightened the top, then knelt before him on the floor. She ran a hand along the sweaty nape of his neck, drawing his face closer to hers.

"How does my breath smell?" she said, exhaling in his face.

It smelled . . . organic. Like the intimate, interior parts of someone. His eyes flicked back toward the partially open bathroom door.

That steam kept roiling out.

"We should leave," she said, standing up.

He didn't move, just stood there staring at the partially open door. He couldn't see anything except a section of the toilet and those cracked and rusty brown tiles.

"We should leave *now*," she said.

Toby got up off the bed.

He asked no questions as he drove her back downtown. She sat alone and silent in the back seat of the Town Car. At one point he glanced up at the rearview mirror, and when he couldn't see her reflection, he was not surprised. But then he repositioned the mirror and saw her slumped against the seat, gazing dreamily out the window at the passing traffic.

After a time, he asked, "Where am I taking you?"

She gave him an address, which he hoped was a residence, but it turned out to be a bus stop. Before he could say anything else, she had gotten out of the car and was crossing the street. He quickly rolled his window down and said, "Won't you tell me your name?"

"You know my name."

"I don't," he said. "You never told me."

She appeared to contemplate this. With her hair out of sorts and her makeup smeared, she looked like some helpless child playing dress up.

"Go home, Renfield," she said. "And thanks for the good time."

"No, wait—"

But she had already vanished, having slipped catlike down a narrow, darkened alleyway, hips ticking back and forth, back and forth, back and forth.

There and then gone.

ELEVEN

"I need to talk to you about something," Maureen said.

Greg was seated in a plush armchair in the living room, a Paul Desmond record on the turntable. The lights in the room were dimmed to a museum brightness, and there was a lowball glass of Macallan beside the armchair on an end table. He had the screenplay to *Hatchet Job* in his lap and a studious expression on his face.

Maureen had waited for Landon to leave the house, dressed in a crisp white shirt, pleated slacks, and his navy-blue blazer, before summoning up the courage to retrieve the scrapbook from Landon's gym bag and approach her soon-to-be husband.

Greg did not even look up at her when he said, almost dismissively, "What?"

She stood in front of him, the scrapbook containing those awful photos held at an angle away from her body, as if to bring it close to her might be to taint and stain her soul. When she didn't immediately respond—

"What is it, Maur?" This time, he looked up at her.

"I found this . . . this scrapbook or photo album or . . . whatever it is . . . in Landon's gym bag in his bedroom. I think you should look at it."

Greg's steely eyes ticked down to the scrapbook she held at waist level. It could have been radioactive, given how she held it so far away from her body.

"What do you mean you found something in Landon's gym bag?" Greg said. "What were you doing going through Landon's stuff?"

"I just need you to look at it," she said, thrusting the book in his direction, "and then I'll explain everything."

"Jesus, Maur, I'm trying to work." Yet he set the screenplay aside and took the album from her.

She watched as he opened it.

Watched as he stared at the glossy photograph pasted to the first page—the one of the dead woman's face, her eyes gouged out, her nose removed so that a bloody, triangular chasm now resided in the center of that face.

She watched as he turned to the next page and stared at the duo of photos there, too, equally as gruesome.

There were more photos—Maureen had looked at every single one—but Greg closed the book without going further. When he looked up at her, there was a strange expression on his face. One she couldn't readily read. It was an expression she'd never seen on him before.

"What the hell is this?" he asked.

"They're photos of a woman who was murdered and whose body was left in the desert outside the city," Maureen explained. "I googled the case. It happened just a few weeks ago."

"Why would you show me something like this?"

"It was in your son's bag, Greg."

"I don't understand what you were doing going through Landon's stuff." He glanced down at the scrapbook that sat closed in his lap now, that odd, unreadable expression still on his face. "I don't understand any of this."

She had promised not to give up Ross as her source, so she said, "I was putting some stuff away in Landon's closet when I saw the book in there."

"Maureen, these photos aren't *real*." Something akin to a chuckle juddered out of him, but the expression on his face did not change. "These are prop shots. You know—like on a movie set. They're fakes."

"I'm not a dummy, Greg. I know what I'm looking at. Go on— look at the rest of the photos, if you're not convinced. That's the corpse of a murdered woman. No one does makeup that good."

Greg sighed. He picked up his scotch, took a healthy swallow, then set the glass back down on a ceramic coaster. "I'm in the movie *business*, babe. Christ, I've made films with special effects just like this. These photos aren't real. I promise you."

Maureen shook her head. She felt suddenly agitated and unsettled, like she wanted to rearrange the curios on the fireplace mantel across the room, or maybe empty the kitchen cupboards and reorganize the glassware by size.

"Okay, look," she said. "I promised I wouldn't tell, but Landon's friend Ross—the kid who came here with him the night of the engagement party?—I ran into him downtown and he told me about the book. He said Landon had showed it to him, said it was of a dead woman who was found murdered in the desert. Ross also told me that Landon had come back to California weeks earlier, that he'd been staying at a motel. He said—"

Greg held up one hand. Said, "Stop."

She stopped.

"I want to get this straight," he said. "My son's stoner friend happened to bump into you somewhere downtown, told you Landon had this book with pictures of a murdered woman, and that he'd actually been back here in the States when he was supposed to be in Europe. Is that it?"

"He was very concerned. I believed what he was telling me."

"So you go hunting around in my son's stuff and find these photographs." It was a statement, not a question, and already Maureen could tell that Greg had poked through the fabricated parts of her story.

"Yes, okay," she admitted. "I went looking for the book after Ross told me about it. It wasn't by accident. But *look* at it, Greg."

"I've looked."

"Those photos are *real*."

"Maur—"

"And the fact that Landon was here in California for weeks—"

"That's not true, babe. He was in Europe the whole time. I saw the credit card statements."

"Ross was using your credit card. He said Landon came back weeks earlier on his own and stayed at a Motel 6 in Glendale for some reason." She didn't want to tell him she'd been to the motel already—it sounded too paranoid, and too much like she'd been snooping around behind his back—so she left that part out.

"What exactly is it that you're implying here, Maureen?"

She knew what she was implying—she knew what she *believed*— but it was harder to speak those words.

"The timeframe when Landon had come back to California lines up with the timeframe when that woman was killed," she said evenly. "The woman's name was Gina Fortunado. She was a schoolteacher from San Bernardino. That's all I'm saying. That's all I know. You can find plenty of news articles about it online, same as I did."

Greg picked up his iPhone from the end table, tapped at the screen.

"I couldn't just ignore this, so I'm bringing it to your attention," Maureen continued. "I think you should know what I know."

Greg read a portion of a news article aloud. Then he scrolled to another one and read that one, too. "Maureen, none of these articles even mention how the woman was killed. She could have been strangled, for all we know, yet you're showing—"

"The articles say she was mutilated, not strangled—"

"—yet you're showing me photos of some woman whose face is all cut up. I don't understand how you've even made the connection."

"Because of what Ross told me. Because of what *Landon* told *him*."

"The stoner kid," Greg mused again.

"He wasn't stoned when he was talking to me. He was nervous. Scared, even."

Greg sighed. "What would you like me to do about this?"

"I don't know," she said, and that was true. She had considered what to do with the book ever since she'd found it, but each scenario—go to the police? talk directly to Landon? make an anonymous phone call to the Sheriff's Department?—felt like she was undermining Greg and going behind his back. She couldn't do any of those things. Only one thing made sense: bring it to Greg's attention and let him decide what was best. Landon was his son; she wanted Greg to handle it from here.

"You know," Greg said, picking up his scotch again, "I could say it serves you right for being so susceptible, and for going off half cocked." He smiled at her, which she found enraged her, because it made her feel like a foolish child. "Maybe that's the fiction writer's part of your brain, elaborating and coming up with . . . I don't know . . . morbid little plots."

"That's not what this is."

"Listen, I'm sure that kid's story spooked you, and when you went rooting through my son's stuff—"

"Greg, it wasn't—"

"—and came upon this book, yes, of course, your imagination ran away with you."

She shook her head. Said, "No." Said, "It's not—"

"But it *is*," Greg said. He took another sip of his drink, the ice cubes knocking audibly together in the glass. Then he set both the drink and the scrapbook down on the end table and stood up. "This is a silly prank, Maureen. That's all it is. It's make believe. These kids were having you on. My son has an awful sense of humor and his friends are lackeys who do whatever he tells them to do."

It was what she had thought at first, too. But still . . .

Greg approached her, rubbed her left forearm with his hand, a warm hand, up and down, three times, which made her cringe because now she needed the *right* forearm rubbed up and down three times, but at the same time, didn't really want Greg to touch her in that moment. She was angry with him.

In her head, she heard Landon saying, *What dark secret are you trying to escape by wearing my father's life as a mask to cover it up?*

"My Funny Valentine" started playing on the phonograph, and Greg collected Maureen up in his arms.

She went stiffly.

He kissed the left side of her neck, down to the shoulder.

"What do we do about this?" she insinuated into his ear.

"What would you like me to do?"

"I think you should talk to Landon about it, see what he says."

"And tell him his soon-to-be stepmother went digging through his personal belongings? That she's accusing him of being a homicidal killer?"

"I didn't say that."

"It's what you're thinking."

She couldn't deny it.

"Tell him you found it," she said. "Or that Lucinda found it when she was cleaning his room."

Greg laughed. "Blame it on the housekeeper, huh? That old chestnut?"

"Ask him about returning from Europe weeks early, and staying at the Motel 6 in Glendale."

"My son wouldn't be caught dead in a Motel 6 in Glendale."

But he was there! her mind screamed, although she knew she could not say it.

"He also has a copy of my novel. He defaced my author photo."

"Jesus, Maureen, you're starting to sound paranoid."

"Go up and look at the book. It's in his gym bag, along with some drugs in his socks."

"Oh, for fuck's sake, babe," Greg said, expelling hot breath against her neck. Maureen felt his body stiffen against hers. He stopped swaying to the music.

"However you decide to do it, and whatever it is you decide to say," she said, "I think you should talk to him. Greg, those pictures in that book are real. And I can't imagine how he got them."

Greg detached himself from her. The song was still playing, Paul Desmond's alto sax a breathy anesthetic, yet Maureen's body felt tight and hot and ready to spin out of control. She looked at Greg's face as he pulled back from her, taking in the firm set of his jaw, the swivel of his eyes as they took her in—took all of her in.

"He's my *son*, Maureen. Pain-in-the-ass burden as he is, he's my son. And do you know what I'm desperately trying to do here?"

She shook her head.

"I'm trying to make us a *family*."

"Greg—"

"He's a problem kid, I know it, but he's not some . . . some . . . " He trailed off. "He's not whatever it is you think he is," he finished.

She thought of Landon advancing toward her that day in his bedroom, like some predatory animal about to pounce. Saying, *Maybe you love him, maybe you don't. But you certainly don't* know *him. And it makes me wonder why this marriage thing is happening so quickly.*

"I just thought you should know," she said. "I didn't know what else to do."

"Well," Greg said. "Then that's that." He pivoted back toward the end table and picked up his drink. "You want me to talk to him, then I'll talk to him. I'll talk to Landon. But I'm letting you know right now, Maureen—this is not the way to start things."

"Start what?"

"This life together."

She wanted to tell him about the uncomfortable and aggressive confrontation she'd had with Landon in his bedroom, wanted to tell him about how Landon had masturbated on the back porch that night by the pool even though he knew she was down in the kitchen where she could see him. She *couldn't*, of course—*couldn't* tell Greg those things—but they were shuttling through her mind nonetheless.

Ross's voice coming back to her now, echoing through the bleak chamber of her skull—

You only answer Landon's questions, you don't ask him questions of your own.

Greg finished his drink in one final swallow. Turning to her, he said, "I'm not a dummy, either, Maureen. I know this whole thing has moved very quickly between us. I didn't expect to fall in love with you like I did. It was so fast."

She shook her head. "What does that mean? What does that have to do with anything?"

"I'm saying that if you're having a change of heart, I'll understand," he said.

"No, Greg. That's not what I'm saying at all."

"Maybe it's too fast. Maybe there have been too many changes too quickly."

"That's not what this is about."

"Maybe this whole thing makes you uncomfortable."

"No, that's not—"

"I love you, Maur. If it's moving quickly, it's because I'm no spring chicken, and I want to hurry up and spend the rest of my life with you."

"I want that, too."

"Do you? Because I feel like you're hunting for a reason to put a wedge between us."

"That's not what this is at all."

"If you want to slow things down—"

"No!" She hadn't meant to shout it. More quietly, then: "No, Greg. I just thought . . . I just thought you should know about it. That scrapbook. Those pictures. About Landon and the motel."

"Well, now I know," he said.

He came to her, kissed her on her forehead, then slipped away into the kitchen where she could hear him begin to fix another drink.

She did something risky later that night, once Greg had gone to sleep: she got into her car and drove to a twenty-four-hour convenience store downtown where she purchased a burner phone and a prepaid SIM card. Then she drove out to a park, which was in the opposite direction to their home—a good distance from any place she would ordinarily find herself—and called the main line to the Los Angeles County Sheriff's Department. When a woman answered, Maureen asked for the name and phone number of the detective working the Gina Fortunado homicide. She figured it was a long shot, since she didn't give a name or reason for asking for this information, but the woman on the phone returned with a name and phone number. Maureen jotted the number down on a napkin she found in the glove compartment then immediately hung up.

The detective's name was William Renney. She sat behind the wheel of her car for a while, building up the courage to make this second phone call, knowing that at least part of what Greg had said earlier that evening was correct—she actually *didn't* know how Gina Fortunado had been murdered.

She dialed Detective Renney's phone number three times, deleting it three times, before allowing the call to go through.

It was closing on midnight, but the detective's phone rang only once before the call was answered.

The gruff voice said, "Renney."

"The woman whose body was found a few weeks ago in the desert? Gina Fortunado? Was her face all cut up? Her eyes removed? Her fingers cut off?"

There was a pause on the other end of the line before the gruff voice returned: "Can I get your name, ma'am?"

"I'll give you my name if you can confirm for me how that woman was killed."

Another pause, lengthier this time. She could hear the police detective breathing on the other end of the line. Or maybe that was her own breath rushing back to her. She couldn't be sure. Her heart was slamming against the wall of her chest, her palms clammy.

"She was cut up," said the detective, and Maureen could feel the hairs on her head prickle. "Just as you said she was. Can I get your name, ma'am? I'd like to—"

Maureen quickly disconnected the call.

The following day, Greg left for New York to meet with investors. It was an impromptu trip, some crisis he needed to deal with involving the impending production of *Hatchet Job*, and he couldn't be sure how long he'd be gone. This would have left Maureen unnerved if

Landon wasn't also heading to Vegas with some friends; in fact, she watched Landon from the front windows as he languished at the crest of the driveway smoking a cigarette until an SUV came and collected him, shuttling him off. She felt a palpable weight rise off her the second they pulled away.

Since the conversation with Greg about the scrapbook and its awful photos the night before, she had heard nothing more about it. She didn't know if Greg had spoken with Landon yet or not, and when she attempted to broach the subject while he was hastily packing for New York, his agitation was clear: he wasn't in the mood to talk about it.

"These sons of bitches sign contracts then think they can renegotiate the details *after* the fact," he grumbled as he wedged socks into his suitcase, which was propped up on the foot of their bed. "They realize I'm a lawyer, right?"

"I'm sure it'll all work out," she told him as she stood helpless in the bedroom doorway.

With both of them out of the house for a few days, it at least gave her time to clear the sordid business of the scrapbook from her mind and return to the story she was writing, if to only occupy her thoughts:

> There is no one standing there.
>
> No tall, lanky, faceless figure behind her.
>
> There is only the man—her lover—in bed, snoring in great pulls and drags.
>
> Yet when she looks back at the altar mirror, the tall, lanky, faceless figure is back, standing right behind her, his hand on her shoulder. She opens her mouth to say something, but before any words can come out, the figure retreats from her, receding into the darkness of the motel room. Something glints in the figure's hand; it takes her a moment to

realize it is a knife of some kind. A bladed instrument, whose edge gleams with a preternatural light even in the dimness of the motel room.

"Watch this," says the figure in the mirror, as he goes to the bed and peels the pale sheet off the slumbering form of her lover. It is no longer her lover—no longer the man she had come here with in the middle of the afternoon for sex, companionship, what feels like a bit of misplaced self-worth—but a woman instead: right there on the mattress.

"Watch *thisssss*," the figure repeats, stretching out that final word the way a cartoon snake might, *ssssss*, and then he leans over the slumbering, motionless form of the woman, and lowers the gleaming blade to her face.

She can hear the sound of the blade piercing the woman's flesh: an audible *pop!* like a burst soap bubble. The blade sinks in deep, penetrating the cavity of one eye socket. The room around her—the *real* room—is still dark, because the drapes are drawn, and the man (her lover) sleeps in pulls and drags on the bed, but in the mirror, the room brightens, and she watches as the figure slices away pieces of the woman's face: an eye, a nose, the delicate satellite dish of one ear. Blood dribbles down onto the white sheets. As he props open the woman's mouth with the blood-smeared blade to remove her tongue, she can hear him saying, over and over again like a prayer, "You are too young and pretty for my dad."

There is something else reflected in the altar mirror, something slightly out of focus and refusing to cooperate. She sees it there on the small sofa against the opposite wall, an item whose reflection refuses to sharpen, that is determined to remain blurry. She can make out the approximate shape of the thing, no bigger than a laundry basket, really, although the shape is different, and while it refuses to resolve into focus, she knows what it is without question, without having to *see* it with any clarity, because she just *knows*, because it is a part of her in a way, and the knowing makes her heart lurch within the tightening confines of her chest . . .

—◇—

That evening, after a late dinner-for-one of filet mignon, grilled asparagus, and two glasses of Castello di Ama Chianti, Maureen was in the kitchen doing the dishes (she had given Lucinda the week off) while one of Greg's easy jazz records played on the living room stereo. In that moment, there came a sound that, to Maureen's ears, was very much like an infant's yowl, followed by a downbeat in the music that didn't quite jibe. She froze at the sink, hot water running over her hands. When she heard footsteps, she realized the yowl was the squeal of the front door, the out of place downbeat the door itself closing against the jamb.

Drying her hands with a dishtowel, she stepped out into the living room wondering if there had been some change in Greg's plans that would have him returning home at this hour.

The foyer was empty, but she could hear footfalls receding down the hall, in the direction of Greg's home office.

"Greg? Hello?"

Or maybe it was just the music messing with her after all. She went to the stereo system and turned off the phonograph. The music slowed and warbled to a stop, a thick blanket of silence draping over the house.

When she stepped back into the hall, she saw Landon standing there, staring back at her.

She jumped at the sight of him, startled. She felt something catch in her throat, too, but somehow still managed to speak. "Landon. You're supposed to be in Vegas."

"You have no idea what you've done," said Landon. Despite his actual words, Landon's tone was easygoing, almost jovial. She nearly expected him to smile as he stood there, staring at her from the opposite end of the hall.

No, not jovial, she thought. *He's toying with me, the way a cat will toy with a mouse before it eats the thing.*

"I've got a camera set up in my bedroom," Landon said. "Did you know that? Greg doesn't, and Lucinda doesn't, so I guess there's no reason for you to know that." He shrugged one shoulder, as if this was no big deal. He was holding something in his hand, Maureen saw, though she couldn't make out what it was—something small and square and black. "I don't check it every day, but maybe I should start. Point being, you've been a nosy parker, Maureen."

"I seem to recall you telling me you'd gone into my office and looked at the writing on my computer," she said to him. "So I guess that makes us both a couple of nosy parkers."

At this, Landon *did* smile. "Yeah, that's funny. I like that." But then the smile fell away. "I really wish you hadn't gone to Greg with that scrapbook."

"So he spoke to you about it," she said, yet in this moment, that knowledge brought her little relief.

"I wish you would have just come to me instead."

He took a step toward her—not menacingly, but just as casual as you please. Nonetheless, she instinctively took a step back.

"I know what you must be thinking about me," he said. "I know what *I'd* be thinking. And I've read your work, so I know how an idea in your pretty little writer's head must be able to . . . I guess, easily grow wings and take flight, yeah? Like a bird?"

Another step forward.

Another step back.

"If you like that phrase, Maureen, you can feel free to use it in your next book, if you ever write one. We're about to become family, so I guess it's all about share and share alike."

"If that's the case, why don't you share with me where you got those photographs."

"That would have been the perfect question to ask me *before* taking them to Greg."

"All right," she said. "But I'm asking you now instead."

"They're not my photos at all."

"Whose are they?"

"They're *Greg's*," said Landon. That smile insinuated itself across his lips again, but only for a moment—there and then gone, a ripple on the surface of a pond. "Dear old Dad, and your soon-to-be husband."

"Cut it out, Landon. Stop with the games."

"Scout's honor," he said, and held up one hand in that gesture. The item in his other hand looked like an old VHS videocassette. "No games. No lies. I found that scrapbook in Greg's back office, buried at the bottom of a filing cabinet. I took it so I could snap some photos of it on my phone, in case I ever needed to go to the cops with it. I was going to put it back, but I guess I forgot. And now he knows I've seen it. And now he knows *you've* seen it."

"Cut the shit," she said. "Your timeline doesn't add up. I know when that girl was killed." Ross said he'd seen Landon with the scrapbook at the motel, which made Landon's lie impossible—he hadn't been in the house prior to his arrival on the night of their engagement party, so the scrapbook had been with him all along. She didn't want to give up Ross as her source, however, so she said, "I'll get your father on the phone right now and we can have a discussion about it."

"Maybe don't be so quick to involve him any further," he said. He paused in his slow approach toward her. He was wearing a blazer and a button-down shirt, with a blood-red necktie, loosened and slightly askew.

"The woman in those photos was murdered a few weeks ago," Maureen said, "so if you don't tell me where you got those photos, I'm going to call the police, and you can tell *them*."

"You don't scare me, Maureen." He smiled again, then shook his head like he was disappointed in her.

"I'm not playing ar—"

He moved toward her and she backed up against the wall, which only made him laugh. He went right past her, down into the sunken living room, and over to the wet bar that stood against one wall. He proceeded to make himself a drink. "Want one?"

She didn't answer. She patted her pockets for her cell phone, but it wasn't on her. Had she left it in the kitchen? Somewhere else in the house?

Landon shook some ice cubes into a lowball glass, poured in some gin, then a splash of tonic.

"You're wrong about the woman, by the way," he said. He turned and faced her, the drink in one hand, that videotape in the other. "Doesn't really matter, I guess, but in an effort for full honesty, I just want you to know you're wrong."

"I read the news articles about her. About what happened to her. Gina Fortunado. That was her name."

Landon's thin lips twisted around, as if he was chewing on a thought. He said, "You think Greg's got a solid alibi for those twenty-four hours?"

"Jesus Christ, Landon, this is absurd."

"Sometimes," Landon said, "dear old Dad isn't where he claims to be. Maybe even now—maybe he's not really in New York."

"What about you? You don't seem to be where you claim to be, either."

He snorted a laugh, the lowball glass halfway to his lips. "You mean Vegas?"

"I mean Europe. I mean a Motel 6 in Glendale."

He hadn't been expecting that: a ripple of surprise washed across his face. It gave Maureen some mild satisfaction to see it.

"What are you talking about?" he said, the tone of his voice less confident now.

"You know what I'm talking about. You came back from Europe weeks earlier than you said. Do *you* have an alibi? Because that was around the same time that woman was murdered."

He frowned. The expression was nearly childlike, and under different circumstances, Maureen would have either laughed or maybe even felt sorry for him. "Don't talk to me about timelines," he said. "I know all about timelines. I'm meticulous about timelines."

"What were you doing staying at that motel? Why didn't you just come home?"

"It's none of your business what I was doing."

"Really? I thought we were sharing. But if you think you're going to convince me that your father has anything to do—"

"You're not my mother."

It was such a childish and pathetic thing to say that Maureen couldn't help it—despite her rising apprehension, something like a small laugh rose up from her throat. "No," she said, shaking her head. "I'm most certainly not. But if you don't want to tell me what you were doing at that motel, then maybe that's something else you can talk to the police about. Or if you'd prefer, I can—"

"I came home early to *meet* you, Maureen." Landon took a small sip of his drink then smacked his lips together. "Not face-to-face at first, but just to . . . to *watch* you. To *see* you. Maybe begin to piece together the type of person you were from afar—this stranger who was about to become a member of my family—before I actually gave you that big old mama bear hug."

"To spy on me, you mean."

The notion that, for weeks, Landon Dawson had been watching her as she went shopping, ate brunch at restaurants, went running in the evenings, maybe even peered in at her through the windows of this very house as he stood out in the street at night, made her more than just uneasy—it made her feel ill.

"I had a right to know," Landon said. "Do you think I enjoyed reading about your engagement to my father online? Do you think that made me feel good?"

"What are you talking about?"

"Do you think it was fair for me to learn that my father was going to get remarried *again* by reading some poorly written blurb on the *Cosmopolitan* website?"

"That's not true. Your father told you about us months ago."

"Is that what he told you? What a swell guy."

"I don't believe you. I don't believe any of this."

"That's fine." He finished off his drink, smacked his lips again, then set the empty glass down on the top of the bar. "You can believe what you want. I don't care. We all have secrets, Maureen. I've got them, good old Greg's got plenty. Even you've got one. It wasn't that difficult to find out your secret, Maureen, because something like that sticks to a person like a shadow."

It suddenly felt like she had ice water pumping through her veins. "What do you know?"

"The truth," he said, positioning his hands in the air as if pretending to grip an invisible steering wheel. "But that's not important. Point is, if you don't want to believe the things I tell you, then I guess I don't care. In the meantime, why don't you give this a watch? Maybe it'll change your opinion of things."

He tapped a finger against the videocassette which he had previously set down on the bar.

(... *because something like that sticks to a person like a shadow*)

He stretched and yawned wide, like a lion in a zoo, then announced that he was tired and going to bed. Maureen maneuvered out of his way as he slunk across the living room and back down the hall. She didn't move as she listened to him climb the stairs. By the time his bedroom door gently closed, she was trembling.

She went over to the wet bar and stared down at the videocassette. It was blank, no markings of any kind on it.

(If you don't want to believe the things I tell you, then I guess I don't care. In the meantime, why don't you give this a watch? Maybe it'll change your opinion of things.)

Where was her phone?

It was in the kitchen, beside the rack of drying pans and glassware.

She picked it up, set it down.

Picked it up, set it down.

Picked it up—

She should call Greg. Or maybe she should just call the fucking police. Truth was, she didn't know *what* to do. She was even considering leaving the house and getting a room at the Marriott because she certainly didn't want to spend the night alone in this house with Greg's son.

(In the meantime, why don't you give this a watch?)

She set the phone down then stepped back out into the living room. Her eyes locked on that blank videocassette. She didn't want to know what was on it—didn't want to even touch it—yet something seemed to draw her toward it. Instead of picking it up, she began to frantically reorganize the glasses atop the bar—the lowball glasses out front in a tidy row, highball glasses behind, some drinker's version of a chessboard. Then she reversed it: highball glasses in front, lowball behind. Then various other arrangements, high low high low, low high low high, as her heartbeat continued to race and sweat caused her armpits to go swampy.

(In the meantime, why don't you)

I'm having a panic attack.

She rushed down the hall, snatching her car keys from the ceramic bowl beside the door. She bolted out into the night and ran across the driveway to her car. Unlocked the door remotely, *beep-boop*, then flung open the rear passenger door.

Snapped and unsnapped the seatbelt.

Furiously.

In a panic.

Over and over.

And over.

And over.

And over.

And—

—until her heartbeat regulated. When she finally extracted herself from the back seat of the car, tears were standing in her eyes, and her body felt wounded somehow, like she'd taken a beating and was covered in bruises.

She felt a bit more at ease by the time she re-entered the house. Even when she saw that blank videocassette sitting on the corner of the wet bar, she still felt a strange serenity shuttling through her entire body. Swiping the tears from her eyes, she went over to the bar and picked up the tape.

Greg's office doubled as a small screening room. There was a VCR in here, as well as all sorts of other equipment—DVD and LaserDisc players, several television sets, a film projector and screen, even an old Betamax machine. There were four leather recliners in here, too, similar to the type that were now found in movie theaters. Maureen switched on one of the TVs and the VCR. Her anxiety was ramping up again, so she switched the VCR on and off several times before she forced herself to stop. Then she slid the videocassette into the machine's mouth, where it was automatically gobbled up. She could hear the gears begin to whir.

She sat in one of the leather chairs. Her hands were wrestling with each other, and she kept her knees pressed so tightly together she could feel her calf muscles beginning to strain.

Please don't be what I think this is, she prayed.

Because what she was thinking was photographs in a scrapbook are bad enough, but actual live videotape of such a thing—

But that was not what it was at all.

It was a movie.

An old one, shot maybe on 16mm film stock. Grainy in places. An opening aerial shot of a bright, desert wasteland. A cheap production, because she caught a glimpse of the helicoptor's shadow briefly against a mesa, which, back then, was how such aerial footage would have been shot.

Then the film's title appeared, superimposed over that bleached, barren landscape:

HIGH DESERT

No musical score or accompanying soundtrack, except for the incessant mechanical pulsing of a heartbeat that seemed to intensify with each passing second—*whuh-WHUMP, whuh-WHUMP, whuh-WHUMP!*

Cast and crew names came and went as the camera navigated high over the desert floor. After a time, however, the meandering nature of the shot appeared to lock into focus: there was something out-of-place on the ground down there, strewn about among the desert plants and bone-colored stones. Something that did not belong.

Maureen sat forward in her seat.

The camera drew in closer to the thing on the ground, and in the upper right-hand corner of the screen, Maureen glimpsed the blink-and-you'd-miss-it shadow of the helicopter again.

It's a dead body. She realized this even before the image of the thing came into focus. *It's the dead body of a woman.*

The camera drew closer, closer.

She could see the way the head was twisted around on the neck, the way the limbs were splayed at unnatural angles. She could see blood on one hand where the fingers should have been—where they had been hastily cut away.

Jump cut to a close-up of the woman's mutilated face, just as the final card of the opening credits flashed across the screen:

Written & Directed by
GREGORY DAWSON

And for several moments, Maureen heard nothing but the steady rush of blood in her ears.

It was a film about a serial killer who stalked and murdered women in Southern California. The copyright date on the movie was 1990, although the grainy quality of the film make it look like something shot in the 1970s. It was a low-budget production, with copious amounts of gore, a lackluster script, and stilted acting, yet Maureen watched it until the final credits rolled. When it was over, she felt as though a fist had formed in the center of her belly, and was now squeezing her insides. After she got up and shut off the television, she stood there for a moment in Greg's darkened office, a sheen of sweat covering every inch of her body.

The women in the film were all murdered in a variety of increasingly ludicrous ways, yet that opening shot of the dead woman in the desert haunted her. It seemed out of place with the rest of the film—a bit of *cinéma vérité*, overlit yet understated in all its gruesomeness compared to the rest of the film. Moreover, the way the woman's face had been cut up was too similar to the photos in Landon's scrapbook. She might have convinced herself this was all part of Landon's elaborate prank at her expense—that the photos in the scrapbook *were* special effects shots, just as Greg had suggested when she'd showed them to him, and possibly from this very movie—except for the fact that she had made that anonymous call to the detective working the homicide in the desert. The detective had confirmed that the woman in the desert had been cut up.

The detective could've been lying. He could have been saying what I wanted to hear, in an effort to get me to tell him who I was and why I was calling.

But she didn't think that was the case.

If the photos in Landon's scrapbook were scenes from Greg's movie, why didn't Greg recognize them when I showed them to him?

Because he had made that movie over thirty years ago. Maybe he didn't remember.

If the photos are real, then what is their connection to a thirty-four-year-old low-budget slasher movie that Greg wrote and directed early in his career?

The answer to that came unbidden into her mind, swift as a bullet fired from a gun: Landon had seen the film, had been inspired by it, and had committed a murder that copied the murder in the opening scene of the movie. And now that she caught him with those photos, he was trying to lay the blame on Greg.

She left Greg's office and moved quietly down the hall toward her writing room. The house was dark and silent, which meant either Landon had gone back out, or he was upstairs in his bedroom. In her writing room, she locked the door, then switched on the small lamp on the desk beside her laptop. When she ran a finger across the track pad, her work-in-progress appeared on the screen. She was about to close out the document, but instead, in a fury, she wrote:

> She can *hear* the steadfast pounding of her heart as she stares at the thing on the motel couch reflected in the altar mirror. It's blurry, as if the mirror cannot bring it into focus. On the bed, the tall, swarthy figure continues to mutilate the woman while, beside the woman, her lover sleeps.
>
> She turns and looks into the darkened motel room at her back. Everything is as it should be, with her lover sleeping soundly, and no one else in the room. But when she turns back to the altar mirror, the tall, dark figure is still there, curled like a vulture or maybe a question mark over the body of the woman on the mattress. The blurry, indistinct shape on the couch is still there, too, and somehow that disturbs her more than the tall man with the knife and the dead woman bleeding out on the mattress. These images—they are like reverse vampires, she realizes, visible only in the mirrored surface of the altar glass.
>
> With one bloodied hand, the killer points to the sofa, and at the blurry, indistinct thing sitting there—
>
> —a thing that moves slightly in all its blurriness.
>
> "Maybe you've got dirty secrets of your own," says the figure.
>
> She wants to scream.
>
> She brings her hands to her mouth.
>
> The tall, swarthy figure laughs. Then he turns back to the woman on the bed and goes back to work.

She forced herself to stop. Her hands were shaking and she could hear that rush of blood funneling through her ears again. There was half a mug of cold coffee on the desk; she swallowed it down in two gulps then grimaced at the taste.

She pulled up a browser and typed Landon's name into the search bar. What appeared on the screen were mostly articles about Greg which happened to mention Landon in some capacity. There was a photo from a Hollywood premiere that featured Greg and Callie Tulane, Greg's wife from his short-lived third marriage. Maureen had seen this photo before, back when she and Greg had first started dating—like any red-blooded American woman, she had googled him—and she had been intimidated by his third wife's beauty (not to mention intimidated by the prospect of a third wife, period). Callie Tulane was an actress in her mid-twenties, slim and gorgeous; even now, the sight of Greg with his arm around this woman's hourglass waist made Maureen feel like the butt of some cruel joke.

What she hadn't realized at the time she'd first come across this photo was that Landon stood just slightly out of focus in the background. He was taller than both his father and his stepmother, his height exaggerated all the more by a wavy pompadour of hair. He held his head slightly downturned, so that he was gazing at the photographer with a pair of steely eyes beneath his brow. It was not a grin he wore on his face, but rather some semblance of predatory smirk. The sight of him in that photo caused her to get up and check the lock on the door.

She scrolled through several more pages until the headline of a newspaper article caused her to stop:

WIFE OF HOLLYWOOD PRODUCER DROWNS IN POOL

This was Charity Sloane, Greg's second wife. Greg had told her that Charity had drowned in the swimming pool of their Santa Monica home. A terrible accident, he had said, and that was about *all* he had said. What Greg had left out—and what the article made clear—was that the medical examiner believed she had drowned due to a combination of excessive alcohol and barbiturates in her system. The article also mentioned that it had been nineteen-year-old Landon who had discovered his stepmother's body floating face down in the swimming pool.

Why didn't Greg tell me that part?

Because Greg Dawson seldom spoke about his son.

There was a photo of Charity included with the article—another young bombshell—as well as a photo of the house where she had drowned.

It was not some house in Santa Monica.

It was this very house.

Why lie to me about that?

Because maybe Greg thought she wouldn't want to live in a house where his ex-wife had died.

Why do you keep making excuses?

She had no answer for that. Instead, she silently chastised herself for having done only a cursory search of Greg online when they'd first started dating—all the cheery, positive headlines that made her feel good about the man she had so quickly agreed to marry. It was as if some part of her knew that everyone carried darkness within them, and she hadn't truly wanted to unearth anything like that about Greg.

Does that make me a fool?

She searched online for Gale Dawson, Landon's birth mother and Greg's first wife. And while there were plenty of Gale Dawsons online, none of them appeared to be the person she was looking for.

I should stop this. I'm making things worse for myself. I'm scaring myself for no reason.

But wasn't there a reason?

She was about to close the laptop when one final thought occurred to her.

She pulled up the website for public arrest records in Los Angeles County. As she typed in Landon's name, she was thinking of the story his friend Ross—Uptown—had told her that day at the coffee shop, about the girl they'd gone to college with, and how Landon had done something to her one night that had upset her greatly. She wasn't sure what she expected to find, but she thought there was a good chance Landon had been arrested for some indiscretion in the past.

One hit came back.

A little over a year ago, Landon Dawson was charged with assault and battery. According to the website, the charges were ultimately dropped, which did not surprise Maureen. What surprised her was the name of the person who had filed the charges.

Callie Tulane.

Greg's third wife.

Maureen sat back in her chair and stared at the computer screen for several moments. The empty coffee mug was still beside the laptop, and she absently began turning the mug around, repositioning the direction the mug's handle was pointing—around and around and around. She stopped only when she placed her fingers back on the keyboard and typed in Callie Tulane's name.

She was an actress in her mid-twenties who had intuited (Maureen supposed) that a relationship with a movie producer might advance her career. It didn't: the marriage lasted less than a year, and according to the tabloid articles Maureen read, the relationship was rife with discord and infidelity on both sides. Callie owned a small acting studio in Sherman Oaks, and there was a photo of Callie on the studio's website, an airbrushed glamour shot, hazy around the edges, though her beauty was not lost on Maureen, just as it hadn't been in the photo from the Hollywood premiere with Landon leering over her shoulder.

She jotted down the address of the studio on a slip of paper, then paused.

What am I doing?

She didn't know.

The house still dark and quiet, she found her cell phone in the kitchen. Dialed Greg's number. It did not ring, but instead went immediately to voicemail.

It's three hours later in New York, she reminded herself. *He's probably asleep.*

On the heels of that, she heard Landon whisper in her head—*maybe he's not really in New York.*

"Stop it," she scolded herself aloud.

On the pool deck, a motion sensor light came on. Maureen froze. Through the window over the kitchen sink, she could see the tall, slender frame of Landon Dawson standing by the edge of the pool. He was nude, his body practically hairless except for a thatch of thick black pubic hair at his groin. When he positioned his arms out in preparation to dive, Maureen turned quickly away.

Still, she heard the splash.

TWELVE

Toby Kampen returned to The Coffin on a wave of excited anticipation, desperate to see the nameless vampire again. This time, he'd even brought her a gift—a hardback copy of *Dracula* that he had stolen from the public library earlier in the day, his favorite passages meticulously underlined. He waited for her in the club that night on his usual barstool, a tepid bottle of beer in one hand, a tequila drink (with real lemon) on the bar beside him should she arrive thirsty. But she did not appear to him that night. He stayed until the club closed at two in the morning, and he couldn't deny the deflated sense of disappointment he felt as he drove the Town Car back to the apartment complex on Chamber Street.

Over the next several nights, he returned to The Coffin. When she failed to show herself, he began to wonder if she'd abandoned this club for good. Perhaps she was being cautious: she had used this place as a hunting ground, had absconded with a victim— Michaund—whom she had devoured in the steamy bathroom of that awful motel, and perhaps now she was staying away to keep some distance from the place. It was smart. Maybe he should be staying away, too.

On the fifth night, as he scanned the smoky dance floor while absently peeling the label off his bottle of beer, Michaund approached him. The sight of her startled him, and he bolted off his stool, his instinct to flee from her sudden and undeniable. Yet he didn't. He just stood there as she confronted him, thumping him not-so-friendly on the chest with one fist. Two other women stood behind her, decidedly more muscular than Michaund, more masculine than Toby, thick arms folded over their broad chests. To Toby, they looked disconcertingly like bodyguards.

He had suffered nightmares over the past several nights of Michaund, dead and gutted in a bathtub filling with pinkish water. Her throat shredded to bloody ribbons, eyes wide and blindly staring into the spray of the showerhead. Enveloped in steam.

"Where's your friend?" Michaund asked, and Toby could tell she was angry.

He thought, *She's undead. She's been turned. She's a creature of the night now, too, just like the nameless vampire herself.*

He studied her neck for signs of puncture wounds but couldn't see any in the darkness of the club.

"She stole my coke and then you two fuckers left me in that rat-hole motel," Michaund said. "That was some bullshit. So where *is* she?"

"I don't know."

Michaund looked at the tequila drink beside him at the bar, untouched.

"I don't believe you," she said. "Tell me where she is."

"I don't know where she is."

"Tell me her name."

"I don't know her name."

"You are full of shit, fuck boy." She struck him again, this time with a closed fist across the left side of his face. The force of it rocked him to one side, and he gripped the edge of the bar so he wouldn't topple to the floor. "Tell that cunt she owes me. And if I see her in here again, I'll cut her face."

She shoved the tequila drink off the bar, the booze splashing against the front of his shorts, the glass breaking on the floor at his feet. The bartender noticed but didn't say anything. Then Michaund and her two bodyguards wove through the crowd toward the club's exit.

"Hey," the bartender said, tapping Toby hard between the shoulder blades while Toby massaged the left side of his jaw. "I think it's time you get the fuck out of here. You don't belong here, anyway."

"I didn't do anything."

"I said get the fuck out."

Toby got the fuck out.

He drove around for an unknowable amount of time, carving passageways up and down the boulevards, prowling shark-like in that massive champagne-colored automobile. The left side of his jaw had begun to swell and there was a split in his lower lip that dribbled a thread of blood, but it wasn't the pain that aggrieved him; rather, it was the sense that the vampire had slipped through his fingers, having vanished unencumbered into the night. He drove now with a sense of desperation, studying the clientele standing outside the clubs, the bouncers beneath the neon lights, the raucous catcalls and shrill curses lobbed into the air from every intersection. Someone threw a glass bottle at the windshield of his car; the bottle shattered, some sudsy liquid sprayed across the glass, and Toby jerked the wheel hard enough to hop a curb.

The bartender was right, of course: he didn't belong here.

He didn't belong *anywhere.*

At one particular intersection, as he eased the Town Car to a stop before a red light, he peered out the open driver's-side window. On the corner stood two homeless men squabbling over something, backlit against the neon lights in the window of a Chinese food joint. There was an alley that ran behind the joint, and a figure stood there in the gloom, staring back at Toby. It was boy, maybe twelve or thirteen years old, although Toby had never been very good at guessing ages. The kid took one step closer to the mouth of the alley, and that was when Toby could see that the kid was actually Puke-Breath Donald, the sometimes-friend/sometimes-bully from Toby's childhood. Donald hadn't aged a day in all these intervening years. He stood there in the smoky darkness of the alleyway staring at Toby with eyes that seemed to be filling up with a preternatural—

A car horn blared.

Toby glanced up to see that the traffic light had turned green.

He turned back toward the alley, but the boy—Donald—was gone.

It was closing on midnight, and he was about to give up for the night when he happened to turn down one particular street that was dark except for a lighted marquee over a set of iron doors. The single word on the marquee caught his eye:

FIST

Spray-painted on the iron doors was a symbol of a fist—an identical match to the tattoo he'd spied along the swell of the vampire's breast that night at the motel.

Much like The Coffin, this club had no bouncer at the door, no queue of people lined up along the sidewalk to get in. For all Toby could tell, the place was closed, a relic from some bygone era. Yet that lighted marquee coupled with the spray-painted fist on the doors called to him.

She's in there.

He suddenly knew this without question.

He parked the Town Car a few blocks away, then hurried up the street with the stolen copy of *Dracula* tucked under one arm. When he gripped the iron handle of the door, he feared he'd find it locked, but it wasn't. He pulled it open then slipped inside a long, dark corridor with dim museum lights in the ceiling and a lush crimson carpet beneath his sneakers. At the far end of the corridor was a red velvet curtain. There was also what looked like a ticket window beside the curtain, a woman behind it wearing a facemask over her nose and mouth.

As he approached the window, the woman asked, "Are you alone?"

"Yeah."

"Tat?"

"What?"

"You have the tat?"

"What's a tat?"

"Tattoo," the woman said, clearly annoyed.

"Uh, no. I don't have any tattoos."

"Hundred bucks."

"For what?" he said. "A tattoo?"

"Hundred bucks to get in," she said, and then she actually leaned forward to observe him from head to toe. He was wearing grubby Converse, tube socks, cargo shorts, and a black T-shirt that said GO FUCK YOURSELF. "What are you supposed to be, anyway? Do you even know where you are?" the woman asked him, then nodded at the book under his arm. "This isn't a library."

"I'm looking for someone."

The woman laughed, the fabric of her facemask puffing in and out. "Oh, you'll find someone, all right," she said. Then added, "Or *they'll* find *you*."

He dug the remaining cash he'd stolen from the Spider from the pocket of his cargo shorts, peeled off five twenties, then passed them through the slot in the ticket window. The woman was wearing a T-shirt that said CRUST PUNKS VS. RIOT GRRRLS and she was missing the tip of her left index finger. The gauges in her ears stretched her lobes to ungodly proportions.

"Through the curtain," she said.

He passed through the red velvet curtain and into another dimly lit corridor. There was a second curtain at the end of this hall, scarlet as blood, and he passed through that one as well. He came out into a dark, circular room, thick with pot smoke. Soft piano music was tinkling from hidden speakers. Plush sofas lined the circumference of the room, while at the center, spotlighted on a raised platform, an emaciated woman was contorting in a variety of impossible positions. She was nude, and the thinness of her frame coupled with those acrobatic positions she was twisting herself into revealed a stark, xylophonic display of ribs, elbows, knees. Some of the people on the sofas smoked hookah pipes, others were pouring drinks from a silver cart in front of them. Everyone was dressed in evening wear—suits and ties, cocktail dresses, expensive wristwatches and shiny shoes. There was a bar at the far side of the room, the bartenders—even the women—bare-chested.

Long glass tables were set before each of the sofas. On those tables, Toby could see a variety of disparate items, things he might expect to find at a yard sale or estate sale, rather than in a place like this—old books, glass boxes, some jewelry, even a long-barreled revolver. The items were being examined by the patrons seated at each of the sofas, one by one, and with a reverence that struck Toby as nearly sycophantic.

Toby clung to one wall and roved slowly along the room's perimeter, gliding like a shadow or maybe like smoke behind each of the sofas. He saw a door at the opposite side of the room, a sign above it that said, simply:

Fuck Room

When he made it all the way around to the bar, he debated whether or not to order his usual beer. At a place like The Coffin, he could fade into the background. No one paid him any attention. He could have set his hair on fire and no one would have noticed. In this place, however, he stood out like a lump of shit in a punchbowl. There weren't even any barstools at the bar upon which he could perch.

You're a fly, he reminded himself. *Just a fly on the wall. No one pays you any attention, remember? No one bothers with you unless you bother with them. You are a creature nonexistent.*

When the topless female bartender met his eyes, Toby averted his gaze. He looked out upon the room, and at the well-dressed people on the sofas. On that platform under the spotlight, the contortionist was balancing on one leg, flamingo-style, her spine bent all the way backward so that the back of her head touched her ass. Her body was all sharp angles and pointy, jutting hips and ribs. Her shaved pudendum looked to Toby like a delicate scalpel incision drawn through a mound of modeling clay.

He almost didn't see her. She was dressed in a frilly, blood-red ball gown with a veil over her face, and was seated on one of those sofas surrounded by similarly dressed women and a couple of men in sharp black suits. She wore none of the dark makeup she had each time he'd seen her at The Coffin, but the intricate tattoos along her arms were unmistakable.

He floated more than walked in her direction. Lingered like a bad odor in the vicinity of her party. A few people glanced in his direction, and Toby could sense them eyeing him up. He felt like dinner. For a moment, he wondered if he was in the presence of an entire clan of vampires—if this club was, in fact, their den.

She was in mid-laugh when she turned her head and saw him standing there. He watched the laughter dry up, the judder of her larynx cranking to a slow stop as she recognized him. She looked different behind that veil and without all that makeup on, sure, but that didn't give him pause: Toby Kampen was used to people wearing masks. The Spider wore the mask of his mother, after all. And Toby himself, of course, was actually a Human Fly. No one was truly as they seemed.

He smiled and held up a hand in salutation, but did not deign to approach the sofa and her entourage. Everyone in the vampire's party was looking at him now. One of the dark-suited men leaned over to one of the women and whispered something into her ear. The woman broke out in a sly smile, then squeezed the dark-suited man high on the upper thigh.

This is not how a fly blends, he scolded himself, suddenly feeling targeted—foolishly, dangerously so. *This is not how a fly remains a creature nonexistent.*

The vampire excused herself from her party and rose from the sofa in that frilly, blood-red gown. She drifted over to him, and even though he could not see her feet beneath the hem of that dress, he imagined her hovering inches off the floor, like something divorced from the rules of gravity.

"What are you doing here?"

"I came to find you," he said. "I brought you a gift."

She glanced down at the book in his hands. He saw that the pupils of her eyes were no longer repositories of that dim, yellow light.

"Your fangs are gone, too," he said.

"What?"

He bared his own teeth at her and pointed to them, as if in explanation.

"This is not a place for you," she told him, and he looked around, suddenly confused, suddenly disoriented, suddenly thinking they were in The Coffin, so where had all these people in suits and ball gowns suddenly come from?

"I'm . . . I'm . . . confused," he said.

"Be a good Renfield," she said, "and go on home. I'll find you another night. When I need you."

He lowered his voice, and brought his face so close to hers that his nose brushed the fabric of the veil she wore. "I thought you killed and ate that woman from the motel the other night," he said. "But then I saw her tonight, and I thought maybe you had . . . " His voice trailed off. For some reason, his head was beginning to hurt. No, not exactly hurt: it felt as though his head was filling with a furious, burning hot gas that was stretching out the boundaries of his skull.

"Thought maybe I had what?" she said.

"Turned her," he said. "Turned her into one of you." And he looked out upon the club, and at all the handsome and beautiful people on those plush sofas, examining the strange grouping of items on those long, glass tables. The woman on the platform beneath the spotlight, wrenching her body into impossible shapes, was suddenly the cog at the center of this mystifying machine.

"Maybe I did, maybe I didn't," said the vampire. "But that's not talk for a place like this. Go home, Renfield."

"Turn *me*," he said, and he was not ignorant to the whiny quality of his plea. "I'm tired of being a fly. I want to be what you are instead. What you *all* are."

"That's a big ask."

"It's what I want."

"I have use for you otherwise," she told him, and then she brought up a hand and caressed his bare arm.

The feel of her fingernails on him sent a ripple through his body. A chill through his soul.

"How did it happen for *you*?" he asked. "How did you get turned?"

"This is not talk for tonight, Renfield. Go home."

He didn't move.

"Go," she said.

He extended the book out to her, and though she glanced at it, she did not take it.

He watched her—

(float)

—drift back over to her party. When she arrived, everyone clapped, like she'd just accomplished some great and difficult task. Drinks were bandied about. A dark, smallish man in a tuxedo wheeled over a silver cart with an intricate hookah pipe on it, and everyone seated on the sofa applauded again. One of the men picked up an item off the glass table—it was a silver-plated revolver, something a cowboy in an old Western might haul around in his rawhide holster—and studied it, turning it this way and that, with all the others looked on. Rapt.

She met his eyes one last time. Her voice then, in his head, borne on that vampiric telepathy she no doubt possessed—

Go home, Renfield.

Defeated, he left.

She *did* find him. Several nights later, as he cruised by the entrance of Fist (as he had been doing every night since), he saw her standing by herself on the street corner beneath the glow of a lamppost. No blood-red ball gown this evening; as he slowed the car and she glided down the curb and across the street in his direction, he could see she wore a man's sleeveless, button-down shirt, jet-black, and tight-fitting gray jeans. She wore a spiked collar around her neck and those silver bracelets at her wrists. The hair along the right side of her head was greased back with some kind of gel, hanging like the fan of a mermaid's tail over her right shoulder. The way she approached the car, an onlooker might assume this was some preplanned choreography.

She climbed into the back of the Town Car.

Said, "Drive."

He drove, not asking where they were going, his mind reeling with the possibilities. The level of elation—of pure, childish glee—that overtook him as he traversed the darkened downtown streets felt like some alien intrusion into his body, albeit one that made him nearly euphoric.

"What is that place?" he asked after a time.

"You mean the club?" she said. Her shape—her face—was a mere black smudge in the rear of the car. It was as if she were only *partly* here with him. "It's a sex club, mostly."

"What were all those things on the tables?"

"You shouldn't have gone in there," she said. And though Toby did not ask about the place—or those items—further, she volunteered: "They're pieces of . . . I guess you'd say, historic significance. To a certain population."

"To vampires?"

He sensed rather than heard her laugh.

"To the initiated, let's say," she replied. "A gun used in a mass shooting. A hatpin someone had driven through the throat of a former lover. The gloves worn to strangle the life from another human being."

The notion of this delighted him. "Where do they all come from?"

"Collectors, mostly."

"What do you do with them?"

"We hold them. Feel their power. If the moment is right—if the stars align, or however you like to think of it—you can close your eyes and actually *feel* the destruction, the pure life-taking devastation, in a particular piece. It vibrates like something alive. You can feel it course through your hands, up your arms, and radiate throughout the entirety of your body."

"That's pretty fucking cool," Toby said.

"Take the 405 North," she said.

He took the 405 to the Valley. From the back seat of the Town Car, the vampire instructed him to turn down a series of dark, suburban streets. The houses were all cookie-cutter beige, single-family homes. The streets wound in loops, and there were the dim pinpoints of streetlamps on every corner. At one point, she leaned forward, her mouth very close to his ear—

—and he could feel the warmth of her breath along the side of his face, smell the scent of her skin, lilac-heavy, infiltrating his nostrils, the electric sizzle in the air from such a proximity causing the delicate hairs along the rim of his ear and this side of his neck to prick up at attention—

—and she said, "That house right there. On the left. See it? Pull up along the curb. Keep the car running."

He did as he was told.

Without another word, she climbed out of the back of the Town Car and scampered up the driveway. He was able to see her for a brief moment longer, until she disappeared behind a stand of valley oaks.

There was nothing significant about the house, as far as Toby could tell. It looked exactly like all the other houses on this block—all the other houses in the neighborhood, to be honest—with the exception that all the windows were dark.

The car was hot. The A/C didn't work (neither did the radio), so Toby had driven out here with the front windows cracked; it was fine while cruising along the 405, but now, parked in this stagnant, nondescript neighborhood, he could feel the heat of the night permeating the vehicle. His armpits felt soupy, and the longer he sat there (unsure why they had driven all the way out here to begin with), the more agitated he became. There was a faint and distant droning in the center of his head, a sound that reminded him of the—

(buzzing of a fly)

—mechanical grinding of invisible gears.

For a moment, he thought maybe he was in some therapist's office, and that this was actually some fantasy, or maybe a past memory, and not something that was actually unfolding right now in real time. The series of events that would have conspired to dump him here at this point—returning to the Spider's web, cajoling the car from her, stalking a nameless woman with rattlesnake teeth through the seedy, underground nightclubs of downtown L.A.— seemed impossible. He peeled his hands off the steering wheel and examined his palms in the moonlight coming through the car's windshield. For a moment, he thought he could see the red rope-burn abrasions on his palms from walking the dogs. When the big dogs would run, the leashes would floss right through his hands, igniting the flesh.

Toby walks the dog.

He wasn't still walking dogs, was he?

The rear door slammed. She was suddenly back there, breathless, her scent pheromonal, her respiration audibly hissing as she gasped for air.

Shouting, "Drive! Drive! Drive!"

He dropped his foot on the accelerator and the massive vehicle lurched away from the curb. In the back seat, she was giggling to herself now, and clutching something in a small black case— possibly leather, possibly vinyl—to her chest.

"Where do I go?"

"Just get back to the freeway."

"What'd you just do?"

"Got the *good shit*," she said. "I need to go to Glendale."

He glanced at the gas gauge. Quarter of a tank. He was running out of the Spider's money fast.

"Do you hear me?" she said. "Don't punk out on me now, Renfield."

He glanced at her reflection in the rearview mirror, wondering what superpowers she possessed to reflect in the first place. As he drove out of the neighborhood and left those streetlamps behind, he could see nothing of her back there except the vague silhouette of her form, and—briefly—the firefly-yellow glow of her pupils.

That night, he drove her to an apartment complex in Glendale. She slipped silently from the car and ghosted down an alleyway. She was gone for a while, much longer than she'd been back at the house in the Valley. When she returned, she moved with a lobotomized lethargy, and even lingered just outside the car before finding the door handle and spilling into the back seat of the Town Car. She slumped across the seats, leaving the door open behind her. Agitated, Toby climbed out, closed the rear door, then slipped back behind the wheel.

"Where now?" he asked her.

"Take me back downtown."

"Where?"

After a long pause, she said, "The club. The club."

He took that to mean Fist, so that was the direction he headed.

"How did you get like this?" he asked as they drove. He could see her head back on the headrest in the rearview mirror, like she was staring up at the sky through the rear windshield.

"What are you, my mother?" she said.

When they arrived at the club, he saw that the marquee was dark, and the street was deserted. The vampire was asleep in the back seat, snoring soundly. Toby sat behind the wheel for an inordinate amount of time, wondering what he should do.

Said, "Hey."

Said, "Wake up."

Said, "Hello? Hello?"

But the thing back there was undead and unresponsive.

He was tired, and his body was jittery. Too much contemplation made his head hurt. Flies, he understood, were not cut out for such work. So he did the only thing he knew to do: he drove the vampire to the Spider's den, the apartment on Chamber Street.

He parked in the space behind the building, shut down the engine, then leaned over the headrest to peer at the vampire's slumbering form splayed across the back seat of the car. Thinking, *How did you arrive here?* And not just here as in *his car*, or even *California*, but *here*. He imagined a great ship, like the *Demeter* in Stoker's novel, chugging through countless miles of cold, dark oceans beneath a star-speckled sky, while this woman—this creature of the night— slept soundly in a makeshift wooden coffin filled with dirt from the grave, buried far below in the damp, creaky depths of the ship's cargo hold.

How did you get here?

How did you become what you are?

Or, more apropos: *How can I be what you are?*

He left her there, asleep in the back seat of the Spider's champagne-colored Lincoln Town Car. There was a moment of concern for her well-being, leaving her overnight in the car in this neighborhood, but then he realized the foolishness of such a concern: she was a *thing* with *teeth* that was perfectly capable of taking care of herself.

He yearned for that, too.

Taking care of himself.

In his bedroom, he thought of her for a while, attempting to take care of himself in an altogether physical manner while he did so. When that didn't work—when he found his imagination erratic and unsteady and incapable of sexual fantasy—he switched on the small lamp at his desk, opened his closet, and removed THE WONDERFUL THING from the box where it was hidden. After a few moments spent with THE WONDERFUL THING, he had finished, was spent. It had happened quickly, before he even realized it had. He cleaned himself with an unwashed sock he scooped up off his bedroom floor, then replaced THE WONDERFUL THING back in the box. There was an alarm clock on the cluttered desk beside his bed. He set the alarm for two hours from now; it would still be dark by then. He needed to get the vampire back to wherever she hid during the day before the sun rose.

Satisfied, he skulked back to his bed where, exhausted, he collapsed in a heap.

Two hours later, with the world still snared in the throes of darkness, he went down to the car to check on her and drive her back to wherever she needed to go, but the back seat was empty. The vampire had fled at some point while he slept.

THIRTEEN

C allie Tulane's studio was small, with a claustrophobic lobby whose walls were blanketed with framed, black-and-white photographs of stage and screen performances—actors who Maureen surmised were some of Callie's students. There was a desk behind a counter in the lobby, but it was unmanned, so Maureen lingered before those photographs, staring more at her own reflection in the glass frames than at the photographs themselves. The place smelled like a gym.

A woman came down the hall, startled to find Maureen standing there. It was Callie Tulane—Maureen could tell right away, despite the fact that she looked nothing like the woman in the glamour shot on the website or in the photo from the Hollywood premiere. Callie was slim, attractive, but wore no makeup. She was dressed in neon tights, a tank top, and a sports bra, as if she'd just finished working out, and was carrying a salad in a plastic container. Her hair, which in the glamour shot on the website was full and luxurious and highlighted with streaks of blonde, was now a mousy brown and pulled back in a simple ponytail.

"Hello," Callie said, offering Maureen a perfect smile. Maureen felt a twinge of inferiority just looking at the woman, knowing she'd once been married to Greg, and had brought that perfect smile and that perfect body into his life, if for just a short time. She watched as Callie slid behind the desk and set her salad down next to a stack of brochures on the counter. "Can I help you?"

Maureen could feel the old compulsion rise in her in that moment—a desire, a *craving*, to rearrange the brochures on the counter, to go around the room and methodically straighten every single crooked picture frame on the wall. Instead, she dug her fingernails into the soft meat of her palms and tried to look normal.

"My name is Maureen Park. I'm engaged to your ex-husband, Greg Dawson. I hope I haven't made a mistake coming here—I'm still not sure it's the right thing—but Greg is out of town and I didn't know what else to—"

The smile vanished. Callie's face was stoic. "I can't talk about Greg."

"It's not so much Greg that I wanted to talk to you about. It's—"

"His son," Callie finished.

"Yes."

"I can't talk about him, either."

"What do you mean, you can't?"

"Legally," Callie said. "There was a settlement as part of the divorce. Greg paid me a lot of money to not talk about him. Or his son."

"To the tabloids?"

"To anyone."

"Please," Maureen pressed, digging her fingernails deeper into the flesh of her palms. "I've been having some trouble with his son, Landon. I know you had some trouble with him in the past, too, and I was just hoping you might—"

"Stop." Callie held up one hand and turned her face to the side, no longer meeting her eyes. She suddenly looked about as green as her salad. "Don't even say his name."

"I don't understand. What exactly happened with him?"

Callie turned back to face her, but just slightly. "Did someone send you here?"

"No. I came to talk to you. Greg doesn't know I'm here."

"Maybe you should talk to Greg about it instead."

"I've tried. He's not very receptive when it comes to his son."

"How long have you known him?"

"Greg? Only a few months."

"And you're engaged already?"

It was Landon's voice that rose to the surface of Maureen's thoughts in that moment, a thing he'd said to her the day he caught her snooping around in his bedroom: *what dark secret are you trying to escape by wearing my father's life as a mask to cover it up?* She chose to ignore both Landon's voice and Callie's question, and instead said, "Landon is making me uncomfortable. Something has . . . happened . . . and I'm trying to figure out what to do about it. I feel like he might be dangerous."

"Has he hit you?"

"No. It's just this threatening, menacing behavior, plus some . . . some strange items I found in his room."

Callie's lips tightened. In fact, it looked like her entire body suddenly stiffened. In a low voice, she asked, "Have you met the Monkey?"

Maureen thought she'd misheard her. "What monkey?"

Callie blinked her eyes, as if waking from a trance. "Never mind." She looked down, began fidgeting with items on her desk. "I told you, I can't talk about this."

"I just wanted to—"

"My advice to you is to *leave*," Callie said, and for a moment Maureen thought she meant for her to leave the studio. "Pack up your stuff and leave them both. That's all I can tell you. I'm sorry, but that's all."

"Just please tell me what you—"

"I can't talk about this anymore. Please go. Please."

Callie fumbled a stapler to the floor. When she turned, her elbow knocked over the rack of brochures.

"Please go and don't come back."

"I just—"

"*Please.*"

Panic tightening around Maureen's throat, she fled back out into the daylight.

In the car, she called Greg's phone. Just like the night before, her call went straight to voicemail. The automated voicemail voice informed her Greg's mailbox was full, so she couldn't leave a message. She sent him a text instead, typing, erasing, then retyping again, over and over, until she settled on a two-word missive that explained nothing yet delivered the proper amount of urgency:

call me

She sat for a moment behind the wheel, her body a jangle of nerves, the palms of her hands indented with little crescent moons from digging her fingernails into the soft flesh there. She knew Greg was staying at the St. Regis in New York, so she googled the number, then called the hotel's front desk.

"Hello, I'm trying to reach my husband, Gregory Dawson."

"One moment," said the clerk on the other end of the line. There was the clattering of fingers on computer keys, and then the voice returned: "What was that name again, ma'am?"

"Gregory Dawson. D-A-W-S-O-N."

"We have no one staying here by that name."

"Are you sure? Can you check again."

The clerk sighed audibly, and those fingers began clacking on the keyboard again. "No, ma'am. No one named Dawson has checked into this hotel."

Her cell phone felt like a hot brick of iron against the side of her face.

"Okay, thank you," she said, and disconnected the call.

Landon's voice in her head again, jeering—*maybe he's not really in New York.*

She drove home in a circuitous fashion, her OCD disallowing her to take anything but right turns. Three times she stopped the car, got out, and furiously buckled then unbuckled the seatbelts in the back of the car. Her hands ached, her mind was a tornado of thought.

Back at the house, she was relieved to find that Landon was still not there. Maybe he'd gone to Vegas with his friends after all.

He has no friends, she told herself, thinking of what Ross had told her about Landon that day at the coffee shop.

She went around making sure all the doors in the house were locked. Her anxiety was running in the red, so she fixed herself a vodka tonic at the bar. Sliced up a lemon, then panicked at the asymmetry of the wedges, so she cut them up some more. Then some more. Then some more. Finally, after the wedges were nothing but pulp and seeds on the cutting board, she rearranged the glassware on the bar, finished her drink, then made herself another one.

We all have secrets, Maureen. I've got them, good old Greg's got plenty. Even you've got one. It wasn't that difficult to find out your secret, Maureen, because something like that sticks to a person like a shadow.

The silence in the house was driving her mad, so she turned on the TV.

Even you've got one . . .

Trembling, she moved from the bar and proceeded to straighten the pillows on the sofa, the record albums on the shelves, the creases in the drapes over the windows, while a cool gray fog swept in over her thoughts and the television prattled endlessly in the background: " . . . several weeks now since Fortunado's body was discovered in the desert and there's been little word from the Los Angeles County Sheriff's Department. And while very little information has been released regarding the details of Fortunado's death, police have intimated that her murder may be related to the killing of Melissa Jean Andressen, whose body was discovered in nearly the same location one year prior."

Maureen glanced up at the TV to see the still images of two women, side by side, staring out at her from the screen.

"Andressen's murder remains unsolved," the reporter continued, "and while there appear to be no leads or suspects in either case, officials from the Los Angeles County Sheriff's Department have suggested that the two deaths could be the work of the same man."

Maureen felt like she was losing her mind.

She staggered to the TV to switch it off, but the world went dark and hazy before she reached it.

When she awoke hours later, it was fully dark, and she was in bed. Disoriented, she rolled onto her side and stared out the bedroom windows at the confusion of city lights below. For a moment, she was back in Wyoming, and everything about Los Angeles was just a dream, even the lights outside the window—all of it. But then reality caught up to her and she sat up in bed.

Her head was pounding and her mouth was dry. Something felt . . . *off.*

She peeled the damp sheet from her body to find her blouse open and her bra gone. She kicked her legs and saw she was only wearing her panties, no pants. She tried to remember coming up here, getting partially undressed, and climbing into bed, but couldn't. How many drinks had she had? Two? Three? She wasn't such a lightweight that those few vodka tonics should have knocked her on her ass and robbed her of a swatch of time. It wasn't as if—

A terrible notion came to her.

Head still pounding, she peeled herself out of bed, groped around in the darkness of her bedroom for her pants, but couldn't find them. The bedroom door stood open, though she had no memory of locking it or not. She had no memory of coming up here at all.

She went into the master bath, switched on the light, then winced at its harshness. Her reflection stared at her from above the sink, a wraith in a parted silk blouse and panties, hair a mess. She could see bruises on her upper arms—small dark patches in the flesh that hadn't been there before. When she looked down, she could see similar bruises along her upper thighs. One set of bruises looked incriminatingly like a set of fingerprints.

She hastily buttoned her shirt, then went back into the bedroom and climbed into a pair of sweatpants.

Thinking: *No no no no no . . .*

She went out onto the landing, not yet ready to turn on any lights, and just listened to the sounds of the big house all around her. When the thermostat kicked on, she nearly jumped out of her skin.

Downstairs, the living room lights were still on. The glassware at the bar was just how she remembered arranging it, as were Greg's records, and everything else she could recall doing before she'd . . . what? Passed out?

Someone else might not have noticed, but Maureen's OCD was in hyperdrive; when she looked back at the bar, she noticed something amiss. A second later, she realized what it was: the bottle of vodka was gone.

She had no memory of drinking the whole bottle, but she checked the kitchen trash nonetheless.

No bottle.

A confluence of thoughts was swirling through her head, determined to arrive at some terrible explanation, but she was doing her damnedest not to allow them to cohere.

The last thing she did was to check the front door, because she *knew* she had locked it upon returning to the house earlier that day.

(you've been a nosy parker, Maureen)

The front door was not only unlocked, but stood partway open.

FOURTEEN

The woman whose body was found a few weeks ago in the desert? Gina Fortunado? Was her face all cut up? Her eyes removed? Her fingers cut off?

That call had come in two nights ago, rousing Renney from a turbulent slumber, and he had spent the next twenty-four hours working with his cell phone carrier to see if they could pinpoint the cell tower where the anonymous phone call had come from. So far: no dice.

It had been a woman's voice, so Renney dug through the case file to review the list of women he'd spoken with throughout the course of the Fortunado murder investigation: friends, former roommates, coworkers. He recalled Gina's older sister—what had her name been?—who'd come up behind him as he'd stood in Gina's parents' house looking at photographs on the wall. How she'd pointed out a watercolor painting Gina had made as a child—a painting of a single red rose—and said, *She wanted to be an artist.*

The woman had sounded nervous. Afraid. Of course she had. She'd had the foresight to purchase a burner phone.

Was her face all cut up? Her eyes removed?

Who could know that?

Renney's office was a square shithole with a single window, a desk, and countless paper files stacked in towers around the room. The department had gone to an online case management system years ago, but Renney, whose age was hanging at the half-century mark, kept hardcopies of every case he ever worked. Looking upon the sea of manila folders and bristling papers made the younger officers cringe, but hell, it kept them out of his office. Mostly.

Politano poked his head in, flashing a Tupperware container. "Brought you some cheesecake."

"From where?"

"Homemade."

"You make cheesecake?"

"My girlfriend does." He came into the office, maneuvering around towers of paper case files, and set the container on the corner of Renney's cluttered desk.

"I didn't know you had a girlfriend."

"I won't if I keep working these hours."

Renney looked up at him. He could see the wheels turning behind A.J. Politano's eyes. "Spit it out," he said.

"That mechanic who you were looking at for the Andressen murder? Well, I figured he'd be in the DNA database, given his rap sheet, and I was right. I had the hair samples and trace DNA found on Fortunado's body against his."

"And?"

"No match."

"Like I said, I didn't think the guy would swoop in a year later just to kill again. But good job."

"Also," Politano said, and Renney could hear his throat click, "I ran Alan Andressen's DNA against what was found on the body as well."

Renney leaned back in his chair.

"No match there, either," Politano said quickly. "I just wanted you to know."

"You should have told me before you went running around doing all this," Renney said.

"I know, you're right. I should have. I just knew you were busy, and I wanted to rule it out."

"Yeah, well, next time you want to rule something out, come talk to me about it first."

"I will."

"How'd you get Andressen's DNA, anyway?"

Politano hoisted one shoulder in a halfhearted shrug. "I just went to his house, explained the situation, and asked him. He let me take a swab."

Jesus fucking Christ, Renney thought.

"Check with me first next time," Renney said.

"Right."

"This cheesecake your girlfriend made any good?"

"Not really."

"Go home and spend some time with her. I'll see you tomorrow."

"Have a good night," Politano said, then negotiated his way around a tower of case files until he found his way out the door.

Either Alan wasn't at home, or he wasn't answering the buzzer at the foot of the driveway. Renney got back in his car and eased down the hillside, drifting past a conga line of stone-and-glass houses, toward the main road. Broad Street boasted a rank of decent restaurants, and as Renney coasted past, he saw Alan's silver BMW parked outside a place called Carolina's. Renney grunted, shook his head, then pulled a U-turn. He double-parked outside the restaurant, threw a police placard on the dash, then ratcheted himself out of his car.

Alan was alone at the bar, eating some pasta dish. There was a glass of red wine beside his plate. He was absently scrolling through something on his phone when Renney approached.

"Mind if I sit?"

Startled, Alan twisted himself around on his barstool. Renney could tell by his face that it took him a moment to reconcile him standing here.

"Uh ... " Alan said.

Renney sat.

"Have you been following me?" Alan asked, his voice barely above a whisper. "How'd you know I was here?"

"Relax," Renney said. "I saw your car out front."

"What do you want now?"

"What are you doing turning over your DNA? I told you before —if anyone comes asking you for *anything*, you talk to me first."

"Officer came to the house. I have nothing to hide."

"You *do*," Renney reminded him. "You *do* have something to hide."

Alan's nostrils flared. He balled his hands into fists on the top of the bar. "Meaning I didn't do anything to that girl. I just want this whole thing behind me so I can move on with my life."

"Yeah, well, your DNA's not on that girl, but it's damn sure on the body of that mechanic buried in the desert. Mine, too."

Alan grunted and turned away from him. Those fists with their pale white knuckles were beginning to tremble on the bar top.

"I'm telling you one last time, doc: anyone else comes barking, you come to me first. This ain't just your ass in the sling. You got me?"

Still not looking at him, Alan nodded. There was moisture collecting in the corner of his eye. In a small voice, he asked, "What's going to happen now?"

"Nothing, far as I know," Renney said. Then he got up off the stool and smiled at the female bartender who had been making her way toward him down the length of the bar. "Enjoy your dinner, doc."

He left.

FIFTEEN

Toby Kampen found himself falling into a routine.

He spent his nights ferrying the vampire to various locations throughout the city. These were drug runs, he came to understand—she was buying, selling, probably both—and sometimes she would return to the Town Car looking half asleep, her face paler than normal, her pupils dilated. On these occasions, she would usually fall asleep in the back seat of the Town Car— she never sat beside him in the empty passenger, never—but Toby never took her back to the apartment complex on Chamber Street: he feared for the time he might oversleep and forget to drive her back before the sun rose, finding only a grayish pile of ash on the back seat of the car. So on these nights, he would drive her back to the city, to the club called Fist, and rouse her from her drug-induced slumber. Wordlessly, she would peel herself out of the car and Toby would walk with her to the club. She sometimes smelled bad on these nights—a combination of pot smoke and body odor— but Toby didn't necessarily find this off-putting; in fact, he liked having to wind an arm around her waist and help her across the street. Once there, he would try to bring her into the club, but even in her less-than-there state, she would stop him with a gentle hand to his chest. She'd shake her head, whisper, "No."

"I want to come inside again."

"This place is not for you."

"Because I'm not one of you," he said, not a question.

She would pat the side of his face or rake her—

(claws)

—fingernails down the length of his chest. Then she would vanish into the club unassisted, leaving Toby standing there on the sidewalk, alone, in the dark. Sometimes, when steam from an open grate drifted across her wake, Toby wondered if perhaps *she* had turned to steam. Had turned to smoke.

Other nights, she returned from these exchanges—from these modest suburban homes and downtown tenements alike—the same as she'd left him, her body moving with a liquid seductiveness, her wolfish eyes sly and alert.

On one of these nights, as they drove back from some expensive-looking mansion in the Hollywood Hills, Toby asked, "How did it happen?"

There were several beats of silence before her response came to him, warm against the back of his neck (or so he imagined): "You want to know how I was turned, don't you?"

"I do," he said. Then added, "Please."

"Ohhh," she hummed, and drummed her overlong fingernails along the window glass—*clackity-clackity-clack*. "It was like a rite of passage. A campaign. Communion. Something I had to seek out and believe would happen to me in order for it to happen at all."

I want to believe that, too, Toby thought.

"There is a little stone church," she told him. "It's deep in the desert, deeper than you'd think a church should be. It looks like a mirage, and it is filled with ghosts. I took the nameless dirt road all the way out to it, and I stayed there for three days and three nights. I surrendered myself to the rite."

"How?"

There was a pause of silence. Then: "I built a fire, then I opened my wrist. I bled on the items I had brought with me—things from the life I was willing to give up in order to become something different."

"What happened?"

"I had a vision."

"Of what?"

She made a clicking sound with her tongue. "Everyone's vision is personal, Renfield. We don't kiss and tell."

"Then what happened?"

She said, "On the third night, he came to me."

"Who?"

"Who do you think?"

Toby said nothing, just swallowed a hard lump of spit that hurt his throat. He glanced up and saw her reflection—

(how does she reflect?)

—in the rearview mirror. It was pure darkness back there, but her eyes were two luminescent, golden discs of light, hypnotic in their luminosity. He could lose himself in eyes like that, he knew. When she grinned at him, he could see her fangs.

"We made love in the church, and then we feasted upon each other's blood. He took mine, consumed it, and I took his. Communion. And when we were done, he disappeared back into the desert, and I went through the change."

"What did that feel like?"

It was quiet back there for a moment, except for the *clackity-clack* of her fingernails on the window. "It felt like I was an insect going through a metamorphosis. Something in a cocoon, only my body was the cocoon, and the thing that was changing was buried deep inside."

"Did it hurt?"

"Yes."

"What did he look like? The thing that changed you."

She said, "The devil."

He imagined his own internal organs undergoing such a metamorphosis—ribs readjusting, lungs repositioning, the substance and quality of his blood altogether changing. "Could *you* change me?"

"We've already discussed this, Renfield. You're too important to me the way you are."

"Could I come to the club with you tonight?"

"No. I've told you that before, too—it's not a place for you."

In some form or fashion, Toby Kampen had been hearing that his entire life. *This is not a place for you.*

Could that be changed?

Could things be different for him?

"I think you and I should take a break for a while," she added.

"What do you mean?"

"I mean I'm going to lay low for a bit. Hang at the club, maybe make the rounds to some other places, you know? I don't like to sit still, or hang in any one place for too long; I like to get out there and move around in the night. Do you know what I'm talking about?"

"Who will take you to the houses?" *To buy and sell drugs*, he wanted to add, but didn't.

"I'm taking a break from the houses, too. A break from you, a break from the houses, a break from all the bullshit in this lousy city. It's poetic. It's tiresome, too. A life change. Something's gotta give."

Toby didn't like that.

He didn't even know what that meant.

"How do I find that church in the desert?" he asked her.

The vampire laughed languidly. There was something liquid about the sound of her back there in the dark—not just her laughter, but in the way her body moved and shifted about along the car's back seats. Toby imagined that would be the sound of smoke if it had substance. "Don't be silly, Renfield. You won't find it. That place is not for you, either. It doesn't want you there, and so it will hide from you."

They drove for a while longer in silence, until Toby summoned the courage to say, "I've got a gift for you."

"Is that right, Renfield?"

He felt her lean forward and twirl a finger in the lengthening curls of his hair. This caused a shiver to gallop down the length of his spine.

He reached over and picked up THE WONDERFUL THING from the passenger seat. He felt a spark of doubt while doing this—a momentary uncertainty that made him reconsider what he was about to do—and he even set it back down on the seat beside him. His heart was suddenly beating in his throat. But in the end, he ignored that feeling, because he felt sure that this act would lead to bigger and better things for him. Without taking his eyes from the road, he passed THE WONDERFUL THING back to her in the dark.

She laughed at first—a masculine, almost garrulous chuckle, way in the back of her throat.

But then she went quiet for a time.

Quiet still.

In those moments, it felt like someone was using Toby's heart as a punching bag.

"What is this?" she said after a long moment of silence. The tone of her voice had changed. Something, he could tell, had shifted. Was that a good thing? "Are these real? Where did you get this?"

He didn't tell her where he had gotten it. Instead, quite genuinely, he said, "It's a gift. From me to you."

"Jesus Christ, Renfield," she said from the back seat, and the words came out shaky and breathless.

Filled, Toby knew, with awe.

For the next several nights, he drove out to the club, but true to her word, the vampire did not appear to him. One night, he double-parked the Town Car and attempted to gain entrance to the club, but on this night, the woman in the ticket-booth window would not permit him entry. When he asked her why, her only response was, "She says not to let you in."

A white-hot fury began to burn inside his belly.

It's not a place for you.

He walked back down the corridor, but didn't slip out into the night; instead, he lingered in the vestibule of the cloud like a foul odor, absently picking at the scabs along his forearms, staring mostly down at his grubby sneakers. He didn't know where to go, didn't know what to do. At one point, he looked up to find the ticket-booth window empty. A moment later, the woman reappeared through the red velvet curtain, followed by two others. One of the women—a pale, slender woman with a cascade of pitch-black hair trailing down one side of her face—Toby didn't recognize; the other woman was the vampire, *his* vampire, only she was once again dressed in a gown that made her look like a princess from some barely remembered childhood nightmare.

She floated over to him.

Said, "I told you not to come back here."

"I just thought—"

"You need to *leave.*"

He stared at her. For a moment, he was a child again, back in the Chamber Street apartment with the Spider.

The vampire brought a hand up, caressed the warm side of his face with the knuckles of her cold, white fingers. Behind her, the dark-haired woman stared at him with laser-like precision, something like a cool smirk on her lips. He abruptly felt like a fool.

"You'll see me again, Renfield. Someday. But this place isn't for you."

He wanted to scream. He wanted to swat her hand away from his face, maybe grab her wrist and twist her arm behind her back. He wanted to do a million terrible things.

But in the end, he only bolted from that place as if his heels were on fire.

SIXTEEN

Greg's return from New York was heralded by a pounding on the front door. Maureen heard his knocking echo throughout the big, empty house, a steady drumming that rivaled the drumming inside her head. She floated rather than walked to the front door, then peered out of the window beside the door to confirm that it was, indeed, Greg Dawson standing there on the front porch. He saw her gazing out at him, a roller bag at his feet, his Pierre Cardin shirt with the first two buttons undone, a look of consternation on his face. It was early evening, and the headlights from the Uber that had dropped him off were already receding down the long driveway toward the street.

Maureen undid the deadbolt and the chain, then pulled the door open.

"My key doesn't work," he said, dragging his roller bag into the house. He administered a perfunctory kiss to the side of her face. He smelled of booze and good times, and when he pulled away from that kiss, a wan smile on his face, she could see that he'd clearly had more than one cocktail on the plane.

"I had the locks changed," she told him.

He rolled his bag across the vestibule floor, then tossed his house keys into a ceramic bowl that sat on a low, decorative table in the foyer. "You did what?"

She took a deep breath and said, "I know you're probably tired from your trip. But you and I need to have a serious talk."

A look of genuine concern washed across his face. "Is everything okay?"

"No, Greg. Everything is not okay."

"What's this about?"

"Landon," she said.

Greg stiffened. He peered up to the second-floor landing, as if to spy his son standing there, staring down at him.

"He isn't home," she said. "I don't know where he is, but he isn't here."

"What's been going on, Maur?"

"First of all, how come you haven't called me? I tried reaching you. I sent you a text to call me."

"Did you? I didn't realize. My phone died while I was out there and I didn't even notice until I was heading back to the airport. I can't even power it on. I'm sorry, babe."

"I called the St. Regis but they said you weren't there."

"What are you talking about?"

"I called the hotel. They said no one by your name was staying there."

"Jesus, Maur." He chuckled. "I never stay under my real name when I travel. You know that. We were Mr. and Mrs. Smith when we were in Bali, remember?"

"No. I don't remember that."

He cocked his head to one side, then reached out and touched the side of her face. His palm was cool against her flushed cheek. "You look awful, babe. Tell me what's been going on."

"Landon's been saying things, doing things, and I don't feel safe in this house with him."

Greg appeared to physically deflate. "What'd that goddamn kid do now?"

"He's deliberately making me uncomfortable for some reason."

"Jesus Christ." His hand dropped away from her face. He turned and wandered down into the living room. At the wet bar, he proceeded to fix himself a drink. Maureen felt a wavering sense of déjà vu as she watched him, as if Greg were destined to mimic his son's actions, that maybe they were even the same person, a single generation apart. "Tell me what happened."

"What did he say when you confronted him about that scrapbook?"

Ice cubes tumbling into a lowball glass, *clink clink clink.* "He said it was a goof. Fake photos that he got from a friend. I told you they didn't look real, remember? I'm in the goddamn movie biz, for Christ's sake."

"He told *me* those photos were yours. That he found them in your study."

He poured some vermouth into a martini glass. Said, "Where's the vodka?"

"That's something else entirely." Hugging herself, she sank down into the living room, but remained a healthy distance from him. "Last night, I think he put something in the vodka. It knocked me out. I woke up hours later, half dressed in bed. There're bruises on my arms and legs."

Greg froze. A moment later, he turned to face her, a quizzical look on his face. "What does *that* mean?"

"I think he drugged the vodka then . . . then did something to me while I was unconscious."

He set the glass he was holding down on the bar. Hard.

"He gave me a videotape of a movie you'd written and directed years ago. *High Desert.* The opening scene with the dead woman, her face all cut up, it looks just like the photos in that scrapbook."

"Yeah," he said. "I told you they looked like prop shots from a movie, remember?"

"No, Greg. He was trying to make me believe you were some . . . some killer."

"Wait, wait—hold on. What is it . . . what are you saying . . . ?"

"Something happened between him and your ex-wife. Callie? She pressed charges for assault, but they were dropped. What happened?"

"How the hell do you know about that?"

"It's public record," she said.

"You looked my kid up online?"

"He's not a fucking *kid*, Greg! Are you even *listening* to me?"

"I'm listening to you overreact. You haven't said a single thing to me that suggests my son has done *anything* to you—"

"The fucking vodka bottle is gone! He got rid of it because he'd drugged it! To knock me out!"

"For what reason? To feel you up? Christ, Maureen . . . "

"To scare me," she said. "I don't know why, but he's trying to frighten me off. What happened between him and your ex-wife Callie?"

Greg hung his head. "I can't believe we're even having this conversation."

"He said he learned about our engagement online. That you never called him to tell him about us. Is that true?"

"He was in *Europe.* I was going to tell him when he came back. If he ever *did* come back."

"You told me you spoke to him about us."

"Things moved fast, Maureen. I didn't have time to do everything the right way."

"So you lied to me?"

"I've been trying to get this movie off the ground. I've been *working.* Do you think I'm sitting around here, having a good time? Cut me some slack."

"I don't like how you're handling this," she said. "I don't like how you don't think that scrapbook and those photos are a big deal."

"They're *not* a big deal."

"Those are photos of a woman who was murdered a few weeks ago, Greg. She was cut up in real life the same way she's cut up in those photographs."

"We've been *through* this," he countered. "You don't *know* that."

"I *do*! I *do* know it! I called the police and they confirmed it."

He took a step toward her, then took a step back. His hip bumped against the wet bar, jangling the glassware. He seemed confused. "What . . . what are you *talking* about? You went to the *police*?"

"I made an anonymous call. The detective confirmed that the woman who was found dead in the desert a few weeks ago was killed in the exact same way as the victim in those photographs."

"I can't believe this," he said, running a hand through his hair. "I'm out of town for two days and you've upended my entire life. What is it you're trying to do here, Maureen? Destroy me?"

"You're not *listening* to me! Your son had that scrapbook in his closet. *He* said they belonged to *you*. But *you* say they're just part of some prank he's playing on me, and for what fucking reason?" She took a step toward him. "Greg, he said he came back early from Europe so he could *spy* on me. He's got some vendetta against me, and I don't know why. And your ex-wife didn't want to talk about whatever happened between the two of—"

"Stop," he said. His voice was even, calm. Yet his face was nearly purple. "Did you have a conversation with my ex?"

An expulsion of breath shuddered out of her.

"Goddamn it, Maureen, *did you*?"

In a measured voice, she said, "I went to talk to her, but she didn't want to tell me anything."

"Son of a bitch."

"I'm *scared*, Greg."

"Yeah? And I'm fucking *betrayed*."

"Please," she said. "Don't be like that."

He pointed a finger in her direction. "You're doing exactly what he wants you to do, which is to make a big deal out of this. He's bored and angry and you're his toy. Don't you get it? He's pushing your buttons just like he pushes mine. Don't give him the satisfaction, Maureen. Ignoring him is the best thing you could do. You don't have kids so you don't know what it's like."

"*He's not a fucking kid!*"

A beat of silence fell upon the room. Somewhere, a clock ticked.

"Enough," he said, raising one hand like someone about to take an oath. "Enough of this nonsense, Maureen. I'm tired of hearing it." He marched across the room and stalked past her, heading down the hall toward his office. When he returned a handful of seconds later, he was carrying the scrapbook containing those awful photos.

"I'm sorry," Maureen said. "I didn't want to do it like this . . . "

Greg paused halfway across the room. He held up the scrapbook, so she could see the single word behind the panel of clear plastic on the cover:

MEMORIES

"The photos in this book are fake," Greg said, his voice surprisingly calm, despite the beads of sweat that now dotted his forehead. "Landon has issues. I acknowledge that. I told him to stop messing around with you, and I hoped he'd listen and abide."

"He didn't listen," she said. "He fucking *hates* me."

"Jesus Christ. Quit overreacting."

"What about the movie you wrote and directed? The way that girl in the beginning was killed?"

"What about it?" he said.

"I just feel there are connections here that I should be making, but I can't."

"That's because there *are* no connections. The whole thing is senseless, Maureen. Get out of your own fucking head for once and listen to what I'm telling you—*there is nothing here.*"

"The woman in your movie was killed the same way as the woman in real life. The same way she's depicted in those photos . . . "

"So what?" he said, shaking his head. "Am I to be punished because some lunatic saw a movie I made over thirty years ago and decided to kill someone in the same fashion? Because my son's got it in his sick little head that he's going to fuck with you about it? Don't be so goddamn naive. Tell me right now—what exactly is it that you think is going on here?"

She shook her head. Felt hot tears welling up in her eyes. Said, "I don't know . . . "

"Yes, you do. Say it."

"I think Landon did something to that woman."

"*Something?*"

"I think he killed her!"

Greg took a deep breath. His nostrils flared. He lowered the scrapbook, which he'd been holding above his head like a preacher with a Bible, and looked down at it.

"Greg, please . . . " She took a breath. Steadied herself. "I don't expect you to love me more than your son. But my words should count for something."

He allowed his steely gaze to linger on her for the length of a single heartbeat. Then, without a word, he went over to the fireplace. Turned the knob, and flames burst from the fake logs in the hearth with an audible *WHOOMP!*

"She's right, you know," came a voice from the foyer.

They both turned to see Landon standing there in the doorway. He was dressed in a crisp white shirt, slim black necktie, black blazer and pants. He looked like a mortician, or maybe someone going door-to-door spreading the word of God.

"I *do* hate you, Maureen," he said. But his eyes weren't on her; they were on his father. "But I hate you more, Greg."

"Landon," Greg said, but said no more.

Landon descended into the living room; he walked with the lethargic, medicated gait of someone just released from a psychiatric ward. "I'm tired, Greg," he said.

"Tired of what, Landon?"

"Tired of always being an extra in the movie of your life."

He stood there, the cuffs of his white shirt too long, the hem of his suit jacket sleeves too short. His eyes looked red and bleary. "It would be the best thing in the world for you if I never came home from Europe," he said. "If I just disappeared like smoke. Like Mom."

"You're talking crazy."

"Marriage after marriage after marriage. You never wanted me to be a part of any of them. Admit it, Greg. You just kept stuffing my pockets with cash and sending me away. Europe, Mexico, wherever. Just as long as I remained an extra. No speaking roles for Landon Dawson."

"Landon, that's not true," Greg said.

Landon just shook his head. That smirk was back on his face, condescending as ever. "You don't want me *around*, Gregory. You don't want the extra standing in the spotlight. You don't want me rewriting the script. But what happens when I *do*?"

"Please don't do this, Landon," Greg said.

"Act One," Landon said. "The prodigal son returns. Act Two, all hell breaks loose. Act Three . . . well, Greg, I think we both know what happens in Act Three."

"Landon," Greg said.

"Fuck this," Landon said, dejected. "I'm getting the Monkey." He turned and walked back up the stairs—

"Landon, goddamn it, don't you do it!"

—and down the hall.

Have you met the Monkey?

Greg turned to her, his face beet-red. A vein pulsed in his temple. "See what you've started? You couldn't have just left well enough alone?"

"I . . . " she began, but what could she say?

Greg leaned over the hearth and was about to drop the scrapbook into the fire.

"No!" she shouted, and rushed at him.

She grabbed a section of the scrapbook, and for several seconds, they played a frantic game of tug-of-war. Greg was stronger, and when he finally yanked the book from her grasp, she fell back on her ass and nearly clocked her head on one corner of the coffee table.

"You fucked it all up, Maureen," Greg lambasted her. "I hope you're satisfied."

Just then, a shrill cry echoed throughout the house. Maureen scooted back against one wall, eyes wide. Greg shouted for Landon not to do it, to stop, stop, stop, but Landon did not stop: Landon appeared in the doorway once more in his black suit and tie, his white shirt . . .

. . . and the rubbery mask of a monkey on his head.

He screeched, stomped his feet, pounding his fists against his chest.

"Goddamn it, Landon, no!" Greg shouted back at him. "No more! No more!"

But the thing in the doorway was no longer Landon Dawson; the Monkey released an ear-splitting shriek, flailing its arms around, stomping its feet. As Maureen watched, the Monkey jumped down into the living room. It swatted a vase off the coffee table, shattering it against one wall. Over and over again, the Monkey cried out—

"*Reeet! Reeet! Reeet!*"

—and it kicked over the coffee table.

"Landon, *please!*" shouted Greg.

"*Reeet! Reeet! Reeeeeeeet!*"

The Monkey tumbled over to the wet bar. Limbs thrashing, all the glassware and bottles shattered to the floor, a rain of crystal and booze, *smash smash smash!* That rubber monkey mask swung in Maureen's direction next, and she felt her heart momentarily seize in her chest. The Monkey cocked its head, as if struck by curiosity, and then—

"*Reeeeet! Reeeeeeeeet!*"

—it cartwheeled across the room in her direction.

Greg cried out, "*Don't you dare!*" and tackled the beast, driving them both to the floor. In the melee, the scrapbook struck the carpet with a thump.

The Monkey squealed, "*Rheeeeeeeee,*" as it began to pummel Greg with its fists.

Maureen crawled across the carpet and snatched the scrapbook up off the floor.

The Monkey swung its gaze in her direction. The eyeholes in the mask were larger than they should have been, giving the simian face a crude, jack-o'-lantern appearance. She could see the rubber mask flexing in and out with Landon's frantic respiration, could hear the muffled sounds of his breathing behind that horrid thing.

"*Hooo! Hooo! Hooo! Hooo!*"

The Monkey jumped up and down, swatting its own chest with its fists.

Maureen bolted to her feet and staggered toward the hallway, the scrapbook clutched to her chest. She felt the thing rushing up behind her—could even smell the animal stink of it somehow, as if it had truly descended upon this house from some remote jungle—and could feel the heat of its breathy exhalations prickling the hairs along the nape of her neck.

"*Hooo-hooo! Rheee-rheee!*"

A set of claws raked down her spine.

She cried out, yet kept running for the front door, which stood open onto the night.

Something smashed behind her. She heard Greg cry out. The Monkey—

(Have you met the Monkey?)

—screamed and screamed and screamed, until Maureen thought Landon's throat might rupture—

—until she was out in the night, and running down the driveway toward the street, then running *through* the street, her eyes streaming tears, her heart slamming in her chest, her mind somewhere outside of herself, lest she go insane given the—

(monkey)

—level of horror she had just witnessed.

SEVENTEEN

Toby Kampen walked out of his apartment on Chamber Street and into the midday sunshine to find two of the four tires on the Spider's Lincoln Town Car flattened. This caused in him some momentary consternation, until he looked over at the white panel van parked in the spot next to the Town Car. The van belonged to the apartment complex, and was primarily used by George Zebka, in Apartment 121, who served as the maintenance man for the Chamber Street complex. He was also a raging alcoholic, Toby knew, and was likely at this very moment sleeping off a massive hangover in his apartment.

Toby himself had driven the van on occasion. Whenever Zebka awoke to find his head pounding too harshly from a night of drinking, he would summon Toby to his apartment, hand him a fistful of cash, and tell him to run some errands. Toby always happily obliged (despite his lack of a driver's license), and it became routine for him to go into the maintenance room on the ground floor of the complex and snatch the van's keys from the corkboard on the wall. (Zebka had also maintained a collection of nude photos of what Toby presumed were his girlfriends pinned to the corkboard, which Toby, in his younger days, would pause to appreciate. Once, he'd even stolen one, and if Zebka ever realized it was missing, he had never questioned Toby about it.)

On this morning, the door to the maintenance room was locked, but Toby knew from experience that if he turned the knob and *lifted* the door in its frame, it would unlatch. He did this now, then quickly hurried inside the room without turning on any of the lights. The keys to the van were not on the corkboard, which caused a column of panic to momentarily rise up in the center of Toby's body. But then he saw them on the workbench, surrounded by about half a dozen empty bottles of Schlitz. Toby snatched them up and hurried back outside.

Earlier that morning, he had packed a cooler with some food (bottles of water, packets of beef jerky, trail mix, a packet of Oreo cookies, other such items) and a backpack with some additional supplies (mouthwash, toilet paper, sunscreen, bug spray, a pocketknife, a tatty old quilt). The cooler and the backpack were sitting on the bottom step of the apartment complex where he'd left them, only now, as Toby came out of the maintenance room, he saw the Spider standing there, staring down at those items.

A measure of disquietude crept through Toby's body.

"What is this?" the Spider wanted to know. She was standing there in her floral housedress, pointing down at the cooler and the backpack with one plump, pale-white finger. "Where are you going?"

"I'm going to work," he lied.

"With a backpack and a cooler? Don't you lie to me, boy."

Who's the liar? he thought. *Who's the thing dressed up as something it's not?*

He gathered up the cooler and the backpack without affording the Spider even the most cursory of glances. When he turned away, the Spider reached out and grabbed hold of one of the backpack's straps.

"Don't you lie to me, Toby. Tell me what you're up to."

He jerked the backpack out of her grasp, hard enough to cause her to stumble down the stairs, although she managed to catch hold of the railing before she fell.

"You've been working nights. What is this new job?"

"None of your business."

"You *are* my business! My *car* is my business!"

"I'm not using your fucking car, so go the fuck back inside."

He unlocked the driver's door of the van, tossed the backpack inside, then slid the cooler over onto the passenger seat.

The Spider was suddenly upon him, slamming her meager, doughy fists into the small of his back. He turned to her and knocked her aside with a wave of his arm. She staggered backward, her buttocks slamming against the Town Car in the next space over.

"Don't ever fucking touch me again, you crazy bitch. Do you hear me?"

"*TOBEEEEE!*"

"Go on and cry, see if I care."

He climbed behind the wheel and slammed the driver's door shut.

An instant later, the Spider's face was filling the window. She was not crying, was not sobbing or begging; rather, for the first time in a long time, her face was revealed as a true mask, for Toby could now clearly see the Spider behind it—the glossy, obsidian eyes; spiny hairs as thick as quills; the quivering, tubular chelicerae tipped with hooked, black fangs. A pale greenish poison dripped from the left fang, snot-like in its consistency.

"*TOBEEEEE!*"

That hand kept slamming against the window.

Toby rolled down the window—it had a manual crank; the van was very old—and just as the Spider attempted to reach inside and hook her claws into him, he pressed the heel of his hand against that false face and gave her a shove.

The Spider fell backward against the Town Car then dropped to the pavement.

Toby got the hell out of there.

Two and a half hours later, he was motoring through an empty stretch of desert, having left the Los Angeles County limits in his rearview mirror. He had passed many churches on his way out here—the Calvary Chapel, the Road Church, the Church of the Redeemer and of All Saints, the Church of Good Hope, the Church of the Sand, the Church of the Sky—but he knew none of these were the one the vampire had been speaking of. As he drove east, he could hear her voice, verbatim, clear as the ringing of a bell, inside his head: *There is a little stone church. It's deep in the desert, deeper than you'd think a church should be. It looks like a mirage and it is filled with ghosts. I took the nameless dirt road all the way out to it, and I stayed there for three days and three nights. On the third night, he came to me.*

The desert was vast, yet he had little doubt that he wouldn't find the church; as it was, he felt like he was being drawn by some magnetic force. A human divining rod, seeking out not water but . . . what? Salvation?

Yes.

The van was hardly an upgrade from the Town Car. The tape deck worked, but there was a Lynyrd Skynyrd cassette stuck in there on repeat, so he shut it off after a while. There were multiple cup holders, too, and before he'd begun his journey, he'd grabbed a Coke-flavored Slurpee from 7-Eleven, and then peed in the empty container when he was done.

She says not to let you in, the woman back at Fist had said to him.

He wasn't interested in the club anymore. He wanted to find the church.

Don't be silly, Renfield, the vampire herself had said to him. She might even have been using her vampiric telepathy to speak free and clear in his head now. *You won't find it. That place is not for you, either. It doesn't want you there, and so it will hide from you.*

After a time, he saw what looked like a nameless dirt road that branched off the main roadway and arced straight out toward a horizon crenellated with mesas. That magnetic pull tugged at him. He reversed the van and spun the steering wheel, taking the nameless dirt road toward some hopeful oblivion. The interior of the van smelled like piss and body odor, and the A/C didn't work, so sweat popped from his pores, soaking his shirt, yet he hardly noticed. He drove for another forty minutes or so, grit and gravel raining down upon the van's cracked and mucky windshield. His head began to throb. He couldn't remember if he had vomited up his meds this morning, had swallowed them, or had taken them at all. The Spider possessed an amnesiac quality that made him forget many things that happened in that claustrophobic little apartment.

At one point, when disorientation got the better of him, he eased the van to a stop, slipped the gearshift into Park, and staggered out into the waning daylight. Straddling above a mound of sagebrush, he unzipped his fly and unleashed a stream of bright orange urine. He was suddenly confused and unsure about what he was doing or even how he had gotten out here. For a moment, he didn't recognize the white van at his back—had someone kidnapped him and driven him out here for some reason?—but then he recalled swiping the keys from the maintenance room. He recalled Mr. Zebka and the errands he used to run for him. He remembered, too, how the Spider had slapped a hand to the window of the vehicle just hours ago and had bared its true arachnidan face to him.

He shook his head, as if to actively clear his mind, zipped up his fly, then hoofed it back toward the van. He was about to climb into the driver's seat when Donald, the sometimes-friend/sometimes-bully from his youth whose breath always reeked of vomit, grabbed him from behind. A meaty, red-freckled arm snaked its way around Toby's throat, and he could feel the bigger boy lifting his sneakers off the ground. Toby struggled, swung his legs, tried to take out Donald's shins, tried to butt him in the face with the back of his head. But it was futile: the struggle lasted only a moment before the world turned gray, gray, grayer, black.

He dreamed a dark shape stood above him, eclipsing the sun.

Toby came to on his back, lying face up on the desert floor, the crotch of his pants wet. The sun had repositioned itself farther west while Toby had lain here unconscious, and in doing so, the topography looked to have changed. Horizon lay in every direction he looked. Shadows were misaligned. Desert plants appeared to have uprooted themselves and scurried about like children playing musical chairs. All of this: just to confuse and unmoor him.

He sat up and brushed sand from his arms. There was a clot of flies hovering above his dampened crotch, so he swatted them away, too. He heard the vampire's voice yet again, a more taunting quality to it now: *You don't belong here. You don't belong anywhere.*

He stood, focusing on a particular Joshua tree that grew against an outcropping of white stone in the distance, in order to anchor himself. He was dizzy and dehydrated. His head felt funny—untrustworthy, even. Desperately, he tried to remember what had caused him to pass out but couldn't.

Maybe you're not here at all, said a voice in his head. Not the vampire this time, but some unnamed, nebulous thing. *Maybe you're under hypnosis in some therapist's office somewhere right now. Or maybe you're suffering a terrible nightmare on that sodden mattress in the self-storage container in the city, strips of flypaper dangling above your head like party streamers, and none of this is actually happening.*

It was not an outcropping of white stone behind the Joshua tree, but a stone chapel: he could see it clearly enough even from this distance, despite how much his mind tried to convince him it was a mirage. He could make out the warped, sun-bleached arcade over the massive double doors, the Spanish tile on a section of the wavy roof, the empty bell tower rising up from behind the Joshua tree, formidable even in its bell-less-ness. For a moment, as he stood there catching his bearings, he thought he caught the oily scent of incense on the air.

He climbed back into the van and covered the distance to the church behind the wheel. The church filled up the van's windshield as he approached, hazy behind a cloud of risen dust. Somehow, it looked even more like a mirage the closer he got, while simultaneously looking all the more real, too.

"If I don't belong here," he said aloud, unaware that he was actually doing so, "then how was I able to find it?"

And not just *find it*—the sensation that he was being *drawn* to it was now unmistakable.

When he was close enough, he shut down the engine and hopped out of the van. He felt instantly renewed, a live wire. The sun was hot, nearly sizzling the sweat on his skin, but he didn't notice. He was in the middle of nowhere, and this just felt *right*. Heart pounding, he stared up at the church, and at an iron cross nailed above the threshold. Not wasting another moment, he hurried up the crumbling, warped steps toward the church's double doors. Thinking—

(don't be silly Renfield that place is not for you)

—of a series of puzzle pieces all falling neatly into place. Or maybe tumblers in a lock—*click!*

"Click," he uttered, the word sticking dryly to the back of his throat.

He reached out, grasped the wrought-iron handles, tugged on them. They didn't open, but the iron cross above the door swung as if on a hinge, and now hung upside down directly above his head.

Applying a bit more force, Toby wrenched open the sturdy wooden doors. They shrieked.

A hazy interior took shape before his eyes; not so much the interior of a church but the resolution of churchlike accoutrements that conspired to convince his mind that he was standing *within* a church, or at least some place that held a measure of sacred tenor. There were two columns of oak pews, maybe a dozen deep, furry with desert dust and garlanded in spiders' webs. The floorboards were the same—wooden, dusty, ancient. Sunlight filtered in through the cracked and grime-streaked windows that flanked the nave, running panels of geometric daylight along the church's floor; Toby passed through these crisscrossing beams of light as he moved beyond the narthex, progressed down the nave, and finally stood before the pulpit.

An altar of sorts stood at its center—a thing constructed of crude white stone that looked to Toby very much like bone. He stepped up to it, ran a hand along its cool, uneven surface. Felt the power that it held.

He was *here.*

"This is a sacred place," said a voice behind him.

Toby whirled around to find Donald sitting in one of the pews. He suddenly remembered the chokehold outside the van, which was what had caused him to fall unconscious. What in the world was Puke-Breath Donald doing all the way out here?

He began to ask: "What are you do—"

"A *turning* place," Donald added, interrupting him. He hadn't aged a day since he and Toby were kids, back in Palmdale, and Toby knew that couldn't be normal. Donald's face was round and sweaty, his bright orange clown's hair like a fitted cap on his head, shaggy enough to cover his ears. He was wearing a striped, sweat-stained polo shirt, and when he leaned forward and rested his arms on the back of the pew in front of him, Toby could see that his elbows were dirty.

"That's what I want," Toby said to the ghost, or whatever Donald was. "To be turned."

"Transmogrification," said Donald.

Toby nodded. "Yes. Whatever you want to call it. Just *yes*."

Donald got up and slid out of the pew. His jeans were filthy, and Toby could see that the boy's clothing—his whole body, really—was covered in a diaphanous cloak of spider webs, just like the pews; they drifted about him like smoke as he moved. "Three days, three nights," Donald said. "Do you think you can make it? Do you think the devil will come to you and set you free?"

Toby opened his mouth to speak, but nothing came out.

His heart was hammering in his chest.

"If you're going to commit, then commit, Dumbo," said Donald. "But if this doesn't work out, what's your backup plan? What will you do then?"

Without waiting for a response, Donald turned and walked out of the chapel and into the desert.

Toby blinked, sweat stinging his eyes. After a moment, he hurried outside after Donald, but by the time he staggered back out into the daylight, heels of his sneakers punching divots into the hard-packed sand, Puke-Breath Donald was already long gone.

—◇—

He set up camp inside the church that first night. His bedroll spread out beside the altar on the pulpit, a series of candles around him to give some light. Wind came howling through the desert sometime around midnight, a sound that was very nearly alive; it summoned Toby to his feet and out into the night, desperate to see if the creature had come to him early. Sand whipped his face like buckshot and stung his eyes. Above, the moon glowered down at him behind a membrane of clouds. Eyes tearing, he scanned the darkness for any sign of movement, of a thing approaching, but could see nothing.

But wait—

There were mesas in the distance, a whole file of them. In the darkness and beneath the light of the moon, they looked like the massive, segmented backbone of some prehistoric creature. Something moved along the top of one of the mesas, or so Toby thought—the sand was whipping at his face and stinging his eyes and he couldn't watch it for very long.

It's too soon, anyway, Donald whispered in his head. *Three days and three nights, remember?*

"I belong here," Toby whispered back, as if Donald had been arguing this fact.

Of course you do, Donald said again in his head . . . and although Toby could not see him—not like earlier that day, when he'd spied him seated in the pew inside the church, dirty elbows and all—he knew that Donald was grinning at him. *Of course you do.*

He recalled what the vampire had told him, and so he set to work building a fire in the sand. Once it burned brightly, he sat cross-legged on the ground. The temperature had dropped considerably, and the ratty concert tee and cargo shorts he wore were barely enough to keep him warm. The fire did little to help, but this was part of the process as it had been told to him.

He owned very little that defined him as a human being. He had to give great thought to what items he could open his wrist and bleed upon, though when it occurred to him, it had snapped perfectly into place, as if he should have always known.

The shoebox sat on his lap now. He pulled the lid off and tossed it into the fire. The flames grew as it burned, and the world brightened for a moment all around him. He could feel the heat from it against the clammy, waxen flesh of his face.

Inside the shoebox were countless Polaroid photographs, each one of Toby himself, childlike but aging, taken one day after the next. When he compared them against each other now, he could actually see the physical change, subtle as the change was: the widening of the space between his eyes, the deepening of his brow, the darkening of his hair. His mouth was a mouth in every photo, yet he knew it was really just a facade to mask the tube-like proboscis buried underneath. Everyone wore a mask. The Spider had taught him that.

There was a Swiss Army knife clipped to the van's key ring. It looked old and rusted, so he ran the blade through the flames to sterilize it. A meager blade; an embarrassment of a knife. He wondered, not for the first time, if this was the actual weapon of choice of the Swiss Army.

Something fluttered in the darkness over his head. He glanced skyward, kinking his neck, but saw nothing but a vast canopy of stars.

The fire crackled.

He rested his left hand on his knee, wrist up. He knew it would be foolish to cut too deep—there was a first-aid kit in his backpack back in the church, but little good that would do him if he bled out while sitting out here—so he only poked the tip of the knife blade against the tender flesh of his wrist at first, watching the flesh dimple, studying how it yielded beneath the dullish point of the impotent little knife.

He wondered what was inside him.

"Fuck it," he said, and insinuated the blade into the flesh of his wrist.

He felt no pain at first. There wasn't even any blood. In fact, he wondered if he'd actually cut himself at all, or if he was just imagining all of this. But when he withdrew the blade, he could clearly see the narrow slit in the pale skin. A moment later, a thread of dark blood oozed out, running all the way down to the crook of his elbow. A moment after *that*, he could feel the pain of the incision—a sharp, acerbic rupture to the fabric of his human form.

He raised his arm and let the blood speckle down onto the Polaroid pictures jumbled inside the shoebox. He wasn't sure how much blood he was supposed to give—she hadn't been specific on that score—but when he began to feel ill, he figured that was enough. He tossed the shoebox of Polaroid pictures onto the fire.

The flames flashed momentarily green.

That fluttering sound was back, somewhere above his head.

He kept his eyes trained on the flames.

On the flames.

On the *flames*.

The vision that came to him was not of the variety he had been expecting. Instead, what he saw before his eyes was the Spider, back in the kitchen of the Chamber Street apartment, the old rotary phone pressed to her ear. She was speaking to someone about him—the police, maybe, or perhaps a neighbor who had called to expel a complaint—and she was moving back and forth throughout the kitchen as she spoke. The phone was a terrible mustard yellow, as was the cord, and as she paced and paced and paced while speaking, that mustardy umbilicus snagged on chair backs and appliances, on a broom handle and the sink faucet. She created a mustard-yellow—

(web)

—cat's cradle as she paced back and forth, back and forth, throughout the kitchen. At one point, when the crisscrossing cord became too cumbersome to pass through, the Spider extended one pale, fuzzy-slippered foot, and pressed down upon the suspended cord like a tightrope walker. The slipper fell away, and Toby could see the bare foot, the crusty calluses on the heel and sole, the hammertoes, the bouquet of bulging varicose veins blooming from the Spider's ankle and traversing up the pale, doughy trunk of a shin, a thigh. A second foot upon another strand of cord, and then she was walking that web, all the while speaking his name over and over again into the telephone receiver.

Toby made an aggrieved sound way back in his throat, and it was as if this vision of the Spider could *hear* him; she froze atop her bed, her head cocked at an angle that caused her eyes to gleam. She was staring at him, even though she was there on her web in her kitchen and he was . . . well, on his way to oblivion.

She thrust the telephone at him. He could see smoke rising in tendrils through the vents in the receiver's mouthpiece. A static shushing sound began to emanate from the phone. It was nothing but a jumble of whispers at first—distant, muted voices, each of them tangled together like bits of twine, and unintelligible—but after a while, Toby began to discern what they were saying:

What do you have?

A set of fingers: fingers for feeling, for touching, for probing into unseen places.

A nose: for sniffing out injustice, corruption, dislocation.

A pair of eyes: for skirting past the things you should have seen to prevent all of this from happening in the first place.

A tongue: for speaking your truth.

A duo of ears: for hearing what I'm saying to you.

Do you hear what I'm saying to you?

Hear me —
What I'm saying to you.

He was thinking of THE WONDERFUL THING.

When he opened his eyes, he found himself staring at the stars. He had passed out, or at least fallen into a momentary fugue state. He sat up, cold and shivering. No idea how long he had been lying here, but the fire had dwindled to a collection of smoldering embers, and he could see no remnants of the cardboard shoebox or the Polaroid pictures he had tossed upon it.

He felt woozy. His wrist was still bleeding. In fact, the entirety of his inner arm was black with blood. Flies swarmed in the air around him, hungry to feast.

Urging himself to his feet, he felt the world tilt once more, and staggered in the direction of the chapel. There was hydrogen peroxide and bandages in the first-aid kit in his backpack, so the wound at his wrist wouldn't be a problem. His disappointment, however, was in the vision itself—that of the Spider walking her mustard-yellow web, and the strange conglomeration of voices that had hissed like steam out of the telephone—and he could not reconcile what that had to do with why he was out here.

He was about to enter the church when, once again, he heard that fluttery, windswept sound. He glanced behind him, and thought—

—for just a moment—

—that he saw something large and humanoid swoop down from the sky before sailing off toward the moonlit horizon.

He went hiking the next day beneath the blazing summer sun. He told himself it was to keep away the boredom, but in reality, he was hunting for evidence of where the desert devil might reside— hoofed tracks in the sand; the yawning, pitch-black mouth of a cave;

a glimpse of a shape far in the distance, wavy behind a curtain of rising desert heat. He recalled glimpsing something moving atop the mesas last night, so he headed in that direction. He drank minimal water and ate little food; a sacrifice had to be made during this ritual. At one point, he came across buzzards picking apart the remains of a deer, snapping pink, sinewy tendrils from the deer's flyblown carcass in their hooked beaks. He assumed it had been a buzzard that had flown over his head last night, after he'd hallucinated that vision of the Spider and the voices hissing from the telephone. What else could it have been? He shouted at them now, flailed his arms, even barked like a dog, but the buzzards hardly acknowledged him. Another time, he saw a rattlesnake that possessed a pair of gold, illuminative eyes; wondering if this might be a form the devil-vampire creature might take, Toby dropped to his knees in supplication before the reptile. The rattler coiled back, tight as a spring. Its tail began to make that terrible maraca sound, *chigga chigga chigga chigga*, moving so fast it blurred. Toby's eyes leaked tears as he waited—as he *hoped*— for it to strike. But the snake only fled from him, rapidly carving its way through the sand and between the springs of dry, marrow-hued underbrush that covered much of the desert floor.

By the time he reached the base of the mesas, the sun was directly overhead. Sweat rolled down his face and his hair felt like a damp wig on his head. There would be no climbing these smooth-walled monoliths, so he resigned to circumnavigating their base, searching for any evidence of the creature he thought he'd seen the night before. After a while, he realized he'd been hearing an unusual ringing sound for some time. What could be making such a sound way out here? He slipped around the side of a pillar of brown stone and saw, tucked down what appeared to be a narrow alleyway carved into the rock formation, a yellow rotary phone—just right there, stuck to the wall of rock.

It was ringing.

He knew the sight of this thing should bother him—this was not normal or even natural, after all—yet he went to it anyway, and with a tempered tranquility. He picked up the receiver—the plastic was hot against the palm of his hand, having been out here baking in the sun all morning—and placed it to his ear.

That papery whispering was on the line—the same whispery voice that had issued from the Spider's telephone in last night's hallucination:

What do you see?

The city below at night from the cusp of a hillside, a dizzying blur of efficient sodium lights, of vehicular traffic shushing by in a bleary stream of headlights and taillights. The flickering neon behind crowded shop windows, the spiral of fireflies in the dark and bottomless desert. The sight of pale moon-faces gaping at you; the sight of the moon itself, high and mighty, overseeing all things in the strip of emptiness that separates our cities. These are two worlds collided—you understand that, don't you? Maybe you see it, maybe you don't. I am not your eyes; therefore, I cannot tell.

What I can see is you creeping stealthily through that city, from street corner to street corner, observing the worn faces, the resignation, the apathy, all within the stricture of that urban depot, the city, the city, the city, where everyone survives in a trembling hive of overloaded senses— of sightssss and soundsss and smellssss and tastessss and feelingsss grazed upon the fingertips.

Or maybe you see me.

Do you see me?

If I wore your body and looked out of your eyes, how would I perceive myself?

Maybe you see me for the thing I am, the thing I'm becoming. What do you think? What do I look like to you?

There is a traffic light at the intersection of First and Denmark that never turns green.

There is a Chinese food restaurant in Inglewood that also exists simultaneously in Las Vegas, in New York City, in Paris, in Siberia, while also floating endlessly in the gassy atmosphere of Jupiter.

What do you see?

There is a fly trembling in a spider's web within the curled armrest of a pew at Our Lady Queen of Angels.

What do you see?

Maybe, when I'm done with you, you'll see everything.

Then the line went dead.

Toby peeled the phone from his ear and stared at it, perhaps expecting to witness tendrils of smoke or steam spiraling out of the holes in the mouthpiece. But it was just a regular phone (albeit fixed to the wall of a mesa), so he hung it up. As he retreated out of that narrow stone alleyway, he was aware that he should have been more unnerved by what had just happened, but that tranquility was overtaking his entire body now.

He felt, for once in his life, somewhat at peace.

At the hottest point of the day, he turned and headed back to the shelter of the church. The water in his thermos was no longer cold; it felt oily against his lips and tasted foul as he dumped it down his throat. When he rubbed his bandaged arm across his mouth, he saw his arm and the back of his hand were slick with blood. Panic shuttled through him—had he injured himself somehow? Had the incision in his wrist reopened and was now bleeding through the bandage? But then he realized it wasn't *his* blood; he upended the thermos and watched blood spill out. It pattered to the desert floor, soaking into the sand, then spread with an eerie sentience in multiple directions, the puddle gradually widening at Toby's feet. He could see the sun reflected in that crimson pool, his own face, too. And behind him—a glimpse of some amorphous, fleeting thing swifting at his back. He spun around, but he was alone. And when he looked back down at the ground, he saw that the blood was gone, too, and there was only the remainder of his water soaking into the sand.

At one point, he walked directly over a shallow grave, but was none the wiser.

That night—his second night—as he sat on his bedroll beside the altar reading *Dracula* by candlelight, an open container of peanut butter in his lap, he heard a whispery, fluttery movement somewhere in the nave of the church. To Toby, it sounded like the leathery flapping of bats' wings. He looked up, but of course it was too dark for him to make out anything up there, even with all the candles lit and the scant moonlight ghosting in through the windows.

But wait—

A pair of luminous golden eyes stared back at him from the far end of the nave. He could not discern the shape of the thing those eyes belonged to, but something—some animal part of his brain— warned him that it was very *big*.

He rose shakily to his feet just as the thing at the far end of the church rose, too. He watched as those beacon headlight eyes ascended, higher, higher, higher, until Toby was certain the thing was either levitating or silently scaling the wall of the church toward the ceiling. Strands of gossamer wafted down from the rafters; when one strand touched a candle flame, it popped and sizzled and the flame briefly flashed green.

Toby picked up one of the candles and carried it down off the pulpit. He advanced down the center aisle of the church toward the place where those shining yellow eyes continued to levitate.

"My name," he said, his voice shaking, "is Toby Kampen. I've come here to seek you out. *Please...*"

More gossamer strands drifted down from the rafters, draping like snakeskin over the backs of the pews. One fell on Toby's right shoulder, and when he brushed it off, he was unnerved to find that it had a tacky, adhesive quality that caused it momentarily to adhere to his fingertips.

Those yellow eyes were high above him now, the thing itself tucked away in some corner where the walls of the church met the ceiling. In the daytime, the ceiling of the church was only a scant few feet above Toby's head; but now, with nothing but darkness and shadow up there, the church had grown taller, perhaps infinitely tall. Toby could not see the rafters or the ceiling for all that height and darkness.

"Please," he begged, and wondered for the first time if this creature might actually be afraid of *him*.

He sensed it shifting about up there, its massive body knocking those gossamer strands from the rafters, its flesh—whatever passed for its flesh—rustling against the stone walls with a sound like dead leaves sliding along pavement. He could smell it, too—the coppery scent of blood.

The eyes dimmed to darkness.

Toby waited for them to reappear.

They did not.

The following day, he awoke on the floor of the church, slimy with perspiration and wracked with the shakes. He felt feverish and cold at the same time, his teeth clacking together uncontrollably in his skull. He crawled to one of the jugs of water, tore the cap from it, then upended the contents down his throat. A moment later, he was gagging and vomiting a stream of blood onto the floor of the church. He looked at the jug, dropping it when he saw it was half filled with a deep crimson liquid. Blood splashed up in a geyser, and the jug rolled away.

He dragged himself on his hands and knees to the other jugs, but each of them was filled with blood as well. He could feel his thirst pulsing in his throat, dehydration wringing the last vestiges of moisture from his hot, steaming sweat. Unless *he* was turned by whatever was out there taunting him, that blood was undrinkable.

He rummaged through the back of the van, found a half-empty bottle of Gatorade, and guzzled it down. It had been in there boiling in the heat of the van, so it tasted like liquid fire as Toby poured it down his throat, but he didn't care. When he was done, he licked the remaining droplets off the plastic cap.

It was there, squatting down like some homunculus in the back of that steamy van, his skin baking and his body trembling with chills, that he recognized he had a choice: he could continue on to the third and final night, or he could get behind the wheel of the van and drive the hell back home. It was a fleeting thought, one that lingered no longer than that flash of green flame from last night when the fallen strand of gossamer came in contact with the candle, and he did not even humor it.

There would be no going back home.

If the vampire did not come for him tonight, then he was prepared to die out here.

He tossed the empty Gatorade bottle aside and was about to climb down out of the van when he heard a muted thumping, followed by a scratching sound against the floor—as if something was underneath the van, raking a set of claws against the undercarriage. Toby placed one ear to the floor of the van and listened.

Those tangled whispers floating up to greet him:

What do you smell?

The decay of a city long past its prime? The walking corpses of the upper class cluttering the boulevards, washing up bloated and flyblown along the shores of Michelin Star restaurants, their hideous, thickened corpses decaying behind the wheels of overpriced luxury automobiles?

Let me take you far away from that living graveyard, straight out to the high desert, where there is only the wind's unscented breeze and the aroma of flowering desert plants. Get on your knees, touch the earth, and inhale its rich scent. There is something greater than you can fathom, far down below—the rich, coppery smell of a bloodline that gives life to the scant few of us who know where to find it and how to extract the lifeblood from it. Puncture this vein with me.

That is the smell of lifeblood.

Do you smell it?

Do you?

It is all for you.

Toby suddenly felt queasy. He glanced at the empty bottle of Gatorade and wondered what, exactly, had been in it.

Back out beneath the blazing desert sun, as Toby staggered back to the church, he looked up and saw Donald standing beneath the minimal shade of the Joshua tree. Donald was still just a kid, but now there were sets of puncture wounds along the exposed flesh of his arms, as if from several dozen snakebites. His face was even rounder than usual—swollen, particularly around the neck—and the skin there was a deep bluish purple, like one giant bruise.

"Maybe you don't belong here after all," Donald said. Some black, tarry substance oozed out of one corner of his mouth, but he was grinning at Toby all the same. "Maybe you don't belong *anywhere*."

"Fuck you, Donald."

"You'll die out here. Nothing is coming for you. There will be no salvation."

"You don't know that." His voice was a dry rasp.

"Maybe you're already dead. Do you remember the buzzards? The ones that were eating the deer? You couldn't scare them off. It was as if you were just a ghost, or maybe a gust of desert wind. I mean, did you really take a good look at that deer those things were eating? Are you *sure* it was a deer? Because maybe it was *really* just a dumb guy in a Megadeth T-shirt who thinks he's a fly."

"It was a deer," Toby countered . . . although, admittedly, he couldn't remember all that well. *Had* it been a deer? Could the dark, dusty hide of that animal carcass actually have been his own *shirt*? No, he wouldn't fall for such bullshit. "I know what you're doing, Donald. This is a test to see if I'll turn around and leave. Well, that's not going to happen."

"Can't leave if you're already dead, Dumbo," Donald said, more of that black tarry stuff dribbling down from his mouth. It came from both corners now, which gave the appearance that his mouth was on a hinge, like a ventriloquist's dummy. "But come here, and I'll tell you a secret."

"No," Toby said, and continued toward the church.

"I wasn't asking."

A shadow coasted along the ground—something large flying overhead. Toby looked up but got an eyeful of the sun. He winced, turned his head, then suddenly smelled Donald's hot, fetid puke breath against the side of his face.

"You big dumb stupid," Donald laughed, giddy, and wrapped Toby up in a chokehold.

This time, Toby fought harder. His body was slick with sweat, which enabled him to slip his chin down beneath the crook of

Donald's elbow. The arm, dotted with all its little puncture wounds, was suddenly right against Toby's parched, peeling lips.

He opened his mouth and bit down. Hard. Shook his head from side to side like a crocodile. He felt a hunk of Donald's flesh tear off in his mouth, and Donald himself staggered backward.

"Jerk," the bully said, somewhat nonplussed.

Toby spat out the hunk of flesh, his own spit dyed black by the strange liquid that pumped through Donald and dribbled out of his mouth. He clambered up the steps toward the church's double doors—they stood wide open like a pair of arms ready to greet him—but he was driven down onto the wooden planks by a knee to the small of his back. Donald straddled him, somehow bigger and stronger than Toby despite him still being a child. Those arms snaked around Toby's throat again, and Toby, even in his panic, managed to glimpse the wound from where he'd bitten Donald: protruding from the wound and matted in that oozing black viscous was the bristling, segmented trochanter of a massive spider.

Before Toby could scream, he was choked once more into unconsciousness.

When he awoke hours later, it was fully dark. He was no longer on the church steps, but splayed out on the desert floor equidistant from the church and the white van. His flesh burned, and when he sat up, he saw his arms and shins crawling with fire ants. He shrieked, swiped them off, and clumsily rose to his feet.

He was about to creep back into the church when he was overcome by the sensation that someone—or something—was watching him from some impossible distance.

Toby Kampen, the Human Fly, felt his antennae prick up.

Yet there was nothing out here that he could see. There was nothing behind the church, either, except a cadre of tumbleweeds ambulating across the desert floor. The moon was full and the sky was clear, and he could see straight out to the flat-topped mesas in the distance. He heard a gust of wind kick up, then felt it come, bullying the sagebrush and casting fine grains of sand against his abraded, ant-bitten flesh. It was a warm wind, almost preternatural. He thought he heard, too, the nearby maraca of a rattlesnake—a sound that reminded him of his collection of jumping beans and how, when he was younger, he would sometimes shake them in their little wooden container in hopes of stirring them to life.

Something whisked through the air above his head—something large enough and close enough to cause him to drop to his knees to avoid it. He heard the flapping of giant wings then felt that warm breeze again. Grains of sand once more peppered his face. He looked up in time to glimpse a dark shape soaring through the night sky out toward the mesas, visible only as a definitive shade of black against a backdrop that appeared even blacker. The thing came to rest atop a mesa, and Toby thought he could make out the shape of its body—bat-like and humanoid all at once—though maybe it was just his imagination. It moved swiftly along the tops of the mesas, from one end to the other. For an instant, Toby lost sight of the creature—it vanished within a patch of darkness too dense—but then it reappeared at the cusp of the final mesa. He stopped there, its body crouched low, and in the moonlight Toby could make out the triangular plane of massive wings spread across his back.

As he stared at it, the thing took to the sky again. It was a black, nondescript smudge for many seconds . . . but then he could see the simmering yellow glow of its eyes, the tremendous span of his bat-like wings, the multitude of limbs that were retracted beneath its body as it soared faster and faster in Toby's direction.

He couldn't help it: some animal instant part of the Human Fly caused him to run back inside the church. He pulled the large wooden doors closed, then staggered backward down the aisle toward the pulpit, his breath searing the trembling, parched stovepipe of his throat. His flesh felt on fire from the ants and there was a sudden pounding at the epicenter of his skull.

"It's already in here with you," Donald said, startling him. Toby turned and saw the boy seated once more in one of the pews. His face was still purple and swollen, his beefy arms poking through the sleeves of his too-tight polo shirt riddled with snakebites. Toby felt the world tilt to one side as Donald stood from the pew and inched his way toward the aisle.

Outside, the wind picked up, tossing debris against the exterior of the church. Those massive wooden doors rattled in their frame.

Sand blew against the stained-glass windows of the church.

More strands of gossamer drifted down from that impossibly high ceiling, causing Toby to peer up into that abyss, holding his breath.

"Not up there, Dumbo," Donald said. "Right *here*."

Toby turned and looked at Donald, who still stood there in his filthy, sweat-stained, too-small clothes—a boy who should no longer still be a boy, yet was one nonetheless. As Toby stared at him, Donald reached up, dug a set of fingernails into the ridge of his own forehead, and peeled away a thick strip of flesh. It came away with a sound like tearing a paper grocery bag in two, and as the flap of skin fell away, Toby could see part of the thing's *real* face underneath— the glowing amber orb of an eye within a nest of spiny black quills.

The thing beneath the Donald-face took a step in his direction. Black, syrupy blood drooled out of the rent in the thing's false face and splattered to the church floor in dark, wet clumps.

There was a cracking sound, and the doors of the church buckled inward; a skirl of wind and desert sand whipped through the chapel, jagged little granules shotgunning against the back of the wooden pews. Toby slammed his palms to his ears and squeezed his eyes shut just as the debris rained against his face.

A creaking, moaning sound filled the chapel. Eyes still closed, Toby backed himself into one corner of the church, the heels of his hands still pressed against his ears, thinking—

(what do you hear what do you see)

—a whirlwind of confused and claustrophobic thoughts, a swirl of them, a desperation of thoughts—

(what do you have what do you have what do you have)

(?????)

—until he heard what sounded terribly like the breaking of bone.

He opened his eyes.

His hands dropped away from his ears.

His heart galloped in his chest.

The Donald-thing was no more; what stood now in the chapel with him was a creature of impossible design, a thing that had wrenched itself through a rip in the fabric of the universe, using Donald as the doorway for its arrival. The waxen, rubbery tendrils of Donald's flesh lay in loops and coils at the creature's clawed feet, along with the boy's grimy, sweat-sodden clothes. As Toby stared at the thing, it shambled forward in a simulacrum of ambulation—an orchestration of stuttering limbs that at once appeared (to Toby) as arachnidan yet somehow human all at once, an unfurling of gray, spiny appendages, a rolling undulation of limbs, a *shuddering* of limbs, that rustled like autumn leaves in their movement, fluid yet ungainly, precise yet distempered and aloof and unholy. It was a thing, Toby knew instantly, that had full self-awareness of its alienness—a thing that knew it did not belong, shouldn't be here on this plane, shouldn't exist in the same story as the hypodermic thorns of a desert cactus, the furtive chuckwallas, the oppressive heat of the California summer sun.

A spider in man-form.

A man in spider-form.

A devil and a vampire all in one, with a face like a corral of burning embers, and a leathery wingspan that widened and widened and widened until the membrane of those wings occupied the totality of the chapel at its back.

Toby's breath rasped from his throat. Impossibly, he felt himself take a step toward the creature.

"Please," Toby hissed, then knelt to the floor in front of the creature, raising his head to expose his jugular for the beast.

The vampire—

(shuffled gusted floated fluttered rushed breezed ghosted)

—advanced toward him. The topography of the creature's membranous wings looked like the desert floor, as if the flesh was also a map, only one that Toby could not decipher. Those simmering, ember-like eyes burned with a heat that Toby could feel on his skin the closer the creature drew.

He could smell the creature—

(what do you smell?)

—and his eyes watered from the reek of it.

And then it was looming above him, encompassing his entire world. Toby could hear its respiration, a labored suck-pull-exhale that wheezed like a bellows. He could see the coarse black hairs around a maw of serrated fangs billowing as it breathed. He felt hypnotized by the amber glow of its spidery eyes.

The massive wings curled around him in an embrace.

The thick, spiny appendage that swelled between the creature's legs rose and pressed against Toby's inner thigh.

He could *smell* it: charred logs and coppery pennies.

Yessssss, Toby thought, and more tears purled from the corners of his eyes.

The vampire lowered its face toward Toby's.

That phallic appendage prodded against his abdomen.

He could feel the creature's hot exhalations along the pale, sweaty, quivering slope of his neck.

Yesssssssssss!

His mind spun. For a moment, he was back in the apartment on Chamber Street, watching the Spider motorvate back and forth within the confines of that tiny kitchen, the mustard-yellow cord of the rotary phone forming a geometric cat's-cradle web as it snared around the tops of the kitchen chairs, the appliances, a solitary doorknob.

Something . . .

Something—

He felt the vampire's fangs sink into his flesh.

The world went gray.

What do you have?

An empty existence, where your body is a husk and your husk is a body? Where all the conventions of humanity conspire to falsify your front to the world at large? A heart that beats like the flapping of hummingbird wings? A tongue that laps at the salty bulbs of perspiration that bulge and quiver out from the pores of your upper lip? Fingers that tremble at the thought of a touch?

> *What*

do

> > *you*

> > > *have*

> *?*

—◇—

There was daylight pressing its face against the church windows when he awoke.

He staggered to his feet, pawing at his neck. He expected his fingers to come away wet and red with blood, but they were dry and colorless. He could feel no wound along his jugular. This, however, did not discourage him, for he understood that vampires had the ability to heal quickly and miraculously. There wouldn't *be* a wound from last night's escapade, he knew . . .

Yet he felt no different than the night before. His body was sore and weak and dehydrated. He looked to the place in the church where the vampire had ripped its way out of the Donald-thing, but there was no evidence of that having occurred, either.

Had he been turned?

Had he been *accepted*?

There was only one way to know . . .

He gathered himself into some semblance of a walk and negotiated the length of the narthex toward the chapel's double doors. They had been blown open by the force of the—

(vampire)

—wind the night before, and they remained open now: a sunlit yawn with an exposed throat of yellow desert beyond.

He approached the threshold, still cloaked in shadow, and stood there for several seconds. Maybe minutes. Maybe longer.

His mind went—

tickticktickticktickticktickticktickticktickticktickticktick

—as if he was something wound up and made of clockwork.

(what do you have?)

He was thinking of THE WONDERFUL THING as he took another step closer to the open doorway. He could feel the heat of the early morning just beyond the threshold. He kept pawing absently at his neck.

His head hurt.

Go for it, said Donald, *and if you catch fire and burn, then you catch fire and burn* ... But when Toby glanced back toward the dark section of the church, he couldn't see the boy anywhere. Still, the sentiment carried with it all the weight of the world: *Go. For. It.*

Toby Kampen, Human Fly and possible vampire, took a deep breath and stepped out into the daylight.

PART FOUR:

DEMETER

EIGHTEEN

1

Renney hunched over a scrapbook that sat on the corner of his desk, staring at the photos within, and felt that old familiar serpent coiling into a ball at the center of his gut. Behind him, Politano came into the office and peered over Renney's shoulder.

"Jesus Christ," Politano muttered.

"You know what these are, don't you," Renney said.

"I do."

"This isn't Gina Fortunado."

"No, it's not," Politano agreed. "It's the Andressen woman. But how did . . . ?"

Renney turned his head and peered out his office door, to where the woman—Maureen Park—was seated in a chair against the wall. She was clutching a paper cup of coffee in her hands, and she wore a pale, haunted expression on her face.

"You learn anything about these people?" Renney asked.

"Her fiancé is a movie producer. He's got money. Had a wife who drowned in a swimming pool. The son had some assault charges filed against him from a different stepmother—"

"Guy gets around."

"—but they were dropped."

Renney jerked his head in Maureen's direction, still perched motionless on that chair, clutching her coffee. "What about her?"

"She's a writer, published a novel several years ago," Politano said. "Young son was killed in a car accident in Wyoming, where she used to live. Other than that, her background is squeaky clean."

"Nice work," Renney said.

Politano leaned over and turned another page of the scrapbook. "Jesus Christ, Bill," he said again, and then said no more.

2

EXCERPT FROM TRANSCRIPT OF LANDON DAWSON INTERVIEW

RENNEY: State your full name for the recording, please.

DAWSON: Landon Emory Dawson.

RENNEY: Also present, for the record, is myself, Detective William Renney, and Sergeant A.J. Politano, Los Angeles County Sheriff's Department. Landon, could you confirm for the record that you are aware this is a voluntary interview, you are not in custody, and anything you say can potentially be used against you in a legal proceeding?

DAWSON: I'm aware.

RENNEY: I'm going to ask you about this scrapbook in a minute, but first I want to ask about your relationship with Maureen Park.

DAWSON: I have no relationship with Maureen Park.

RENNEY: She told us the two of you have a somewhat acrimonious situation.

DAWSON: That sounds like her.

RENNEY: Would you say that's true?

DAWSON: I told you, we don't have a relationship.

RENNEY: Ms. Park alleges that you put some sort of narcotic in a bottle of vodka two nights ago, which ultimately rendered her unconscious.

DAWSON: Are you kidding me?

RENNEY: Did you put any narcotics in a bottle of vodka, or any other substance in the house?

DAWSON: Narcotics?

POLITANO: Did you drug the vodka, Landon?

DAWSON: I did not.

RENNEY: Do you have any illegal narcotics in the house?

DAWSON: Did your guys find any when they tore the place apart?

RENNEY: Have you ever had any illegal narcotics in your possession?

DAWSON: [laughs] Next question.

RENNEY: Do you know what happened to the bottle of vodka?

DAWSON: I don't even know what this is about. How should I know what happened to it? What are you even asking?

RENNEY: Ms. Park said that when she regained consciousness, the bottle of vodka that she believed was drugged was no longer in the house.

DAWSON: She probably drank it. She's a drunk.

RENNEY: She said she didn't.

DAWSON: Well, I don't know what to tell you. I didn't do anything.

RENNEY: Two nights ago, did you come into physical contact with Ms. Park?

DAWSON: Is that what she's saying? I've never come into physical contact with her. What is she saying I did?

RENNEY: She says you came into physical contact with her while she was unconscious.

DAWSON: The fuck is "physical contact"? You mean, did I feel her up while she was blackout drunk? Did I poke my cock in her? No, man, I didn't do those things. I wasn't even in the house two nights ago. I was out with a friend.

POLITANO: Which friend would that be? Give us a name?

DAWSON: Ross Kline.

POLITANO: Anyone else?

DAWSON: Just Ross.

RENNEY: He could vouch for you?

DAWSON: Yes.

RENNEY: What'd the two of you do all night?

DAWSON: Went to a movie. I was never at the house and I didn't do anything to her. She's crazy.

RENNEY: She says you've been tormenting her. Saying things that make her uncomfortable.

DAWSON: She's welcome to leave if she's uncomfortable.

RENNEY: Have you ever threatened Ms. Park with bodily harm?

DAWSON: Nope.

RENNEY: Where were you between [dates redacted]?

DAWSON: I was staying at a motel in Glendale.

RENNEY: Your father said you were supposed to be in Europe. Why did you come home early and stay at a motel and not tell him? Why not just go home?

DAWSON: That place isn't my home. It's never been my home. It's a zoo. A circus.

RENNEY: What'd you do for those days while you were staying at the motel?

DAWSON: Ran around with some friends, hit a few bars, a few clubs.

RENNEY: Ms. Park said you told her you had been stalking her.

DAWSON: I didn't say that. "Stalking."

RENNEY: Did you tell her you followed her around for a few days?

DAWSON: I don't know if I said, "for a few days," but yes, I told her I followed her around.

RENNEY: Did you, in fact, follow her around?

DAWSON: In fact, yes.

POLITANO: Can you elaborate?

DAWSON: You guys talk like you're reading a dictionary. Elaborate on following someone around? It means I followed them around. What the fuck do you think it means?

RENNEY: Why did you follow her around?

DAWSON: I wanted to see who she was. I wanted to watch her in her natural habitat.

POLITANO: So you just followed her around the city? Watched her run errands, that sort of thing?

DAWSON: Is that a crime?

POLITANO: It's stalking.

DAWSON: I wouldn't call it that.

POLITANO: Yeah? What would you call it?

DAWSON: I'd call it being smart. Wanting to know who this woman was who Greg was so quick to want to marry.

RENNEY: Did you ever return to the house to watch her? Go into the house without her knowing?

DAWSON: It's my house.

RENNEY: Really? Because you just said it wasn't. Said it was a zoo, a circus. Not a home.

DAWSON: A home and a house are two different things.

RENNEY: Meaning what?

DAWSON: Listen, I followed her around, dug up some stuff about her on the internet. I wasn't breaking any laws. And I didn't attack her, or whatever it is she's claiming I did. I just wanted to know why this woman was marrying my father after only knowing him for a few months. I don't trust her, and I don't like her. And Greg doesn't exactly have a stellar reputation when it comes to holy matrimony.

RENNEY: Did you come into contact with Gina Fortunado during the time period you were staying at the motel in Glendale?

DAWSON: I don't know who that is.

RENNEY: You don't know Gina Fortunado? Here, look at this picture. You don't know that woman?

DAWSON: Oh, right. Yeah. I know her from the news. I know she was killed.

POLITANO: But you've never seen this woman in real life before? Think about it, Landon. I want you to be sure.

DAWSON: I don't have to think about it. I've never seen this woman before. She's cute, though.

RENNEY: What about this woman? Look at her photo. Recognize her?

DAWSON: Yes, I recognize her. I know who she is. Anderson.

RENNEY: Andressen. Melissa Jean Andressen.

DAWSON: Yes, that's right.

POLITANO: Tell us how you know her.

DAWSON: She was that woman who was killed last year.

RENNEY: Did you know her?

DAWSON: Just from her pictures on the news back when it happened. And from the photographs in that scrapbook, too. I guess that's where this is headed.

POLITANO: Did you ever come into contact with her?

DAWSON: Nope.

RENNEY: Where did you get those photographs?

DAWSON: They came with the scrapbook.

RENNEY: Okay, Landon. Then where did you get the scrapbook?

DAWSON: I bought it off this chick I know.

POLITANO: Who's that?

DAWSON: Her name's Freyja. I don't know her last name. I don't even know if that's her real first name.

RENNEY: Who is she?

DAWSON: A freaky deaky. I don't know her too well.

RENNEY: How do you know her?

DAWSON: From a club downtown.

POLITANO: This is like pulling teeth, Landon. What club?

DAWSON: Place called Fist.

RENNEY: What kind of club is that?

DAWSON: It's an everything club.

POLITANO: What's that mean?

DAWSON: Means anything goes. You wanna fuck? You can fuck. You wanna do drugs, you can do drugs. Bunch of weirdoes hang out there.

POLITANO: Including you?

DAWSON: Hilarious. I go sometimes. I don't mind weirdoes.

RENNEY: Let's get back to the scrapbook. You said you bought it off this woman?

DAWSON: A thousand bucks.

RENNEY: How'd you find out she had it?

DAWSON: It was making its way around the club.

POLITANO: People were passing this scrapbook around at this Fist place?

DAWSON: They pass around everything there. These weirdoes, they think if you touch an object that has some trauma attached to it, you can feel its power. Siphon it into yourself. Get strong—or maybe get off—from it.

RENNEY: So this scrapbook was just one of the items that was passed around for people to touch?

DAWSON: Exactly.

RENNEY: And you just happened to see it, and so you bought it from this Freyja gal?

DAWSON: No. Freyja told me about it. Said, "Remember that chick who was killed last year in the desert?" I sort of did. So then she showed me the scrapbook.

RENNEY: When was this?

DAWSON: Back when I was staying at the motel.

RENNEY: Why did she think you'd be interested in something like that?

DAWSON: Do either of you know who Greg is?

POLITANO: You mean your father?

DAWSON: He's a film producer, which means he's got zero talent to do anything else in the industry. He <u>did</u> write and direct one movie early in his career, a low-brow piece of garbage called <u>High Desert</u>. It's become an underground cult thing, but really, it's a piece of trash. Freyja and those other loonies, they love that movie. They're like sheep that way—they like anything they think is edgy or dark. Anyway, there's an opening scene of a dead woman in the desert, all five of her senses removed.

RENNEY: What?

DAWSON: You know, the five senses—see, hear, smell, taste, touch. Victim's got her eyes, ears, nose, fingers, and tongue cut out. The camera

just slowly closes in on this dead woman from
an aerial shot for the entirety of the opening
credits. Those weirdoes at Fist think it's high
art, but really, it's exploitative garbage.
Anyway, she showed me the pictures in that book,
and I could see the chick was cut up the same
way that actress was in the opening shot of the
movie.

RENNEY: Where did Freyja say she got the scrapbook?

DAWSON: She didn't.

RENNEY: You didn't ask her?

DAWSON: Didn't matter to me.

POLITANO: Why did you want it? Must've had a good
reason to pay a thousand bucks for it.

DAWSON: I thought it might come in handy down the
road.

RENNEY: Handy how?

DAWSON: Well, hasn't it? Scared the shit out of
Maureen.

RENNEY: Ms. Park said you told her your father had
killed that girl.

DAWSON: Yes. I lied. I told her the scrapbook was
Greg's. I suggested he might not be the man
she thinks he is. That sort of thing. I don't
remember exactly.

RENNEY: Why did you tell her that?

DAWSON: To scare her.

RENNEY: Why did you want to scare her?

DAWSON: So she'd leave.

RENNEY: Why would you want her to leave?

DAWSON: Because she makes Greg happy, and I can't abide Greg being happy. Hey, do you think she's coming back?

RENNEY: No, I don't think she's coming back. You wanted to scare her? Mission accomplished. That little stunt you pulled last night did the trick, Landon.

DAWSON: Stunt?

POLITANO: Ms. Park told us about what happened at the house. She said you threw a fit wearing a . . . was it a monkey mask?

DAWSON: [inaudible]

RENNEY: What was that?

DAWSON: The Monkey.

RENNEY: Right. That's what she said. A monkey mask.

DAWSON: Act Three. You meet the Monkey.

RENNEY: The hell does that mean?

DAWSON: It means this is all scripted bullshit. You'd think Greg would understand that, seeing how he's this big shot Hollywood producer. But he doesn't. He's blind.

RENNEY: I don't get what you mean. What's scripted?

DAWSON: Life. But there are only so many scenes. That's why shit ultimately repeats, you know? You remember a million years ago when a bunch

of movies all came out at the same time about
kids and parents switching bodies, or Tom Hanks
getting hair on his nut sack overnight? That
ain't coincidence. Time runs in a circle, like
a reel of film, and there's only so much of it.
Sooner or later, shit's gonna repeat.

RENNEY: That's an interesting theory. I knew
someone once who believed a similar thing.

POLITANO: Ms. Park said you attacked your father.
The guy's got a busted nose, broken jaw, not to
mention a good bit of damage to the house, but
he's not pressing charges. Told us Ms. Park was
mistaken, and that he'd fallen down the stairs.
He's covering for you, in other words.

DAWSON: That tracks.

POLITANO: Why do you say that?

DAWSON: The only thing Greg Dawson cares about is
his reputation. He can't press charges against
me, it would look bad. He'd rather just send me
off somewhere and forget about me.

POLITANO: Why not just go off somewhere on your
own?

DAWSON: And give that cocksucker the satisfaction?
You fellas don't understand—I fucking <u>hate</u> that
man. He keeps hoping for a happy ending to this
little tale, but I'm not gonna let that happen.

3

Excerpt from Transcript
of Ross Kline Interview

RENNEY: Tell us about when Landon decided to leave
Europe. What reason did he give for coming back
to the States so early?

KLINE: Well, something upset him, something that
had to do with his dad. I didn't know what it was
at the time, but when I got back home—back to the
States, I mean—and hooked back up with him, he
told me his father had gotten engaged.

RENNEY: This was why he cut the trip to Europe
short?

KLINE: He's got a weird relationship with his
father. But I guess I'd be upset if I learned
about my dad getting remarried from some internet
article.

RENNEY: Why didn't you go home with him?

KLINE: To be honest, I wanted to. What was I gonna
do hanging around Europe on my own? I mean, I
didn't have the money. Landon bankrolled the
whole trip. Well, his dad did. Anyway, he gave me
his credit card and told me to hang around.

RENNEY: Why'd he want you to stay?

KLINE: Well, again, I didn't know until I came back
home, but he said he wanted it to look like he
was still in Europe in case his dad checked the
credit card statements.

RENNEY: Where was he staying when he came back from Europe?

KLINE: Some motel in Glendale. Motel 6.

RENNEY: Did you visit him at that motel when you got back.

KLINE: Yeah. Just once, though.

RENNEY: What was the state of things in that motel room?

KLINE: What do you mean?

RENNEY: What was he doing there all that time?

KLINE: The truth? Drugs. Drinking. When I got there, he had a bunch of E and was googling crazy shit on his laptop.

RENNEY: What crazy shit?

KLINE: Some of it was porn, some of it was shit about serial killers from Wikipedia. He also pulled up some website and showed me a picture of the woman his dad was going to marry. It was some book review website, and he said she was a writer. He bought one of her books, showed it to me. Then he says, "Hey, you wanna see something wild?" And then he shows me this, like, photo album, with all these pictures of some dead woman, all cut up. I asked him, hey, what is this, and he says they're photos of a murder victim. I asked him where he got it, and he said some freaky chick with rattlesnake teeth gave it to him.

POLITANO: What'd you do after he showed you the scrapbook?

KLINE: Had a couple of drinks. He asked if I wanted

to crash his dad's engagement party, and I said sure, let me know when. Then I left.

POLITANO: You weren't more concerned about those photos?

KLINE: To be honest, I thought he was full of shit. Landon is like that, always fucking with your head, trying to make you uncomfortable, keep you off-balance. You know guys like that?

RENNEY: Sure.

KLINE: But then I heard something about this dead girl found in the desert on the radio, and so I googled her. It made me think about that photo album. I realized Landon had been back in the States when that girl was killed.

RENNEY: What'd you do after that?

KLINE: I went and spoke to Landon's dad's fiancée.

RENNEY: Why her? Why not come to us?

KLINE: Because I didn't want to get mixed up in any of this. Although, well, I guess here I am.

RENNEY: Why not Landon's father?

KLINE: Why didn't I go to him instead, you mean? I don't know him all that good, and he's, I guess, a little intimidating. I guess I didn't want to have that conversation with him.

RENNEY: You thought Ms. Park was the best bet?

KLINE: I didn't know her, only met her briefly at the party at Landon's house. But she looked like someone who might listen to what I had to say.

RENNEY: And what'd you have to say?

KLINE: That I thought Landon might have killed that girl.

POLITANO: Has he ever done anything else to anyone in the past that would make you think he murdered that girl?

KLINE: He's never killed anyone, far as I know, if that's what you're asking. I've never seen him be . . . physical . . . with anyone, really. Except . . .

RENNEY: Except what?

KLINE: He's just got a way of making people uncomfortable.

RENNEY: Anything specific come to mind?

KLINE: No. I mean, he makes me uncomfortable.

POLITANO: Yet you still hang around with him.

KLINE: He's got a lot of money.

POLITANO: So he's a generous guy? A free spender? You like that about him?

KLINE: No, he's not a generous guy. He buys his friends. I got a free trip to Europe out of it.

RENNEY: Were you with Landon two nights ago?

KLINE: Yeah. We went to a movie, then hit some bars.

RENNEY: What movie did you see?

KLINE: It was a double feature. The Thing and some movie called Dead Rabbit.

RENNEY: He was with you the whole night?

KLINE: Yeah. Why?

RENNEY: The two of you ever go back to Landon's house that night?

KLINE: His house? Not that I remember.

RENNEY: Not that you remember?

KLINE: I mean, I was pretty drunk. Landon did the driving. I'm pretty sure I blacked out at some point. Woke up in my apartment.

RENNEY: Where was Landon during that time?

KLINE: With me. He was sleeping on my futon when I woke up.

RENNEY: Is it possible he drove back to his house while you were blacked out?

KLINE: I don't understand what this is about. Was he not allowed at his house?

RENNEY: Ms. Park claims he came into the house and drugged her drink.

KLINE: Oh.

POLITANO: Are you aware of anything like that, Ross?

KLINE: No. No way. But it sounds like something Landon would do.

POLITANO: Yeah?

KLINE: He would think it's funny.

4

EXCERPT FROM TRANSCRIPT
OF FREYJA GLEESON INTERVIEW

RENNEY: Please state your full name for the record.

GLEESON: Freyja Leigh Gleeson.

RENNEY: Age?

GLEESON: Twenty-three.

RENNEY: Where do you live?

GLEESON: I'm sort of between places at the moment. Been crashing on a friend's couch.

RENNEY: Are you currently employed, Ms. Gleeson?

GLEESON: No.

RENNEY: Your last place of employment was at a veterinary clinic on Boyle Street, is that right?

GLEESON: How'd you know that?

RENNEY: We ran your background. You were fired for stealing ketamine, then charged criminally. A felony, knocked down to a misdemeanor. That correct?

GLEESON: Yes.

RENNEY: What did you do with the ketamine?

GLEESON: I thought this was about that scrapbook?

POLITANO: We'll get there.

RENNEY: What did you do with the ketamine?

GLEESON: Sold it. Used some of it.

RENNEY: You ever provide any to Landon Dawson?

GLEESON: No.

RENNEY: Are you sure?

GLEESON: I'm sure.

POLITANO: His father's fiancée says Landon drugged her, put something in her drink. If you sold him anything, you'd want to tell us now, and get yourself on the right side of this thing.

GLEESON: The only thing Landon ever bought from me was that book. I swear.

RENNEY: Right. Okay, let's talk about that scrapbook. Where'd you get it?

GLEESON: It was a gift.

RENNEY: A gift?

POLITANO: From who?

GLEESON: This . . . well, this guy I know. Used to know.

RENNEY: Who's the guy?

GLEESON: I never knew his real name. I just called him Renfield.

POLITANO: That's from Dracula, right?

GLEESON: Yeah.

RENNEY: Why'd you call him that?

GLEESON: Because that's what he was—a Renfield.
He thought I was an actual vampire. I guess
I let him believe it. I sometimes wear these
porcelain fangs and colored contact lenses when
I go to certain clubs. This guy thought I was
the real deal. So I let him hang around, drive
me around the city, that sort of thing. It
was fun at first, messing with him and playing
along, making up stories about how I became a
vampire, stuff like that. But then things got
. . . well, they got weird. He started making me
uncomfortable. I realized this guy was actually
crazy, you know? He gave me the scrapbook as a
gift, and yeah, it was cool and all, but that's
when I tried to, you know, put some distance
between myself and him.

RENNEY: You look upset talking about him.

GLEESON: He upsets me. I don't like to think about
him. It was a mistake messing around with him
like that, and I wish I'd never met him.

RENNEY: Did he say where he got the photos in that
scrapbook?

GLEESON: No. I wondered about that, too, after a
while. All he said was that they were photos of a
woman who was murdered last year and her body was
found in the desert. He called it the "wonderful
thing," that scrapbook, and said it was a gift
for me. I looked at the photos and knew they were
real. That's when I knew I had to stop hanging
around with the guy.

RENNEY: Can you describe the scrapbook?

GLEESON: It was like a plush photo album. It said "Memories" on the cover. The pictures inside it were behind, like, a film of plastic. Just like a photo album I had as a kid.

RENNEY: Is this it?

GLEESON: Jesus. Yes.

POLITANO: How did Landon Dawson ultimately come to have this scrapbook in his possession?

GLEESON: He got it from me.

RENNEY: Walk us through how that happened.

GLEESON: Well, I told him about it. I showed it to him. The photos of the dead woman looked just like the opening scene in a movie Landon's father directed a bunch of years ago—<u>High Desert</u>. You ever seen it?

RENNEY: No.

POLITANO: No.

GLEESON: Well, at first I thought, how fucking wild. When I showed it to Landon, he said he'd buy it from me, and to name my price. So I did. One thousand bucks.

RENNEY: Did he say why he wanted the book?

GLEESON: No. And I didn't ask. Landon's a little weird, too. Not flat-out crazy like that Renfield guy, just a little off, you know? But he's loaded. Well, his father is.

RENNEY: This guy you call Renfield—where did you meet him?

GLEESON: At some club. I don't remember where.

RENNEY: He ever have anyone else hanging around with him?

GLEESON: Never. I don't think he had any friends or anything. Like I said, he was real strange.

POLITANO: Is there anything you could tell us about him that would help us find out who he is?

GLEESON: I don't know. I mean, I know the car he drove, but I don't know a license plate number or anything. Oh, and I've been to his apartment building once.

RENNEY: Really?

GLEESON: Not inside. I fell asleep in his car and I guess he just left me there in the back seat overnight.

POLITANO: Do you remember the address of the apartment building?

GLEESON: I don't remember it, but it would be in my Uber app history. I got an Uber to take me home from there.

POLITANO: You could get that for us?

GLEESON: Yes. I can check right now.

POLITANO: Perfect.

RENNEY: Is there anything else about this guy you think we should know?

[long pause]

RENNEY: Freyja?

GLEESON: Listen, I don't like cops, okay? And I know some of this might be . . . you know, might be my fault. That's why I didn't report what he did. It freaked me the fuck out and I didn't want to get involved and I didn't want to go to jail for anything. I just wanted to forget about it.

POLITANO: You're talking about the scrapbook?

GLEESON: No, not the scrapbook. The girl. He had a girl tied up. When I freaked out about it, he said it was just a joke, that they were friends, but I didn't believe him. He has no friends. And that girl, she didn't look like it was some joke. She had something over her mouth but I could tell she was trying to scream. I know I should have said something, called the police, but I was too scared, and I didn't want to get fucked up in any of it. I wanted to forget about it. I didn't want to get involved with whatever that was.

RENNEY: What girl?

POLITANO: What girl?

NINETEEN

Around dusk, a young man fitting the description given by Freyja Gleeson pulled into the parking lot of the Chamber Street apartment complex behind the wheel of a white panel van. There were two cracks on the van's windshield that came together to form what, to Renney, looked like an inverted cross; for a moment, the waning sunlight struck the cracks at just the right angle, and the cross seemed to radiate with an ethereal light. The young man parked the van next to a champagne-colored Lincoln Town Car (sporting two flat tires), which matched the description of the vehicle Freyja Gleeson had also given. Renney watched the kid hop out of the van, a greasy paper sack from a fast food joint tucked under one arm. He was scrawny and pale, swimming inside an oversized Slayer T-shirt and stained cargo shorts that hung a good five inches past his knees.

Renney approached him from across the parking lot. When he was within about twenty feet of the kid—just before the kid began to mount the stairs—he called out, quite amiably, "Hi! Hello! How are you?"

The kid stopped and looked around, visibly confused.

"Over here," Renney said. "Is your name Toby Kampen?"

"Who are you?"

Renney held his commission book up with his left hand, so that the kid could see his shield. (His right hand hovered peaceably beside his firearm, hidden discreetly beneath his sports coat; and goddamn, this weather was too hot for sports coats.)

"Detective William Renney, Los Angeles County Sheriff's Department. I'm gonna have to ask you to come with me, Toby."

The kid's eyes narrowed. He turned his head and peered up at the second-floor landing of the Chamber Street apartment complex, to where A.J. Politano stood peering down over the railing, along with a handful of uniformed officers.

"You're gonna have to come with me, Toby," Renney repeated. "That means dropping your lunch and putting your hands behind your back, son."

"Oh," said the kid. He glanced down at the pouch of food cradled beneath one arm, and looked instantly disappointed that he wasn't going to get to eat. He set the bag on the hood of the white van, then glanced down at his palms. Flexed his fingers.

"Put your hands up and turn around," Renney instructed, just as three uniformed officers came down the stairs and surrounded the kid.

"I guess this is about the girl," the kid said.

Renney's right hand slipped farther beneath his sports coat, until his palm came to rest on the hilt of his Smith & Wesson.

"Okay," the kid said.

He raised his hands above his head and turned around.

The officers fell upon him.

Renney let the kid sit and stew in the interrogation room for some time while he and Politano watched him on the observation camera. He'd had no weapons on him and had been surprisingly cooperative; the kid sat now in that shoebox of a room, uncuffed, his hands fidgeting in his lap. His eyes were locked on the camera in the upper corner of the room, which made it appear as if he were staring directly at Renney through the monitor. After a time, Renney said, "What's a Renfield?"

"He's like Dracula's lackey. Eats bugs and does his bidding. Didn't you at least see the movie?"

It was suddenly very warm and claustrophobic in that cramped, stuffy hallway. Renney, thinking of the photographs in the scrapbook that he held under one arm, felt that long-dormant snake twist about in his guts once again.

Politano frowned at him. "You okay?"

"Me? I'm fine. Let's get in there and do this."

Renney went down the hall, filled a paper cup with water from the water cooler, then shouldered his way back into the interrogation room. He set the water on the desk in front of Kampen just as Politano came in behind him, carrying a yellow legal pad and a stack of documents in a manila folder.

"Hey, thanks," Kampen said, like some schoolboy, but he didn't touch it. Renney had run the kid's background and knew he was twenty-two years old, yet in that moment he seemed no older than fifteen.

"Mr. Kampen, I'm Detective William Renney, and this is my partner, Sergeant Politano. You are currently under arrest, so I need to advise you of your rights."

"I know what they are. From the cop shows."

"That's right, from the cop shows." He read Kampen his rights anyway. Then he set the scrapbook on the desk and sat down beside Politano, who was balancing his notebook and his folder on one thigh. "Is this the book you gave to Freyja Gleeson?"

"Who's that?"

"The girl you thought was a vampire."

"Oh. I never knew her name."

"Is this the book you gave to her?"

"Yes."

"Where'd you get it?"

"I'm embarrassed to say."

"No judgment here, Toby. Everyone does embarrassing things. So tell me—where'd you get it?"

"I stole it."

"From who?"

"My doctor."

"Your doctor?"

"My psychiatrist."

"Who's your psychiatrist?"

Kampen nodded toward the scrapbook. Said, "The dead woman's husband. Dr. Andressen."

"Dr. Alan Andressen is your psychiatrist?"

"Was," Kampen said. "Not anymore. I stopped going."

Renney felt Politano's eyes drift in his direction.

"When did you stop?" Renney asked.

"I don't remember. I'm not very good with timelines. They sometimes . . . blur . . . in my head. It's hard to explain, but even now, I can't say for sure if I'm in *your* timeline or one completely separate. It's like being displaced. Disjointed."

"Where exactly was this scrapbook when you stole it?"

"I didn't steal the *scrapbook*," Kampen said, and Renney caught a measure of contempt in the kid's voice, as if he thought Renney was a moron. "I stole the *photos* and then I *put them* in the scrapbook."

"Then tell me how you got the photos."

"There's a waiting room when you first go to see Dr. Andressen. There's a door that goes right from the waiting room into his office. The door is usually locked, but sometimes it's not, because when patients leave, sometimes they don't latch it all the way. So sometimes I'd go in there and look around."

"In Dr. Andressen's office?"

"Yes."

"Why would you do that?"

"I don't do it anymore."

"Why did you *used to* do it?"

"Just to look around. Sometimes I'd look to see if he had any drugs in his desk, or anything like that. I don't take drugs—I can't stand to feel, I guess you'd say, out of myself anymore than I already do—but sometimes I thought I might sell them if I could find any."

"Did you ever find any?"

"No. Only those pictures. That's all I found."

"Where'd you find them?"

"In a desk drawer. They were in a folder with a bunch of other papers. I wasn't interested in the papers, so I don't know what they said. The photos, though, they were *very* interesting. So I took them."

"Did you know what they were photos of?"

"Dr. Andressen's wife. She'd been murdered and he'd stopped seeing me—stopped seeing all his patients, I guess—for a while. It was all over the news. So, yeah, I knew who she was."

"But then he started seeing you again as a patient sometime after his wife's murder?"

"Yes. I don't know when—like I said, I'm bad with timelines—but I remember being kind of excited to go back, which was a rare thing for me."

"How come?"

"I'd never known anyone whose spouse was murdered before. It was exciting."

"Was Dr. Andressen aware that you took those photos from his desk?"

"I didn't say anything to him, if that's what you mean. He didn't know I took them."

"Did he ever say anything to *you* about his wife?"

Kampen appeared to consider this. In the end, he just shook his head. "No, he never did. But I wish he had."

"Why's that?"

"I guess I'd just be interested in talking about what happened to her."

"Had you ever seen Dr. Andressen's wife before?"

"Her picture on the news. And on a billboard, once, I think."

"I meant in real life."

Politano opened his folder and slid out the headshot of Melissa Jean Andressen—the photo of her in tennis whites and with that luxurious chestnut hair. He set it on the table in front of Kampen. The kid leaned over and stared down at it, his nose mere inches from the top of the table.

"Yes. I saw her once before."

"Where?" Renney asked.

"At the house, after a session with Dr. Andressen. I saw her in the driveway. She was very pretty."

"Did you kill Dr. Andressen's wife?" Politano asked, and Renney looked at him.

Kampen's eyes went wide. "Me? Why would I? Jesus, no."

Renney readjusted himself in his chair, causing the legs to screech briefly along the linoleum floor. To Kampen, he said, "Tell us about Gina Fortunado."

Politano removed a photo of Gina from his folder and set that on the table next to the one of Melissa Jean. Kampen gazed down at it, then shifted uncomfortably behind the table. He rubbed at his chin with the heel of one hand. His eyes flitted back toward the camera on the opposite side of the room before returning to the image of Gina Fortunado. "Hmmm. She's pretty, too. I guess I didn't notice at the time."

"Tell us what happened," Renney said.

"I will," Kampen said, "but you need to know the details of what got me to her in order to understand the whole story. Is that okay?"

"That's okay," Renney said.

"It's going to sound . . . strange," Kampen said.

"That's okay, too," Renney said.

"All right," Kampen said. "Here goes."

And he began to talk.

TWENTY

THE MURDER OF GINA FORTUNADO

I

H e stood in broad daylight, not burning.

His eyes gummy with tears, Toby stared down at his palms, vaguely shaking, and wondered why tendrils of black smoke weren't spiraling up from the pores in his flesh. Wondered why he could stand here in the stark, unforgiving light of day and not burst into flames.

The devil-vampire had come to him last night in the chapel, had sunk its fangs into Toby's jugular. Had swiped a glistening contrail of mucus across the front of his shirt from a suppurating eyelet in the crown of that terrible, spiny, throbbing appendage that swayed between its legs. He had been *turned*, hadn't he?

Please, he thought.

No—he *begged*.

Please. Please. Please.

He glanced over his shoulder and back at the church's doorway through which he had just staggered, dehydrated and sunblind. The magic of this place was instantaneously gone, he realized;

something had changed the temperature of the world in the night. He could see the church now for what it truly was—a rundown adobe hovel in the middle of some godforsaken lunar landscape, with the only sign of life his own footprints impressed upon the hard-packed earth.

He felt no different than he had the night before.

His body had not undergone transmogrification.

His cells still felt the same. The molecular structure of his being still felt the same. His *body* still felt the same. Something was wrong, and the wrongness was that he was—

Still.

The.

Same.

Yet . . .

He crept back inside the church and gathered up his belongings. The jugs of water that had turned to blood had turned back into water. He unscrewed one of them, dumping nearly half the container down his raw, parched throat. The church was silent around him, the floor blanketed in dust, the pews garlanded in the gossamer strands of spider webs. If the Donald-thing had actually been in here with him, there was no evidence of it now.

Toby packed his belongings in the back of the white panel van. Before cranking over the key in the ignition, he scanned the horizon for signs of . . . well, anything. A pair of massive wings superimposed against the blazing backdrop of the sun, or perhaps a dark, indistinct figure loping furtively from mesa to mesa in the distance.

But he was all alone out here.

There must be another way, he thought. *There must be something else I can do.*

He considered the possibilities.

It was a long drive back to Central City East.

2

He entered the Chamber Street apartment to find great membranous panels of webbing draped from the ceiling and stretching from wall to wall. The furniture was entwined in it, the tacky, threadlike substance twisted around chair backs and wound around the legs of end tables. Strands of webbing hung from the chandelier and light fixtures, and there were translucent sheets of the stuff over the windows as if to mute the daylight.

He could hear the Spider's voice even though he could not see her:

"My God, Toby, where have you *been*? Why did you run off again? And what . . . what happened to your *skin*?"

His skin was sunburned and blistered. His lips were crusty and peeling from dehydration, and he could feel himself hobbling along on achy, damaged feet. He'd drank an entire jug of water on the drive back from Antelope Valley, but he still craved more.

"Toby, what's the matter with you? Where have you been?"

He didn't respond; instead, he brushed aside the tendrils of webbing and broke through the gauzy ropes strung like tripwire as he advanced through the apartment. Wisps of web clung to him, sticking to his T-shirt, his shorts, his sunburned skin. Strands collected in his hair and tickled down the length of his face.

"Toby? Toby? *Where have you BEEEEEEN?*"

A shadow moved on the other side of the kitchen doorway. The doorway itself was crisscrossed with so many gray, sticky cords of webbing that it looked nearly impenetrable. He went to it anyway, digging his fingernails into each flimsy, diaphanous sheet. Pulled the webbing away. Strands wafted to the floor in whispers, and lay there in a colorless heap like some giant reptile's sloughed skin.

He entered the kitchen.

"*TOBEEEE! TOBEEEEEE!*"

The Spider had shed its mother-suit, revealing to him her truest self. The massive arachnid clung to the ceiling, its segmented legs rippling and drumming against the walls. Its pedipalps pawed noiselessly in the air, behind which Toby could see himself reflected in an arrangement of glossy, obsidian eyes. As he stared at the thing, the Spider's abdomen jerked spasmodically, and expelled a clot of webbing along the ceiling; the strands fired across the room then drifted down to the kitchen floor like party streamers.

"*TOBEEE! TOBEEE! TOBEEEEEE!*"

And then the world went black.

3

Somehow, it was night, and he was back behind the steering wheel of the white panel van. He couldn't remember how he'd gotten here, nor could he comprehend what he was supposed to be doing. Framed in the van's windshield was the neon glitter of downtown's club scene—not the seedy, back-alley fetish clubs the vampire liked to frequent, but the popular ones, where people (mostly men) stood queued up at the front doors, and where Toby could glimpse flashing lights and smoke just beyond the clubs' thresholds.

He didn't know what day it was. He couldn't remember the last time he had taken his medication.

When a group of young women spilled out of one of the clubs, Toby readjusted the gear shift on the steering column. He rolled alongside them, incriminatingly slow, and studied each one of them.

They were bright, shiny things, all midriff, tits, and ass. When they looked in his direction (and one of them called him a fucking pervert), he pressed down a bit more on the accelerator and the white panel van shuddered its way through the next intersection.

At some point, he got the sense that he had been doing this for some time—for days, maybe weeks. When he glanced over at the passenger seat, he could see a heap of greasy fast food wrappers and empty soda bottles. Cans of Red Bull rolled back and forth in the footwell of the passenger seat, and there was an overall smell of desperation in here with him.

This area was too crowded. Too popular. He maneuvered the van up and down side streets, leaving the thriving section of the city behind. The boulevards here were dark, less populated. The clubs looked dingier, the clientele a bit more hopeless and apathetic. A stray dog watched him from a street corner as the van glided by, tracking Toby with its glowing, moonlit eyes.

At one point, he found himself the sole vehicle at an intersection where the traffic light never turned green. Eventually, he rolled the van right through it.

4

He entered places like The Coffin, claiming a seat at one darkened corner of the bar. From there, nursing a solitary beer for the entirety of his stay, he observed women gyrating on the dance floor. He studied the shine of the glitter on their cheekbones, the cat-claw fingernails, the stiletto heels and patent leather hot pants. He watched them go to the bar and cheer as they tossed back shots of grain alcohol. He watched them find men, or sometimes other women, locking their faces together, their mouths, hands roaming up and down the trunks of their bodies, a leg bent, a section of thong exposed.

He approached a woman with a silver hoop pierced through her lower lip. Asked to buy her a drink—

(with a real lemon)

—but she shunned him.

He approached a woman in a denim vest and repeated the process. She visibly recoiled at him, looked him up and down, then vanished into the crowd without a single word.

Another woman, who possessed the complexion of a broiled ham hock, actually laughed in his face when he asked about her name.

He was not good at this.

At another club, he purchased a drink ahead of time, then attempted to offer it to any woman who deigned to come near him. This, he learned, was not a good approach, nor did the bartender approve: he was asked to leave the club.

One woman struck him across the face just for opening his mouth.

At another club, he was approached by security and asked to leave. He hadn't even spoken to a woman in this particular place yet, which meant that his sheer presence was disconcerting enough to warrant proactive intervention. As the two bouncers led him out of the establishment, Toby happened to glance up and spy the shiny cyclopean eye of a security camera directly above the bar. How could he have been so careless? Security cameras hadn't even occurred to him. What if he'd left here with one of those women? That would have spelled T-R-O-U-B-L-E, trouble. He considered the bouncers' intervention a blessing in disguise.

He was not *good* at this. Perhaps he exuded some off-putting pheromone? Perhaps his clothing—heavy metal T-shirts and stained cargo shorts—suggested he was of a different ilk than these women? True, he had not been turned into a vampire, yet he was still the Human Fly, which meant he was adept at quickly vacating one location for another while remaining practically invisible. And that's what he did: buzzed around those bleak and forgotten clubs, hunting for some bleak and forgotten woman.

He remembered nothing about the daylight hours.

Only the night.

And a part of him wondered, *Maybe I have been changed. Maybe the transmogrification is still taking place. From fly to vampire. Maybe, maybe . . .*

At one point, he looked down at himself to find he was wearing different clothes.

Then, on some random midnight, two in the morning to be more precise, as he was pulling away from the last club of the night, he spied a woman walking by herself up the block in the dark. He spun the van's steering wheel and coasted in her direction, keeping the headlights off so as not to alert her to his presence.

She wore a turquoise halter top and frayed denim shorts. There was a tattoo of a rose running down the length of her left thigh.

He eased the van alongside the curb then glided past her, glancing at her through the passenger window of the van as he went. She paid him no attention, didn't turn her head, which allowed him to fully digest the lines of her profile, the sweep of her hair, the thrust of her tits beneath that halter.

She looked *delicious.*

He gently pushed down on the brake and parked the van a good twenty, thirty yards in front of the woman, right against the curb. Leaving the engine running, he popped the driver's-side door and hopped out into an unusually cool night for this time of the year. The street, he noticed, was empty. There was a row of warehouses across the street, their windows dark as pitch, and a parking lot beside the van. He went around to the rear of the van and popped open the doors, then chanced a glance over his shoulder.

The woman was approaching, staring down now at her cell phone. The light from the screen cast her face in a white, angelic light. As he watched her, he saw her nearly stumble, though she did not look up from her phone.

She's drunk and looking for her car. Or maybe she's walking home and got lost.

He didn't care; all he cared about was *getting it done.*

He pretended to busy himself with something in the back of the van. When the woman walked by, he extracted himself from the back of the van, then silently came up behind her. The lamppost at their backs threw his shadow alongside hers, but she was too drunk—or too preoccupied with her cell phone—to notice.

He thought of Puke-Breath Donald, and those summers spent playing the victim. Of Donald's meaty, freckled arm snaking around his throat. Of Donald hoisting him off the ground and squeezing him about the neck until he lost consciousness.

She turned just as he brought his arm up.

Opened her mouth to speak.

But he was already on her, one arm squeezing her windpipe, the other slipping beneath her left armpit. Her cell phone clattered to the ground. She dug a set of fingernails into his forearm, but he hardly noticed. A moment later, she went limp.

Toby carried her around the back of the van and placed her on the floor inside. Then she shut the doors, and was about to climb into the driver's seat when he recalled her cell phone. He hurried over to it, picked it up, then slipped it through the bars of a storm drain. The sound of it splashing into the water below gave him some dim satisfaction.

His arm was bleeding from where she'd dug in her nails, but he didn't care.

In the end, this would all be worth the T-R-O-U-B-L-E, trouble.

5

According to the driver's license he found in the pocket of her jeans, her name was Gina Fortunado, from San Bernardino. She had no purse or keys with her, so Toby wondered if maybe she'd been mugged, or had just left her stuff behind in some bar. Whatever the case, it didn't matter much to him.

As he drove, the woman in the back of the van began to moan and move around. No problem there, either, since he'd bound and gagged her while she was still unconscious. He could hear empty Red Bull cans rolling around back there as the woman tried to free herself of her bindings.

He drove out to the E-Z-Storage facility, where he still had a few months left on the unit that he'd once used as a home, back when he'd first run away from the Spider's den. He hadn't been here since returning home, and for a moment, he worried his key might no longer fit the lock. But the key fit, and he was able to slide open the door without incident.

A smell rushed out at him—his own sour body odor, mostly, but also decomposing food and whatever else might have been rotting away in there. He ducked beneath the streamers of flypaper that hung from the ceiling of that small, metal box, then knelt before the stiff, crusty mattress where, for a time, he had slept. He straightened it, patted it to make it more comfortable. It reeked of his perspiration.

Well, she won't be in here long, he rationalized.

When he opened the back doors of the van, the woman began bucking her hips and moaning through the strip of flypaper he had stretched across her mouth to keep her quiet. She was curled like a prawn back there, and Toby thought he could smell the fear coming off her in waves. Either that, or she had pissed herself, just as Toby had whenever Puke-Breath Donald would do the old chokehold routine.

He reached in, grabbed her by the ankle with two hands, and dragged her toward him.

Behind that strip of flypaper, her panicked cries went shrill as a power drill.

No one was here at this hour, but still, Toby wasn't eager to draw any attention to himself. He climbed into the back of the van and knelt beside the woman's head. He even smoothed back a lock of her sweat-damp hair to sooth her.

"You gotta not fight me and try to keep quiet, okay? It'll be best for you if you could do that."

He could have been talking to a door for all the good it did: she kept bucking her hips and struggling with the rope that bound her wrists behind her back. Kept making a *mmhnn mmhnn* noise behind that flypaper barricade, too.

"Suit yourself, then. I'll just have to be quick and not as careful."

He grabbed her beneath her sweaty armpits and dragged her out of the van. Her feet, lashed with a bungee cord at the ankles, struck the cement floor and Toby felt her whole body shudder in pain. He dragged her farther into the storage container and ultimately dumped her onto the mattress. The back of her head hit the wall as she went down, eliciting a sound like a mallet to a gong, and then she rolled over onto her side. She was whimpering, and there was snot streaming from her nose and down the strip of flypaper covering her mouth.

"You probably don't want to get yourself too worked up. With your mouth taped up and all that snot clogging your nose, it might be best to, well . . . "

He thought it best not to finish the sentiment.

"See you soon," he said, and pulled down the metal door.

6

Time continued to blur. There were no days into nights, but rather *nights* into nights, an unending reel of moonlit boulevards and alleyways. It could have been that very first night after he'd abducted Gina Fortunado and tucked her away for safe keeping, or it could have been days or weeks later, when he saw the vampire again.

She came out of the club Fist upon a cloud of smoke. She wasn't alone—there was another—

(vampire?)

—woman with her, and the two of them loitered around the street corner for the length of time it took them to share a cigarette. Toby watched them from across the street, tucked behind the van's steering column, that Lynyrd Skynyrd cassette warbling through the van's fuzzy speakers. When the smoke was done, the vampires kissed, embraced, and then Toby's vampire was left alone beneath the pearlescent glow of a nearby streetlamp. She whipped out her cell phone and was staring at the screen as Toby got out of the van and crossed the street in her direction.

Hypersensitive to her surroundings, she sensed his approach and looked up at him.

"Hey," he said, smiling. "Hi. Hey there."

"What are you doing here?"

"I've been thinking about you."

"I told you, we need to take a break," she said. Her speech, he noticed, was a bit slurred. Her eyes, too, which normally shone with a dull golden hue, looked teary and rimmed in red, as if she'd spent a portion of the night crying.

"You also said you were leaving the city," he reminded her.

"Yeah, well, I did for a bit."

"Do you need a ride somewhere?"

She slipped her phone into the back pocket of her jeans. No frilly ball gown tonight. "Where's your car?" She was searching for it across the street.

He jerked a thumb over his shoulder at the white panel van. "Driving that for a while now."

"Really? Looks like it should say 'Free Candy' on the side."

"Come on," he said, and started walking back across the street toward the van.

Follow me, he willed her, refusing to turn and look back. *Follow me, follow me, follow me.*

When he climbed back into the driver's seat, he could see she was already halfway across the street and heading in his direction. He felt a smile crack his dry, blistered lips. Vampires, he knew, had the ability to telepathically coerce someone to do their bidding. Again, he wondered if he'd been turned in the desert after all, and the process inside him was still . . . processing.

He gathered up the old fast food wrappers, empty bottles and cans, from the passenger seat, and flung them into the back of the van. He shut off the Lynyrd Skynyrd cassette, too.

She opened the passenger door and got in.

"It smells so bad in here, Renfield."

"I've got air fresheners," he replied, and pointed to the cluster of cardboard pine trees dangling from the radio's volume knob.

"Let's just go."

"Where to?"

She checked her phone again. "There's another house up in the hills. It won't take long. I just have to pick something up."

"Okay," he said. "But first, there's something I want to show you."

She looked at him, and he glanced at her. She was mesmeric in her beautifulness, with those impossibly dark eyes set within her pale, porcelain skin, offset by black lipstick and great, bruise-like patches of eye shadow. She was watching him with her mouth closed—not even grinning—so he could not see her fangs.

"What?" she said. "What is it you want to show me?"

"I got you another present."

She shifted in her seat. Turned her head to peer out the passenger window. "Who's the girl in those pictures?" she asked him, not looking at him. He turned his head and saw her breath fogging against the passenger window.

"In the memories book?"

"Yes."

"A murder victim. Someone killed her last year and left her body in the desert."

"Are you the someone?"

He didn't answer her.

She looked at him.

Said, "Well?"

"Would you be more inclined if I said yes?"

"Inclined to do what?"

"Turn me," he said . . . although now, he was wondering if he still needed turning. Could he feel the change taking place inside him? It was hard to tell. He still felt like a common housefly.

"I told you, Renfield, that's not going to—"

"I went out to that church in the desert," he said, cutting her off. "Stayed there for three days, just like you said."

"Oh, yeah?" she said. Her head lulled against the headrest and her eyelids fluttered.

"I saw him," he said.

"Who?"

He grinned to himself. Said, "Who do you think?"

She shifted again in her seat. Her eyes were closed. "I don't like this game, Renfield. Just take me to the house. It's late and I'm tired."

"I want to give you your gift first."

"I don't want any more gifts."

"You'll want this one," he promised her.

7

The parking lot of E-Z-Storage facility was a ghost town when they arrived. The clock on the van's dashboard didn't work, and Toby owned no watch, so he had no idea what time it was. Or what day, for that matter.

The vampire was asleep beside him in the passenger seat, her head rocking back and forth on her neck every time he took a turn too sharply. He drove down the rows of storage units, each square metal container with a number above it, until he arrived at his— unit 168. He twisted the keys out of the ignition and the engine shuddered then died. The vampire opened her eyes.

"Where are we?"

"Come on," he said. "You'll like this."

Without another word, he got out of the van and headed to his unit, already fishing around in his pocket for the key to unlock it. He heard the passenger door open a moment later, heard the hollow thud of the vampire's boot heels as she dropped down to the cement floor.

Toby's heart was racing.

"I don't feel so good," said the vampire.

"That's because you have to feed," he told her, slipping the key into the lock. The lock popped, and he shoved the large metal door up on its tracks to reveal the interior of the unit.

The woman lay curled in a fetal position on the filthy mattress. Her hands were still bound behind her back, her ankles still lashed together with a bungee cord. That strip of flypaper was still stretched across the lower half of her face, like some hideous brown smile. It occurred to Toby that he didn't know how long the woman had been in here—a night? a week?—and that he hadn't been back to feed or water her. To him, she looked dead lying there, her eyes staring blindly out at him.

But then those eyes blinked. She began making that terrible sound again from behind the flypaper—*mmhnn mmhnn*—as she started to struggle.

Toby turned to the vampire, expecting to see a fiery hunger burning in her eyes, her mouth unhinged and those elongated fangs dripping with saliva.

But the look on the vampire's face was one of stunned terror.

"For you," he explained. "So you can eat and feel better. And then, to thank me, you can turn me."

The vampire looked at him. Took a step back. Not hunger in those eyes, but *fear*.

In the metal box, the woman on the mattress tried to scream and break herself free of her bonds. She kept banging the back of her head against the metal siding of her prison.

Toby raised his hand and reached out toward the vampire, but she quickly took a step away from him. Shaking her head, she said, "What . . . what the *fuck* . . . "

"I'm *Renfield*," he reminded her.

"*This isn't real!*" she suddenly screamed at him—so loud, he clamped his hands over his ears. "*I'm not a vampire, you fucking lunatic!*"

She turned to look back at the woman in the storage unit, that fear building, building, building in her eyes.

"No," Toby said. "That's not right."

"You fucking psychopath, *who is she?*"

Dinner, he thought, but could no longer say.

Suddenly, nothing made sense.

"She's . . . " he began, while—

—behind him, the woman kept trying to scream, kept trying to break free from the rope around her wrists and the cord around her ankles. Her head kept knocking monotonously against the side of the storage unit: *WONG! WONG! WONG! WONG! WONG!*

"You are *sick*! You fucking *lunatic*, you are out of your goddamn—"

"Hey, hey," he said, brightening up—smiling and holding his hands up to profess his innocence. "Hey, listen—really? You think . . . you think this is real? Hey, now . . . " and he reached up and pulled the unit door down until it slammed against the concrete floor, closed, "hey, come on, *this was just a joke*. Get it? It's just a joke. I didn't mean to upset you. It's only—"

"Who the fuck is that woman in there?"

"A friend. This was all just . . . hey, don't be upset. It was all just a bad joke. I'm sorry. I'm sorry. I'm not funny. I know that."

"You're fucking *sick*, is what you are." She kept looking past him at the storage unit. A tear escaped one eye and traveled down the length of the vampire's right cheek. He thought vampires cried blood—he'd heard or read that somewhere, hadn't he?—but her tears looked like normal tears.

That's because she's right, he thought, and felt a welling of anger and humiliation building inside his stomach. *She's not a vampire. This whole thing was a game to humiliate me. The fucking whore.*

The smile on his face ached.

"Just a joke," he repeated, as calm as you'd please. "Just a dumb and ugly joke."

"Go fuck yourself," she spat at him. "You better untie that woman. And you better never come near me again, you sick fuck. Do you understand?"

"Hey, hey, come on—"

"*Do you understand, motherfucker?*"

She didn't wait for a reply; she turned and ran down the rows of storage units, the heels of her boots clacking hollowly on the cement. Toby thought about giving chase, but in the end, what good would that do? Probably best just to let her go and never see her again. After all, she'd lied to him and played him for the fool. She didn't look so mesmeric in her beautifulness with tears in her eyes and terror on her face.

"Fuck you," he muttered, just as the sound of her heels faded into the night.

Silence, then.

Except—*WONG! WONG! WONG! WONG! WONG!*

Shit, he thought, and pushed open the door to the storage unit again.

The woman had managed to crawl off the mattress and shrimp her way to the door. What good that would have done her had she reached it, Toby had no idea, but he had to applaud the fortitude.

He stood above her, hands dangling limply at his sides. His clothes were soaked with sweat and he could smell himself—a smell worse than whatever stink was seeping out of the storage unit.

"I'm sorry," he told the woman, staring down at her. "This was a mistake."

He stepped inside the unit and tugged a strip of flypaper off the ceiling. When he knelt beside the woman, she began to squeal and shake, trying to fight him off with just the thrusting movement of her body.

"Really," he said. "I'm sorry."

He pulled the strip of flypaper taut over the woman's nostrils.

"*Mmhnn! Mmhnn!*"

Bucking.

Flailing.

Head striking the wall one last time with a resounding *WONG!*

"*Mmhnn! Mmhnn!*"

"Shhhh."

"*Mmhnn! Mmmmmhnnn!*"

"Shhhh. Stop. Stop."

"*Mmmmm —*"

"Stop."

8

He stayed with her until she stopped breathing.

9

It was THE WONDERFUL THING he was thinking about as he drove the van back to the Chamber Street apartment that night. THE WONDERFUL THING, so cherished, which he now regretted giving away. THE WONDERFUL THING that, in moments of stress or discomfort or agitation, had always brought him peace.

Where would his peace come from now?

We'll fix it, said a voice in his head. Puke-Breath Donald's voice, it sounded like.

The apartment complex was silent and dark at this hour. Even the homeless had vacated to wherever the homeless go during the deepest, witchingest hours of the night. He did not pull into the parking lot for fear someone might hear the van's engine and rise to a window and look out, but instead parked in the alley between his building and the next. He hurried soundlessly across the quad and dipped into the tiny, nearly hidden alcove, then slipped inside the maintenance room. He rummaged through George Zebka's stuff until he found two items that would suffice.

A retractable razor and a pair of large bolt cutters.

Before leaving, he grabbed a pair of work gloves off Zebka's bench, stuffing them into the rear pocket of his shorts.

Back outside, he paused and glanced up at the apartment building's second story. Long streamers of spider web blew out from the Spider's apartment and flapped and fluttered like pennants above the parking lot.

He didn't want to set foot in that apartment again, but there was something up there in his room that he now wanted. That he *needed*.

Only a foolish fly returns to the spider's web once he's escaped.

In that moment, however, he felt *more* than a fly.

A change, it seemed, *was* taking hold.

He took a deep breath then raced up the stairs to the Spider's apartment.

10

Ten minutes later, on the drive back to E-Z-Storage, Toby began to feel a little woozy. Despite the profusion of fast food wrappers and empty cans and bottles jouncing around in the back of the van, he couldn't remember the last time he'd eaten or drank anything. Was he even hungry? Thirsty? He couldn't tell.

A part of him wondered if he might arrive at the storage facility and into the waiting arms of a battalion of policemen. But the place was just as quiet and desolate as it had been earlier that night, and Toby felt himself begin to relax, little by little.

He unlocked the storage unit, slid the door up on its rattling track, then set the three items down on the floor—the bolt cutters, the retractable razor, and the Polaroid camera he'd owned since his youth. There was a time when he had used that camera every single day, taking pictures of himself to document the transformation from common boy to common housefly. Now, in this moment, a different sort of transformation was taking place; he was beginning to feel it graduating throughout his body, altering the DNA of every one of his cells. He could feel his mitochondria swelling as alterations were made to their biochemical reactions, could feel a tightening of his entire musculature. Could feel a rush of heat at the center of his being, pulsing there like a heartbeat.

He knew those photos that made up THE WONDERFUL THING by heart. Knew every nuance of them, every cut, every empty socket, every snapshot of bone and flesh and gristle.

He pulled on the work gloves, knelt over Gina Fortunado's body, and began to cut.

II

What do you have?

There was a set of fingers—fingers for feeling, for touching, for probing into unseen places.

He opened the bolt cutters and insinuated a finger between those yawning, hungry claspers. An index finger, right hand. He saw it there so easily. Was it really that easy? His face was ten inches from the digit, hovering above it, looking down; all he had to do was—

—pull the handles of the bolt cutters together.

There was hardly any resistance.

Not even the crunch of bone.

The finger fell away.

He did this nine more times.

Until—

What do you have?

A nose: for sniffing out injustice, corruption, dislocation.

Yes. That's exactly what this is. Dislocate — amputate — the nose.

No bolt cutters for this. He remembered the photos in THE WONDERFUL THING, knew from memory the grand artwork he was mimicking, and so he picked up the retractable razor. He thumbed the blade into position, then inserted it just above the bulb of the left nostril while holding the side of the head with his other hand to keep things steady. He felt the flesh give way as he punctured it, felt the tip of the blade sink in. Blood spilled down the side of the face; it pooled in the concavity of the supra-alar crease. As an incision, perhaps not as neat, not as careful or diligent, as the cuts in THE WONDERFUL THING, but he did his best: tracing the outline of the nose, slicing through the wall of cartilage at the base of the nose, back around the other side, then right up over the bridge. The bridge was the toughest part, because he couldn't tell just from pressing down with the blade what was bone and what was cartilage. But in the end, he got through it. *Sawed* through it. The blood that spurted out was furious—he wouldn't have thought there was so much blood beneath a nose—and it leaked down both sides of the face, where it pooled on the floor of the storage unit. Toby plucked the nose away from the face, feeling some minor resistance from the bits of cartilage and sinew that were still attached, but then it finally came free, revealing a pulpy triangular chasm bisected by a sliver of pale white bone. The blood in those dual channels was as black as ink.

What do you have?

A pair of eyes: for skirting past the things that should have been seen to prevent all this from happening in the first place. How she stared at the glowing spectral screen of her cell phone as she swayed drunkenly down that otherwise empty sidewalk. How she'd paid him zero attention—and he, a lone stranger opening up the rear doors of a nondescript white panel van along the shoulder of a desolate Hollywood boulevard. How careless were those eyes? How pointless and futile?

They were not so easy to remove. He used the razor to dig them out, but they did not come out whole, like they do in the movies: he inadvertently punctured the first one, and a stream of greenish fluid spilled down the side of the dead woman's face. The eyeball itself deflated, retreating into the orbital socket. A piece of the retina sloughed away like jelly. In the end, he had to reach in with his fingers and pluck it out. It came with a snap, as the sinewy strands of muscles detached from the orbital pocket.

The second eyeball fared no better: it, too, burst upon being punctured, and sank into that gooey, viscous pocket. He dug that one out as well, noting its texture was quite similar to a peeled grape.

What do you have?

A tongue: for speaking truth—yet what *was* truth, exactly?

Toby didn't know. Truth—the truth of the world, anyway—had seemed to evade him his entire existence.

All he knew—all he learned—was how difficult it was to snag the tip of a tongue with his gloved fingers and pull it out between the teeth, because the nature of a tongue is to retract and hide, a lizard in a hole, and it kept slipping, slipping, slipping through his fingers and falling farther and farther down the dead woman's throat. Finally, he committed to a hasty job, and two swipes of the razorblade liberated that pulpy, Braille-studded organ from the dead woman's mouth.

What do you have?

A duo of ears: for hearing what was being said.

"For hearing what I'm saying to you," Toby whispered into one of the dead girl's ears. He saw the way his breath made her hair flutter. "Do you hear what I'm saying to you?"

No response, of course.

"Hear me," he whispered. "What I'm saying to you."

He cut both ears away.

And when he was done, he thought, *What do you have?*

And the answer returned to him, unbidden:

Nothing.

Nothing.

12

When he was done, he took a number of photos with the Polaroid, then stashed the photos, the bloody bolt cutters, and the retractable razor in a plastic five-gallon bucket at the back of the storage unit. (The Polaroid camera he tossed on the passenger seat of the van— he wasn't quite done with it yet.) He considered what to do with the body parts he'd removed from her—the fingers that lay in a coagulating pool of dark red blood, the eyeballs trailing ribbons of muscle and nerves, a severed tongue like a thick, fat slug—and in the end, decided just to leave them in the storage unit. Souvenirs, he supposed.

Gloves back on his hands, he carried what remained of Gina Fortunado to the van, where he rolled her into the back. He realized he hadn't had the foresight to grab a sheet or a bunch of towels or a roll of plastic tarpaulin, but it was too late to fret over such stuff now.

There were still a few jugs of water in the van from his trip to the church, so he cleaned himself up as best he could before gently closing the rear doors of the van then sliding back behind the wheel. He cranked over the ignition, and "Call Me the Breeze" came shaking out of the speakers.

He drove.

13

He considered for a moment driving all the way out to the desert church, but in the end, that wasn't what he did. Instead, he drove until he saw the sign that read LOS ANGELES COUNTY LINE. There was a photo in THE WONDERFUL THING where, in the background, he could see that sign, and so it seemed fitting to leave Gina Fortunado here where, a year earlier, THE WONDERFUL THING was born.

He parked along that desolate strip of pitch-black highway, opened the rear doors of the van, then pulled on the work gloves, which were saturated in blood by this point. Silent as a ghost, he carried Gina's body straight out into the desert. He stopped only when his arms grew tired and his calf muscles ached. He set her down gently in the sand, took some more photos of her, the Polaroid camera whirring and whining with each shot, *shhht-FZZZ*, the built-in flash leaving afterimages dancing before his eyes. When he was done, he sauntered back toward the road, flapping the freshly printed photos in the cool desert air so they would develop faster.

Before he crept back into the van and headed back toward civilization, he glanced toward the sky where he saw a pair of massive bat wings sail across the face of the three-quarter moon.

TWENTY-ONE

A momentary silence fell upon the room once Kampen had finished his story. Politano had stopped making notes on the yellow legal pad somewhere around the time the kid started talking about his communion with a devil in an old, abandoned church deep in the desert.

"Those Polaroids you took," Renney said, "and the pieces you cut off of Ms. Fortunado's body—where are those things now, Toby?"

"They're still in the storage unit."

Politano was scrolling through his phone. There was a map on the screen. "E-Z-Storage. This the one on Pine Hill Road?"

"Yes," said Kampen.

"That was . . . " Politano looked down at his notepad. "Unit one-six-eight, correct?"

"Yes."

"You give us permission to search it?"

"I guess so."

"Yeah?"

"Yes, you can search it. It's not pretty. It smells really bad, and there are a lot of flies. I'm sorry about that."

"Toby," Renney said, leaning forward in his chair. "At what point in all of this did you kill your mother?"

Something in the kid's face changed in that moment—a subtle shifting of musculature, a dimming way back in his eyes. Renney could see the change even if he could not define it.

"You mean the Spider," Kampen said, his voice suddenly low, as if they were sharing secrets.

"Why do you call her that?"

"Because that's what she is. Or *was.* A giant Spider walking around in mother-skin. I've known this for years, just as I've known I'm not really a *man*, but a common housefly, *Musca domestica Linnaeus.* I struggled in that web of hers for *years.*"

Kampen's lower lip began to tremble.

The kid had relayed the entire story about the kidnapping, murder, and dismemberment of Gina Fortunado with stoic, almost casual detachment, yet now, talking about his mother, Renney could see emotion leaking to the surface.

"At what point in your story did you kill her, Toby?" Renney asked again. "You didn't tell us that part. You never said anything to us in your story about your mother's death."

Once again, Kampen looked up and at the small camera mounted high in one corner of the room. Stared at it in silence for a length of time.

"I don't really know," he said after a while. "She was still alive when I went out to the desert to spend those three days in that church. I remember her trying to stop me, slamming a hand on the window of the van."

"What about when you came back from the church?" Politano asked.

"When I came back from the church," Kampen mused, still staring directly at the camera. "When I came back from the church . . . the apartment was full of spider webs. Every room, just . . . just *filled* with spider webs. They were sticky, and they stuck to my body as I moved through the apartment."

Suddenly, the kid's eyes went wide.

"She was in the kitchen. I remember that now. She had shed her mother-skin and was fully the Spider. She was on the ceiling, and she was still making webs. I could *hear* the silk excreting from her spinnerets. It sounded like when you take a spoon and mush it around in a bowl of macaroni and cheese. You know that sound? All moist and thick?

"I think maybe I blacked out then. Or . . . what's it called when you go into a blind rage? There's a word for it, I just can't think of it. Ordinarily I'm very good with words. It's one of the few things I'm good at. It's timelines . . . it's *time* and *place* and *things* and *events* . . . that tend to sometimes trip me up."

"Tell us about what happened in the kitchen," Renney said.

"You know, I'm only remembering just now," Kampen said. The kid's eyes, which were still locked on the camera, were quickly filling with tears. "It's like my mind wanted to block that part out for some reason. Not that . . . you know, not that I'm ashamed or even sorry for what I did, because believe me, it *had* to be done. There was no way I'd ever be free if I hadn't done it."

"Tell us what it is you did," Renney said, although he already knew; he'd seen the state of things in that apartment when they'd first arrived on Chamber Street looking for Kampen.

"I guess I took the phone off the wall and wrapped the cord around her neck," Kampen said. "She was somehow still the Spider on the ceiling making its webs, but also the Spider in the mother-skin again, and it was that version—the mother-skin version—that I'd wrapped the cord around. Around and around and around. I just keep pulling the cord tighter and tighter."

"Why did you do that, Toby?" Renney asked.

"Because a Spider that big, you can't step on with your shoe. You can't swat with a rolled-up newspaper. You have to take alternative measures."

"I mean, why did you kill her in the first place?"

"I told you: so I could be set free."

"And you've just been living in that apartment with her body in the kitchen all this time?" Politano asked.

Kampen shrugged, then swiped an errant tear from one cheek. "I guess I didn't notice."

"Okay." Renney leaned over to Politano and said, "Let's talk in the hall for a sec."

They excused themselves, then slipped quietly out into the hallway just as Kampen picked up the paper cup of water and brought it with one trembling hand to his lips. His eyes were still locked on the camera high up on the wall, and there were tears leaking down the sides of his face.

"Jesus, that was some story," Politano said once they'd both stepped out into the hall and Renney had shut the door behind them.

"Yeah, well, I see where this is headed. He'll claim insanity."

"I'm not so sure that'd be wrong."

"Which means a good defense attorney will say the kid isn't in the right frame of mind to grant consent for us to search that storage unit. Let's get a warrant just to cover our asses."

"Okay. I think we should also get his consent to turn over some DNA. No question it'll match whatever trace DNA was found on Fortunado's body. Just to tighten things up."

"Good idea."

"I also wanna charge Gleeson with obstruction. I don't give a shit how scared she was, she should have called in what she saw that night. Things could've ended differently."

"I'm good with that," Renney said.

"How the hell do you think Andressen got copies of his wife's crime scene photos, anyway?"

"I don't know. But I've got a rapport with the guy. I'll pay him a visit later today."

"You think we should push this kid more on the Andressen murder? He's so off the wall, who the hell knows what he's capable of?"

"I think everything is exactly as he told us. I don't want to muddy his confession on Fortunado. We press him too hard on something else, he might cop to the Kennedy assassination. Let's keep it clean."

"I guess you're right."

"Meantime, I'll finish up with the kid on my own."

Politano nodded, then hurried off down the hall.

He'll make a good detective one day, Renney thought, watching him go. Then he went around to a small console and switched off the camera in the interview room.

Back in the interview room, Renney pulled his chair out and sat down with a grunt. Across the table from him, Kampen was clutching the paper cup in both hands, the way a squirrel would hold an acorn. He had been staring down at the folder Politano had left in the room, at the photographs in it, but his eyes flicked up toward the camera again once Renney sat down.

"The little green light is off," Kampen said, nodding toward the camera on the wall.

"It does that sometimes."

"What do you think that thing sees?"

Renney glanced around at the camera, then back at Kampen. *Sees nothing now*, he thought. Said, "Sees whatever happens in this room. Records the audio, too. I told you that when I first brought you in here, remember?"

"I don't mean just that," Kampen said. "I mean, what do you think it *sees*? Like, does it see me for what I really am? The changes in me that are happening just below the surface? Just below the flesh? Does it see *you* for what *you* really are?"

"What am I?"

Kampen's eyes jittered in Renney's direction.

"I'm not really sure," the kid said. "Haunted, I think."

"Hey," said Renney, leaning forward. "Dr. Andressen's wife."

"What about her?"

"You copied the way she was murdered when you killed and cut up Gina Fortunado."

"Yes."

"You did it that way because of those pictures in that scrapbook."

"Yes."

"Is that really how it happened?"

"What do you mean?"

"Are you sure you didn't kill Melissa Jean Andressen?"

"Me? Of course not. That's silly."

"Is it? Because you couldn't remember killing your mother until we asked you about it."

Kampen shifted around in his seat, looking instantly uncomfortable again. "That's different," he muttered.

"Because she was your mother?"

"Because she was the Spider wearing a mask. Her true face was rarely visible to me, and so it confused me. But I can remember other people's faces, when they're not hidden behind anything." He pointed to the photograph of Gina Fortunado that was still on the table in front of him. "I remember her face." Then he nodded at the photo of Melissa Jean Andressen. "I remember her, too, and I'd only seen her that one time."

"Because they didn't wear masks," Renney said.

"That's right." Kampen leaned over and pinched the edge of another photo between his thumb and forefinger, sliding it out from beneath the photo of Melissa Jean. "I even recognize this guy," Kampen said.

Renney stiffened in his seat.

It was a photograph—a mugshot—of Lucas Priest.

"How do you recognize him?" Renney asked.

"I saw him at Dr. Andressen's house. Same day I saw Mrs. Andressen. Dr. Andressen walked me out of the house to the street where the Spider was waiting for me in the car. I looked over and saw Mrs. Andressen standing there in the driveway. This man was with her. He was touching her arm and she was laughing."

"Did Dr. Andressen see this, too?"

"Yes. He didn't look happy about it."

"Why do you say that?"

"He just looked angry. Or . . . maybe upset? I didn't know the woman was his wife until after she'd been murdered and I saw her picture on the news. I've got a good memory for faces when they're not wearing masks, and I knew who she was right away."

When Renney spoke, it was as if, to his own ears, his voice was coming from the end of some long pipe. "When exactly was this?"

"I'm not sure . . . " Kampen began, but then his words seized up. He was back to staring up at the camera on the wall. "I mean, I'm not good with time. And events. Remember? I told you that already."

"But you're sure it's this guy?" Renney tapped a finger against the photo of Lucas Priest.

"Oh, yes. I'm positive. Like I said, I've got a good memory for things like *that*."

His voice just above a whisper, Renney said, "Did Dr. Andressen ever talk to you about his wife?"

"No."

"Are you sure?"

"I don't think so."

"You don't *think*? Is it possible?"

"Anything is possible. I know that now," Kampen said.

Still staring at that camera.

Suddenly grinning.

TWENTY-TWO

I

Toby Kampen's holding cell was very nearly the same size as the storage unit at E-Z-Storage that he'd lived in for a time, so in that sense, it was rather cozy. What he *didn't* like was that one of the light fixtures in the ceiling kept blinking on and off, on and off, as though it were imparting some undecipherable message to him. It was enough to drive a person crazy.

He sat there by himself on a wooden bench that was bolted to the cinderblock wall and thought for a while about his current predicament. A part of Toby still wondered if this all wasn't just some part of a dream, and that maybe right now he was actually sitting, daydreaming, in Dr. Andressen's waiting room, or maybe slouched in the comfortable leather chair in Dr. Andressen's home office. He *was* a little drowsy, after all.

He was thinking of the Spider. He tried to recall his final confrontation with the beast, just as he'd relayed it to that detective, but found himself confused about the details now as well. Somehow the Spider had been on the ceiling spinning its web . . . yet also standing there in front of him in its mother-suit, which was how he'd . . .

What?

He tried to summon an image of her in his head, but got confused by the images he'd been shown of Dr. Andressen's wife. Had he cut off the Spider's fingers or had he strangled it to death?

He couldn't remember.

Everything in his head, it seemed, was suddenly jumbled.

There was another holding cell directly across from his, only there were no lights on in there. Yet even in the dark, Toby could see a figure seated opposite him on another wooden bench. He could have sworn the figure hadn't been there before, but then again, what did he know? Toby leaned forward, allowing his eyes to adjust and the figure to reconcile itself.

Puke-Breath Donald sat, his shoulders slumped and his feet barely touching the floor. He stared at Toby with eyes that were glowing white pinpoints of light.

"*Spiders don't have fingers, Dumbo,*" said Donald. Although Toby couldn't see any details of the boy's face due to the darkness of that holding cell, he could tell that he was grinning.

"*Maybe,*" suggested Donald, "*you're like the* Demeter, *the creaky old ship that carries Dracula to Europe. Maybe you're not a common housefly at all, and never have been. Maybe you're the* Demeter, *bringing literal death to the shore.*"

Out in the hall, the ceiling light flickered.

Toby Kampen touched his tongue to one of his incisors, and was happy to find it sharp as a knife blade.

2

Somewhere along a barren, midnight stretch of Nevada desert, Maureen Park pulled her car into the parking lot of a nameless roadside bar. She had been driving for hours, and her exhaustion was so great she feared that without some caffeine pumping through her system, she risked falling asleep behind the wheel. The bar was in the middle of nowhere and looked like a grungy, neon-lit mirage. Beyond, the sky was impossibly vast and spangled with countless stars.

Her phone rang just as she was about to slide out of her car. Greg. He had been calling her since the incident at the house, leaving voicemails that she deleted without listening to them, text messages she erased without reading.

This time, she answered the phone.

"Jesus, Maur, where the hell *are* you?"

"I don't know, Greg. In the middle of nowhere."

"Are you okay? I've been trying to reach you ever since . . . well, ever since that all went down."

"You sound funny," she said.

"My nose is busted. So is my jaw."

"Oh, Greg."

"Come back, Maureen. Please."

"I don't think I can."

"You can do anything you want. We can do it together. The two of us."

"What about Landon?"

There was a brief pause on the other end of the line. "I've been doing a lot of thinking about that. I'm going to insist he goes to counseling. And he's moving out. In fact, he's already gone. It's time he takes responsibility for himself and his actions. And it's time I stop ignoring and making excuses for his behavior."

"That's good, Greg. I hope you stick to that and hold him accountable."

"I am. I will. I'm sticking to it. Please, Maur—please come home."

Home, she thought. *Where is that? Back to Wyoming or back to Los Angeles? The lady or the tiger?*

Or maybe, she thought, they were *both* tigers.

"I haven't been honest with you, Greg. I've got something that I've been running from, something I've never told you, and that's not fair to you."

"Then tell me. Whatever it is, we can deal with it together."

"I don't know, Greg," she said. "I think it might be something I need to come to terms with on my own."

"Maureen, please. Don't do this alone. I love you."

But do I love you, Greg? Or were you just as Landon said—a mask for me to hide behind? A completely different life so I could forget the old one that I fucked up so badly? The one thing I wish had never, ever happened.

"I have to go now, Greg."

"At least please think about it, Maureen. Can you do that for me? Can you think about coming home?"

"I'll think about it. I promise. Goodnight, Greg."

"Goodbye, Maureen. I love y—"

She disconnected the call.

Felt her heart racing in her chest.

Inside the bar, an old Kris Kristofferson song played on an actual jukebox above which hung a framed photo of a young Kris Kristofferson. Her hands were shaking and Greg's voice still echoed in her ear.

The bar was shaped like a horseshoe, with only a few barstools occupied. The bartender was a busty middle-aged woman in a leather corset and an outdated beehive hairdo, clown-nose-red. Beyond the bar were a few empty booths. Two men in faded dungarees and leather vests huddled around a pool table, pool cues and bottles of Bud in their hands.

Maureen took a seat at the bar. There was a condiments caddy nearby, and she couldn't help herself—she began to frantically rearrange the items by size, then by color, then by symmetry. Salt shaker, pepper shaker, hot sauce, ketchup bottle, mustard bottle, plastic container of various sugars, an aluminum box containing too-thin paper napkins.

Stop it, she willed herself. *Stop it, stop it, stop it.*

The bartender drifted over, noticed her handiwork with the caddy, but decided not to comment on it. "What can I get you, darling?"

"Do you have any coffee?"

"Might be cold, but I can nuke it for you."

"That'd be perfect. Thank you."

When the coffee came, she wrapped her hands around it despite the fact that it was warm in the bar: something *inside* her was cold.

The Kristofferson song ended, and Miley Cyrus came on.

Halfway through her coffee, she happened to look up to find a woman staring back at her from the opposite end of the bar. The woman was dark-skinned, with a wave of short black hair sculpted across her forehead. The black tapered pantsuit she wore looked wholly out of place in this dingy roadside watering hole. The woman's eyes, when they locked on Maureen, almost seemed to flash with a deep, ethereal light.

It took Maureen a moment to recognize the woman. And by then, she had already gotten up from her barstool and was sauntering over in Maureen's direction, the inverted cross hanging from her neck glinting in the dim lights of the tavern. She was smiling, her head cocked in an inviting manner. Once again, Maureen thought she recognized this woman, although she could not tell why.

The woman approached, addressing the empty barstool beside Maureen with a coy nod of her head. "Hello, Maureen. Do you mind if I join you?"

Maureen, momentarily speechless, waved a hand at the empty barstool. She cleared her throat, discovered her voice, and said, "Not at all. Please."

The woman folded herself neatly onto the stool beside her.

"You were at my engagement party," Maureen said. "You commented on my book."

"Ah, you remember? It was such a wonderful book. And it was such a pleasure to meet you and your fiancé."

"Meet us both? I just assumed you knew Greg from the movie business."

"I'm not in the movie business."

"Then . . . if you don't mind me asking . . . who invited you to our engagement party?"

The woman smiled decorously. Her eyes looked impossibly luminous beneath the muted lights of the bar. This close, Maureen could smell her perfume—sandalwood, and beneath that, something earthier, she thought. Of the desert.

"Let's just say I invited myself."

"Why would you do that?"

"To see you."

"Me? Why?" She leaned closer to the woman and said, "How do we know each other?"

"Oh, Maureen. I think you know. Tell me—tell me more about that story you started telling at the party."

Maureen turned away from her. "I don't want to talk about that story."

"Why is that? Does it frighten you?"

"Frighten me?"

"With its weight."

She fought the urge to adjust the items in the caddy again. "I've been running from something," she said instead. "I've known it all along, of course. That's what my story is about. Greg's got a son. Landon." She felt herself shudder as she spoke his name; she kept seeing him going berserk in that terrible monkey mask, smashing things and striking Greg over and over again. *My nose is busted. So is my jaw.* "He said something to me that was true, although I didn't want to admit it at the time."

"And what was that?"

"He said he could tell I was running from something, and that I was using the marriage to his father as a means of escape. As a way to cover up my own past. He didn't say it quite like that, but that's what he meant."

"So tell me the rest of your story," the woman said.

"I can't. It's confusing. It doesn't make sense."

"Of course it does," said the woman.

Maureen finished her coffee. Then she looked back at the woman, and could still smell the sandalwood and the earthy scent of the desert. That inverted cross, peculiar as it was, nearly transfixed her. The woman was beautiful, otherworldly. Those *eyes* . . .

She told her—

As the tall, swarthy man continues to disfigure the woman on the bed with that sharp, unforgiving blade, her lover rises. He is covered in the dead woman's blood, yet he does not seem to notice; in fact, he does not seem to know the dead woman and her assailant are even in the room with him. Sleepily, he rubs his eyes, tells her to come back to bed, because she is still standing before the altar mirror.

She turns and looks back at him in real life, and he is there, sitting up, rubbing his eyes. There is no blood on him in the real world, just as there is no dead woman in bed beside him, no tall, dark assailant with a blade. Yet when she looks back at the mirror, those things are all still there.

That other thing, too.

That out-of-focus thing seated on the sofa.

Furry, hazy. Indistinct.

"We've all got dark secrets," says the assailant in the mirror. The mirror version of her lover—the version covered in the dead woman's blood—does not hear him. "Even you. Even you've got your own dark secret."

And then he points with the dripping blade of the knife to the thing on the sofa.

To the . . .

. . . boy on the sofa.

A little boy.

Suddenly in focus.

Suddenly there.

He is sitting on the sofa against the wall in the motel room, yes, but in actuality he's sitting in the back seat of a car. She knows this.

As she watches this scene, her *own* reflection peels away from the glass, and moves toward the boy. She moves slowly, as if in a dream . . . and what is it to be living inside mirror glass if it's not living inside a dream?

Her reflection kneels down before the boy. The boy smiles. Says, "Mom," just like that, just one sound that is a word that is a name, "Mom," like that, and her reflection reaches out and simply buckles the boy's seatbelt.

Snap.

"See?" her reflection says to the boy as her eyes fill with tears. "Now you're safe. Now nothing terrible will happen and you can stay with me always."

417

And she hugs the boy, kisses his brow. Dampens the fringe of his hair with her tears.

And then the woman wakes. She's lying in the motel bed, next to her sleeping lover.

She climbs out of bed and goes to the altar. Stands before its mirrored glass. Peers *into* it, hoping to see the boy one last time . . .

But no: it's only a reflection of the real world. Of the truth in things. The absence of things.

She takes one last look at her lover sleeping in the bed. And then she gathers her things and leaves him there in silence.

There were tears in Maureen's eyes.

"I'm sorry," Maureen said, and grabbed a handful of napkins from the nearby dispenser. "I'm so embarrassed."

"There's nothing in this world to be embarrassed about."

Maureen crumpled up the damp napkins then set them beside her drink. "Who the hell are you, anyway? What are you doing out here in this bar, in the middle of nowhere? Tell me how it is we know each other."

"You might say looking at me is like gazing into an altar mirror," the woman suggested. One of her thin, raven-black eyebrows arched, and she added, "*Alter* mirror."

"I don't understand," Maureen said, shaking her head. "Tell me who you are."

"You know who I am. Just like you know what your story is really about. The man with the knife—the killer—isn't the important part of the story. It's the *woman's* story."

"Tell me how we know each other . . . "

"Don't be blind, my love. And don't go back to him. Move forward, Maureen. Not backward."

"*What?*"

And then the woman leaned over and kissed Maureen softly on the lips.

When she drew away, she excused herself and walked across the bar toward the exit. She pushed against the door and drifted out into the night on a cool desert breeze.

Maureen sat in stunned silence for several minutes. When the bartender returned and asked if she wanted another cup of coffee, it took her a moment to find her voice before telling her no. "Do you know the woman who was sitting right here?" she asked.

"Sweetheart, you're the only gal been in here all week," said the bartender. "Maybe all month."

Maureen felt a nerve twitch in her eyelid. She dug out some folded bills from her purse and set them on the bar, then got up and went to the door. She took a breath, then pushed against it, opening up a chasm of nightfall before her. That cool desert breeze chilled the droplets of sweat along her forehead.

There was no sign of the woman anywhere.

Maureen stood there for several minutes, breathing in the crisp night air, before climbing back inside her car. Behind the wheel, she glanced up at her reflection in the—

(altar/alter)

—rearview mirror.

The ghost of her.

And behind her: that empty back seat.

She crawled out of the car, opened the rear door, and leaned inside.

"I'm sorry," she whispered. "I miss you, baby."

Suddenly, she recalled being pulled from her overturned vehicle, dazed and bloodied, sirens wailing in the distance. A dark-skinned woman with sculpted hair in a tapered black pantsuit, dragging her across the roadway upon a carpet of broken glass. The cross around her neck appeared to hang upside down. The woman kept saying, over and over again, *you'll be okay, you'll be okay.* In return, Maureen had only managed two words—*my son*—before falling into unconsciousness.

Feeling cold, Maureen buckled the rear seatbelt, then got back behind the wheel. She turned over the engine, and pulled toward the exit of the parking lot. In both directions, the highway looked impossibly long, impossibly straight, impossibly dark.

Wyoming or Los Angeles?

The lady or the tiger?

Swiping tears from her eyes, Maureen pulled onto the highway.

3

At a little after six o'clock on an unusually cool summer evening, Bill Renney pulled his sedan up to the automated gate at the foot of Alan Andressen's driveway. He hit the buzzer on the gate, then waited for Alan's voice to come over the speaker. No voice came, but the gate shuddered open.

Alan was waiting for him at the top of the hill, standing in the open doorway of the house. He was wearing gray sweatpants, running shoes, and a Lakers T-shirt, the front of which was dark with sweat.

"I just got back from a run," Alan said, as if his condition required explanation.

"Can I come in?"

"Please."

He followed Alan into the house—that wide, cold, sterile house—and it was in that moment that something Landon Dawson had said during his interview came back to him: *A home and a house are two different things.* He hadn't understood what the kid had meant at the time, but he thought now he did.

"I left you a voicemail but never heard back," Renney said, following Alan into the kitchen.

"I got your message. I saw the news, too."

"How long did you treat that kid?"

"Kampen? Just a few months, on and off. He was one of my pro bono cases."

"What's your diagnosis?"

"Hard to say."

"Is it?"

"It's not a black-and-white science, Bill."

Alan went to the refrigerator and took out a bottle of Perrier while Renney continued down the hall to where the large shelf of DVDs still stood. Melissa Jean Andressen's movie collection. Alphabetized.

"He had a problem taking his meds," Alan went on. "I can tell you that much. Had a strange relationship with his mother, too."

Not anymore, Renney thought, running his finger along the spines of the DVDs.

"I never suspected him to be the violent type," Alan said. "He was actually quite polite and well behaved, from what I remember. Extremely intelligent and introspective, too."

Renney said nothing. He found the DVD he was looking for and pulled it off the shelf.

"I'll admit, I'm a little taken aback by the whole thing," Alan continued.

"You ever seen this movie?" Renney asked, holding up the DVD.

Alan looked at it. Said, "*High Desert*? Doesn't ring a bell. Why? You want to borrow it?"

"I think maybe I do," Renney said. He turned the DVD over and gazed at the ghoulish images on the back.

"Can I get you something to drink?"

"No, thanks. I just need to talk to you about something."

"Why don't we step outside?"

"All right," Renney said.

It was unseasonably chilly on the back deck. Renney could see the city lights down below winking on, not in gridded patterns like they do when there is a power outage or restoration on a movie, but in small, tidy pockets and increments—*wink* and *wink* and *wink*—here and there. Like a slyness to those lights. Like an entire city built on individual secrets, fragile as an eggshell.

"So what is it you need to talk to me about now?" Alan asked.

"Kampen had duplicates of the crime scene photos from your wife's case file," Renney said. "He said he stole them from your office. Found them in your desk drawer."

Alan had gone to the railing and was gazing down at the canyon below, but Renney could see him stiffen now, as if every muscle in his body had suddenly turned to stone.

"You wanna tell me anything?" Renney said.

Alan's knuckles whitened and his grip on the railing tightened. "It felt wrong having those pictures of her in some file in a police station somewhere. There were copies and I thought you wouldn't miss them. I needed those photos here in this house with me. I had every right to have them, and I told you that at the time." He shook his head but didn't meet Renney's eyes. "I wasn't in a very good place back then. I wasn't thinking clearly."

"Those photos are going to be evidence in this kid's trial. We should get our story straight on why you had them."

"I just told you why I had them."

"It's more like I brought that case file over one night for you to take a look, see if anything in there might jog your memory about something," Renney said. "Same as we did with those emails and phone records and credit card statements, remember? After I left, you noticed some of those photos had slipped out and had fallen on the floor. You stuck them in a desk drawer to give them back to me at a later date, but then you just forgot."

"It's basically the same thing."

"In this version you're not a thief and I'm not so careless," Renney said.

Alan hung his head and shook it, as if disappointed in the whole situation.

"There's something else, too," Renney went on. "Something that probably won't come up in the trial, but something I'd like an answer to nonetheless."

"Yeah, what's that?"

"I'd like to know why you didn't tell me you'd seen Lucas Priest at your house."

Alan's head swiveled in Renney's direction. His face was mottled in red patches, which could have been from his run. "What are you talking about?"

"Kampen positively identified a photo of Priest. Said he saw Priest one afternoon at your house, after a session with you. That Priest was standing in the driveway with your wife. That he had his hand on her arm."

He expected Alan to prevaricate, but instead, the doctor said, "Yes, that's right."

"So, you knew who he was," Renney stated.

"No, not that day. That day, he was just a guy called to fix a flat on M.J.'s car. I didn't know he was the same guy you were talking to at that mechanic shop in Reseda until I went there and put my eyes on him."

"And what'd you think in that moment? When you saw him?"

"That I knew without a doubt he'd killed my wife." He leveraged himself off the deck railing, his eyes still hinged on Renney's. The sweat stain on the front of his shirt was in the shape of bat wings.

"Everything clicked the second I saw him. I realized he'd been stalking my wife, coming around, smiling at her, chatting her up. And when he saw an opportunity to do something fucking terrible to her, well, that's exactly what the son of a bitch did."

"Why didn't you tell me this the night we buried him?"

"What was the fucking point? He was gone, he was dead. My mind was going a million miles a second and I wasn't thinking too clearheaded. And after that night, you and I hardly spoke again."

"Let me ask you straight out," Renney said. "Did you kill Priest because you believed he murdered your wife, or did you kill him because he was fooling around with her?"

A crease appeared between Alan's eyebrows. "*What?*"

"You know what I'm getting at, doc."

"My wife was not *fooling around* with that piece of trash. She was being *stalked* and she was *murdered* by him. All of that was clear to me the second I saw that piece of garbage standing outside the mechanic shop. I drove him out to the desert to beat that confession out of him, but in the end, I just couldn't control myself. And we both know how that ended."

"Maybe you couldn't control yourself with your wife, either."

"What the hell are you talking about?"

"I'm talking about looking at this thing through a different lens, doc," Renney said. "You were the one who put me onto that mechanic shop in Reseda in the first place. Said it was unusual she'd take her car there—"

"It *was* unusual—"

"—and so I went there and that's how Priest got on my radar in the first place. And when you killed that guy, I thought about arresting you, but then I thought, you know what? Fuck it. He's probably the guy who did your wife in anyway, so good fucking riddance. Because I felt sorry for you, Alan. But you were smart there, too, because you used my sympathy against me and got me dirty. The second I picked up a shovel instead of putting cuffs on you, you got me dirty."

"You *told* me he killed her!" Alan suddenly shouted. His face had grown redder and thick cords stood out along the sides of his neck. "You told me you were sure! I fucking *asked* if you were *sure*! And now you're coming back around putting this thing on me again? *I wasn't in town when my wife was killed!*"

My wife, Renney thought. *Not Melissa Jean. Not M.J.*

"Maybe you didn't need to be in town," Renney said. "Maybe for you it was better if you *weren't* in town."

Alan threw his hands up and wheeled back toward the railing. "You're losing your fucking mind, Bill."

"That Kampen kid," Renney said. "I've spent some time with him in a closed room, and there is no question—he's got more than just a few screws loose. Maybe he's delusional. Maybe it's even better because he doesn't want to take his meds. Nothing he says or does when he's off his meds makes any sense. Goddamn kid thinks his girlfriend was a vampire, can you believe that? Maybe you can. You spent more time with him than me. Hell, you're his psychiatrist of record. Which means you'll likely be called to serve as an expert witness at this kid's trial."

"Where the hell are you going with this?"

"Maybe you showed this kid a movie," Renney said, tapping the plastic DVD case against the palm of his hand. "Maybe you crawled inside his head. Maybe you told him things about your wife, things that would set him off. And then maybe, when you were conveniently out of town, this kid does exactly what you told him to do."

"Is that what he told you?"

"Yes," Renney said. It was a lie, but he wanted to see Alan's face as he said it.

But Alan's face remained expressionless.

"What do you have to say about that, doc?"

The tendons were still sharp as knife blades along the sides of Alan's neck, but when he spoke, it was with a quiet calculation. "I don't believe you. Lucas Priest killed my wife. And if you weren't so fucked up over the loss of your *own* wife last year, you would have solved M.J.'s case just like you've solved this one." Alan's eyes suddenly looked like steel pins. "You should have taken a leave of absence from work, but instead, you used my wife's murder as some grieving tool to get over your own loss. You weren't up for the challenge and so I stepped in and did what had to be done. And now a year later, you're coming back around to accuse me all over again—*when the whole reason we're here is your fault.* So, if you want to arrest me for a murder," Alan went on, taking a step in Renney's direction, "then arrest me for the one I *actually* committed. And then let's see how well that shakes out for you, too."

They stood there staring at each other for an unknowable length of time. Renney could feel sweat slipping down the sides of his face. In that moment, he happened to look past Alan and at the small secuirty camera mounted just beneath the eaves, a SPY-X sticker on it. A little green light on it, too.

Alan realized what Renney was looking at. "Took your advice, Bill. Got 'em fixed. Video *and* audio. I'm safe as milk now."

Alan returned to the deck railing and hung his head. In a voice that trembled, he said, "I think it's time you go away, Bill, and never come back."

Renney stood there for a moment longer. His eyes kept volleying between Alan Andressen's trembling shoulders and the little green light on the SPY-X camera.

"Leave," Alan said, refusing to look at him.

Renney left.

—◇—

That night, for the first time in a year, the Roy Orbison record started playing again. The sound of it dragged Renney from a fitful sleep, and for several seconds, he just lay there on his damp, dream-sweated mattress, listening to Orbison's achy, heartfelt vocals echoing down the hall from the living room into his bedroom. He could feel his heart racing in his chest. After a couple seconds more, he got out of bed.

Linda was sitting on the couch this time instead of the recliner. The room was dark, with only the barest light from the streetlamp poking its way between the slats in the blinds. Yet Renney could see her with perfect clarity—the old Linda, before the cancer. She was in her wedding gown, which looked luminescent in the dark, and her hair was done up the way it had been on the day she'd said her vows, and he'd said his.

"Am I dreaming?" he asked her, but then quickly amended, "Wait, never mind. Don't tell me. I don't want to know."

He joined her on the couch, side by side. The fabric of Linda's wedding gown rustled, but it was cool, smooth silk against Renney's side. After a time, he reached over and took her hand in his. Her fingers were stiff, her palm like ice. He squeezed her hand nonetheless.

"He's right, you know," he whispered over the music. "I was in a bad place after you died. In a lot of ways, I still am."

"Yeah?" she said, turning to face him.

"Yeah," he said. He stared into her eyes, took in her entire heart-shaped face. The delicate beauty of her clavicles was no longer lost on him. "I've made some mistakes."

"That's okay, baby."

He remembered her in the final stage of her death, a living skeleton with parchment skin stretched taut across her skull. In those terrible, final days, she'd lost her sight, her hearing, the ability to feel. All her senses.

"I'm just going to have to live with this one," he told her.

"That's all right, baby."

"I miss you."

"I miss you, too."

"It's been a hard year without you," he said, and could feel his eyes beginning to burn. He squeezed her hand tighter. "I didn't want to let you go. I wasn't ready. I'm still not ready."

"You are," she told him. "It's time."

He smiled as he felt a tear trickle down the left side of his face. He was thinking about the cosmic echo of things—how the universe repeats itself after a time, bringing things back together, content in such harmony. "I'll see you again, Lin." It was not a question.

And when the record ended and the needle started crackling in the groove, Bill Renney leaned over and kissed the side of his dead wife's face.

ACKNOWLEDGEMENTS

t.k.

ABOUT THE AUTHOR

Ronald Malfi is the award-winning author of several horror novels and thrillers, including the bestseller *Come with Me*, published by Titan Books in 2021. He is the recipient of two Independent Publisher Book Awards, the Beverly Hills Book Award, the Vincent Preis Horror Award, the Benjamin Franklin Award, and his novel *Floating Staircase* was a finalist for the Bram Stoker Award®. He lives with his family along the Chesapeake Bay, and when he's not writing, he's performing in the rock band VEER.

ronaldmalfi.com
@RonaldMalfi

For more fantastic fiction, author events,
exclusive excerpts, competitions, limited editions and more

VISIT OUR WEBSITE
titanbooks.com

LIKE US ON FACEBOOK
facebook.com/titanbooks

FOLLOW US ON TWITTER AND INSTAGRAM
@TitanBooks

EMAIL US
readerfeedback@titanemail.com